ACCLAIM FOR MIRRORS

"*Mirrors* is an absolutely magical story with stunning imagery, rich symbolism, and beautiful prose... Brittany's writing always makes me feel like I'm curled inside a poem. I was enchanted from beginning to end!"

—RACHEL LAWRENCE, author of *Seashells and Other Souvenirs*

"A tale almost as old as time that will leave you absolutely enchanted, Eden's *Mirrors* takes us on a journey to crumbling castles, dusty libraries, and warm hearths as romance blossoms between two searching souls finding their way home."

—KAITLYN CARTER BROWN, author of *Queen of Shifting Sands*

"Heartfelt and poetic, *Mirrors* weaves a tantalizing mystery where past and present collide in a tale of books, musings, and romance. For anyone who has fallen in love with fairytales, *Mirrors* promises a treasure hunting adventure sure to sweep you off your feet."

—ASHLEY SCHALLER, author of *R.E.M.* and *Riley + Sam*

ACCLAIM FOR HEARTS

"Our hearts are fragile things, just as prone to shatter as they are to swell. Brittany Eden captures that beautiful dichotomy in her aptly named novel, *Hearts*. It features an art-loving main character who seems to stray between the lines of reality while asking the questions we are often too scared to ask. A creative, fascinating debut for fans of whimsy and wonder."

—AUTUMN KRAUSE, author of *A Dress for the Wicked*

"*Hearts* slowly and surely, like the unfolding of a breathless romance, captured my own heart. Few words could encompass the beauty of this story, but one is this: needed. Our world with its broken pieces and shattered hearts needs these words. And in an unexpected way, this story spoke to places of my heart that needed healing and hope, and I've found it—and my heart is on the mend. If you choose to read one book this year, let it be Hearts. Reminiscent of Caroline George and Amanda Dykes' masterful storytelling, Hearts is not to be missed."

—CAITLIN MILLER, author of *The Memories We Painted* and *Our Yellow Tape Letters: A WWII Novel*

"Like any well-crafted novel, *Hearts* is a story that must be savored like a steaming cup of afternoon tea. Through Elizabeth's artistic eye, we are brought into a world of whimsical wonder with tea parties and swoon-worthy landscapers. But the depth of *Hearts* is in the details. Through Eden's poetic and lyrical prose, the severity of lies, mental health and isolation take on new life. With beloved fairytale elements intertwined, we are taught in *Hearts* that dreams and wonder are meant to take root in your mind, life is not meant to be lived alone, and the truth really does set you free."

—V. ROMAS BURTON, author of the Heartmaker trilogy

"After her outstanding debut novella *Wishes*, *Hearts* has everything I have come to expect from an Eden book. A thoughtful exploration of mental health, darkness and light, and achingly romantic, this lyrical novel is an experience to savor with many pots of tea. Lincoln is a leading man to yearn for and Elizabeth gives us an intriguing mix of fragility and strength while learning a lifelong lesson: Be strong, not bitter."

—AMBER KIRKPATRICK, author of *Until The Rising* and *Unleashed*

"I was instantly transported into this beautiful world Eden has created. It sparkles with hauntingly gorgeous prose, a deliciously swoony romance, and sheds light on matters of the heart and mind often left bereft in corners unattended. A poignant, timeless tale for the ages."

—AJ SKELLY, bestselling author of The Wolves of Rock Falls

BRITTANY EDEN

Acclaim for Wishes

"Charming and inventive, *Wishes* offers a romance that tiptoes between reality and fairytale. A smart, heartfelt retelling perfect for fans of Kiera Cass and Melanie Dickerson!"
—CAROLINE GEORGE, author of *Dearest Josephine*

"Eden's melodic and vivid prose invites readers into a heart-warming reimagining of one of my favorite fairy tales. She paints pictures with her words, not only with her moving descriptions but with poetic and visual details I've never seen before in fiction. A timely and tender read for fans of Hallmark and fairytale retellings alike!"
—TARA K. ROSS, author of *Fade to White*

"Enchanting and unique, Eden's prose in *Wishes* is a paintbrush, creating a masterpiece depicting grief and sorrow and how love can overcome them in time. By carefully combining two beloved fairytales—Cinderella and Pinocchio—Eden has written a beautiful novella that will capture the hearts of readers, young and old."
—V. ROMAS BURTON, author of the Heartmaker Trilogy

"*Wishes* is a beautiful glimpse into the fairytale world Eden is creating with her Heartbooks series. It is filled with such poetic prose and wonderful little hints of the familiar stories from which it drew inspiration. I believe fans of The Selection Series and all things Cinderella will find this an absolutely lovely story of romance, royal intrigue, and overcoming loss."
—TABITHA CAPLINGER, author of *The Wolf Queen*

"*Wishes*—this book had my heart from beginning to end. The writing as beautiful as poetry and as stirring as a timeless classic, I couldn't not fall in love with this beautifully moving story. I adored this book and absolutely cannot wait for future releases by the author. It's five glowing stars from me."
—CAITLIN MILLER, author of *The Memories We Painted*

"Brittany Eden's *Wishes* mingles Cinderella tropes and modern monarchy for a fast and fun fairy-tale drama... Surprising twists and complex relationships grant Brittany Eden's *Wishes* a fulfilling and fast-paced read."
—LOREHAVEN MAGAZINE

MIRRORS

ALSO BY BRITTANY EDEN

THE HEARTBOOKS SERIES

Welcome to Loirehall and Gabreville, where fairytale hints hide in sparkling corners and nostalgia seeps under doorways when you're least expecting it. In this series of standalone novels and novellas, you can read each book on its own or start the series with whichever book strikes your fancy, though the reading experience is richer if you read them all! Dreamy and lyrical, each vintage-inspired story has a new featured romance and is written in Eden's signature poetic prose.

SEASONAL READING ORDER:

Winter ~ *Wishes*

Spring ~ *Mirrors*

Summer ~ *Hearts*

Autumn ~ *Curses*

Winter ~ *Endings*

BRITTANY EDEN

MIRRORS

Quill & Flame
EmberLight

Quill & Flame
Emberlight

Mirrors

Copyright ©2025 by Brittany Eden

Published by Quill & Flame Publishing House, an imprint of Book Bash Media, LLC.

www.quillandflame.com

Cover design by Ashley Bustamante

There is a friend…and without her, this book might not be here.

To Brigitte Cromey, a woman of kindness, valor, and strength. It may be a stretch to say that the best friend in this book is inspired by you, but only because you're funnier, better, and more loyal—if that were possible.

sickly-sweet the wicked breath,
heavy heart and dagger depth.
death or sleep all seeking vain,
the unsaved story-telling pain.
'til fair like eve in Eden new,
love's unfinished radiant hue.
healing heart so softly fell,
hope turned hurt with whispered spell.
this vow ever sweetly sends,
true love 'wakened never ends.

part one

the beast and the rose

Prologue

The Gated Library, Loirehall University

NOT LONG AFTER DAWN, I ENTERED THE quiet heart of Loirehall's historic University district and arrived at the first place I fell in love—with books, of course.

I walked alone through the echoing arcade in the center of the massive building, which hosted the library but also the administrative offices and auditorium only used for dignitaries and graduations with overlong council speeches. The building's façade was simple but grand on the outside, but inside every surface was ornate. Tales from Loirehall and Gabreville's shared history were embellished on detailed frescoes and on the painted domed ceiling.

For all their bickering, the towns shared the university in uncharacteristic cordiality. The students...not entirely. First-years usually kept to their side of the twinned stairs, where carvings lined the walls bracketing each respective staircase. They kept to their own side, that was, until they inevitably made friends from the other side of the river. Lecture boredom and unceasing essays made comrades across the division the two staircases represented—not for me, though. My real-life friends were few, but there was a whole world of characters waiting for me between bookshelves.

Paige, they called, *come up here.*

Those fables told on frescoes towered above where flying buttresses met in the middle, creating four curved white domes. The painted ceiling was an opulent collision of history and stories and art. A fitting entrance to a library. I took the left staircase as I always did, where Gabreville's rich inheritance of mining, hunting, and all things mountainous and grand was represented by statues at even intervals along the walls.

Who were they? What did they do to deserve their bust in marble? Something good, or evil?

I shifted the pile of books in my arms and ascended to the second floor, past the magnificent arches at the entrance to the library, diverting to another polished set of stairs then up again one more time on another less grand—and increasingly narrow—to finally arrive at my favorite part of the library. The fourth floor. The Gated Library. Then, bowing inward in that particular hunch of a bookworm around their overly-tall stack of books, I lost my grip on the heavy load, leading to the inevitable—

"Oomph!" The books left my arms as if they meant to, toppling to the ground.

"Sorry!" a male voice replied, deep and husky and dark, like he hadn't appeared around the corner out of nowhere and nearly knocked me down.

Aghast at my scattered books, I stood insulted at their abandonment and his hurried manner. "You shouldn't rush through the library," I retorted, kneeling to grab the farthest book first.

"Aren't you also supposed to be quiet?" The young man spoke above me with eerie calm, the opposite of my racing heart so soon after he'd barrelled me down. But my surprise had good reason. We were in the corridor farthest into the secluded, light-and-air controlled, and usually *locked* section of the topmost floor of the joint Gabreville and Loirehall Memorial Library. The Gated Library, called such not just for the fragile books, but for the locked case containing the literal Crown Jewels.

"How are you even up here?" I snapped. "It's locked." There was a reason those curving iron steps leading up here were narrow. They kept out intruders and allowed only the most ambitious readers deep into the heights at the heart of book heaven. And my poor books, strewn across the floor. Reaching for my papers scattered beyond, I mumbled, "Saturday morning curse. I should have known..."

Then I finally looked up.

I'd always dreamed of love at first sight. I even believed it was possible, especially if it involved haughty cheekbones beneath beautiful brown eyes and a hint of scruff over a dimpled chin and mesmerizing bold lips refusing to smile. His face was angled and proud. Pale, freckled skin, perfectly clear but for a scar clear through the far edge of one eyebrow and a similar white line on his jaw. I had always hoped for my own heart-stopping moment, like any good lover of stories. Until now, as my heart skipped a beat with annoyance.

Disdain at first sight.

I continued collecting my books with painstaking care. This was *not* the ambitious reader type. But it wasn't just his lack of etiquette, or the detachment in his voice, that made me want to pull away. I was also avoiding the cut of his jaw, attractive like unforeseen danger or the suspenseful chapter that ends amidst dialogue. To admit enjoyment in the study felt akin to jumping off a cliff, and I was far too poised for that. So, I spoke with the tone of Cleopatra—the real one, the legendary queen full of guile, not Shakespeare's iteration or any other fictional one.

"There are priceless books in this section," I informed his feet. "Aged, preserved, and special. I was just going to file them." One by one, I turned each treasure upright and checked for ruined pages. This old section, the Gated Library, was no longer a functioning library so much as storage for literal antiques—including the forsaken scepter of power and crown of Loirehall with its diamond-speared tips pointing to the stars, all gilt and golden with endless diamonds like a casual aside from a bygone age. I huffed a short breath. "There's a reason one should speak only in hushed tones in a library."

He talked to the top of my head. "Would my voice really wreck the texture of those books? They've already survived longer than us."

I was inordinately pleased that this rude apparition in my part of the library at least recognized our small place in history. Old stories mattered. Gently unbending a page from a book that had fallen facedown, the sound of his voice having suspended, I was about to look up before large hands—strong looking, with a smattering of freckles across the knuckles—reached over mine to help. Now on his knees on the waxed-wood floor, he took care in closing a leather-bound journal that was over two hundred years old. I couldn't help but be pleasantly surprised.

"It's not about that," I said finally, after pondering the concepts of long ages, memory, and survival.

His question came after another moment of carefully arranging books in such a way as to begin stacking them. "What is it about, then?" His voice had an unusual tone, a little bit raw.

As he gathered the lost papers from my folio case and handed them to me, I took the loose pages before he examined their contents too closely. He surrendered easily. It was hard to quiet my humming thoughts, caught red-handed for being in possession of sketches ripped from my late mother's diary. As if guilty, for having ripped a single page from a dead woman's book. I'd ripped out *ten*. On the other hand, I felt silly to feel let down in the face of his disinterest, as if having this stranger intrigued with these old pages could validate me.

I almost said they were sacred, but I sighed instead beneath the weight of the books piled once again in my arms, tired and suddenly lonely in the face of their longevity. Beneath the stack were the pages of repeated drawings of a crest of sorts, the symbol in my mother's diaries I'd been researching on my own, alone. I hadn't yet found trace of it, no matter where I'd looked.

"Books...they're like family." Heat bloomed across the skin of my throat. *Why did that come out so honestly?*

"Are they now?" Teasing failed to hide the uncomfortable end of the question in his husky voice. It was intriguing to hear him sound so deliberately unattached. Surely there was great value to whatever question had led him on some quest into the highest and loneliest part of the Gated Library. It was obvious to me even through the scratchy timbre in his baritone. Neither too high nor too deep, but implacably centered. "Isn't this a bit much to be carrying?"

I huffed to standing, back ramrod-straight, refusing to swoon at his husky voice. For all I knew, it was the dangerous surface above fathomless waters. *No one gets to see me struggle.* "Do I look weak to you?"

One straight eyebrow raised. "The *books* look heavy to me." His arms crossed, light brown eyes darkening, and I resisted the urge to step back. With the build of a young man whose shoulders had nearly filled in to match his height, his seemed the kind of face that was hard to place in time. He was probably a few years older than me, and if he was a student here at the university, he could already have been one for years. There was a prominent line between his brows that remained, even as his forehead smoothed, a haughty expression transforming into a smile. A rare grin, it seemed, but because I was determined to not be charmed and he couldn't hold it through our silence, and it fell.

"Books are heavy because they carry the weight of imagination and history. Much weightier than your life or mine. So yes," I said, accepting the final book from him without flinching. "They're heavy."

The smile returned briefly, slightly too sad for a smirk, as if he was truly trying to see beyond the books, the weight, I'd grown used to holding. "Whatever you say," he said, the straight edge to his broad shoulders lifting in a shrug.

His acquiescence wasn't what I wanted, now that I had it. And I was annoyed at not being *annoyed* so much as *intrigued*. "Intrigue" was a dangerous word. Both a fascination and a plot. A curiosity, or a conspiracy.

Which meaning would the word come to mean between us?

Either way, he was confounding. Morning sun lit strands of cropped hair. Too-long at the top, as if hacked by hand, but short on the sides, rough edges turning golden. His fair eyelashes squinted as the rays struck his face, as if the stained-glass windows lining the upper portions of the hallway meant to blind him. His brown eyes glowed bronze, for a moment.

I shook my head. "You never answered my question." *Why* was he alone with me on an early Saturday morning on the fourth floor in the Gated Library that *should have been locked*?

"I did not," he replied. "How could I, with the tomes of history piling insignificance on my head?" His tone gave the truest signal that he—and his questions—were far from aimless. At my answering expression, a heady feeling of my smile trying very hard *not* to smile, his countenance lightened.

I thought—irrationally, and likely due to the irresistible hue of his eyes—that he might *actually* understand the search for meaning plaguing me, the search for what truth could only be found in books. The history and love that every intangible word was seeking to draw with type and ink. Could he hear it too? The sound of possibility in pages? At the tilt of his golden head and an ageless hint of gilt in his bronze-brown eyes, I inhaled dust motes and scents of dust jackets and a deeper breath found its way inside, behind my heart, filling me with air and life. Like dawn breaking after a cold night.

He...*saw* me.

"Why are you here?" I asked again. His open expression shuttered at the repetition, and he stepped back, turning and walking away before I had a chance to rescue this one song, these impossible paragraphs, this fascinating first chapter of my day that I was not quite ready to let end. I hurried after him saying, "Wait, please."

At my *please*, he stopped.

I didn't need his name. I didn't care if his finely cut, white-collared shirt was rumpled or that the shoes beneath his jeans were the muddiest oxfords I'd ever seen. My pulse spiked. I just didn't want him to *leave*. Afraid that my library haven had forever shifted, the ache of loneliness threatened to burn the back of my throat if he were to go. *I can't be lonely in a library.*

"Tell me what you need." I rushed, and risking, took a step toward him. Leaning in with all the hope I could muster. "I won't tell my supervisor, and if no books will tell...have we really done anything wrong?" I half-giggled awkwardly; his face didn't even crack a smile. "I'll help you if I can." I inhaled thinly, because the looseness in my chest from moments before was long gone.

The pause was an interminable millisecond before he turned his head to speak to the rows of tomes bracketing our convergence. "I'm looking for a rare book. The *Oirdera*."

I released my breath gently. "I don't recognize it." I blinked at the name, though. It *was* familiar—like each flower in spring was familiar but new—but I couldn't place it. "But," I said, gazing down the hall, "I can find it if it's here. I know my way through all the codex listings almost as well as I know the rest of the books in the Double Sea."

His fair hair was so haphazard, nothing like heroes with wavy locks of hair grazing their cheekbones. The uneven long bit at the top slanted as he tilted his head, gilded gaze back on me. "The what?"

But I smiled, because he *wasn't leaving*. I hoped my answer would make him let me in on his search. "Welcome to the so-called 'boring' Catalogue and Chronicles section." With books in my hand, I couldn't gesture grandly to the three long straits of rows or the nearby bracketed room—a collection of thousands of volumes and periodicals dating centuries back to the first king of Loirehall. Vast, valuable. The reason the Gated Library wasn't open to the public. "A place I lovingly call the Double Sea." Which absolutely no one deigned to use as a nickname. Merciful shame, that.

"Sounds like a place you could get lost." Words like that, in a sad, husky voice like his, felt heavy in the quiet place.

Every person's voice is a story in itself, my mother had said in her diary. *Every inhale an expectation of a happy ending, every shuddered exhale a tale of woe.*

If she thought of voices as music, then right now, whatever this young man was hiding about his purpose was discordant, the adjacent note lilting beside the resolved chord, unable to let the dissonance go. Unfinished. She'd been gone many years, but I'd read enough of her abundant diaries and handwritten stories to believe that Mother would call his story lonely, as if the harmony trying to survive without a melody was merely missing the appropriate character for the hero to complete their journey. And for a young man I'd disdained at first sight, I was hard-pressed to imagine him with anyone but me beside him right now, because he exuded *alone* like a brand.

Just like me.

His half-smile wasn't going to be enough to make him stay—his motion was controlled hesitation—and I could just tell. It took a recluse to recognize one. My original disdain was now turned to desperation to keep a fellow lost soul nearby.

He'd stopped at the break between the narrow aisle dividing the alphabet of Legislative Orders. It was my first catalogue assignment last semester, and I had checked every single pre-war measure with its post-war counterpart in the opposite rows. Little did I know the job was repeated every academic year by each new, unknowing apprentice, assigned by bitter teachers' assistants who'd suffered the years before. It was the most hated row in the library for those of us apprentice archivists who'd spent too many unfortunate—and ultimately pointless—hours there. People trying to someday become professors should be kinder, yet I never knew if the assignment had been because I was from Gabreville or because I was worth initiating.

Hateful uncertainty. *I can't be lonely in a library,* I reminded myself and said, "Chronicles of all kinds of histories are always forgotten until people need the information preserved in their oceanic depths." I hurried forward, closer to his tall frame and crossed arms, pausing at the rows between "P" and "Q." "I'm only a first year, but I know these seas." I still couldn't close the distance between us, struck by a strong sense of unease. Of wanting to avoid making him feel as lost as I had at the beginning of the academic year last September. Now, in March, I was one of three others from the university library who had access to the Gated Library's inner room, and hopefully information about this mysterious *Oirdera*. My shift was first in the day—was it twisted fate that we should run into one another?

Straight eyebrows rose, brow furrowing, his scar twisting. His gaze was hope distressed, and something like gold fleck sparked in his eyes as he looked down on me. Heavy gaze, heavy gold. Those hopeful embers lit within his gilded eyes, and in the chemistry of dusty bookends and filtered morning bright for once, a different sort of warmth filled me. Instead of jewel tones of burgundy and aged green and burnt leather, the irises of his gorgeous eyes were hidden treasure, bronze edges tarnished. An overlay darker than it should be, on golden, precious metal.

Inhaling a lost sunshine scent that didn't belong in the musty library, I asked, "Other than a very rare, nearly unfindable book, is there anything else you're looking for?"

THE BOUQUET STINGS

Two hours later, present time, on an unseasonably freezing March morning

"**Y**OU DON'T BELONG HERE," calls a refined voice, rudely.

I stop in front of *Azalea's Treasures* while my companion deftly avoids the petite woman currently shoving a bouquet in my face.

A thorn snags my scarf, and another scratches my jaw. *Who gives white roses in winter?* I lift my gaze, dreading but knowing. I recognize her just by her stiletto heels, impractical and stark white on the cobblestoned sidewalk. Here is my father's landlord in an all-white ensemble, looking like a frosty, aged cupcake with absolutely no frosting or sweetness to speak of.

Lenora Hayes, that's who.

The space beside me empties as the young man from the library with the sad gold eyes continues walking, ducking his head as if we were strangers on the sidewalk. I glimpse his reflection in a shop window as he leaves, shoulders hunched, as if to hide his strength and stature. What a transformation from the enigmatic aura of mystery he had in the library earlier, the princeliness. Not only is that not a word; it isn't even a *thing*. *Too many books, Paige.*

I don't know him, but I see the lie. The broken image distorting reality. The reflection disguising his air of confidence into a cloak seeking invisibility. He reminds me of rare, nearly unfindable books, and the dim light we need to read them.

"Mrs. Hayes," I say with a shudder, feeling quite alone now that he's left me alone. And to her. Though the weather's warming, no other souls brave the sidewalks on this frigid morning during the lull between get-to-work traffic and go-to-lunch outings.

"Call me Lenora. Declan and I split. Though no one knows yet. Don't tell anyone; it's our little, joyous secret." She shrugs one shoulder, her white winter coat nearly blending with the bright, pale sky. "I came all this way to find you. Gabreville is a long way over the river."

It's a ten-minute walk to the bridge. "I was at the university." Though I left earlier than I should've.

"I hear you're always at the library."

So I can avoid people like you. "I study there," I say.

Lacquered white nails tap her narrow chin. "Percy studies there too, but Darragh mentioned he rarely sees you on campus." Lenora's lashes fan perfectly around dark brown eyes. They should be pretty, but they're just cold. "Do you hide in the library daily? Books don't bite?" Her tone mocks.

Pulling my hair over my shoulder with my free hand, I'm thankful for the gloves protecting my fingers—*morbid white bouquet.* Fear snakes like a stray thought around my lungs, so real I can't tell if it's emotion or an allergic reaction. I can't stifle the thoughts.

"Asphyxiation" is a lot of letters for not being able to breathe, which I know intimately. Asthma, allergies…lack of air. *Is this how my mother felt before she died?* I keep my eyes averted from our reflection in the window, afraid it shows my trembling hand, or if the knot in my stomach twists my lips. I'm not ready for this. I hate this woman. Why has she sought me out? Is something wrong?

"Haven't you grown into a fair beauty? I was too, before a terrible man drained my energy." Lenora steps closer. "I heard that my estranged husband"—she grimaces—"was visiting your father at the shop." She says *shop* haughtily, disdaining clock working and tinkering and antique gear-fixing in a word. "If he can't make this month's payment, we'll have to report him to the bank. Your father is six months behind on rent, and your home is collateral."

Six? I choke on a gasp.

"You didn't know?" she asks haughtily.

Declan and Lenora Hayes are Papa's landlords. They overcharge for rent of the publishing offices of *The Loirehall Times,* a building that's all thin walls and broken radiators and mildew in abandoned storage corners. They arranged the contract so that they co-owned the printing press itself, which my papa had inherited from his father, and his father before that. That old thing can't be moved out of the building without ruining it, which is why my papa works in Loirehall and not Gabreville. It's the mainstay of my father's income. The *Gabreville Gazette* has always been printed there, alongside *The Loirehall Times.* Save for special editions, both papers are now relegated to weekend editions only, which comes out on Sundays. It irks me when I look at Papa's ledgers only to see that

Lenora and Declan Hayes profit off all his printing jobs with the cranky printing press that is at least a century too old. No one else could operate that crotchety thing, never mind fix it.

Papa hasn't told me about his debts—*six months of them*—which means they've probably accrued since I'd started university and stopped helping with his accounting. Like a painful stab of a thorn, Lenora clearly enjoys rubbing my face in his secrets behind his back.

She continues. "Do you know, I've always hated that building. But even though Declan and I are going to quietly divorce, we're sharing ownership. People might talk." She pulls her gloves from a pocket and waves them dismissively, but I refuse to even raise an eyebrow. "The boys might stay with me, but I rarely see them. Good thing our estate is enough to keep Declan in another wing of the manor." She sounds relieved, explaining her separation from Mr. Hayes.

I blink and sniff, not wanting to hear about their family breakup but unable to stop to wave of pity for her two sons. Percy isn't so bad, but his older brother Darragh is a class-A jerk.

Bursts of light glance off the windowed storefront of *Azalea's Treasures*, and Lenora looks appreciatively at her reflection. I avoid my own mirror image, but then something beyond catches my eye. Across the road, the young man from earlier stands at the corner of University Road on the way to Russet Bridge. His form seems less worn from here than it had been as he'd very deliberately avoided Lenora. A hint of strength shows again in the lift of his chin and across his shoulders, squared toward the river. The Valais bisects our towns, a river between two worlds along the northern edges of Loirehall, snaking east, then south, to meander between both towns. I know the route well from walking to work with my father. It's as natural as breathing. Over Russet Bridge in an inhale, back for an exhale, our daily commute.

The young man pauses at the edge of the Valais River, just for a second. A second feels long when you're unable to breathe. Then he's gone, and I decide I don't want to hear any more from Lenora about their family drama.

"What is this for?" I ask boldly, shaking the bouquet. A pale rose petal falls to the ground.

"Your father seems willing to help Declan—who apparently threatened you, my dear. Daughters are a good motivator, after all. So I thought you could find something for *me*. Us ladies should stick together, hmm?" I feel only duress from Lenora, who to me seems the evilest of queens. Women can sparkle, but sometimes the diamond is a dagger and white roses are blood-red poison. "Wouldn't want to leave your father in the cold, would you?"

I don't doubt her threat. They could evict Father's business, which would leave him not only without income but without his beloved shop, printer, work. Without purpose. Guilt niggles my mind. My university tuition. My dreams. *Papa didn't tell me because he loves me.* "If this is about money—"

Lenora interrupts, "I don't need money. I have a terrible ex-husband for that."

I stomp my feet in the cold, thinking I glimpse a person watching our exchange from behind the reflection of the bookshop. But when I focus, the window is empty. "What do you need?" I gaze in the window's reflection again, but there's nothing. Imaginations are powerful things.

"It isn't what *I* need, girl, it's what *you* need."

"And what is that?"

There's an edge to her voice as she says, "To save your father."

I start. "What do you mean?"

"Declan is forcing him to go get...something. But I think *you're* more likely to find it, dear daughter of a sad old man. Wouldn't want your father to get lost in that old death trap, would you? And I suspect you're like me. Books aren't enough—it's what they lead us to."

Where? I feel myself caught up in her drama, her story, her threats. I've been spellbound and clutched beneath talons like hers my entire life—neighbors who ignored me and Papa, schoolmates walking to the other side of the road to avoid brushing past—shunned, yet chased by claws of regret like a lifelong stain. "What do you want from me?"

"Declan and I—"

"I thought you hated him."

"Oh, I do. But one can work well against what they hate. You can even work *with* them for a time, if you must." Her eyes darken. "If I have to, so will you." Lenora looks down my frame like an unsatisfying photo of a bad memory, then reaches to twine a lock of my hair between her fingers. "Beauty comes at a price."

"I don't think that's the saying—"

"*I'm* saying it. Your price is your father's shop, his livelihood. His stake in the printing business. And doesn't he love those precious little contraptions in that dusty shop of his? His inventions, his bits and bobs. History taunts us with memories and newspapers and books." She sneers, fingers having trailed down my arm and now digging into my wrist. "The only thing he loves more is *you*, which is why you need to go after him. You can save him, if you do what I ask."

"What do you need me to find?" I try and tone my voice to be submissive, but her eyes harden. I wouldn't believe me either.

"Take this from someone who learnt that her reflection never matched her nature. You are broken like me, girl. Don't hide who you are, and"—she flicks my shoulder—"don't pretend you're just a nice, sweet girl. You do not want to make an enemy of me."

Are we not already? I don't understand why she's dragging me into this, but she's right. I don't care why or for what; I *will* chase my father and make sure he's safe from whatever he's gotten himself into. Whatever it takes. "Fine."

"Good choice." She nods, blonde hair flicking against her chin.

"*My* choice." I lift my chin, repeating my question, "What do you need me to find?"

"Find the *Oirdera*." She speaks low, and I can feel my eyelashes flutter at hearing the unusual name for the second time that morning. "Old books *are* your forte."

"What do you want with it?" My fingers choke the strap of my book bag. I hope my lungs don't choke *me*. Deadly flowers. Stupid allergies. Stupid asthma.

"That's none of your concern."

"Why do you think I can find it?"

"Because you'll worry about your father, wandering without a clue in the broken-down castle—"

"It's *there*?"

"—searching for something he wouldn't recognize, liable to choke on ash or fall down a set of unseen stairs." Lenora tuts, dismissing the grandeur of the ruined castle that is Fairhavens.

Fairhavens. The name sits on the tip of my tongue. That's what it used to be called, the white stone castle built by the Lord of Gabreville long ago. Now, it lies in its own waste, a haven for only those wild enough to go that deep into the woods, that high on the mountain. But how does one un-ruin a castle? It lies in disrepair. Neglected.

Lenora continues. "Any manner of ill might befall an old man like him there, that high up, where the air is thin." She places a palm above her heart and I swallow the lump in my throat. I will face the same issue as Father, at that elevation. "Declan doesn't know this, but the *Oirdera* was last known to be in the library there, which means it *may* be untouched by the fires. Of anyone, the bookish daughter of Gabreville's genius inventor will know what to do with it once she's found it." She flicks a flower in my bouquet menacingly, making my sinuses revolt.

Just because you can't see it doesn't mean it isn't there. I shudder at what she might do with the *Oirdera*, and at what this has to do with the young man with golden eyes, but I push down worries that aren't mine. There is no one else to look out for my father.

I glance toward Gabreville, toward home, toward the young

man who has by now disappeared. Uncaring that Lenora sees my heart aching that direction. She might tear it apart or keep it from me, whatever she sees fit, if I don't do this. But now that I know the White Forest is where Papa's going, I'll follow. "If I succeed, we keep our home, and my father doesn't lose his stake in the printing press or *Wrenley & Sons*."

"So eager for him to keep that business, when you're a daughter with no claim to it." Her dig hits closer to my heart than I dare admit. "Do all I ask, and all will be well, for you, your father, *and* your home that the bank is about to foreclose on." Lenora stops short of grabbing my chin, tapping it gently instead. "Tell no one, and find an excuse to get yourself into the castle. You swear to everyone that you know nothing. The *Oirdera* isn't our goal, it's the map it contains, which I trust you can discern. They've only ever mined nickel, cobalt, and valuable copper there... Did you know rumors of gold were unproven? I think it's because it wasn't from this region at all, just hidden beneath the castle. But even treasure isn't enough unless you can carry it away."

There's a map? In the *Oirdera*? To treasure? I don't believe her, but I hold my tongue nonetheless.

"Declan truly has no vision. Once you find it, give him the *Oirdera* without telling him what it's worth. *He* thinks it records the name of a forgotten heir, but I doubt it. If he's right and the heir exists, they won't for much longer." I feel sorry for the heir, if they exist. The threat in her tone, for once not directed at me, is scary. She continues. "With the requisite decade now complete, and no direct firstborn son of a firstborn steward son to be found,

Declan wants Gabreville Council to recognize *him* as the next of kin when council sits again in session."

"Didn't the steward's son survive the fire?" I ask dumbly. I honestly couldn't remember.

"My nephew is gone," she says harshly.

That didn't help. What would happen if the son came back? If he was still alive? Would these people—his aunt and uncle—have allowed him as steward even all those years ago? Unlikely. But I don't allow the questions to emerge, not just because of my reticence to discuss a decade-old fire, but because I don't want to give her the chance to show how truly evil they might be.

Lenora shakes the bouquet in my hands. "You have until the first day of spring to find the book, or you lose your house—boring proceedings, big consequences. I want that treasure out of there before Declan takes stewardship, so you need high stakes just like I do."

"How is this possible?" Find a book, then find a treasure it *might* lead to? "I have no idea what I'm looking for!"

Raising her hand as if to slap me, she pauses and says calmly, "You must find anything that matches this design." Taking a small paper out of her coat pocket, she unfolds it to reveal a title page bearing the words *Charta: Punctum Temporis*. Upon wrinkled ivory paper, fading ink shows a rock hammer and sword forming a cross, atop a single rose.

The very symbol from my mother's diaries, the exact crest that I saw beside the missing pages this morning. The symbol I'd hidden from the young man in the library. "Where did you get this?"

"Old families have long memories," she says, tapping the page, making the old paper make a hollow sound. "Follow this motif. Find the *Oirdera*, then figure out the map. From there, treasure. Don't tell a soul."

I take the proffered paper, careful not to brush her fingers. Just because the fire doesn't touch you doesn't mean you won't get burned. *I will save my father.* I close my eyes and count to three. Then I say, "I'll do it," because I don't have to believe in the treasure to find a lost book.

I will find the *Oirdera* and whatever secrets it leads to. But first, I need to stop Papa. Save him. Take his place—because she's not wrong. He's weak, and I can do this better than him.

Lenora leaves with a stiff nod and a swift gait. I fold the sketch twice and put it in my book bag. It feels like my hope from this morning was a handful of fluffy dandelions, a gust likely to blow it all away. Now, all I have is a bouquet of white roses with thorns that sting.

Not a minute later, outside azalea's treasures

"DO THESE FLOWERS HAVE A DEATH WISH?"

At the thorny tone, I whip around, speechless, dropping the bouquet.

"Oh, stop clutching your coat like a damsel in distress." My best friend's voice is mocking and concerned at the same time; she's that complex. Like her impossibly tight ringlets. But her brow creases as a tear falls from my itchy, weepy eyes, blurring my view of our reflection in the storefront of *Azalea's Treasures*, the bookshop where my friend lives and works and must have just walked out of.

"Juniper!" I say her name on the world's shortest exhale, which is a feat, because *syllables. Did she see Lenora?* "You don't need to hate the poor things with that vehemence on my behalf, though I appreciate it."

Juniper's delicate hands reach menacingly for the bouquet I'd dropped. "Flowers! Are you listening?" She grabs the offending apple blossom branch, tossing it away down the cobblestoned sidewalk. "What do you wish for, evil stalks?" She yanks a thistle with a violent flourish, making my smile return. "It's too early in the year for this!" she berates the white roses, all that's left of the pale bouquet. "It isn't spring yet! Not for six days! Why are you tempting my wrath by tormenting my dearest friend?"

On cue, I sniff back a sneeze. It's coming, whether I want it or not—*ACHOO!*

"Poor thing," Juniper purrs to me, stroking the petal of a perfect white rose then snapping it off. She lifts long-lashed, wide brown eyes, all innocent braided-hair beauty. How she braids the curls at the crown of her head is a magical feat. "Who gave you a bouquet of rare white roses with apple blossoms and thistles?" She near spits the question. She must not have seen Lenora after all, so my mind seeks a clever way to avoid telling her about the encounter as she continues. "It's so white, it's evil. Like whoever gave it to you knew you were allergic."

I wipe tears from my eyes as if they were merely due to the flowers. "You have a thing against roses? Tell that to your earrings," I deflect and sniffle, smiling. I'm so glad she's here, rescuing me from stupid flowers. I do not want to explain the conversation with Lenora Hayes I just had until I understand it myself.

Juniper flings the last white rose onto the street, where a taxi runs over it. "Not at all." Her smooth alto has a jagged edge, which if aimed my way would make me antsy. "Roses merely need tending with a gauntlet."

"Why do I feel like you're talking about me and not the roses?"

"Paige, you're nothing like a rose. Not a thorn on your loveliness or fair skin or petal-like fragility—even when you decide not to tell me who gave you these." She blinks, innocent yet knowing. "Because *stubborn*. And morose? You're definitely something."

I huff. Not a blemish on my olive-toned but still pale skin. There's not a hint of warmth in my cheeks, which I notice whenever I spend too long in front of a mirror. Nothing like the spitfire freckles waterfalling over Juniper's nose and tawny cheeks, or the life coiled in her naturally vivid-hued mahogany hair. With a sidelong look, I stare at my reflection in the storefront window.

Juniper meets my gaze in the window, opaque, and it's as if her body is semi-filled with the books from the window display on the opposite side of the glass. *Azalea's Treasures* lettering fills the window, and we find the mirrors of ourselves between the gold and white words, surrounded and safe. I love this bookshop.

Juniper's head tilts, stray curls bouncing above her shoulders. "History was made here."

"History is made everywhere," I say, taking her arm and looking at our reflection but imagining the storybook moment captured on camera here forty years ago.

I love that old picture—I have a copy stuck in my vanity mirror at home from when the newspaper did a special edition on the former king when he passed a few years ago. It had been so simple that I hadn't given it much thought. I cut out that picture, walked from Gabreville to this Loirehall shop, and asked Madame Garcon for a job at her bookstore.

I read well, if a bit too much, I'd said, *but I love books.* She'd smiled, serene with possibly a tear in her eye, and replied, *I love stories too,* and set me free to reorganize the shelf of collectors sets. By the time I'd made it through fantasy, philosophy, and poetry, she'd made me call her Penelope and we'd become friends.

I'd never been close to my grandmother, my mother's mother, even before fate ended our relationship. Father's mother was gone before I was born. But books...books have a way finding and filling spaces. In lieu of family, Penelope filled a corner of my heart I hadn't known needed filling. She let me spend hours doing home-work in hidden nooks, curled in a Queen Anne armchair that feels soft as a cloud.

I sigh and toe a rose petal off the sidewalk to the street, because Penelope's love story was beautiful and it isn't in the bookshop books, but resides in all our hearts. "Who decides what moments deserve memory?"

"And why can't we take the bad ones away?" Juniper murmurs, her voice unusually tight.

"Who's morose now?" I ask, elbowing her to bring her back.

She returns, sparing me a smile then squinting into the too-bright sky. For a strained moment, it feels like we're both trying to see something—anything better, or different—than the version of ourselves in the reflection, like the calligraphy of *Azalea's Treasures* could wrap around us and make us better, stronger, wiser, kinder.

Those words sound a lot like how I imagine my mother would encourage us.

Stop looking, I tell myself. I turn away from the light mottling our mirrored selves and the way I've started looking so much like my mother. Resembling her visage in the small oval frame sitting on a windowsill at home. Long, dark brunette hair that only curls at the end on rainy days, average height for my age, the feeling that an eighteen-year-old should have a better grasp on makeup instead of covering her face with scarves all winter. It makes me both love and avoid my reflection. Mirrors, showing me what I am and what I've lost.

"The sun feels so nice," Juniper says, tilting her face to the slanted late-March sun for a quiet moment. Then she tugs the end of my red scarf, shaking her gloved hands around me like an aura. "What's with you? Really? How was work this morning at the library? You're here too early. I can read your face like a book, and it tells me there's a story."

"You don't like books, June." But I swallow a lump in my throat at her sensitivity to my mood, and admit a half-truth. "I'm just worried about Papa." Light from a passing car shimmers behind my reflection.

She nods. "You always are. You take good care of him, but maybe too much." She sighs. "It's made you look older than your age"—she mimes poking her own eye—"in here."

I flick her black-and-yellow-clad hands. "I don't like stripes. Or bumblebees. Keeping flowers alive and all."

She breathes deep of the fresh, looks-warm-but-still-wintry, sun-tinged air. "Fashion is not your gifting, and bees keep me sane. Such a tragedy that your love of the *look* of flowers is so at odds with your—"

ACHOO! I sneeze again, allergic reaction and my asthma and the cold and my emotions still bothering my nose. "You and your honey, bees keeping flowers alive that want to kill me."

Now Juniper smiles, eyes perfectly lined and lips stained with really pretty makeup. "We're arriving at tea, then, to begin your story. The prologue was that bad, huh?"

It wasn't the prologue that was the problem, actually. It was the chapters after...but I choose to address the earlier part of my morning, which though equally confusing, is leaving a less bitter taste. "Have you ever met someone you've never seen before and felt like you knew them?"

"Wow, you sound dreamy, and no. That's not sweet, that's creepy."

"It isn't! He was—"

"It *could* be. That's all I'm saying." Her hands buzz between us. "Who is *he*?"

"I don't know." Unintentionally, my voice sharpens in his defense. "And it wasn't him who gave me the flowers."

"Was it a Hayes?" Bitterness laces her voice. The needling words don't suit the natural tone of her voice, which is like alto maple syrup. A puckered frown mars her round, angelic face.

"Wow, Juniper. Way to jump to conclusions." *Not that she doesn't have grounds.* I loose a breath, seeing the puff of steam for only a split second. Warm-winter, indeed, but spring is coming. "I told you, I don't know who he is." But yes, a Hayes did indeed give me *these* flowers a few minutes ago.

"Okay, but obviously, he made an impression. Did this something—wait." She deflates. "How bad or amazing a thing can happen in a boring library?"

I smirk at her disappointment in the romantic setting. "Breaking and entering."

Her eyebrows rise with interest. "He broke something! Was it the crown? Was it stolen? Wow, can you even imagine? Even without the scepter, that thing must be worth a fortune and heavy to boot because all that real gold—"

"No," I hedge, unsure if telling her about the book Nolan was searching for is a good idea. After our encounter two hours ago, I'm feeling the need to keep our search secret. *Why was Lenora asking me not five minutes ago for the same book?* "He asked for an...unusual book." I flap my hands. "And don't look at me like it's the straightest way to my heart, it's just my expertise. And it's a title I've never heard of before—"

"This is literally just about books?" Juniper sighs in disappointment; dramatic, even for her. "Nothing broken? And entering on its own is decidedly less exciting. Or criminal. And in a library it's less—"

"He was in the staff-only area of the fourth floor." I've told Juniper about the Gated Library, and the Double Sea, but she always forgets the significance of the different sections of the library.

"See? How perfectly boring."

"It's breaking the rules!"

"Surely, *surely*, there is more fun in the world than breaking library codes of conduct."

A throat behind us clears, deep and resonant even without words, calling me out formally, "Miss Wrenley. Visiting her namesake? Or running away from her duties at the library?"

THE FOURTH STORY

In the Gated Library, two hours earlier

THE YOUNG MAN WITH GOLDEN EYES tilted his head and brushed that cropped hair at the top of his forehead impatiently. "I heard the *Oirdera* might be referenced in Gabreville civil records from a hundred years ago."

"You're a historian?" I asked. Any mention of past centuries brightened my mood, but I doubted he was a student here. I practically lived in the library, haunting the university at odd hours because of my filing duties for Professor Sterling Figgleston. Old fellow must have secrets in that eclectic, overstuffed office that I refused to enter on principle because it had no chairs. He left my work in an old copper-plated mailbox outside the door. I appreciated the extra cash to support my papa, whose work wasn't as busy as it used to be.

So, here at the library, between the professor's tasks, my frequent perusal of outdated overdue lists, and random bits of research to aid Madame Garcon with her bookshop's difficult customers, I was familiar with nearly every broken book spine. I knew which dusty corners to avoid, and how to find hidden books. This young man most certainly would be the type to be on said overdue list, were he a student here. I didn't think he was. I would've remembered him, because now that I'd met him, I would never forget him.

I chafed at the romantic notion, which should only be relegated to stories, instead saying, "What's your name?"

"Nolan Neville Carter," he said, low and rough.

Hiding my grin almost hurt. I tamped it down, not wanting him to know how much his name suited him, all troubled nobility vibes with his beastly mannerisms and fair good looks. Perfect fodder for a story. A cloud passed in front of the window, or possibly in front of the sun. It didn't matter; either way, it blocked the rays burnishing his fair, hewn-edged hair.

Nolan cleared his throat. "I have...interest in history."

I smiled fully for the first time today. I should be suspicious or even alarmed at being with a stranger, but noises below-stairs assured me the awakening of the day had begun, and the safety of this library haven wasn't compromised with this young man. He was too aloof and stuffy to be a threat, though fit enough around the shoulders—with corded forearms beneath his rolled sleeves and an intimidating sense of presence—to feel dangerous. Yet, he seemed too reserved for anything but the most serious of destinies, and he needed a guide through the treacherous waters of our region's largest library. That sounded like a good enough fate for my morning. "And?" I prompted.

"And what?" He frowned, an expression he seemed comfortable in.

Rude! "Finding a reference to this mysterious *Oirdera* in all those civil files is like finding a single word in a stack of books." I hefted my arms, which were tiring with the load of tomes I carried. "We need to be specific. What category of record? Law? Politics? Crown land? Elections? The Accords? There's even a section on—"

"Crown land."

"Why do you think this *Oirdera* will be referenced in there?" I asked, and he shrugged. I was just glad I didn't have to mention sewage systems. "All right. This way." I swept past him toward the conference room, as if my piles of books were featherlight instead of making me sweat. As I thought it, he swooped the books from my hands, balancing them like they really weren't that heavy. Murmuring a thank you and ignoring the niggling thought that Nolan somehow also possessed a key, to have gotten up here, I slipped *my* key through the aged notch and entered the bracketed side room—what I think of as the knave of the Double Sea—with familiar awe.

In a vignette of history, I imagined professors sharing hours of silence poring over books on the massive mahogany table. Lemony, sun-washed light spilled from the windows, warm and unhindered. Waist-high windows framed the room like book covers, the spine a stained-glass rectangle of alternating red and gold diamonds—Gabreville colors. The wrought iron between the stained panes was black and perfect, all clean lines and bright color dancing along the table to the opposite wall. There was a tall partition to block direct light from damaging the old books; ornate cherrywood, catching prisms. Behind it, overflowing bookshelves reached clear to the double-storied ceiling.

What a dream.

I didn't notice Nolan wasn't following until I put down my book bag. The expansive view always eased the hold on my chest, and while the illusion of flying can be falling with the wrong inclination, I always gloried in the view of the courtyard below and open skies above. Turning, I found Nolan stock-still at the threshold.

"What a wretched place," he muttered stiffly under his breath.

I stayed still, afraid he'd leave and I'd never discover his purpose. If I pretended he was a book-worthy hero with a tragic backstory, his handsomeness might come across less jarring. One could even edit out his patronizing raised brows and melancholy vocal tones. I almost laughed, but his grave countenance had turned sickly and compassion led my words instead. "What's wrong?"

He didn't answer, not taking a single step inside. He might as well have been climbing an impossible mountain. Whatever clouds obstructed the sun briefly earlier were long gone, and the fresh morning light flooding the room revealed a fleck of sweat near the ridge of his unkept hair.

"It's the windows," he ground out like the words cost him.

But why? I tried to see the amazingly tall set of iron-lined glass panes from his point of view. It was beautiful to me, as if they framed the world from on high, eager to let the light in. That perfect natural light was part of the reason this room was often used most by academics, what with electricity being only a recent invention in the light of the centuries-long history of the campus and this building. "They're lovely to me. But not for you?"

His expression bordered on stricken. "The height."

I stopped the teasing comment I wanted to make. Self-editing wasn't as fun in real-life as it was in writing. *How many levels high are we again?*

"Four stories up," I said on a breath, suddenly understanding. And that was more than your average four levels of a building, given the eleven-foot-tall bookcases on every floor of the library that served Loirehall University, Loirehall's Mayor and government, and the Gabreville Council.

He nodded. Afraid and ashamed, I thought.

My gaze wandered, wondering how my dream world could be his nightmare. How my perception of freedom felt to him like fear. The view would be a terrible thing if you weren't comfortable seeing the faraway ground from over fifty feet up. I inhaled deeply, thinking of how I handled my own limitations. "What if I tell you four stories to get to here?" I tapped the solid chair beside where I'd placed my book bag, farthest from the windows. "You can't see the view when you're sitting, just the sky. I tell good stories, I promise."

He met my gaze steadily, hopefully sensing my lack of judgement and harnessing that determination building in his eyes. I took the lack of retort as a yes, and began. "The first story is about a little girl who gets lost in the woods."

"Heard that," he grunted, eyes down, taking a single step forward.

I raised an eyebrow, allowing the rudeness for the moment. Uncommon grace and all that. I considered my storytelling options. "Okay. Second story. Once upon a time—"

"I hate those." Second step.

"Wow, tough crowd." But, progress. I bit my lip.

"You have no idea." The half-smile looked uncomfortable on his face, which was mostly stuck in a painful grimace. Actually, he had one of those faces that looked more beautiful when sad. How discomforting.

Third step.

I raised an eyebrow. "There wasn't a third story yet."

He grinned wider beneath a knotted forehead, taking the last step and turning the chair in one swoop, sitting as heavily as if he'd run a marathon. He huffed, but not in victory. "Tell *no one*." He fairly slammed my books from his arms onto the table.

"I don't know you. And I don't know anyone important to tell." I shrugged, giving him space, flitting behind the tall barrier to the beloved bookshelf, browsing the tall faded-bronze books and their gilt titles in renaissance typeface for the appropriate section of land records for the Crown. Instead of scouring the far end, where tiny drawers held assorted fragments so dust-covered that last time I was in this catalogue room they'd sent me into a coughing fit, I focused on the sepia-toned pages hiding behind book spines. *A single title can hide a whole book of pages...*

Once, I glanced over my shoulder to find his eyes following me, sitting there at the edge of the room and glued to the view opposite the evil windows. Hard work to ignore the heat of his gaze. *Focus, Paige,* I chastised myself. *Ceded land? Or unceded?*

Without turning, I asked, "You said over a hundred years ago, but do you know what exact year?" I fingered the new labels attached to the shelving, listing ranges of years.

"Exactly one hundred fifty years ago."

Unceded, then. I looked over my shoulder and caught his grave expression. He was seriously looking for something specifically in the Dark Year? And what was this *Oirdera*? Surely more than a random, rare book.

Even the castle, Fairhavens, the periphery treasure of Gabreville, was on unceded land with no inheritor. Long had it stood near the top of the mountains. The town survived, and the nobility either joined the Gabreville council or faded away in the annals of history, scratched out by the most equal of straight lines: bureaucracy. The castle's mine had been overseen by the richest bidder—after the Dark Year that meant the stewards, the Hayes family—as no inheritors came forward to claim the land. Seven generations of Hayes stewards. And if memory served, the decades-long wait was about to end for the next Hayes steward to control the mine, which had lain dormant since the fire ten years ago. What was the Gabreville Council to do, indeed?

Good thing that's not my business.

Nolan stared back and dipped his chin. I turned away, thinking of a story to suit the somber time we were apparently going to be digging around in. "An evil sorceress in a faraway land," I began, but then I remembered a tune, a memory of a melody that started a better tale, and stopped my story. "A sorceress in a neighbouring land," I tried again, beginning the third story differently, "came to the last daughter of a peasant, promising her riches and true love if she abandoned the life she hated and went to live in a castle with a forgotten library." I stopped because that third story sounded too much like a wish, and because that story was about to introduce a cursed prince, but then Nolan's breath of laughter applauded my efforts as I skimmed higher on the shelf. Five-foot-five sounds perfectly reasonable until you're reaching for the second-to-top shelf on an eleven-foot-tall bookcase.

Oh well. Nolan didn't need the fourth and final story. Hopefully he'd recovered from that fear of heights that made him a statue; as he was watching me search this shelf and his horizon would not be skies, but books.

"Found it!" Up two steps on the sliding ladder, I stretched my arm, pointing to the correct tome as I strained to keep my balance. "None for the Dark Year itself, but there's two from the year directly after, but I can't—"

Suddenly, he was behind me. Heat radiated from his body as he stepped onto the ladder as well, a scent like the yellow sunlight streaming around me, catching my breath. Lemon, and freshly dried cotton, and something warm. His chest skimmed my back as a strong forearm reached above my outstretched arm, sturdy fingers easily, gently, touching the book spine. The vision of his hand covering mine and finding home shook me, as much as the displaced air between our bodies made me aware of every slow, fast, long heartbeat. And for a thrumming moment, we were so close that I *did* feel his heart, pounding as mine stopped for a precious standstill, drawn out and gone in a second, forgetting to beat or breathe.

"Chronicles" were a more exciting section than they got credit for.

As quickly as he came, he left and sat with the tomes, efficiently putting one to the side—for my research, I presumed—and began scaling the index of his book for whatever secret he was searching for.

He looked unaffected. So could I. I returned to the table and surveyed the book. I had A-L, his was M-Z. They were alphabetical, so perhaps one would lead us to O, not that I thought our search could be that simple. "Oh, there's always a story when we're missing pages," I hummed as I took my seat, settling at the head of the long table a few chairs away from him; an acceptable distance. Couldn't have the professor coming in and finding anything untoward.

Sterling knew I spent early weekend mornings here, weekends beginning on Fridays and excluding Sundays per university schedules. Saturdays like today were usually quiet. He called it "research." I called it desperation to find answers to the sketches mother left, safetly stored in my folio—and the professor gave me free reign. I was the keeper of his spare key ring; he came up here that rarely. But he had a knack for showing up unexpectedly, and I'd rather not be caught in a web I couldn't explain. Still, sitting across from this blond-haired mystery, I found myself longing for more from the unknown caverns deep inside my heart.

"Missing pages?" Nolan inquired.

I smiled secretly. "Only the best libraries have books with missing pages." I ran a finger over the spine and headband of the old book that had a harsh space, ragged in seams that didn't lie just so. Someone had torn the pages from this book as desperately as I had torn pages from my mother's diary.

His gaze was steady. I was impressed how he'd calmed after his struggle to merely enter the room. "And I suppose you think all the best stories are those with open endings?"

Hair flipped over my shoulders as I opened the other book and said, "Absolutely not." Then a moment passed, silent reading. Handwritten scratches listed landowners and families. Some of the surnames had survived to the present day. "We have no context for these lists. No other books survived that year, and nothing mentions it."

"You're sure?"

"Not that I know of, but the Dark Year is sort of a legend in my university program. Archivists hate a good mystery."

"Sounds like you're well acquainted with the frustration."

I keep silent a moment, fingertip grazing the names with no context. People whose lives ended long ago, people who had families and stories worth remembering.

Nolan's voice intruded on my sad thoughts. "Happily ever after, then, for your stories?"

"Not really." I glanced from beneath my hair at him. "But I do like when characters have unusual names." I didn't even get a smile for my attempt. He was distracted. Something had caught his eye in the book and mercies, I couldn't complain about that, being *me*. "I don't know about finding references to this *Oirdera* in the

Dark Year. Sometimes history can't be known." I turned a page to where there should be more. The end of the L section. "With these missing pages, we can't even know..."

My voice trailed off as I considered another angle, shocked at what appeared before me, and in that instant firmly submitted to following Nolan on a wild book chase.

Either you yield to destiny, or it comes like a hound for you.

I blinked and rubbed my eye. It's for the *books*. That's what I could tell myself. And...for the symbol sketched beneath a hand-written name that I'd only heard in dark whispers. *Ludovici*. So innocuous, this little volume of Crown land records in my hands. Such a boring book chronicling landholding, yet it felt like it was about to burst into flames. My hands shook, fingers lifting away from the edges of the book with missing pages like it might burn me.

White roses...I couldn't believe my eyes.

I thwacked the book shut.

THE MIRROR LIES

Present time, a freezing Saturday morning in March in front of a bookshop

"P ROFESSOR?" I WHIP AROUND. Sterling Figgleston never enters a scene without, well, an entrance. *What is he doing here?* "What a pleasure to run into you." I manage to sound collected. I think, but then I think I fail. A shrewd line creases his left eye, magically distinguishable from the other many laugh lines etching his dark skin.

"There's trouble brewing, Miss Wrenley," Professor Figgleston says, "and you'll find that I chase it instead of letting it get away—why! Good day, Miss Puddleglum." He nods to Juniper as if only just noticing her before continuing, "Trouble is an oppor-tunity if you look at it upside down. Or backward, in a mirror."

"Trouble?" Juniper asks, ignoring my glare, her eyes tracing the royal blue awning, then skirting past mine with a smirking nod of her head to the shiny-eyed bird on the handle of his umbrella. "There *was* an incident at the library—"

Oh, *no*. Smacking her arm, I swallow a giggle at my disruptive friend. She deserves her recently acquired moniker *Puddleglum*. Sterling ignores our silent exchange with aplomb. I suppose it would take much more than two fluttering girls like us to faze an old man like him, however old he really is. It's hard to tell.

He pins Juniper with wizened eyes beneath a furrowed forehead, then points his pinky finger at me, a gold ring catching rays of sunlight. "My, your imagination is wide, but in this case, we need to look up." His neck stretches as if he could see beyond the storied buildings lining Wrenley Square—named after my father's ancestors, so some say. "Big world out there. But it's not the width of it, not even the depth of it I'm interested in, though treasures often lie deep. It's the heights."

Unbidden, the young man in the library earlier this morning comes to mind, like light sparking behind your closed eyelids when your fingers press too hard. A vision of Nolan's strong frame stilled by fear—a terrible fear of heights—that nearly stopped him on his search for a hidden book. But he didn't stop. He came with me anyway. Stepped forward, though afraid, when it probably killed him inside to admit how it scared him. There was something he wanted more than to give in to the fear. That's how bold I want to be. Regardless of Lenora's threats.

Hesitation thins my breath, so I use bold words. "Where are we looking up to?"

Sterling's umber coloring is stark against the bright of the few vague, unformed white clouds behind him as I look up, up, up to meet his keen gaze. I may feel fear, but one thing I've vowed to never again do is fail without first trying. Really, *really* hard.

Sterling assesses me with his trademark raised gray-black eyebrow. "Fairhavens."

I stifle shock, unbelieving that this place is crisscrossing my path for the third time today.

"The abandoned castle?" Juniper breathes in sharp, like the wind that buffets those empty spires. "Paige? Maybe we should've stuck with the tea plan. Go inside, drink tea, avoid decrepit haunted castles?"

"Normally, I would tend to agree, Miss Puddleglum," Sterling concedes, yet his eyes narrow. "However, our Miss Wrenley seems the right person for this assignment."

Juniper shuffles her feet on the sidewalk. "But Professor, will she get school credit?"

Sterling regards Juniper with bemusement. I've heard tell of their sparring. Juniper is of the ancient variety that holds to the tenants of an eye for an eye, or finder's keepers, but occasionally lacks the tact to keep her keen wit respected instead of mocked. That's what happens when you get a reputation for zinging the professor—during day one of "Introduction to Common Law"—then spilling his tea, and pouting for the next three months about auditorium clean up duty after classes. She's paid with the nickname Puddleglum all over the university since, made all the funnier for her very slight height and the fictional namesake being, well, *over-tall*. It's tragic I wasn't studying Law and had missed out that day.

Sterling refocuses on me. "It's merely a cataloguing job. The library in the castle was remarkably untouched by the fire those years ago. And while Miss Wrenley is a First Year, you and I both know she's spent more time in that library than regular staff.

Paige"—he's using my first name for the first time *ever*, and a nervous sensation flits up my spine—"you know books tell us more than the words on the page. What do you say?"

Hesitation makes my heart race. It's backward, but true. Like thinking of a story you loved from the end to the beginning. Once you know how the pages have turned, you can't help but judge it through the lens of the final words.

I'm still stuck on Fairhavens. Am I so destined to go there? Between Lenora, the evil queen wannabe; Sterling, a mentor with an edge; and Nolan, the mysterious young man in the library, it feels like I don't have a choice but to listen to the call of the castle. Like an ending personified, it has called to me since...well, since always.

Because though my mother's been gone for as long as I can remember, every year it was like finding anew she had died, because I kept asking and asking as if each new year the answer could change. And each time I asked what *really happened*, and *why*, my world fell apart. Over and over, struck by stones and broken by storms, a part of me inside crumbled like Fairhavens, the old castle abandoned since a deadly fire ten years ago. Its ramparts remain, but it's an empty shell of what it used to be—

Realization comes like the snapping shut of a book.

The castle. It's me. "When would we go?"

"Not *we*. Just you, I'm afraid." Sterling sounds remorseful. "I have a dear friend who needs my help...her time is nearing an end."

"Oh, I'm sorry to hear that." I'm sorry for the ending coming—final chapters have a sound, and the professor is reading the closing words with his friend.

He tuts. "I won't tell her you said such a thing. Regret was never in this one's vocabulary, and she won't descend there now that she's lived a full, heartfelt, important life. And her name will carry on…" His voice trails off into a sad sort of hum.

"Well, Professor, I'm sorry for *you*, then," I say sincerely. A hint of pain pools in his eyes. I might even say it looks like regret, just a tinge. "Very sorry." My chest rises and falls with a strong breath. "Shall I do this? What must I find?" I glance north. Loirehall, the Valais, even the Old Forest—it's all fairytale beauty. Then my gaze travels farther, to the east. Gabreville, over the river. Beyond the reaches of the Gray Forest where it creeps up the mountainside cliffs, becoming the White Forest on the Gabreville side of the Valais River. Where the heights of the trees and the mountain embrace the abandoned castle.

Behind Sterling's professorly coat and tall form, I catch Juniper's reflection in the window. She's also lifted her face to the east, nostalgia warring with reticence in a mirror of my own. She's from Gabreville, too. She and I linked arms many a blustery afternoon over either the Russet Bridget or the Concorde Bridge and along Valais Boulevard proper. *Quaint*, they called us. *Stuck-out* and *hand-me-down*, our peers from the Loirehall side of the river mocked. Girls from the town that never grows in the shadow of the mountains. But that wasn't why they teased. Others from Gabreville went to school and had friends on either side of the river without suffering the harsh words. It's just…*someone* had to be a target. Because we were both sad and unwilling to defend ourselves, except to turn to each other. But best friends become strong, under duress.

"Loirehall is Cinderella to the fairytale, sparkling on this side of the river." Juniper jerks her chin in the direction of the crumbling Fairhavens. "What good is up *there*? Is it safe? Walls falling in disrepair and heaven-knows-what creatures who have found castle corners to carve into twisted little abodes? There could be *critters*, Paige."

"You think the search for beauty is safe?" Sterling scoffs, soft but serious, and both Juniper and I return our attention to him. "Who says that's what a fairytale is? Or if that's all it means? Entering darkness, bringing light. That's the fairytale: the rescue, the sacrifice, the saving." He looks up to the east. "Who knows what black thing lurks? Who knows if the treasure exists? What if you stumble upon it?"

I clench my teeth at the mention of the Gabreville treasure. Stuff of nonsense.

"Who knows if good is to be found up there?" Sterling echoes Juniper's question, then pauses until I meet his eyes. "Wouldn't you like to see for yourself?"

I am arrested at the unsaid in his gaze and the unknown of the castle in the distance. What child hasn't dreamt of finding the fabled treasure? *Gems abound*, grandmothers tell busy children in need of a task, sending them to dig in backyards or rustle through imaginary castle towers in their own attics. But that's pretend. This is literal. *Can* the treasure be real? Lenora *is* looking for it.

My mind flits to Nolan's search for the *Oirdera* this morning.

Coincidence? Shouldn't I take this catalogue job and find answers? I may love libraries—and it's amazing that the library there is intact and I'd love to see it—but also, I can certainly leave the library and search the castle while I'm there...

Juniper shakes herself out of her stupor. "No," she intercedes, "this is a very bad, terrible idea."

"It might be," the professor muses, "or it may be the one thing you need. A single night can change your life," he says gravely. "A single choice can save a life. We never know how our decisions make the world unfold. All I've learned is that the deepest pain can point us to seek what's better—love, and truth—if we only look up."

Tears fill my eyes. I didn't learn from my pain and become better. I went straight to broken and stayed there. Isn't that why I couldn't deny Lenora earlier? My poor papa? The force driving me to protect my father isn't righteous, making me move. It just feels like guilt.

"I can't believe that old library isn't dust and ashes." Worry etches around Juniper's eyes, lined with the smoothest black pencil shade.

"The areas the family lived in were modern construction, but the older wings, the original sections, are stone. Centuries old. And the library wing was sealed off before there was even smoke damage. Fire ate the inside of the castle. People left it after it started burning, except for the top floors... I'm sorry if it's hard for you, Paige." As he knows of my loss that night, Professor Figgleston's voice is kind, but firm. "But there are those of us who are *looking* now that the smoke has cleared."

I cringe. The smoke's been clear for ten years, and somehow, it's still making my eyes sting. My mother *died* in that fire. So did my grandmother. An ending, the kind you have no choice for, when you're not ready to close the book. I've been so worried about my papa because he's all I have left to care for. I never went to look for *them* the night of the fire, but I won't let my fears keep me from helping *him* any way I can, even when it feels like I lost him that night, too. Bodies die, hearts do too. My eyes fill, caressed by a cool wind.

"Oh. Well, there are credible rumors it's haunted." Juniper scrunches her nose and wraps wool-clad hands around my arm as if to stop me, or comfort me.

"It's guarded," Sterling responds. "There's a difference."

Juniper huffs, steam in cold air, then it's gone. "So, you're sending my best friend alone to—"

"There are caretakers on the property at the gatehouse who guard the entrance and care for the land," Sterling reassures over her sputtering.

On my behalf, Juniper's not ready to concede. "Webs and dust will aggravate Paige's asthma! And who knows what creaking, forgotten things hide in the castle walls?" She's nothing if not tenacious—but it's helpful in this case. Because I'm too stupefied at the prospect of Sterling's proposition coinciding with the threats from Lenora. All pointing me to return to the place where my mother and grandmother died. It seems too easy. And above it all, my thoughts revolve around the young man I met this morning on the fourth floor of the library, searching for the records of the land the castle rests upon. Searching for the *Oirdera*.

Something about the title of the book Nolan was looking for brushes through my thoughts, like the sweep of a breeze with a scent of story. A scene you're not sure is yours, someone else's, or a memory that belongs to the future. "It sounds hard," I finally say, but my heart says it's *so* hard. It's so hard to move on, it's so hard to let go, it's so hard to see my father caught in the past.

"Then you should probably do it," Sterling replies with certainty.

I know I'll say yes, as I must search for my father at the castle anyway and this provides the perfect opportunity, but I feel stubborn. The last breath of air before going under. "Why?"

"Because it's hard." A pause, then Sterling asks, "What if it's worth it?"

Curiosity has a foothold, but it's less whimsical—more a sense of needling dread for unavoidable questions, like *what if it's worse?* I sigh, struggling to imagine a catalogue job being dramatic, no matter that it's in an old, abandoned castle. "You really think I should go?"

"Me? No, I can't think that for you. You ask the question, you find the answer."

"You make it sound simple."

"I never said that. Good answers are never anything but complicated." He smacks his lips. He's right, so I just nod. Sterling nods back and it feels like a salute. "Don't be afraid."

I tug my scarf. It feels too tight around my neck. "Anything specific you're warning me of?"

His lined face stays completely straight. "Don't fall in love. It's dangerous. The very worst thing other than traipsing through the decrepit parts of a castle. Stay away from the ashes and you'll be fine."

Juniper laughs. "Professor, you're the king of swoony tunes every Friday at the Jazz Club. How often do those songs talk about falling in love?"

"What else good is there to fall for?" He waves a dismissive hand. "Everyone needs a heart-hobby. Have you found yours?"

Juniper squirms. Then looks at me and points at the mountains where the castle lies. "We're talking about my best friend and a dangerous, haunted, castle-thing above a huge mine—"

"*No one* is going searching for ghosts." Sterling leans his tall frame down to peer at her. To her credit, she doesn't step back. "Unless you think books come alive?"

I choke on a laugh. Such an absurd conversation, but what a marvelous idea.

"Okay, maybe it's just *guarded*"—Juniper uses air quotes on Sterling's description—"but it's only a book-list-type job?" She looks at me, dark chocolate eyes wide and worried in that special way only good friends who know your history can. "Are you okay spending that much time there?"

Lenora's voice from earlier rattles by on a wispy breeze. *It's what you need*, she'd said. What if there's truth somewhere in her evil words? What if this *is* what I need? I shake my head, fighting doubt with the call inside—it feels stronger, and I cling to it. "I don't know, but I think I need to go."

"Who knows what treasure you'll find up there?" Sterling murmurs, but if he wants to tempt me with the rumor of lost treasure, he's mistaken, like Lenora was. I've only ever been one to search for lost stories. "One doesn't often get opportunities like this," he continues in his official voice, which seems as binding as a signature. Verbal agreements are valid that way, or so Juniper told me after her third week in his lectures in law. "The antiques in that library are priceless *without* touching the books. But the books..." He narrows his dark gaze at me. "If you want to learn, truly learn, then this is your chance. The castle's library used to rival the university's, and it's older. It is still a private collection, but someone arranged—"

Juniper asks before I can speak, "Who?"

His chest puffs out. "Madame Penelope Beaumont, Miss Puddleglum. She is acquainted with the caretakers, as she's taking some of their items for display with the Crown Jewels at the Gated Library—candelabras taller than you." Sterling lifts a hand to hover above both of our heads. "Yea high?"

Juniper sniffs. "Professor, you do know both of us work here at the bookshop, yes? We're on first-name basis with Loirehall's Cinderella." I snort; Juniper has more snark than me. "And seriously, whose freakish idea was it to have a life-size candelabra?" She shudders from more than cold. "What if it came alive? It could knock you over and bar the doors."

I cough a laugh in the dry, falsely-warm air. "Dramatic much?"

"It's all the books I read," she says conspiratorially to the professor, who taps his umbrella impatiently, as if bored with our conversation.

"You don't read," I mumble through another snort—at best, she skims.

"Mostly true," she admits. "Too many in the world. It's the sheer number of books that's terrifying." Her gaze dwells on me before narrowing on the tall professor. "How large is the library? At Fairhavens?"

"Big enough for Miss Paige to get a semester-long leave from her studies for her time there. Two stories of a collection more than three hundred years old, from what I hear. But it's...sparse. It's not quantity that's the problem, it's quality. Someone wants to catalogue it—they're looking for something. Learning in the real world is incomparable, and in this case"—he swings his umbrella in a circle—"you'll get credit for your work there, as your friend adeptly negotiated. Getting your work experience in your first year instead of waiting until your final year. Does that suit?"

That *is* intriguing. Getting university credit from my professor for a cataloguing assignment at the very place I need to be? Maybe I can learn something for the admittedly gorgeous young man while I'm at it—if I ever see Nolan again. He was searching for the *Oirdera* in the Gated Library, but Lenora seems to think it's in the castle library itself. Could I have asked for a better coincidence?

Here we go. "I'll do it."

"Grand," Professor Figgleston says, as if this task is neither mammoth nor opaque. He taps the unnecessary burgundy umbrella on the ground, sealing the deal. An umbrella only suits one

type of weather, and it isn't this melting-frosted sidewalk kind.
But the mother-of-pearl eye on the handle winks in the slanted
sunlight, and the tall man tips his hat at the person waving through
the window. The sides of his mouth tip up in an impossibly wide
smile. "Penelope will connect you with the caretakers—a Mr. And
Mrs. Lucas. Don't stay in the cold too long. Cheerio," he calls,
confounding the winter with the near hope of spring and his
spritely gait, impressive for one so old.

"Toodle-oo!" replies Juniper, with a charming accent.

Bells chime on the bookshop doors as Penelope's voice calls to
us to come in from the cold.

Catching my reflection, I adjust my ruby scarf so the knitted
edges of warmth are tucked closer to my neck. It looks like I should
be warm, in my overlong navy coat with a thickly-knit sweater
dress brushing knee-high brown boots. Even my long brown hair
falls around my shoulders like a cloak, soft waves and warm tones,
nothing like the harsh threats and cool voice of Lenora, threatening my father and giving me no choice but to do her bidding.

But the truth is, I feel cold—the mirror lies.

THE HIDDEN BOOKS

In the Gated Library, two hours earlier

NOLAN'S DEEP VOICE WAS WRY. "I thought you knew everything in this library."

My head whipped in his direction, away from the white roses and possibilities before me. I may have spent a time or two reading late after hours, or before. It didn't mean he had the right to mock my studiousness.

"This is *research*," I said. "You think it's going to be concrete, but it's all hand-wavy." I fluttered my hands above the book with missing pages before me, distracting myself from what the symbol I'd just seen might mean by gazing at the bookshelves, where the civil law section promised to be long and tedious. "Leave me alone with the uncertainty. The more you read books, the more you know what you don't know." My voice cracked at the thought of the many times I'd read my mother's diaries, but never understood what the words were saying.

"Someone really did a number on you, didn't they?" He raised a brow, and I realized I'd said more than I intended.

"How—" My breath caught on my reply, annoyed that he was

so perceptive. Not just that he'd heard the deep hurt I'd unintentionally recalled, but that he saw it so quickly. *How dare he...* "Tell me about *you*, Nolan. Where you're from, why you're here..."

He rubbed his thumb on his dimpled chin. "No. You've been a help, but you're also free to leave. I have all I need." Eloquent speech, rude words.

What an unusual, beguiling, frustrating combination.

After seeing that symbol on the book margins, I wanted to stay and to help with every possible word contained in my body. Not for him. For *me*. "This book must be important, for you to steal a key—"

"*Borrowed*. I have permission."

"—and seek the unfindable." I shook the explosive book by its spine, pretending that what I'd seen wasn't already seared like an imprint into my mind. Some part of me was appalled at my handling of the old thing, but I needed to prove a point. "There's nothing here. Someone's taken literal pages from the book! Searching for something that doesn't want to be found is pointless." Just like me, with Mother's writing. Her random sketches, now showing up here—

All the words, they told me *nothing*. Why, then, were answers popping up now? Here? With *him*?

"With the cost this excruciating, is it worth it?" I gestured to the windows as I said it, and he flinched.

The sky was as clear as the expanse above the White Forest on the coldest mornings, where the only color left in a white-covered world was the bluest of skies above the Gabreville mountains, and the spires of Fairhavens reaching, reaching.

Mountains. The mines beneath them. My mother, and my grandmother. The missing pages in the index from A-L. The *Oirdera*, whatever it contained, didn't want to be found in this way, apparently. Something else, however, did. A drawing in the margins. In this innocuous old book before me, a book of handwritten lists. Names. Places.

"I told you," he said, interrupting my thoughts with a baritone voice both jagged and harsh, "you're free to leave. I'm not making you stay. I'll find what I need on my own."

I silently called him the names of my favorite villains while holding the open tome toward him. "And I told *you*; something's missing."

He leaned forward and examined the open book I held before him, the ragged edges catching the pad of his fingertip as he traced the missing pages where the *Oirdera* listing might've been referenced among family names and landholding titles. Lost genealogies, referenced between lists. An index with meanings historians hadn't yet determined.

"It isn't listed under 'O'," he said, apparently relieved, "but the section missing in this book is the beginning of the 'H' section."

"Why there?"

"Hayes," he said quietly. "It exists, then."

"If someone went to the effort to rip their pages from the story, possibly," I said, glancing at his fair hair and thinking the only Hayes men I knew were dark-haired. "But it could still just be a story. Not a rare book, just a rumor." Not that I wasn't curious as to *why* he was so determined.

He pushed the unhelpful volume back at me, not seeming to have noticed how I'd been using my thumb to hide the drawing at the end of the torn book, which had a connection to the sketches I'd dropped in our run-in earlier. I traced the indent of hastily scribbled words in the margins before closing the book, its bindings still strong even after all this time, before putting it away with its unhelpful cousin.

"Still want me to leave?" I asked. "You don't have much to go on here."

"Right now," Nolan bit out, "I'm willing to follow a myth. I *need* to find this family line."

Legends and fables had been known to lead many a hero astray. "It's a genealogy then? Whose?"

He inhaled like he'd made a decision he was uncomfortable with, tapping his fingers on the polished chestnut wood. "It's the last mention of citadel lordship."

"The *Oirdera* is the genealogy of the lost lords? *That's* what you're looking for?" I was surprised. The lost lords of Fairhavens had been scrubbed from history, their names lost. "Why would that matter? The castle's been without its original lords for ages and stewarded for more than a century by the Hayes family, who ran the mines until a decade ago..." I paced beside the bookcases, not wanting to think about that family or my own.

Nolan's eyes flashed, light brown like gold. "Doesn't matter. That's who I'm looking for."

I glided a feather-light finger along the precious spines of my favorite collection in the oldest part of the Double Sea: the chronicles of amended law from before the twentieth century. So much history recorded. Many a story could be conjured from the revision of a law, if one's imagination contained the space. And I'd always sensed a story between the pages of the signatures on the city accords of Loirehall and Gabreville, where each year carried a sense of history within its amendments.

Every year, that is, after the Dark Year, when the last Lord of Fairhavens and his family simply vanished. Lost to history. Burned into embers, then ashes, from time passing.

That was a slow process—not like the fire that'd killed my mother in the very castle Nolan was concerned with. Fairhavens, which had a history of bursting into flames. *Indestructible chest. Ruby-red key.* What did the note mean? Who'd written those words in the margins beside a smudged ink drawing—the exact crest from my mother's locket, just as in her diary?

"I'm willing to pay whatever cost," Nolan said to my back.

What others called a lost cause, I called a mystery. From a shelf at the height of my waist, I took the council records—hazarding a glance at the young man who looked fit. Strong, like someone who ran for sheer enjoyment, and yet, he was terrified of heights. I said to him, "Considering you shouldn't be in this room at all *and* I haven't screamed yet, I'd say I can accrue whatever debt I please."

"Well then, I owe you." His straight eyebrows lowered as he tipped his jaw at the book I held. "Please?"

I paused. The flashing storm in his eyes didn't return, but gold was molten and dangerous. The sheen, like a challenge, drew me in. That's how I found myself saying, before I could stop myself, "Here." I hastily handed him the book. "This is the only place I think there might be a clue."

I stood behind him as he flipped pages, my eyes skimming the simple lines of signatures. Used from after the Dark Year until 1914 in council meetings, the ornate book was tall and thin, unlike the thick, damaged leather of the other records from that era that we'd been handling.

Nolan paused at the bottom of the seventh page. Family names in a simple list, witnesses to the very first accord. "See the blotted-out name?" I pointed to where his finger stopped. "That's who you're looking for."

The heir, the lost family of the last Lord of Fairhavens, the forgotten name.

I looked closer. Most others were readable, and a signature within the witnesses stood out: *Neville Richter Hayes.*

"Neville is an unusual name," I prodded, suspicious.

"Coincidence. Gabreville is an old place."

How unsatisfactory. If he *was* a Hayes, some far-off cousin, perhaps, why would he want the *Oirdera*? If that book truly was a rare genealogy of the lost lords...what a prize. Finding it would open the door to allow any lost inheritor from the lordship genealogy to take ownership of the castle and lands, and most richly, the mine. The Hayes family weren't on the council, nor were they descended from the last lords of the castle—they had *bought* rights to the mine after the Dark Year. They'd made riches from the mine for generations. Until ten years ago, to be exact. Until the fire.

Gabreville Council governed the citadel itself by proxy, their only stipulation the decade-long holding pattern between each successive steward, to leave the path open for a lord to return. And lit behind my eyes was the crest my mother had drawn. The blotted-out name in this book of accords. The handwritten name, Ludovici, in the book with missing pages.

The room felt too small. I focused on taking in air, looking out at the sky and imagining my chest opening as wide as the horizon.

No one lived in the castle now. Not since the fire ten years ago. And no one was allowed to mine the mountain—Gabreville Council's orders. Officially, it was *unsafe*. In vernacular typeface, it was haunted, cursed. In practical terms, the mine would have shut down the year of the fire due to structural instability. From all I'd heard as a child, the castle was a wreck—supposed disaster on every step up the soaring spires, though only one tower had actually fallen.

But an outer shell could survive while sheltering brokenness. I would know. Not that anyone ventured up the mountain now; rumors and fear had a way of keeping people away. It couldn't be safe. Crumbling castle walls from the fire, abandoned on the heights of the Gabreville mountains...yet the depths below the towering landscape had caused the Dark Year in the first place. Historians assume there was a conflict, and if so, it'd been over the wealth in the mountain.

Greed, mining. Riches, gems. A tale, older than our time. Fairhavens, the castle with no heir. *Or was that—no.* I stopped myself. "Why...do you want the name of an heir?" I asked.

Nolan snapped the book shut. "Can't tell you that."

My thoughts churned. "It's not like anyone is connected to them anymore."

Nolan was unruffled, leaning back with steepled fingers against his chest. "I have good sources, so it's not a lost cause yet. But today"—he tapped the cover of the book with a ghost of a smile—"someone didn't want to be found."

"I'm sure they had good reason," I said weakly.

"There might be a living heir to the citadel and lands of Fairhavens, and that's all you can say? 'Good reason?' As if they should be left alone?"

"Now that you mention it," I replied while scratching fingers against my throat, "it's quite the thing to be chasing after. Why *are* you looking? No one has found an heir for ages. No one's even been searching..." I raised my eyebrow at his wrinkled shirt, rolled-up sleeves over tense forearms. His lack of having brought a coat on a cold, late-winter morning in March.

He observed my perusal with an aloof brand of annoyance. "What?"

My smile felt tight. "It's just, if there was an heir who'd abandoned a castle and refused to claim it, I think he'd look like you."

Something sharp lit his eyes. A ray of light? "And what, exactly, do I look like?" he asked, something sharp edging his voice.

Weighted, burdened. Discreet, yet disheveled. "Trouble," I said. He was appealing, but also confusing; I wanted to know more, but part of me dreaded it. "I don't know if I like you."

"It's mutual." He held my gaze until a spot on the edge of my vision reminded me to breathe.

"First, find this rare book the *Oirdera*, all to find an inheritor? A long-lost heir?" I laughed lightly. "I thought *I* chased fables, but—*is* it you?"

He shook his head, blond locks straight and sharp like his one-word reply. "No."

I inhaled, not sure I believed him. "I always wondered…" He looked up and the interest in his eyes encouraged me to continue. "After spending so much time here, I've heard rumors. About the library there, the renowned collection. It's even mentioned in these old records." No one seemed to know if it had survived the fire. "Even if it was ruined in the fire, imagine what treasures might reside there, guarded by myths of hauntings and wolves beneath the castle's full moon." I walked to the window and the view of the Gabreville mountains where the citadel resided.

I'd never believed such fearsome tales. Like how I avoided seeing my own reflection in the glass, my focus was on something beyond, and far more important. History and books, always books. "Libraries always seem like a place for a good story." And, I hoped, a better one than I knew.

For a moment Nolan didn't realize I'd turned back to face him. His countenance was crestfallen, broad shoulders and handsome face weighted.

"Libraries are like churches," I said, imagining tall steeples and storied stained-glass. "It's a glorious sanctuary, but it would mean nothing without the people inside."

In the ensuing silence, Nolan hesitantly met my eyes, unguarded. "Sanctuary?" he asked, with a hint of reverence.

"This library makes these little towns fade away. The people in books don't care who I am or who my father is and who my mother was. I can be myself as I let their stories tell themselves in my imagination. I'll never judge them, and they don't judge me." I sighed, allowing myself this one truth. "Books are better friends."

"Maybe you just haven't met the right ones yet." A real smile tilted his full lips, piercing eyes focused on me like he saw beyond the books and stories I held too tight to my chest.

In this moment, I felt bigger, stronger, braver—like I wanted to be a harmony for a beautiful melody, instead of listening to a song that wasn't mine, over and over. Now that I'd heard it, the notes of his story might not let me go. What if this chapter of my day could change *my* story?

It was like scouring aisles of tomes and finding a single stanza of a poem you'd forgotten, there in the hidden books.

The Fairytale Land

Later, inside the bookshop, mid-morning, two hours and one pot of tea after the Gated Library

"THERE *WAS* A FIRE, LONG AGO. It's been abandoned ever since." Enchantress she is, Penelope tells the story like a fairytale. "While the walls of the castle were thick, and cold"—her blue eyes gleam—"most of the furnishings were destroyed by flame and smoke. Blood-red brocade curtains. Centuries-old rugs from the late lord of the land's travels—"

"Did it still smell like smoke when you were there?" Juniper asks, entirely drawn into the dramatic story told by the owner of *Azalea's Treasures*, Madame Penelope Garcon. Loirehall's own Cinderella princess, but now a socialite and philanthropist forty years after her dramatic story, and expert in all things historical. And now she's explaining more about the assignment I've just received from Professor Sterling.

Penelope wrinkles her nose, causing the lines around her eyes to crinkle. "The windows—you know most of them survived the Second World War?—were shattered." Her head shakes. "It's as if someone walked the halls, breaking every window to let in the air and stir the fire. Only one corner of the castle is untouched by the carnage." She leans forward, lifting her teacup but not drinking. Like I can't touch mine, for her tale isn't a fairy story to me—it's the history of the night my mother and my grandmother died. "The caretakers told me the library is kept locked behind a steel door in that old wing of the castle. They wouldn't let me see it."

Juniper bounces. "What are they hiding?" She's standing, as we all are, at the front counter of *Azalea's*, teacups and dainty saucers between us and a teapot in the middle. "Why do they need Paige now?"

Penelope tilts her head. "They said their client is looking for something, like we all are, but something...specific. They need someone with time and experience, which you have now, Paige. And a university dean who speaks highly doesn't hurt either." Her light blue eyes fall on me. "I'm surprised you accepted so readily, but I agree with Sterling. You should go."

I look away. I don't want to give away Lenora's influence on my motivation to go to the citadel. Sterling's and Penelope's roles in arranging this library catalogue job—quest, really—are help enough. It's a perfect complement, the coincidence somehow reassuring. Between the two of them, surely they can contain the storm of what's to come and make it beautiful. I hate to hold back information from either of them, but if they knew I'd agreed because of Declan Hayes's estranged wife, I don't believe they would take the news kindly.

But they didn't hear her threats like I did today. They don't know what I now do about my papa—his bad choices and burdens that are now mine.

"Strange, though," Penelope continues, oblivious to the churning of my gut, her voice calm and curious, "your father was there recently. Fixing an old clock, I believe."

Papa's been to Fairhavens? I bite my cheek to refrain from asking for more details. Papa has been *hiding* things from me lately, and with what I found out earlier from Lenora, this is just one more for the list.

Before his work at the old newspaper print offices and in his own repair shop, my father taught at the university—the Loirehall commute is the one thing that has remained unchanged in his life. I've heard others speak of it—behind their hands, as if that stopped anyone from overhearing—of how after my mother was gone, my father was never the same.

Eccentric. Reclusive. Genius. *Broken.*

My father was from Loirehall, my mother from Gabreville. Him with undying love for my mother, but undying love didn't work—she was gone just when I was old enough to remember her voice clearly, but before I could ask her the difficult questions I have now. All I had was an idea for books of stories that my mother and I would never share.

Since her passing in the fire which we never speak of, Papa found his niche, hiding away with his inventions and tools at *Wrenley & Sons.* Even as a child, I saw the kindness of the Garcons and how the former king—a woodcarver—had taken pains to give Papa enough business. Fixing and creating clocks: grandfather clocks, cuckoo clocks, simple round clocks for a classroom that seemed too polished and detailed for children who would only look at it for escape.

"He didn't tell me." I focus on the kindness of the woman before me. It aches, keeping my voice at an even keel to hide my turmoil. "Was it freestanding or a wall clock?"

"Oh, it was a strange one, with legs to stand on. I wanted it for my wall! Quite unusual, and I've seen my share of outlandish clock designs from the regent—oh, you girls are too young to have known him. Nicholas's uncle—now *there* was a person who lived in a world all their own. Did you know he built hidden treehouses in the Gray Forest?"

"The Old Woods?" Juniper smirks her question and Penelope smiles back, both angelic with a hint of stubborn on either side of the cashier counter.

There's a generational disagreement on both sides of the Valais river about the name of the forest that spans the northwestern edge of Loirehall, travels along former Crown land, and continues over the river to the northern edges of Gabreville proper and halfway up the mountains. Though dark and dense, it's often called the White Forest, likely for the medieval citadel in its center—Fairhavens. Between the mountains and the forest, near a cliff and above the abandoned mine, the castle boasts pale stone turrets from long ago.

What is the view like from way up there? My mind drifts to Nolan, the young many from earlier this morning. Would it make him afraid?

I give myself a mental shake. From Gray to Old to White...if I had to choose, I'd rather stay in the woodlands of the past instead of searching through the darkness of the White Forest. White, the snow-line near the tops of the mountain. White, the rose from Lenora. *Wretched white.*

Juniper pauses spinning the postcard display. "If they won't let *you* see the library, why would they let Paige in now? What's changed? And who *really* asked? The last stewards died in the fire, and wasn't there that law about a ten-year period to wait for the Lost Lord?"

"And you know this how?" I ask as Penelope looks on.

"First year law with Figgleston, friend. It's terrifying. It's also been in the papers. But these old laws date back like a hundred and fifty years ago. Seems archaic to wait a decade just for honor's sake? If I was next in line for the stewardship, I'd be angry, wouldn't you?" Juniper asks, and our gazes lock before swinging to Penelope.

I've read about Gabreville Council's most recent deliberations. Now that a decade has passed since the passing of the previous steward, this land will be deeded to their next closest relative, in this case the younger brother of the family that died in the fire. Unless there's another claim.

It hits me with startling clarity. "And the next closest relative is..."

Penelope's words are solemn. "Declan Hayes."

It's a shame the old steward's son didn't survive the fire. He could stop Declan. Because of my own grief at the time, I don't recall specifics. I was too young, my memories hazy but for my own pain. "Didn't the son die in the fire?" I almost ask, but Penelope's already chatting with Juniper.

"Juniper, did you really read the last weekend edition of the Gazette? I thought you'd sworn off newspapers for life." As Juniper returns to her tea, mumbling under her breath about 'accidental reading,' Penelope elegantly shrugs one slim shoulder. "Badgering of the council aside, the caretakers were gracious to me, allowing me to take some inner décor and the occasional garden statue. Candelabras—"

"The professor told us about those," Juniper interrupts, "to *scare* us."

"The rust on those candelabras is a mountain all its own. My poor nephew helped me restore them." Penelope's eyes travel the heights above the bookshelves around us, where volumes are stacked unreasonably high to touch the ceiling.

"And the heir? The Lord of the Mountain?" Juniper mimes a shudder, but I think her fingertips shaking are real. She's never been sensitive to anything except the dark, jumping at shadows since we were little. "It's been a hundred and fifty years and his ghost has returned? Was it him who wrecked the windows then, like you said? I always heard the fire had almost supernatural speed. Is he a—"

"If you mention ghosts again, I'll send you to the storage room to sort old newspapers. You'll find musty boxes and antiques donated from the Gregson Estate after the passing of their patriarch." Penelope's voice slices on a diamond edge that no one would dare question. "That should be enough to shower you with ghosts of the past in all their dust-moted glory."

Juniper's bangs cover her eyes as she dips her head, muttering obstinately, "I apologize."

Sterling's words from earlier come to mind. *Who says that's what a fairytale is?*

I nudge Juniper's elbow. "Your version of the story is more exciting. All I'm to do is catalogue books. Thrilling inventory, these items." I shake the crisp sheet of paper—a handwritten list Penelope had handed me after pouring my tea—which is full of decidedly boring titles that the caretakers recall from memory. I'm to add to this list so the university can begin negotiating shared ownership of the old collection, and eventually transfer the most valuable items to the Gated Library for safekeeping.

I smooth the slip of paper. I'm a sucker for saving old books.

Penelope smacks her lips together. "You'll find all that, and more."

I place my elbows on either side of my untouched teacup, wary of venturing into the fairytale land of Fairhavens. "You're *certain* the library isn't wrecked too?"

"Yes. And Mr. and Mrs. Lucas are good people, you won't be alone up there." *That's their names, the caretakers of the castle and its grounds.* "Honorable members of Gabreville's community, and *such* a sweet couple. They assured me the library was untouched by the fires. Ruin is hearsay. It's a wholly different wing of the castle, thanks to a long stone corridor. And if that detachment weren't enough, pure luck—and the efforts of firefighters—meant the east side of the castle truly was untouched."

"How can that be?" The only image in my mind since childhood comes from nightmares. It's a twisted gore of the castle on fire. Burning. But then my grandmother's cabin always catches fire in that nightmare too. As if the dream was a twisted metaphor of my grandmother's and my mother's deaths.

"Stone doesn't burn, and the other sections had wood flooring and paneling, and many rugs and tapestries to catch," Penelope says, "and that night's furious wind was a factor." Juniper's concerns of the supernatural tickle my mind as Penelope continues. "The flames consumed all they could in the other corridors and the entrance hall, swift and certain. But the speed of the fire spreading—whether natural or manipulated—saved the library, they say. A castle like Fairhavens does not easily fall—not all of it, at least."

Juniper sips her tea quietly and I lower my head. I want to ask about what happened to others that night. How did the fire start? Whatever happened to the steward's son? They'd said no one but the steward and his wife and my mother and grandmother died. I know, because my father made a big fuss at the time about us not having a funeral. He'd kept everything as quiet as he could. Since no one had seen them there that night, it seems that many have remained unaware all these years. With so many questions now about a time that I've been happy not to remember, I hesitate. Strung up at the thought of Lenora's threats and those awful white roses earlier, and before that, golden-eyed Nolan from the library. Papa, Sterling, Penelope. Where do I fit? What sort of fairytale am I expecting?

Penelope smiles into her teacup.

"What is it?" Juniper prods, never one to stay quiet for long.

"You girls out there in the cold, stomping your feet and chatting with the professor." She points to the window, storybook frosted edges and the calligraphy of *'Azalea's Treasures'*. "All we're missing is swirling, frozen, starry flakes. Something important always happens when it starts to snow," she murmurs.

Is it superstitious? Fanciful? True? Juniper mumbles about the vernal equinox and confused snowflakes, but I agree with Penelope. "There *is* something magical about snow. Even if those silly snowflakes are crazy to fall this time of year."

"Who said it's only falling? Maybe it's flying."

Juniper raises a brow, but it's my turn to smile in my teacup. I like that. But then my smile falls, because for all our talk of the past and dramatic, castle-consuming fires, that old stone citadel is guaranteed to be one thing: cold.

Juniper pipes up. "How *is* Azalea?"

"*Maman?*" Penelope sighs, tracing the fading gold rim of her teacup. "Not well. This past winter was hard for her, and I've nearly forgotten her age she's that old. We're trying to keep her comfortable. She swears she has one more summer in her, and I've learned to believe the woman." Penelope's gaze turns inward. "When I ushered you girls into the bookshop, out of the cold, it reminded me of another time—" Her voice breaks off.

Juniper catches my gaze, raising her brows. *King Nicholas.* The love they shared was legendary, and like their marriage filled pages of the newspapers, so did the state funeral, an honor bestowed by the government. He died two days before Christmas, two years ago, and the funeral for the One-Day King was black but beautiful—parades of black umbrellas on a rainy winter day as townspeople crowded the streets for miles in a somber celebration.

He'd served as Crown Prince Nicholas, King Garcon, and later as an advisor to the government. Eventually, his life was again interrupted by tragedy, but he was well-loved by the people. And the gathering that year—the turn of winter after Christmas had never felt so dark with so much light, or so sad with such a spot of hope. Just like Loirehall's historic midnight blue flag and that silver, teardrop star. The symbol of the crown had eventually been adopted as the city's emblem. I kept my mourning band from his funeral, and use it to bind my journal.

Penelope is frozen in memory, perhaps the same one playing like a movie through my mind.

"Even in passing, he brought people together," I say sincerely, honored, as always, when I remember that the matronly attention bestowed on teenage girls like us from Penelope isn't from just *any* sweet and classy and quirky elderly woman. She is timeless beauty and a nearly perfect checklist of lifetime accomplishments. This woman could have been a queen.

As if aware of my thoughts, Penelope raises her chin. "This isn't the first time the bells have chimed on these doors to welcome in lost girls from the cold. I daresay it won't be the last."

I smile, but can't bring myself to laugh—too many questions remain of Papa's predicament, Declan's scheming, and Lenora's meddling. Yet, Penelope's guidance is a rescue. It feels lovely to be clucked at and admonished by a voice that reminds me of the softness of velvet, with the surety of a brick—fairy godmothering at its finest. If I had to choose my own, it'd be her.

"So," Juniper's voice brings my head up from staring at my teacup as she asks, "are you ready for an adventure?"

"Not before unboxing this shipment of books," Penelope states, leaving her empty teacup. "If people don't get their books, then where will we be? What will they do with their lives? Their minds? Will fictional worlds exist if no one reads of them?"

Juniper drains the rest of her tea in a loud gulp before jumping after Penelope. She calls from the storage room—something about an old box with dresses and an even older chest of who-knows-what blocking the door. Forgetting that I wanted to ask about the steward's son, I laugh at Penelope's unaffected voice instructing Juniper to kick it out of the way, because those old chests are indestructible.

Indestructible. The word pings behind my eyes, bright, inked and smudged in sloping script, like the note beside that mysterious but crudely-drawn crest I saw this morning in the margins of an old book. *Indestructible chest. Ruby-red key.*

My hair falls over my shoulder as I straighten, so I brush it back with more confidence than I feel. Ignoring the reflection in the window. Afraid of what it will show, and wondering if it would be worse if I looked ready for this or anxious. Though I'm not sure I can tell myself, and I wonder which is the truth.

THE TIMELESS JOURNEY

Many hours after the Gated Library, mid-afternoon, and twenty minutes after leaving the bookshop

I AM A COWARD. *No, I am confused.* This is the refrain keeping time with my breaths, as I walk a brisk pace toward home. Breathe in, accept that I will figure things out eventually. Breathe out, deny that the events of today ever happened. Breathe in, ignore the uncomfortable imagining of my father's face if he found out I knew of his impossible choice. *He should have told me.* Why did *Lenora* have to tell me the bank is foreclosing on our home, not him? *I should have been there.* I should have been there to help him. Not that it would've done any good.

He chose his work over our home. Over me.

I can't wish away what happened today—the surprising, the comforting, the awful—just like I can't forget the sad ending to a story I never wanted to hear. Once the words are there, they must land somewhere.

After tea with Penelope, then treasure hunting in the storage room with Juniper, I walked quickly in the cool, clear afternoon to wait outside *Wrenley & Sons*, afraid to face my father and worried about the closed sign prematurely put on the door. He could carry on conversations while fixing anything, which is why I'd come here and not gone straight home, but he *never* closes during working hours. Not since my mother died.

My tragic mother passed too young, making me the sad opening of many a heroic tale. I still resent my childhood beginning overlapping with her story ending, for these new chapters have dragged overlong in the book of our lives that Papa and I have been scraping together word by word, brick by brick, year by lonely year. Now, he's been stuck in his tiny shop that holds his universe of inventive collections between two buildings. He may be a kind of genius, but now I know he might lose it all.

I lift my hand to knock and realize I've forgotten my gloves at the bookshop. But suddenly Papa emerges and locks the shop door behind him too early, greeting me with his usual gruff voice and rushed mannerisms. Like him, I'm not one to prattle, so after a perfunctory overview of my day—coward I am, leaving out anything *important*—he nods and lapses into silence, walking beside me at a crisp pace.

We pass over Concorde Bridge, through the historic quarter, and walk up Main Street in Gabreville. Our path takes us around the medieval cathedral, soaring high with gothic spires outside and a pipe organ that resonates timeless music inside. Each façade has an abundance of stained-glass windows, rainbow-prisms of light. The designs tend to the grotesque, not beautiful.

Red and gold flags flap above in too brisk a breeze. Papa's steps haven't slowed, and now my breaths hover beneath words I wish I could ask. Questions about the woman who gave me white roses. And how long until someone takes away our home? If I leave the unsaid mute one moment longer, it'll grow into a dark wood full of spindly, deadly trees and swallow me whole.

I have to talk with him about Lenora. Pretending I'm writing the bold words, I ask, "Is it true, what she said?"

Papa clears his throat with a ragged cough. "Who said?"

Your landlord, the witchlike woman who owns you. "I ran into Lenora Hayes."

His leather loafers speed along the sidewalk. "You worry too much. About me. About the business. You need to live your own life."

Indignation rises. I care for him because he misses forests for trees, and we all know woods are dangerous places. "Is *this* why you wanted me to stop handling your budget? Now I know you've been hiding extra costs—"

"You had workload from your classes—" he grunts, turning down the street one block from our home. "Wait, how do you know about that?"

Can't he see I'm trying to save our family? Why is he pushing me out? Twice a month, I used to step into the dim, musty back office of his shop—extra sweater, scarf wrapped tight—poring over handwritten receipts and putting them into a laptop. Just because the trinkets and clocks and devices he works with are from fifty, a hundred, *hundreds* of years ago, doesn't mean business today can survive without a spreadsheet. I *tried*.

"I just worry." *About how we'll lose our home in a week to the bank, if what Lenora said today is true.*

He hesitates, then stumbles to say, "You have to do more than care for your old man. I'll be fine. You can't stay with me forever." *I can't stay with you forever*, he probably means to say, but can't.

Papa inhales in a wheeze of narrow, unsatisfying air that isn't deep enough. He passed the asthma on to me. Bitterness laces my breath like thread stitching a wound. He lets me into our home first, closing the door behind him and shutting out the daylight.

I ignore the light switch, plopping down at the kitchen table, which holds a small pot with a sadly drooping fiddle-leaf fern, left unnoticed too many days. It was a pleasant gift from Penelope for completing my extensive archival work last semester. She noticed how tired I was, often bringing me tea when I studied—sometimes napped—in the back of the bookshop on my non-work days. This semester is so new, and with worry about Papa's stress levels so top of my mind lately, I'd forgotten to water or relocate the plant.

Our cozy house reeks with the unavoidable musk of the unsaid.

Papa pauses to deposit his myriad keyrings into the hidden safe inside the old-fashioned family chest we use as a table beside our worn reading chaise. "You work too hard for me," he mumbles.

I step aside as he leaves purposefully to his room. Purposeful, planned. He's been avoiding this conversation as long as I've been hiding in my research at the library, and now it might be too late. "Papa, what's really going on?" I try to turn the page and catch the plot. It's like we're living in two different stories. Good thing I believe stories are meant to be rewritten.

"Nothing," he lies, his narration slipping. As he emerges from his bedroom, he's placing inside his breast pocket a slim, embossed book of lovely colors that I can't completely catch.

I bite the inside of my cheek, my conversation with Lenora this morning having brought me straight here. Her estranged husband, Declan Hayes, Lord Chamberlain of Loirehall, is sending my father to the castle itself, on some wild goose chase, holding unpaid rent over Papa's head. I knew cashflow at his shop was tight, his trade naturally lending itself to too-hard work and too-little pay.

I feel cold, and I just hate that I know where Papa's going. "Mr. Hayes is *threatening* you. He's insane! And awful! It's dangerous!" Papa stiffens, stepping closer to the door, closer to leaving, but I feel no remorse at hurtful words, my ire at the forbidden castle returning like a nightly story, like memories of mother. Sharp, like broken glass. I whisper, "Why didn't you tell me?" *Why won't you let me help?*

"There's nothing I can do." He gathers his bag and an apple from the fruit basket. I relax a little. An apple isn't provisions for an epic journey; maybe I worry too much. He moves to the front door, gaining positive energy as he leaves me behind.

I feel a trail of goosebumps down the back of my neck. "Is it cold to you?"

He sighs, shoulders sagging and forgetting to fill his tailored greatcoat. The seams are frayed, just like his voice and his shop and our relationship. "You're right, as always, dear one." His vocal cords catch on my childhood nickname.

"Papa," I say, trying to turn on the kitchen light and realizing the power is cut off. "Will the bank take our house in a week? Did you not pay the heat and electricity bills?" We have no more time. And he didn't tell me.

He shuffles past me, not meeting my eyes.

Words exist, though, even when we don't say them. But I refuse to accept a stifling story where Papa goes away and leaves me without a say in the ending. Frowning at the memory of his overwork, of losing himself in solving problems with cogs and wheels that can be fixed, I realize I've done the same with books. Neither of our escapes have filled our need for family.

Bereft, I run fingers through my tangled hair, finally ready to say all this out loud, even if he isn't. "You didn't tell me about the clock you fixed at Fairhavens, and you weren't going to tell me about this. If it's about money, I know you refused before, but..." Hand shaking, I point to the cross-studded chest in the living area, and the impenetrable safe within. I want my father back, and not even the fabled buried treasure would be worth my fear that his journey to Fairhavens will not end happily. Will he return? My mother didn't come back.

"You have the locket," I whisper with all the will I can. "It's real and right here and worth a small fortune—"

"No." The same force of will fills his weary voice, but completely deflates what is left of his posture. He turns the doorknob.

"Papa..." My voice stops him at the open door, yet he only turns his head part way, his profile etched in the glare of the stone and storied alleyway outside glowing with splintered, lofty afternoon light. Because nothing we do can bring her back, and he's all I have left, I say something I haven't said for years. "I'll leave a candle on for when you get back."

A nod is all I get for our beloved leave-taking. He leaves the words unfinished, not satisfying the story with a proper goodbye. My father, lover of stories, now willfully forgetting his favorite script he used to say to my mother and I as he left, when we were still a happy family.

He leaves into the sunlit alley behind our home, and everything feels unfinished. Debts. How far will we go to pay for them?

I try to breathe deep, planting my feet before leaving sadness. It's never gotten me anywhere. Shoving open the massive chest, I unlock the sophisticated gears of the safe inside with practiced hands. I found mother's jewelry box—unbeknownst to my father—when I was eight. The year of the fire. Papa never saw the times I observed his quick hands, hands that weren't yet swollen and sore, arthritic and tired. My observations paid off one summer when he'd worked long hours to upgrade the façade on his shop to match Lenora's exacting specifications. I flip the circular gear to the compass rose pattern, then click through the numbered sequence. I still wonder how Papa believes he's hidden the contents of the box from me with his nifty invention. As if his personal safe could withstand the combined genetics of his genius and my mother's imagination.

The safe opens with a soft click, revealing the oversized keyring to the shop, an assortment of papers and passports, faded paraphernalia like cinema passes and train tickets, and a lone oval velvet box. Flipping the lid reveals the tarnished gold locket, which itself opens to what seems like my reflection in the picture of my mother.

I look like her, I really do. *Is that why Papa seems sadder the older I get?* Both her image and my face now resemble the aged woman in the picture on the other side. My grandmother, old and faded, framed in untarnished, heavy gold. I imagine our three generations of women frowning with concern over Papa's refusal to sell the precious metal. Rubies, gold. Of all the things in the world, why leave this one unattended, unclean, unloved, unused?

My frown doesn't match my mother's Mona Lisa grin on her long, delicate face, but otherwise, we're a mirror image of the other. Doesn't every daughter want to look as beautiful as her mother?

Gently lowering the necklace over my head, I cling to this precious thing of my mother's. Papa allowed me to keep her vast collection of storybooks and diaries. I practically have them all memorized, and they're all I have of hers other than the red scarf. Yet with all those books of hers stacked on a large bookshelf in my room, he never gave me this. Why?

Every person's voice is a story in itself, she wrote later, in her final diary. *Every inhale an expectation of a happy ending, every shuddered exhale a tale of woe.*

Heart-pain throbs and I grip the locket above my heart, careful not to pull hard on the delicate, diamond-cut edges of the gold chain, which feels as though the slightest pressure could tear it apart. But the gold is heavy, and the finished edge of the rope design, though tiny, calls to me in the pain, because it's strong.

So much stronger than it looks. To have lived so long through lifetimes I know nothing of. Who owned this locket before my mother did? Did they have hopes and dreams and love and family like my mother, who left only her words and a locket with a link as fragile as the chain holding it around my neck.

What would she call her story, now that the title has been ripped off the cover? Is the title even right? Probably not anymore.

Spurred by the lack of light and the cold, it takes just minutes to ready myself to leave. A bit like my mother, more like my father. Urgency is heady. The design from the title page of the *Oirdera* Lenora showed me this morning is a precise depiction of the engraved face of the locket now so weighty against my breastbone. The design of a family crest exactly like the sketch I hid from Nolan, when I showed him the civil records with missing pages. The very same as the sketches my own mother left in her diaries, which I kept in my folio and have been searching endlessly for until today.

Today, that family crest has found me.

I keep my steps silent as I close the door and lock it. "I'm not sure how long we'll be gone," I whisper to the hanging, hearty ivy plant, tucking my house key beneath the iron cage it rests upon, impervious to the world and its never-ending books with tragic endings. Gripping the strap of my book bag across my chest, I turn away to begin the timeless journey designed for unsure heroes, thankful those stories begin with a familiar path, even though I fear what lies beyond. I hope I'm brave enough to face what's coming.

The Cursed Castle

A few minutes later, at the Endilwood Gate

I'M HIDING BEHIND A TREE, sneaking after Papa as he faces the jagged gate at the base of the mountain. Papa is truly going to let himself be a pawn for Mr. Hayes, so what else can I do but follow him and try to keep him safe? I puff out cool air in the fleeting afternoon light, refusing to think of myself as a pawn for Lenora Hayes. This is my choice. It's different.

I hesitate. I've lost sight of my father—*there*. Beyond a gnarled tree, far enough for the snapping twig beneath me to be unheard over the unused creaking of rain-rotted iron, my father wrestles the Endilwood Gate. Too hurried or too afraid, he doesn't close the towering doors to the forest before he rushes up the ever-narrowing path. He walks with the gait of one unaccustomed to uneven ground—heaven knows he's hardly left the dutiful stool behind the oak counter at his shop that serves as both transaction till and inventor's workbench.

At the base of the mountain, a parallel road to this pedestrian foot path is an equally wandering curve that goes around and up through forested lands. What dignitaries and parties and bustling life once frequented here? Long, overgrown ferns encroach the road, which is lined with tall evergreens. Following in curves beside it, time and forest life have nearly removed this walking trail from memory.

A gatehouse stands here, at the beginning of the road at the base of the mountain. It's a manor house really, the effect homely rather than intimidating, surrounded by manicured hedges and pretty sunrooms and greenhouses adorned with hand-forged iron and sparkling glass. There's a gate for cars nearest the road, and for all the grandeur the title implies, *gatehouse* seems to be the right term. The gate at the road has been left open, too.

The unused worker's entrance to the mine is halfway up the mountain, on the east side. Barricaded since the fire, Penelope had mentioned. And all around, these outskirts of Gabreville's largest parklands are dense forest, with the castle itself far beyond. My heart bottoms out and I push my steps faster. *I can't lose him too.* Papa knows the area; he's taken to walking on the weekends up the mountain. I followed him once this past winter—this isn't my first time sneaking and slipping on the frozen ground and staying hidden as he tapped the blocked shaft once and slowly sat on a boulder to cry.

Mother died from the smoke—her and Grandmother were found at the top of the stairs. I still don't know *why* they were in the castle. I just know that they died there. That my mother left me that night with my grandmother, who, in a wild state, left me as well. Alone, in Grandmother's cabin in the White Forest. *Why?* And my poor papa, out of town that night lecturing in a nearby engineering college, had been told over the phone that his wife and mother-in-law died in the fire. He didn't come get me until the next day.

She didn't care for her life. She grew disdainful of her unconventional husband. She didn't love her daughter enough to stay with her. He was consumed by grief. He didn't love his daughter enough to find her. I shake my head, touching my ears to remind myself that those thoughts aren't truth, they're words of gossip spoken in disdain or spite by people who care nothing for my family.

The Endilwood Gate is lined by manicured hedges, which connect the gently sloping land to the gatehouse proper. A world of its own, and a beacon before the way up the mountain, whomever lives in the gatehouse has created this whole...ambience. A home cast in muted tones at the foot of the cold, dark mountain, not shrinking in the shadow of the old castle.

Mr. and Mrs. Lucas, Penelope said. The loyal caretakers. Beacon-light glows from every window on both the first and second story. All the tall rectangular, shutterless windows on the ground floor reveal rooms inside. I hesitate, because it's inviting: the red door of the manor house, the well-maintained square courtyard. Square step-stones circle the courtyard, swallowed by imposing hedges taller than me.

Don't go up, beckons an arched entrance to the garden. *Stay here.* The ground crunching beneath my feet is not grass, it's gravel. Smooth round stones that make my footfalls feel slower, as if the wild of the forest should be forgotten. The lower courtyard—I suddenly remember that's what they call this. The university rumor mill fed me something helpful after all.

I avoid the path to the manor house. I need to follow Papa on the disused path up the mountain. So, I slip through the pedestrian gate, not bothering to close it and alert Papa to my presence. He wouldn't imagine his daughter following his footsteps—he's so desperate himself that he can't see the same fire inside me. It burns, soaking my soul dry. Wet earth and staggered sunlight and trees from times past whisper about this hopeless mission. Declan's blackmail of Papa, forcing him to search for the same book Nolan wants. Lenora's entrapment of me, her thorny words. She was right. I *must* follow.

The way is nearly obscured, but the weather is fair. No one ventures here, so no one will delay me from following my father, whose determined steps lead us higher, higher, higher. I keep to the trees, placing a hand on each one bracketing the path, as if implanting a memory of each step will someday remind me of how my stubborn nature helped me do the right thing, even though I was scared. Scared of the shadow of the castle, scared of the sunshine exposing my movement in the trees, scared of whatever reason made my mother and my grandmother leave me alone in the woods the night of the fire. *Were they afraid, when they died?*

After pausing a moment to catch my breath, I take one step and then another, up, up, up, where the edge of the forest-lined road steeply veers against gravity. Turrets rise like knights, towering squares with edges of flint. No tall tree can hide peeks of the grandeur, tricking the mind with distance. Up close, are they still sharp? The path beneath my feet is wild. There's a shock of cold wind, the afternoon ending. With the forest like an embrace, it's slightly less fearful. Though, from afar, I've always thought mist blowing in or dark clouds suited the far-off castle better. Sad history, sad story. Do the white walls hold stains from the black smoke, or have decades of rain erased haunting shapes like licking flames?

A crack sounds in the muted air—*Papa?* I dare not speak. I'm trespassing.

I instinctively move a step away from the sound, moving through the underbrush and onto the paved road, toward the imposing white gates. I feel small beneath the towering castle, which I know overlooks the lake on the far side while hugging the cliff, far edges clinging like claws. Part of me is glad to see it, now that I'm so close, but at the same time, tendrils of fear strangle my lungs. Still, nothing will stand between me and saving my father from ruin.

A howl in the distance punctuates the air, fine hairs at the back of my neck stand on end. My chest burns. From the long climb up the mountain. From fear. There are wolves in the distance, this deep in the forest, this close to being near the end of it. Like Nolan this morning, the heights are starting to scare me.

In the shadow of the castle, still Saturday

STIFLED IS THE WORST FEELING. Life, new life, is a gift. A gift I've seen others receive. They have a hope I do not; I just keep looking behind me, looking back, even as I run ahead. My mother, in her diaries, looked back often. Isn't that what a diary is? Looking back? *Just because there are clouds doesn't mean there was a storm,* she wrote on the bottom of every page. I never understood it. If I wrote in a diary on the bottom of every page, I think I'd write *somewhere, there's always a storm.*

There he is—Papa, up the paved drive, where the road is lined with oversized stones, alternating in faded white and black squares. In the weakening light at the end of the afternoon, the castle looms above us, its roof of vaulted towers a blackish sort of olive-green—the northmost one is ruined.

My father pushes open one of the massive black doors, disappearing inside. On the outside, the sandstone façade seems steadfast, yet somehow liable to fall to pieces and knock one down. This once-defensive structure was built long after knights and chivalry were reduced to romanticised medieval culture. It's not a thousand years old, only a few hundred years old. Even portions rebuilt less than a hundred years ago are made to *seem* older. But it's beautiful, and as I walk up the drive I crane my neck to take it all in. Then there's another howl, and I race toward the entrance. I never expected my first time at the castle to feel like a chase—wolves are rare here, but far from extinct.

I thought I was supposed to find my prince in chapter three. This is already the seventh chapter and even with a prologue before it, there's no prince. The woods own the castle, not the other way around.

At the white gate, checkerboard squares are arranged neatly

around the edges of ornate stone pedestals, which bracket the majestic portals. There's an intricate design on the ground, at the threshold between the destitute castle and the world. One large portal for cars remains shut, though the small pedestrian opening is ajar. As is the door to the castle itself. *Papa, I'm coming.*

My heart stalls along with my feet as I stare up at the wrought iron gates. Beautiful gilding trails along the top edges of the stone pillars, matching designs on the unlit lamp-posts atop them. On the principal portal opening, the tallest arc of the gold-plated gate has a mighty metal crest in the center. It combines the gilded motifs into a shield-like coat of arms with a single rose, cut through with a sword crossing over a rock hammer.

Breath leaves me—it's the crest on the title page Lenora showed me, in my pocket. Just like the locket hanging around my neck, that someone drew beside in the civil records above the name *Ludovici*...just like in the Gabreville Accords, where a name starting with "L" was blotted out, deliberately stifled, choking me with the unknown.

Climbing the path made every breath grinding from my body fuel more questions. My legs shake a little now that I've stopped running, finding something like an answer staring me in the face. My eyes trace the roses adorning the gates as I pass beneath, hurrying and alone and denying that I'm afraid, hand covering the locket, heavy on my chest. The rubies have warmed against my skin beneath my scarf, heating my blood red like they are.

Suddenly, I hear something. I pray it isn't going to be followed by another howl—gracious heavens above, that the sky would fall instead of the woods opening to reveal a wolf. But no, it's foot-steps, yet I can't see around the massive stone columns. Papa is already inside—is someone else here?

Just because there are clouds doesn't mean there was a storm.

"You," a familiar, husky voice accuses.

Flipping around, I trip, the castle behind me. "You!" I mimic his haughty tone, willing my heart to calm. "Trespass much?" Fear recedes, because the golden-eyed young man from earlier incites another sort of flurry, making my heart skip a beat.

Nolan smirks, but it doesn't reach his wary eyes. "You really have a knack for seeing the wrong side of a story."

I am testy and tired and thirsty. "I get stories."

"Reading isn't enough. You might tell them. Doesn't mean you understand them."

"This place doesn't look as bad as the stories say." I lift one hand. "Why are you here?"

"It's where I live." His lofty brow quirks, mirth likely for my attempt to school my expression into anything but *surprise*, be-cause though the castle doesn't look as derelict on the outside as I anticipated, it's quiet. A heady stillness that's lonely—there's no life or living here and surely he can't be telling the truth. He continues. "I should ask *you* what you're doing here."

His expression hardens as I continue stepping back. Never walk with strangers in a dark forest. Isn't that the rule in nearly every book, ever? "Special assignment from the university library," I say, feigning innocence while puzzling why *Nolan* is here. "You know me, specializing in boring old rare books. My professor sent me."

Nolan's head tilts, openness now in his gaze. "I knew Mrs. Lucas arranged more visits about the collection, but didn't know it would be so soon... A coincidence, then?"

If he means our meeting this morning? Yes. My being here now, no. Coincidences sound like they happen without you asking, and I'm *choosing* to be here. "Can't believe it," I reply, but it's breathy, my avoidance about plot versus coincidence.

How many people sent me here today? Sterling, but he'll always get you into trouble. And Penelope knew what she was asking—if she believes in me, I need to as well. But it was Lenora who first found me this morning. And to hear *her* story, it was Mr. Hayes who'd been the one to start this whole thing—if one can believe tales from estranged wives.

But Nolan being here, this is unexpected. We've caught each other off-guard, and though I probably know more than him about the others wanting a piece of this castle, I can't let on that I do, not yet. And know nothing of *him*. Isn't one supposed to meet a cute stranger and never see them again? I thought that was the story this morning, when I was drawn to that something *unknowable* about Nolan. Past tense. I can no longer wonder now if it would be worth the trouble to delve that deep, to mine in whatever haunts his soul—only a tortured soul can look this comfortable in the lonely shadow of this castle. I might go too deep, but perhaps Nolan is the kind of trouble worth figuring my way out of? When it all comes crashing down, will I have a choice?

No. This is getting in the way of my story, and most importantly, saving my father.

A howl again from the black of the woods, the White Forest. Hastily, Nolan grabs my arm and in a surge of awful memory from when Lenora dug her nails into my arm and coerced me into this hopeless, dangerous mission, I wrench myself away.

"Sorry." He lifts his hand, but doesn't back off. "Martin said there was a lone wolf—they're the most dangerous. We should go." He turns to the supposed safety of the way down the mountain. The effect of the dimming light is making the empty road curve to nowhere.

My voice is thin, like the air. "I can't leave." *Not until I find my father.*

I clutch the strap of my book bag, the bag holding books and my inhaler and lip balm feeling heavier with each moment. I'm determined to find answers from the mirror images chasing me all day. Ludovici, the locket. Lenora, the treasure. Declan, the mine. The gates Nolan now walks beneath as I walk toward the castle entrance.

All for a lost book. The *Oirdera* both Nolan and Lenora mentioned this morning—

I stop and squeeze my eyes shut and decide I don't care. Why me, why now? Father and I have been grieving my mother in our own ways since forever. Will forever end? I open my eyes, surprised to find Nolan staring at me, blocking my way, statuesque beneath the castle of worn white stone, looking for all the world like he *belonged.*

"Can't leave?" he asks. "And where must you stay? In there?" His voice has that rough-hewn quality I'd forgotten since meeting him this morning. His words though, are smooth with warning. "It's haunted. Haven't you heard?"

Scoffing, I look away. I'm afraid to go into the castle—this close, its white stone and chiseled details remind me of older times, older books, older stories. In real life, beneath tall towers, I suddenly fear the tales. I fear the history in this very real castle. I fear the emptiness, and what has filled that emptiness when no people have lived within to light the darkness. But I'm willing to find a way—any way—to get my father out of this predicament. And myself—I have no home, no warmth, no light, to return to. "I want to see inside. Unless you *own* it, you can't stop me. And didn't we determine this morning that the heir is a lost cause?"

Nolan crosses his arms, glaring at the forest over my shoulder. A hunter would look no less focused.

"The place has been abandoned ten years, and law permits Gabreville Council to sign the deed of stewardship to the closest remaining kin," I explain what Penelope said earlier, when she reminded me that this week was the only time I'd have without outside...interference. "Proceedings begin next week, when the spring session opens."

"I read the newspaper," he growls. The darkening sky loses light like sand slips through an hourglass. It's like the trees ate the sun before it set. "Declan Hayes will take the seat unless someone else makes a claim."

If only Nolan knew that family is threatening my father and me. "You make it sound like a travesty. Why shouldn't Mr. Hayes claim it if he's the nearest relative?" Threads tangle in the air around me, flickering toward Nolan, pulsing back at me. Mr. Hayes is scheming to inherit the stewardship of this castle and lands, Lenora scheming to usurp him by finding a fabled treasure before he knows about or can claim it.

They're all ridiculous.

But...if *I* could find a nearer steward relative—or wilder yet, a literal lost *heir*—would Lenora stop threatening Papa and I? If there were another enemy to distract her? Surely, I can find that book this week and leave her to her treasure hunting. My father wouldn't lose his shop, our house could be warm again, and the Hayes's would ignore us for good if there was someone else for them to fight. Could it end that easily? I examine the weather-worn but ornate stonework beneath our feet. All these people, hunting for riches. What will they destroy? What are they willing to do if something—some*one*—gets in their way?

Somehow, I don't think anything will be enough to satisfy them.

Nolan's eyes narrow, and once again, I feel like I'm in the presence of a hunter. That, or the cursed prince we're all searching for. *What if that steward's boy was lost, and never dead?* Nolan's gaze steadies, trapping me with a look so intense that I wonder if he's reading my thoughts. Scowling, as if *I* were the traitor! I stare back, tension taut between us. *Betrayal* a strange word to come to mind. I don't *know* him. I owe him *nothing*. It isn't a lie to a stranger, to not tell him my whole story, is it? I don't even know who he is—

A tingle of intuition stirs my next question. "Then how do you fit in this story?"

A sharp exhale. "I'm also a Hayes." Nolan's golden eyes seem darker, a soul-lit reflection of the brown hues of soil and tree bark and unending forest. I think I breathe *you're the steward's son*, but he speaks over me. "So, no, Declan shouldn't have it—"

A crash breaks the stillness, and both our heads turn. "Was that up in the tower?" he asks, incredulous, while I cry in horror, "Papa!"

Nolan's head whips around. "Your father is *here*?"

"How can I get in?"

"Do you have any idea how dangerous it is?" Nolan's intense gaze catches mine. "The back balconies don't have doors. You can fall from three stories up. There are chips in every stair. None of the railings are intact. Breathe wrong once, and you topple to your death." He faces me with barely restrained rage—but it's fear in his eyes. Fear for my father, for me, or for himself? I start to speak, but he cuts me off. "It isn't safe."

"I don't care! My father is in there!"

Ignoring Nolan's shouts, I rush around him to the massive carved, blackwood doors ensconced by a white stone arch. Emerging into darkness. Rushing through the castle doors in front of Nolan, who follows my anguished pleas to *save my father*.

There are no lights but the measly glow of the lost afternoon. The entrance leads us into dark shadow, and I am absurdly thankful Nolan hasn't left me alone. He forces past me, muttering scary warnings and instructions with curt words, leading up a grand, curving staircase two stories high beneath vaulted ceilings. An elaborate chandelier of wood and brass hangs, lightless. Carvings race from four triangles to a point at the top of the vast ceiling, animals and humans in wild chases in dark woods. Carvings, of a hunt.

And all of it scorch-marked. Blackened, from smoke and fire.

Inhaling dust and ash and empty shadows that won't abide trespassers, I ascend in Nolan's wake. The middle of the stairs seems safer. Beyond the top of the sweeping staircase, hallways taper into black questions in four directions—up to the west, toward a pair of eastern stairs that go down and up, and this level that stretches north and south. Nolan stays against the wall, away from the edge, calling me toward the servants' tunnels that he explains were untouched by the fire.

I know I shouldn't. It isn't safe, and I'm rushing. But I do it—I look back. Because this is the place where my mother and my grandmother *died*. Stairs curve behind me, tempting me to fall, and a gust of wind slams the front door closed. I shudder. Maybe the castle really *is* haunted.

THE SELFISH SACRIFICE

The castle of Fairhavens

I RAN ACROSS THE THRESHOLD of the castle without a second thought, because losing love is too terrifying to accept.

Through dim light and dusted air, I hear Papa calling for help. It tears me away from staring down the curving staircase, from wondering what lies down darkening corridors littered with rotting fabrics and skewed paintings and fallen statues of bronze. Brokenness lies in every direction. Shattered glass and porcelain, shredded curtains blackened with holes. My foot catches the edge of a wrecked rug. It crunches and crumbles into nothing. Decay and loneliness and burn marks from the fire scar the hallways of ruined parquet floor, branching from the landing at the top of the staircase.

I must have slowed because Nolan returns and grabs my hand. "Don't stop." His confidence is reassuring, but also a dark question for later.

The grand staircase connects with a more usable set of marble-topped stairs that curve up into darkness and then down. "Why aren't we going up there?" Above my panting, I can barely hear Papa's calls from a westerly direction, up a different set of stairs at the apex of the halls. Nolan is not going up.

"That way"—he points to the marble stairs— "is the way to the library wing. He's not going to be there; it's locked. The other stairs are the West Wing, and you can't go there," he warns. "I told you—we'll take the servant stairs." He stands at an innocuous wall, pressing a polished stone. An opening unlatches out of nowhere. I blink away ashy dust as he yanks open a hidden door. He explains calmly, "The south and east end of the castle are older. More stone, less wood. But these inner stairs are safe." Nolan holds the half-width door open and extends his other hand to me. "Trust me."

I hesitate at the invitation. It feels, looks, and sounds like I'm going in the wrong direction to help my father. It's so dark behind Nolan. I read wisdom once, that you only need take one step at a time, that you don't need to see the whole staircase. Does that still apply if the stairs spiral? No matter how far they go?

Nolan's hand grabs mine and he pulls me past, holding me against him as he shuts the door behind us. Dimness suffocates, surrounding. His chest expands against my back as his left arm curves around the front of me, his hand covering my forearm. I can't fully tell if it's my heart racing, or his heart thumping. Our blood pounding in the air, in the silence. He holds my other shoulder with his free hand, and I can't fight, not that he'll hurt me, but...

"I'm afraid—" I begin, but he interrupts, "Listen." His command is hot breath in my hair.

Papa's voice calls, clearly from above, "Someone! Help!"

"Follow me." Nolan's hand slips down my wrist to capture my fingers in a warm grasp, pulling me after him as he descends a flight and finds another new set of narrow stairs to ascend. He doesn't release my hand, and embarrassingly, I'm wildly thankful. I can't see my feet, but my toes hit the ends of the rough, stone-hewn steps, their length short, aged. The air even smells old. Step, step, step. Small square windows above Nolan's head provide tiny breaks of light. His hold never wavers as I miss a step.

At my harsh intake of breath, he explains, "I played here when I was a kid. I know these tunnels inside and out. It doesn't ever feel like it's not dark, though."

"I'm fine. Which way?"

My father's voice leads us until the stairs diverge. The sound seems to echo both directions, but Nolan goes right, which seems opposite my father's weary calls the farther we go up. And my thoughts are still stuck on always-night and lost-son.

"You know this because you're the steward's son?" I venture, asking the loaded question boldly to his back. Which would mean his parents died in the fire. Does he know what happened that night? Was he there? How is he alive? Why did he hide?

Broad shoulders shrug, but he doesn't brush me off. "Yes."

I'm afraid for my father, though his calls now seem closer—Nolan was right, the echo *would* have led me astray—and he doesn't sound injured.

I need a quick breath. "Nolan?"

"You know," he says easily—his breath isn't labored like mine—and he laughs, low. "I still don't know your name."

I huff in response. Maybe I'll tell him, since he admitted who he is. I want to know what really happened. How he left after the fire without anyone knowing for sure if he was even alive, and why he's back. Now *that* sounds like a story I need to hear.

"Who's there?" Nolan's deep voice carries up and down the stairs, rushing through my chest and reaching my father.

"Hello?" My father's voice is earnest. "Oh, thank you. Please, help me. The door closed and the latch snagged from the out-side—"

"Papa!" My voice isn't loud, and not just from my lack of breath, but because we've found the door.

It visibly rattles. "Paige?" My father's voice isn't relieved, it's *distraught*. "You shouldn't be here."

I ignore how those words prick my heart, just like I don't want to think about how high we've climbed, how high we are now in the castle towers. All I see looking out the square windows is a sunset-hued sky. But unlike the fairytales...no clouds, no mist. *No ground.* Nolan's fear isn't unfounded.

"What is this place?" I whisper to Nolan.

"The south guardroom, five stories up," Nolan replies, voice tight. He unhooks the latch and notches it before opening the door, so he and I won't get trapped ourselves.

I rush past him and throw my arms around my father. Grease-stained arms close around me, reminding me how I used to tease that oiling his machines would loosen his joints. His heavy-duty work apron never kept him clean. Familiar and heavy, his stocky frame surrounds me in a cloud of white tea and lemongrass and the tang of oil. A clock and a cup of tea and being inside on a foggy day—my papa.

"How are you here?" Papa admonishes. "It isn't safe."

I extricate myself from his crushing embrace, needing a breath. "Exactly! Why did I have to come running—"

"You should not be here," he says.

"Well, I am now. Let's go home." I turn for the door, and Nolan steps aside to let me pass.

"I can't, sweet Paige."

My feet stop moving, and my heart too. It's an awful second before I escape Nolan's confused, compassionate gaze to face my father's resolute, resigned expression.

"What do you mean?" It's like he's having an entirely different conversation than me, here in this forgotten tower. Damp from drips, smelly and wet from the elements that shouldn't be inside. Something scurrying making noises in discarded paraphernalia.

Papa's anxious. "Does anyone know you're here?"

Nolan steps in. "I just came from visiting with the caretakers in the gatehouse." His words sound practiced; they don't tell the whole story. "Then I heard someone calling—" A question in his eyes at me. "Why did you come up here? The floors are unstable, the stairs cracked, and I wasn't kidding when I told *Paige*"—his deep voice rasps my name, which I'd never told him—"on the way up that—"

"It's none of your business!"

Nolan's countenance hardens. "It is." Spoken like the son who grew up here.

Nolan is a Hayes. Lenora, his aunt. Mr. Hayes, Declan, must be the brother of Nolan's dead father. His uncle.

The steward's son was never dead. The steward's son is back. I swallow, not sure what to say. *Breathe.* "Papa..." I don't want Nolan to hear our family's unspoken pain laid bare, or how my father came to steal something, but what choice is there?

"It isn't any of your business either, Paige." Papa raises his eyes to the square window, where air flows without glass or bars to contain it. "Neither should you help *him*." Papa points at Nolan. "You're a Hayes?" Though frantic enough to have locked himself in a tower, Papa isn't an inventive genius for nothing.

Nolan is implacable, inclining his head a degree, eyes like flint.

Papa turns on me. "Do you really know this boy? Don't trust them. Not any of them!"

Do I even know you? The safety I felt in my father's arms is gone. I'm cold, alone. "I'm not *helping* him, I'm saving you!"

The stoop to Papa's shoulders from before is worse. "Nothing can save me."

A book could. I can be obstinate too. "The book—"

"Books aren't real life, my darling. Debt and mistakes and regrets, those are real life." It's the most cynical my father has ever sounded.

It would be better, if there was rainfall outside the unreachable windows. Then there would be a break in this stony silence. It would be better, if at this glorious height, the angle of the windows didn't make the last of the setting sun shine on my father's disappointment and my determination. It would be better, if we could forget the past and focus on the future.

I pull my leather book bag to the front of my body. "There is more to life, Papa. There are lovely memories, better choices, stronger sacrifices."

Nolan steps between my father and me. A force, a storm, a stone. "You are trespassing, and you need to leave." I wonder if his will is immovable, like the foundations of stone, or unavoidable, like a gale that leaves nothing untouched in its wake.

"I am not trespassing," Papa wheezes. "No one lives here. It's abandoned." He looks pointedly at an unaffected Nolan—*more stone-like, then*. Nolan, who's been hiding his identity, who's a *Hayes*. Papa mumbles, "I need to give him something, or he won't leave me alone. He won't leave *her* alone." Papa's turned so inward, I wonder if he means me or my dead mother. "It isn't anything that matters—you won't miss it. You can trust me!" he beseeches a stoic Nolan.

Nolan scoffs. "What do you owe your enemies? You must have them, to have ventured this high. You're looking for something *worthless*? I doubt it." A straight, fair eyebrow rises, and my father shrinks a little, more frail and more tired than I've seen him. "Who sent you?"

I am relieved Nolan is the one interrogating Papa. I need to hear it too.

Papa kicks aside an empty crate. They're scattered about with mildew-scented, nearly disintegrated packing paper. Their contents have spilled—serving utensils, intricately designed. "He told me to look in the towers, but these crates are tableware. I must find a rare book—truly, I don't know why!" he implores, eyes turning to me. "I just wanted to keep you safe!"

My sad papa isn't going to find what either Hayes villain wants—he doesn't care about rare books or the stewardship of Fairhavens or the lost lords. I doubt he'd even desire the fabled treasure, as if finding wealth would justify our loss. As if my papa would know where the *Oirdera* was, in any case.

How could he, when the book is in my bag?

Was it luck, or something more that led me to that antique chest at *Azalea's Treasures* today? An *indestructible* chest. What enchantment unearthed that book at just the right time? What incalculable odds made me find what they're all looking for, in Penelope's *bookshop storage room*? Those antiques from the Gregson Estate were much more providential than Penelope could have known. More than I can believe, to have found what I needed so quickly, even as I reach into my bag.

Papa is wrong. Everything about this matters. And I *will* save us.

Nolan's patience seems to thin, like the air. "*What* are you meant to find? Who sent you? Who threatened Paige?"

"This." I reach into my book bag and pull out the *Oirdera*. One of two, which I realized when I opened the cover and found an intact title page. One just like the ripped title page Lenora gave me earlier, where the words "Charta: Punctum Temporis" screamed loud, as only words on a page can, that this mystery was larger than I was prepared for. Before me, two men mute with surprise, silent like a chorus of crickets.

"See?" I say. "Everything will be fine. Let me do this, let me help you. Let me do this for you, Papa." They're still speechless at the *Oirdera* in my hand.

Nolan inhales sharply. "Where did you—"

Papa takes the book with reverence. "Paige, you should not... How?"

"And there are two. It's Latin. A second book. See here?" I indicate the book I'd found, with a title page saying "Charta: Primus Omnium." "I found this first one not long after I met you earlier today, Nolan, and now I know what to look for to find the second." I shove it at my father. "Take it. I've already copied what I need from it—dates, the list of poets. A picture. There didn't seem to be anything else useful, but I took pictures too, just in case." At Papa's questioning gaze, I answer, "It's a compilation of poetry."

I don't think that's all it is. It might be a genealogy, like Nolan said in the Gated Library this morning. Like Declan seems to think it is. But it might be something else. A map? Like Lenora thinks?

To Nolan, I explain, "Declan Hayes sent my father to find this. Papa, you can tell him you found it. He'll think it's meaningless, and he probably won't notice that it's half of a pair. This can end."

It can't, but Papa doesn't know that. It's up to me to save our home and Papa's business, and not from Declan, but from Lenora. She doesn't care about an heir, or who the next steward is. She wants treasure. And she told me there was a book in the library...so it's in the library I need to look.

"Meanwhile, I'll look for the second volume, for you, Nolan. If it's here at all." I feel dizzy.

"Why do *you* want this book?" Papa says to Nolan with a pained exhale. "Paige, how do you know about all this?"

Nolan also balks. "Declan *Hayes* is behind this? Your being here? He wants it too?" His deep voice catches. "You're trespassing...for this book? Paige, you really didn't know this morning?" My mind feels fuzzy as I whisper "no", then he asks, "How did you find it?"

I close my eyes, because the light hurts the back of my eyes. "Coincidence?"

"Truly?" Nolan's breath tickles the top of my forehead. His proximity is jarring; I didn't notice he'd come so close.

"Honestly," I admit, eyes on Nolan's chest as it rises and falls, quickly. But not from exhaustion or strain—rather, the physical effort seems focused on keeping his emotions checked. The steward's son with the hard-angled, handsome face who seems a single step away from fury. Not necessarily at me, but it's fearful nonetheless. I just want to shutter myself inside my head and sleep. "I can't believe I came across it right after you told me about it." I inhale and the air doesn't satisfy. *What a long day.*

"Why bring her into this?" Papa glares at Nolan.

"He didn't mean to," I assure him. "It was someone else." Lenora and her awful white roses, threatening my father. I hold back from telling Papa that I'm also looking for a map for her. *Breathe.*

"Who was it?" Papa asks. "Her?" He's right, and by the resignation in his voice, he knows it. "She knew Declan's plans," he states, resigned.

He doesn't know the half of it. He probably doesn't know they're divorcing. But I shake my head, then nod and regret it, for it shocks a delayed wave of pain behind my forehead.

Nolan reaches his hand out, stopping short of touching my arm. Silence soaks into stone walls and my sweaty pores. Loud, loud silence. My fingertips itch. I don't want to tell my father everything. I don't want to tell Nolan everything while Papa is here, either. The slant of Nolan's brow indicates he'll question me when we're alone. Unease flutters against my spine.

"The book isn't enough. Not even two. You should never have come here," Nolan says quietly, sounding for all the world like a privileged son born in a castle. And I realize it isn't the castle he's protecting, so much as himself. The son of the stewards who doesn't want to be found. Though with the way Nolan's hovering around my elbow, I wonder if he's also trying to force my father to leave simply because it isn't safe to be here at nightfall.

"I have nothing left!" My papa sounds desperate. "Let's go, Paige." His brow is knotted, furrowed, at me, for intruding where I should not. Going where I should not. Seeking, when I should not.

It feels like we deserve to sacrifice something for this intrusion into the castle. But do I seek atonement, or forgiveness? My father slumps in the sharp, failing rays of sun. Sunset arrived too swiftly in this tower that has become something more. A cage. A prison. A choice.

Well, I can only be me and hope it's enough to save us.

To Nolan I say, "I will find the other *Oirdera*. With you." He wants to find an heir, just like Declan. Well, they can take their heir and carve them up for all I care. It isn't Nolan's motives that concern me most. Lenora was right that us girls needed to stick together. "We know it isn't at the university, so it must be in the library here. Which must be why *someone*"—I rest my gaze on Nolan, who meets my gaze with a smoldering one of his own—"summoned me to catalogue the collection, right?" I fiddle with my scarf, but my side hurts. "Papa, Nolan knows his way around, so I'll be safe with him—"

Papa blanches, either at my plan or me being alone with a young man. "No!"

I sigh. I don't know which complaint in his tone I'm more annoyed at. "Your lungs, Papa."

Even now, I hear the wheeze. His asthma, his heart. I'm afraid. Afraid because my lungs are like his, because something inside *my* chest is burning. Afraid of the wolves in the forest, afraid of the people trying to destroy my father whose heart has been lost since my mother died. And all I have left of her is all I can carry. Her scarf, her diaries in my book bag, her locket heavy around my neck.

Breathe. I take breaths, exhaustion seeping in. From my run through the forest and the climb up the stairs, to the relief of finding my father and the disappointment that he hasn't changed, not at all.

Nolan takes a step back. Golden eyes lock on mine. "You'll really do this?"

I dip my chin. Of everything, I'm not afraid of this crumbling citadel. Some part of me knows today's roundabout events were leading me here. This isn't about him or my father. It's about *me*.

I need to find what happened to my mother. Why she left me. What was worth dying for. Why I wasn't worth living for. Where else in the world can I get those answers, or discover the true story behind the questions plaguing me? I'd wanted to stay in the Gated Library at the university, safe behind walls and books and unending lines of knowledge. But now, I want more. I want to be out of that cage and afraid in the wild unknown. I'm like her, like a mirrored reflection—she died here, maybe I can find a way to live here.

Maybe this is the something more I've needed all along.

Nolan addresses Papa. "We must leave, before dark. And sir, you don't sound so good."

"Go home, Papa. Let me find what needs to be found." Spring is coming. Lenora's date—the threat hanging over my neck. Her map to the treasure—*can I find something I don't believe exists?* For the first time, I don't want winter to end.

Papa steps away, farther into the guardroom, like he doesn't want to leave. Desperation makes us funny, makes us useless, makes us choose to dive into the dark places where we fear to find answers. Desperation makes us choose fear over freedom. But I'm not staying out of fear—I'm choosing to stay because I *want* freedom.

Spots dance at the edge of my vision. I push them back. "Papa, let me do this." Just as letters don't make words, or words make sense, silence doesn't mean something isn't said. This silence echoes. Truth has a ring to it. It echoes and ripples and shatters illusions.

My father is tired, and he needs to let me go write my own story.

Nolan follows our back and forth, brow furrowing as he misses nothing, sharp gaze roving up and down my body. Not in a lewd way, but with worry. I stop clutching my stomach and hide my shaking hands behind my back, adjusting my book bag.

"Let's go," Nolan says, his body coiled and tense, stone turning to storm.

Papa looks at me. Does he see my trembling? Is he worried like Nolan is? Or does Papa see my mother in my brown eyes and brunette hair and not his daughter, shaking right in front of him?

"We need to leave." Nolan—closer beside me, his hand once again in my periphery. Near, but not touching. A hidden place inside me whispers a hope that he'll catch me, if I fall. "Paige's father? After you." There's an edge to Nolan's tone. Respectful, unyielding, with simmering annoyance. "Bats come out after dark. Hopefully we encounter nothing worse."

Worse?

We spiral down together. Nolan leads, Papa next, then me.

My father regains some of his eccentric curiosity as we exit the servant stairs, but I hear his mumbling as if through a haze. "Paige, did you see these murals? They must be over three hundred years old! I saw that fairytale scene depicted somewhere before..."

Papa's voice fades in my mind. I see his mouth moving. We're at the top of the grand, curving staircase, and I glimpse the opulent black front doors—one of them swung open from when Nolan and I rushed in. *Hadn't it slammed shut?* Nolan pauses at the top of the stairs, waiting for me, framed by half-scorched tapestries telling stories without words: a conquering lord in a red cloak, an enemy at the white-stone gates, a citadel burned.

I can't hear because the blood pounding through my heart is

leaving my aching chest, rushing past my ears, pooling in my toes. Flecks of black edge my vision, but the dance isn't beautiful. It's wicked and dangerous and so, so tiring. Twin vignettes. Splotches of white-hot fire, burning me and I blink away the desire to sleep it all away—

I want to see if someone will catch me, but all I can do is fall.

the hopeful time

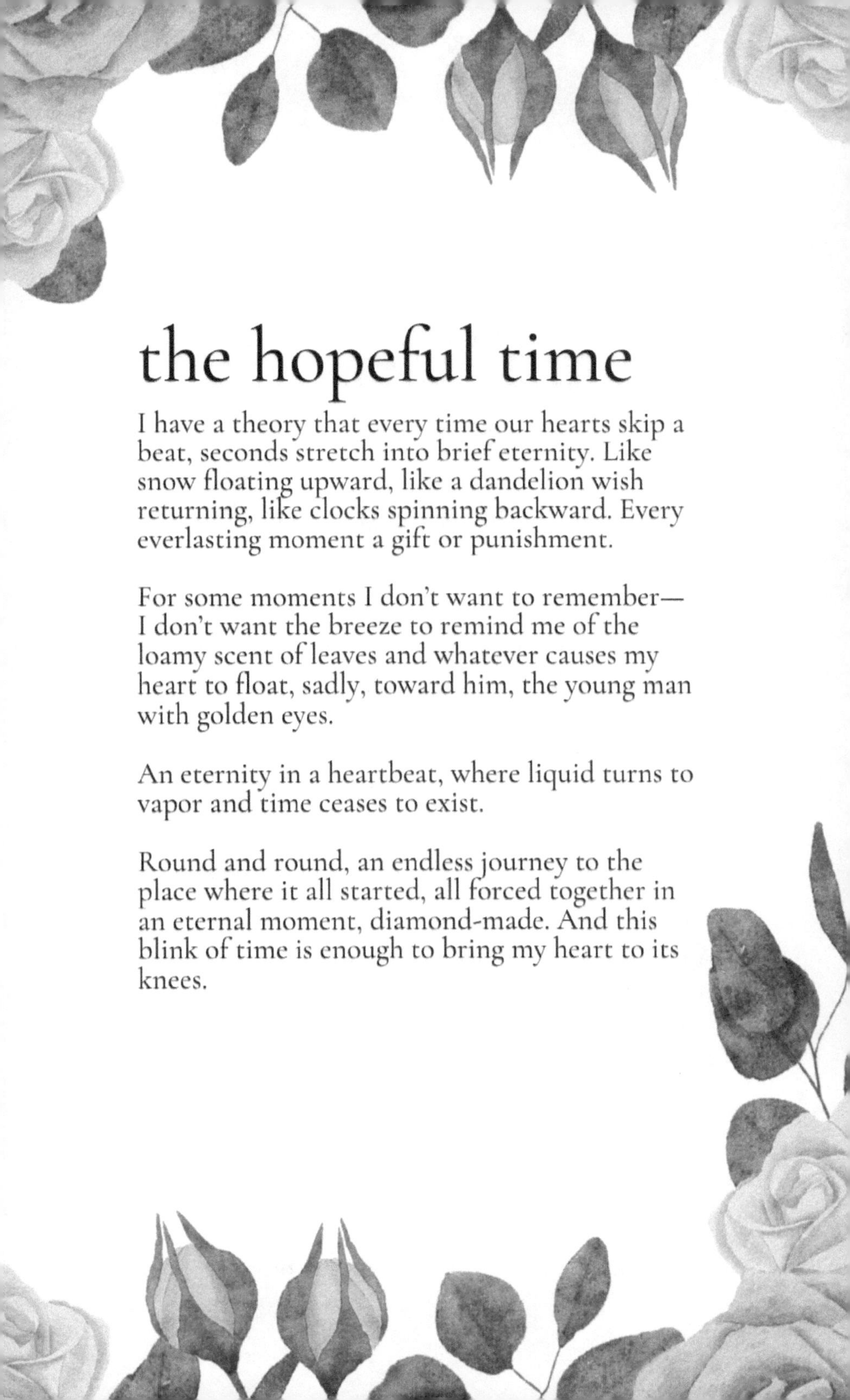

I have a theory that every time our hearts skip a beat, seconds stretch into brief eternity. Like snow floating upward, like a dandelion wish returning, like clocks spinning backward. Every everlasting moment a gift or punishment.

For some moments I don't want to remember—I don't want the breeze to remind me of the loamy scent of leaves and whatever causes my heart to float, sadly, toward him, the young man with golden eyes.

An eternity in a heartbeat, where liquid turns to vapor and time ceases to exist.

Round and round, an endless journey to the place where it all started, all forced together in an eternal moment, diamond-made. And this blink of time is enough to bring my heart to its knees.

THE LOST GIRL

In the square courtyard at the gatehouse, at dusk that same evening

DROWNING IN DARKNESS. I'm not that great a swimmer. *Fainting.* And just like that, I'm sinking. There's probably some connection between lack of sleep and food, physical exertion, and becoming a damsel in distress. I hope to remember what emotional toil made me so exhausted when I properly regain consciousness. Right now, though, I'm treading water in the inky blackness of confusion. Hearing voices from far away, above the waves, speaking about things I don't understand. I want to stay in the dark waters; it's much calmer below, and I know there are storms above.

But then I feel warm, it's all around me. At last, I can rest and forget the memories. It's dark here, and muted, but not scary. A magenta-hued warmth, gilded edges of black waves catching light, golden and weighty. A safe shore where night has fallen and there's someone watching over me. Looking for me. Surely, I'm just dreaming, but the movement is soothing.

We always want to stay in unremembered dreams.

Suddenly the warmth is gone, and I want to protest.

"It's okay Paige, I'm right here." Maybe I *did* protest, but there are arms around me instead of pitch-dark, listing waves. Deep—the young voice rough around the edges is itself a relief, because it makes me feel safe. But there is something amiss in it, something important.

I can't look yet. Sharpness aches behind closed eyes, the backs of my legs shaky as the arms holding me try to make me stand. I crumple, and I think I'm caught by those strong arms. My hands, so cold—and one uncomfortably stuck against what feels like tiny rocks. The top corners of my head hurt, like the inside is square, not curved. It isn't splitting, it's imploding. But there's that tingling warmth fighting the cold, and it feels like safety, it feels like home.

Who knew someone's arms could feel like home?

My brain is truly addled. But I really am coming to, and the more aware I become, the more carefully I keep my eyes shut. Emotionally spent, I scrunch my eyes tighter and pray they will just let me sleep.

My father's voice breaks the illusion. "We helped her breathe with the puffer—why won't she wake up?" he asks, sounding frazzled, like the dust falling from the cracks between chandelier droplets and the broken stairs in—*the castle! The steward's son!*

A moan fills my chest.

"Paige?" Nolan's whisper is as quiet as his fingers lightly brushing my temple. "I know you're awake." I swallow involuntarily, then I imagine warm fingertips tracing a line across my exposed throat. I don't remember the life-saving puffer on my lips, but it *was* in my bag. Papa must've told Nolan to help me when I blacked out. *Let me stay in this unremembered dream.*

"Everything will look better tomorrow. I promise." Nolan sounds shaken, uncertain. And that feels wrong. "But if you're okay, squeeze my hand." In the dark silence, his fingers grip mine.

I open my eyes and exhale painfully—all the head-pounding pain is moving down to torture the back of my neck. Moving to his knees before me, Nolan shifts to help me stand, one sturdy arm supporting around my waist. I'd always dreamed of love at first sight, believed in the impossible for one unexpected moment in the library.

And he appears like this morning, when I first met him. Dangerous cheekbones like the nearby cliffs, straight lips thinned, trying not to smile, and his *eyes*. Arresting my heartbeat with a rich gaze of cold, untouchable gold reflecting bright shards of lamplight. If this morning was disdain at first sight—and even then, he made my heart skip a beat—then all I have left is this confusing magnetism that makes my body sink into his and my hand grip his like he is the way up from the depths, the sinking, the drowning.

But then I realize—I can see him. *Lamplight.* There's light. Lamp-posts. We're at the base of the mountain. There's the edge of a narrow, curving road, the large gate swung open... "Where are we?" I ask, my voice small.

"The gatehouse," Nolan replies quietly, his hands beneath my elbows, holding me steady. "I had my car at the castle, so we drove here." I try and imagine the car snaking down the incline from the castle, but I can't remember how we got here, to the entrance to the estate grounds. "You didn't wake up the whole way down, Paige."

Papa shuffles aside on the shadowy road, hedges turning a crisp corner behind him to keep the shape of the courtyard. And beyond that, there's a glowing house, beckoning with light and warmth, and suddenly I remember that our home has neither.

As I turn to say, "They cut off our house, Papa," my father says over me, "They're good people here. Mr. and Mrs. Lucas. Stay here. You'll be safe in the gatehouse—" He can't finish it, either from pride or embarrassment, but I don't care about any of that. "Besides, the shop is closed early for the weekend. No new requests for cleaning or upkeep this week, no new appraisals until next week. I can stay there."

No goodbye? No gratitude? No worry? "I'll find it," I promise, unease skyrocketing. *I'll make you proud.*

Without another word of love or encouragement, my father takes his leave, heading around that sharp-edged square hedge to get in Nolan's car, just outside the circle of light left by another lamp-post.

To Nolan I ask quietly, "Will you take him home?"

"After I see you safely inside. You can stay here as long as you need. Your father explained your...situation. Mrs. Lucas and her husband Martin are my godparents. You can trust them." Nolan's eyes glimmer with an inner light, or a *trick* of the light, questions behind his eyes that I can't begin to answer. Realizing he's still helping me stand, I pull myself away, his fingers sliding from my elbows.

Taking my focus from the pity on Nolan's face, his sympathy

and understanding only highlighting the embarrassment bordering my heart, I peer over his shoulder. The path is gravel lined with circular stones, and beyond the hedges near the back of the gatehouse, tall windows beckon like a row of mini lighthouses set between layers of trailing ivy. Yet my heart is still pumping too fast, and my stomach is knots. A firestorm of emotion, burning like acid behind my eyes.

Suddenly, Nolan leans forward and wraps his arms around me. My hands are crushed against his chest as I grasp tightly to his coat. My forehead brushes the skin of his neck, citrus and cotton scents overwhelm me. He cradles the back of my head for one surprising moment, and I sense he doesn't want to break me. *Do I look like I'm falling apart?*

"I'm sorry this happened," Nolan says. His hand smooths hair down my back, pressing me in as if our togetherness isn't new. His voice is soft and serious. "You are strong."

"How can you know?" I speak into his chest, face burning in the dark twilight as a single tear soaks into his coat, my flushed cheek pressed against the scratchy navy wool. I should pull away, but if I don't, I can't see his face or be embarrassed at this stranger holding me. Strange, how solace is sometimes found not in the soft, plush comfort of the known, but in the uncomfortable consolation of disquiet and aggravating winter fabrics.

"Let's go to the house. Fainting is no joke." Something like a chuckle rumbles as he turns me out of his embrace.

He keeps me against his side as we walk the gravel path at a slow pace. Just a quiet evening stroll, nothing unusual going on. My thoughts are not so muddled that I don't enjoy the sensation of his strong arm around my shoulder. It's making a memory I don't know how to feel about, because I don't know how this story will end.

Evening has fallen, incoming clouds painting the sky grey, cold. The sound of the gravel beneath our feet seems obnoxious. But then we come to the stairs of the back patio, running the width of the greenspace edging the square courtyard, and the silence is even louder.

One, two, three, four. Four steps up to the terrace. Now all I want is to run inside and be alone. In a room. Any room. And to wash my hands under really warm water. Alone. Walking away from the courtyard path feels like leaving a dream, but have I gotten myself into a nightmare? As if sensing my uneasiness, Nolan drops his arm as we near the first set of French doors, and opens the one on the left for me before stepping back.

"I'll take your father back to town. Seeing as how you're determined to search the castle, rest here. See you tomorrow," he promises vaguely, looking inside and nodding to someone. "Mrs. Lucas, here's Sterling's student," he says, his hand briefly touching my back as I step over the threshold and into a brightly lit sitting room, all white fabric and brass accents.

An older woman walks forward. "Got lost in Fairhavens, did you? Dust like that is hard to come by in the forest." Her voice is composed, and she shoos Nolan away with a calm but commanding air. "I'll take care of her, go on with you."

I feel like I recognize her from somewhere. She is shorter than me, with a plump figure and pleated navy dress, but it's the over-whelmingly *floral* apron that makes me feel at home. Her tawny skin reminds me of leaves forgetting summer, and her painted lips match her nail polish with a vivid color of orchids. She exudes a serenity I so desire, yet another safe harbor after a storm. Will I only remember today as a storm?

Click—I whip around as the door shuts behind me. My heart unceremoniously drops and shrinks, just a little.

Without thought, I dash across toward a hallway, ignoring my chance to peek at the cozy rooms between in my haste to reach the front door of the gatehouse. Throwing it open, I glimpse the black car disappearing down the road to town. *He's already gone.*

I linger. The fading sound of tires, leaving. I have no choice but to trust my papa's safety to Nolan, who I hardly know. Before to-day, I willingly accepted the what-ifs of my story. The unanswered questions, the unfinished pages, the confusing chapters. I don't want to be uncertain anymore. I am ready to experience the dark of the forest my mother wrote stories about in her diaries. I am ready to explore the shadowed paths to a forbidding fortress—not unlike the castles with princes and glorious endings that I read when I put myself to bed, my own bedtime stories as a sleepy little girl.

My life, spent searching books, searching the woods, searching for gems. Are any of those where treasure can be truly found? I worry to myself—*which treasure will save my father? Which will save me?*—until a feminine voice breaks the silence.

A word later

"THEY'LL BE SAFE," she says over my shoulder and I startle. "No one knows Fairhavens or this forest like him." So, the people in this household *know* Nolan goes into the abandoned castle? They must know he's the steward's son, long thought dead. But this woman's words are tinged with affection, a slight remonstration, and unwavering belief—a tone I always wanted to hear, cajoling but loving me.

I shut the door, deliberately slow and gentle, with a clear *click* that sounds like safety. We are at the bottom of the mountain, below the White Forest, the trees between us and the white-stone castle walls. *Fairhavens.*

Turning to the lady who's determined to call the crumbling castle by it's proper name, I face the cozy luxury of the gatehouse and all thoughts of dangerous darkness outside vanish. The rooms are so golden, so brightly lit, that there's nothing to be seen of night beyond the windows. Twilight had fallen, tall trees making the horizon low and the day end early. I admit, I feel cold without Nolan, the stranger who shaped my day, but I brush off this curling need. It makes sense that I feel strange—today has been one revelation after another, and I'm physically and emotionally drained. It's no surprise I'm unusually drawn to rely on the one person who was in every scene. The one person who was *there*, who carried me when I fainted, like a prince in a story.

Does that make me the damsel in distress? I don't want that. The prince though—

"What a rough day you've had, dear." The orchid-lady is sincere and sympathetic. And wearing heels. How did she come up behind me just now without my hearing footsteps? Do I know her? Mrs. Lucas is her name. She seems familiar...

Distress, that's it. Should I be glad it all happened in a day, instead of stretching my father's desperation and my searching any longer? I'm not sure if it makes me angry that Papa left without a word, or relieved to have space to think. I'm no beauty in these uncomfortably dusty, stained clothes. Ashen poofs color my hands.

The woman gives a little laugh. "I'm sorry for Nolan's manners. So abrupt." She shakes her head tolerantly, like he's always been like this. I frown...he wasn't awful to me. He was kind and helped me when I most needed it. *I'm the beastly one who's been difficult.* Her straight, dark hair swishes against her shoulders as she says, "Your face, dear girl, is perfectly lost. How ironic that you've been sent by the professor to catalogue the library up there." I feel my eyebrows rise and she smiles knowingly. "Nolan has his mind set on something, and far be it from me to stop him. I'm sorry, I don't know it—what is your name?"

"Paige. Um, Paige Wrenley."

"Is that a question? Don't ever doubt who you are. I would feel unsorted if I got lost in the castle, too. But the good news is, that you are not." She tugs one of my hands and starts through the hallway, over layered beige-brown knit rugs upon oak wood floors.

Does she know exactly what Nolan's been searching for? What he's asked of me? I can't imagine how she could; it seemed spur of the moment, desperate, impossible, trapped. Not part of a plan for either of us. Yet, at her manners acting like nothing is amiss—as if a strange eighteen-year-old girl *hasn't* appeared on their doorstep, hair and clothes mussed from fainting in the middle of the off-limits, abandoned castle—my returning smile feels genuine. "I feel less lost."

Though there's a fabled forest around the citadel, inside me is a wilderness. What am I doing? Planning on lying to these good people? And for whom? Because Lenora made me swear to find her a map no one knows about to a treasure no one believes is real? Is saving Papa's shop worth it, if someone gets hurt? Is saving our home worth it? I'm not sure who I'm more afraid of. Declan Hayes, or Lenora-estranged-Hayes whose threats drove me here? My father whose frail will made his sadness easy to manipulate?

The lady mutters under her breath about "surprise." If I didn't know better, I'd almost say Nolan surprised *himself*. Come morning, will he want me here, in this place he clearly knows so well? Will he regret giving me leave to search for the other *Oirdera*? Will he truly let me into the castle's library? Thoughts tangle until I notice a familiar brown bag filled with—

"Books!" I exclaim. Pausing in the hallway, Mrs. Lucas looks at me quizzically. I touch the edges of the paper bag, peeking inside. "Mysteries! I knew I recognized you. From *Azalea's Treasures*—I work there!"

Mrs. Lucas, Penelope's most reliable consumer of cozy mysteries, flashes her teeth in a knowing smile. "I knew I knew your face."

Lucas...I close my eyes and imagine the old-fashioned receipts Penelope insists on using. *Anne.* That's her name. "I'm glad to meet you."

"Come now. Upstairs there's a guest room with its own en-suite, and in the drawers are some spare clothes and sleepwear. Up you go," she urges, eyeing my dirty and dusty clothes with a raised eyebrow. Her brown eyes soften when they meet mine, and after I decline dinner, she leads me silently to the staircase, and like the good teapot in the homely house, she pats my hand, telling me "all will be well" with kind instructions to come to the kitchen the moment I awaken tomorrow for tea.

Climbing obediently to the top of the stairs, I walk a wide hall lined with extravagant wallpaper—alternating vertical stripes of ivory and gold with embossed floral print. The delicate design contrasts with dark wood on the floor, on the ceiling, everywhere. It would be *too* dark, but for the warm glow coming from matching piano lamps on a narrow table at the end of the hall. Three square windows, each with bars forming a cross, hang above them. Like black, empty paintings. *The light. Focus on the light.* The last door on the right is my goal, that's what Mrs. Lucas says as she ushers me up, to sleep. She seems prepared for anything, the kind of person who always finds what's lost. If only forgotten stories could be unearthed so easily.

The thickness of a red and brown round rug muffles my steps into the room. I shut the door, turning the ornate brass handle slowly, reveling in the stillness of solitude. Blessed room. After slipping off my brown leather boots—the worst of the dust brushed off on our walk through the courtyard—and placing them under the small bench at the foot of the bed, I look around tentatively. *So tired.*

Averting my eyes from the en-suite mirror, I brush my teeth with borrowed items and confine my hair in a messy braid. Holding my hands as close to the radiator as possible, I promise myself a long, hot bath tomorrow. At least the radiator is on full blast. It's much too hot to touch, but I get close as thoughts churn around the young man whose existence is still a secret.

Who are these people in the gatehouse beneath the mountain? They seem like family to the steward's son...a young man who could challenge Declan Hayes for rights of stewardship. A drama of succession and riches. Have they forgotten where they are, in the shadow of the abandoned castle? I wish I knew my mother's family, because Mrs. Lucas—in a single simple, gentle interaction—brought to mind all the loss a grandmother and mother have been.

Spent, I pray for sleep, sprawled on the softest bed with a white comforter like a pillow beneath me. The last I remember is curling into a ball, mind spinning, my forehead on the soft—

part two

the wolf and the girl

The White Roses

Sunday morning, at the castle gates

LOCKED. The pair of arching wrought-iron gates are at least three feet higher than the top of my head. Intricate designs matching the crest in my pocket make the paper feel heavy. And my mother's locket, weighty too, whose existence or connection to me Lenora seemed unaware of when she handed me the aged page yesterday. First Nolan, then her, then Sterling and Penelope, then Mr. Hayes and my father—all of them sending me here.

It was a long, lonely walk up the mountain this morning.

I'm glad I took Nolan's suggestion to stay at the manor house. I hadn't wanted to go home, and not just because there's no light, or heat. If my father noticed anything was wrong, anxiety might've taken hold, but he left last night so easily. I worried at the unsaid, which was worse, or that my father might *not* notice and my heart might break.

It was cool when I left the gatehouse, not having seen either Mr. or Mrs. Lucas or Nolan. It's colder up here, near the top of the mountain. Winter holds on longer, here. There's a frost line that won't let go, though spring is less than a week away.

You have until the first day of spring. Lenora's threats propel me forward.

Wishing for gloves, I grasp either side of the gates, fingers firm around the posts. I shake the bars. *Did Nolan lock it? Wasn't it open yesterday?*

I don't recall him carrying me out last night. When I awakened from fainting, I was in his arms in the square courtyard behind the gatehouse. A blush heats my neck, humidity and nerves suddenly making me over-warm. But the gate now...it's immovable and stuck, like the discomfort of coming here with so many people wanting me to, without anyone truly *inviting* me. What feels most wrong is that while yesterday's events made me feel spellbound to come, my father desperately wanted *away*. Would he have let me stay so easily, had he known I was following my mother's and my grandmother's footsteps with this locket around my neck?

"It's you and me," I whisper to the castle, chilled fingers covering the ebony motif on the stone post: sword, hammer, rose. There's a divot there, with a keyhole. A key, which Nolan probably has. "Let me in. Tell me your secrets. Please." *Is all I've lost is worth it?*

Swirling designs on the pavement are intact, but hard to discern from here on the ground. It appears heavy objects slammed the front doors. A level above, every second square turret is ruined or missing. As if the stewards didn't care much for exterior care—*did they not have funds to upkeep the castle?* Soaring six levels up is the tallest tower, with the second highest tower five levels high—*I can't believe we were all the way up there yesterday.* All the smaller towers match with rounded, faux-medieval curves.

The rest of the castle is designed with square edges. Four smaller, single-level-height guard towers brace the compass corners of the citadel. White stone that's survived hundreds of years of storms and history. Black accents line the arch of the impressive front doors, an intricate detailing of the rose and vine motif. It's there on the decorative buttresses cornering each watcher-wall, and the crown molding inside that I recall from yesterday. I imagine there used to be painted-gold accents, but all that's left seems black.

I can't see the sky for the misty curtain hanging above the world. Mist coats my face and tickles my eyelashes as it starts to rain. If there's gold on either of us, it's hidden. No sun to shine on us today, the castle broken, cracking at the edges, giving up. "Prove me wrong." *Prove everyone wrong, for both our sakes.*

I startle at a sound, but it isn't a wolf. A bird calls as I draw out the locket and, on a whim, hold it against the indented shape in the centre of the iron gate. It fits, and with a push, something clicks. The gate creaks open and, placing my locket beneath my sweater dress, which I've made extra warm with a borrowed shirt and jeans beneath it, I step through and along the pavement to the blackwood front doors.

They open without a key, unlocked.

Keeping my mind open for the coat of arms, I gingerly step over the threshold. I leave the door open, apologizing to the black and white checkered marble floors for the mist I'm letting in. It's dark, so dark. It felt less oppressive when I was running in here with Nolan yesterday. Today, the silence feels empty and loud, so large I might disappear.

There's a crack on a black marble corner of the floor beside the main staircase—what used to be the central feature for grand families and society parties is no longer. No polished banisters to brush swoops of tulle or the starched edges of dress coats, no, most of the banister is on the ground. Each railing is an intricate carving of a vine, crafted from the same blackwood as the front doors, the top half of which are now broken below. Beyond the graveyard of rotting wood railings, hallways curve to the ballroom, parlours, dining rooms. Beneath my feet are old, moldy-smelling carpets—I presume from the water firefighters used to try and save the building during the fire—and somewhere must be the kitchens that serviced the stewards who once called this home.

The library though, is not here. It's up the stairs. To the east, Penelope had said. Drawing in a fortifying breath, I take one careful step at a time, avoiding a broken vase and a gauntlet from what I hope was a *decorative* suit of armor. It feels there's already a layer of dust as I wipe my face dry with my scarf. Keeping to the center of the stairs, I breathe easier when I reach the second-floor landing, where hallways branch in each direction.

I pass where Nolan had led me through the hidden servants' door yesterday, shivering. The marble-topped stairs from yesterday continue down, then up, past the open air of the grand foyer, where I can see the hallway there leading the east. Other hallways diverge in either direction. One goes west, up another flight of stairs, the parquet floor charred with black from the fire. It's lined with many doors, and tattered pieces of a burnt rug glint with broken glass. I wonder if those doors used to be living quarters.

A rush of wind comes from there, from the west. Wind blows around my feet, as wild in here as it is in the White Woods. *Wind, inside an empty castle?* Sneezing, and blowing my nose with a tissue from my bag, I harness my fear and walk away from the cool air. The glass shattered, I remember. Light's coming in where windows were broken to admit greedy air and turn the fire into an inferno—

I leave behind the light, determined to tempt the dark instead.

I tread down the east hallway, where the scorched wood of staircase and walls and railings fades and the citadel becomes cold, untouchable. Nolan said yesterday the south and eastern wing of the castle was older, constructed of stone by the first builders and unmarred by the fire. And Sterling said the library itself was sealed. Hope heats my veins, and my steps echo in a shimmer of dusty cobwebs. I turn a corner and there's a small set of stone stairs, then a medieval-styled arched metal door. It's a warm, dark charcoal color, styled with overlapping squares that bring to mind the turrets outside. Three hinges and a huge hook that's unlatched—it's swung open, but perhaps on the night of the fire it was closed?

Pristine stained-glass windows filter the dim of the rainy, almost-spring morning as I step inside. I unravel my scarf, pulling my locket out. The red rose, it's here, letting in daylight through the rainbow-filter of gorgeousness every five feet or so. A few steps, another window. They aren't large, maybe two feet square, and they're all different-colored depictions of the same rose. They're intricate, smooth, and untouched by the sadness sleeping in this castle.

"Beautiful, but broken." I place my palm on the smooth stone beneath the last window, but there are no sunrays to press the colours from the glass onto the walls. "Beauty isn't on the outside, but within." The last words in my mother's last diary before she—

I swivel to face a creaking sound.

A single door, twice as wide as any normal door and much taller, pushes against its hinges.

"Is anyone there?" I call. If I'm not bold, the silence will smother me. "I'm coming into the library." My voice echoes down the rose corridor, but there is no answer. The long hall, untouched by the fire, ends here. I can't be afraid of an unopened door; it's the only way forward, the only next step.

And the door—abysmal, if one described this as a mere *door* as if in a book. It's an entrance to heaven in every way, and the noun lets it down. It's iron-hinged, old. Wood, with a human-sized panel of colored glass. Between the curved stencil patterns of the same vine and rose motif, and beneath the safety of the blackest wrought-iron arch is more stained-glass—it's a picture. Starlit sapphire is a sky sprinkled with snow-white orbs the shape of roses—white roses—and there are seven. A forest with deep emerald trees, etched with midnight needles and sharp, poisoned-pine edges. Brimstone hues build a tiered castle of towers, a picture of Fairhavens like a fairytale, and wrapped around the exquisite handle are ruby roses, a bouquet of blood-red.

It's haunted, Juniper's voice whispers in my memory. *It's guarded*, Sterling replied ominously.

"Is there a difference?" I ask the air. With no reply, I grasp the handle and pull the glorious door all the way open.

This is my world. If the castle is broken and beautiful, this is the heart that remains. Alive, beating. It's golden secrets on a rainy day, walls of windows open to the world, and wall-to-wall books. Shelves, not stuffed to the brim, but filled with hundreds of books of many sizes and styles carefully placed. A sanctuary.

Knotted leather hardbacks of indistinguishable age lay in wait. Forest green and royal blue tomes filled with forgotten stories slumber in the cool odor of shadows and old pages. Can I live here? Can I stay? A book is memories for the person who wrote it, the ones who inspired it, and the lucky souls who read it. Memories are someone's history, and I never take the honor lightly.

Warm from the walk and the stairs and excitement, I take off my mother's scarf, giving her memory a place to sit on the worn, buttoned-leather chair situated with the best natural light in a corner beneath a spiraling staircase. Nearby, a dusky-rose settee mingles with two small writing desks, and in the corner a marble-topped table sits low, piled with books and a kintsugi pot containing a very dead fern.

An antique mirror with gilded edges like fiery ivy is set prominently on the west wall, between towering shelves. It's a location where instead I would've expected a monstrously framed portrait, but all the thing does is reflect my wide brown eyes. I look finally out the monstrous second story windows, edged with draping, butter-toned sheers. *We're all a bit worse for wear.* They're towering windows which don't need to open to make you feel like you might fall out into the landscape beyond. They overlook the east-southeast corner, behind the castle, and for a moment I let my eyes relax, searching for the farthest point in the distance beyond the remains of a beautiful balcony below and a courtyard filled with a mind-boggling maze of tall hedges.

Down the side of the mountain, the frost-tipped trees become merely green. This year, unseasonably heavy rains washed most of the snowflakes from Gabreville's mountains, which in the past would have flooded the canal. Though the Valais still rushes, still rises, the dikes constructed since the Yorkson Tragedy long ago leave the roads safe. But winter isn't quite over. With only six days left, spring still isn't ready to take hold, not yet. Precious white in an undaunted line remains near the top of the mountains—*how gorgeous would the landscape be when it snowed?* My mind rests as my gaze settles on the river, the thick forest below. Amidst low-hanging clouds, there's the slightest glimpse of the Valais running into the lake, where a thin layer of mist skates above startling turquoise waters, the opaque green-blue a stunning jewel in center of the valley.

Imagine if someone wrote a book sitting *here*.

Daylight showers the room from those towering east-facing windows filled with the breathtaking view. Even through the clouds and rain, it's beautiful, and I place my palm on the cool glass pane—squinting slightly. There's no window-frame, and it's just the vista, and if the cool glass disappeared beneath my hand and I took a single step, I would be out there in all that mysterious, wondrous beauty. I sniffle at my nonsense. Luckily, I have no fear of heights like Nolan showed yesterday. Penelope would call him a "strapping young man," with his study-looking, rigid shoulders, calloused palms, and that look called *brooding* in books but what actually seemed like anguish beneath an arrogant exterior. I call his bronze-hued eyes sad, like the once-shiny design on the spine of a precious old tome, forgotten on the wrong shelf in the quietest aisle of a library.

From this direction I can't see the front gates. Expansive balconies grace the back edge of the castle—all different heights with their own entrances from rooms within—with mosaic designs on the floor of each balcony. Each one forms the rose motif, but the largest is on the terrace directly adjacent to the center of the castle, where stairs as wide as half the castle extend to the crumbling gardens. The history... Ruffled dresses swirl at a long-ago part and candle smoke flits out the line of doors to the fairy-lit garden and hedge maze, as prettily dressed people flirt and gossip and plot against one another, ready to slit throats or stab one another in the back, possibly not figuratively...

I skitter away from the window, afraid of the past, afraid of *my* past. My mother entered this glittering world for a reason. How much did she belong, if the symbol from her locket is emblazoned on so much of this old castle? Does it mean *I* am meant to be here? Or should I run?

Before I start examining the contents of the library, which I truly want to do—never minding that it's what I *came* here to do—I let my gaze linger once more on the terrace below. From above, it's strange and beautiful, seeing the locket's design as a stony replica, seeing the crest woven throughout the castle, from the tattered coat of arms to the torn tapestries. I slide my fingers around the chain. There is no sun to make it sparkle, and muted cloud-light makes the world too big and the sky too small, like a castle in a dusty snow globe, never shaken up. The solitary rose, like the door to this library and the stained-glass windows, all blood-stained ruby atop a sword and a rock hammer, seems to scream *wealth, love* and *death.*

"Trespassing again, Paige?" a deep voice asks directly behind me.

The same moment, in the library

I SCREAM, THEN SPIN, clutching my throat and forgetting I have no scarf to grip for dear life.

"Nolan?" I manage, refusing to lose my head but *oh my word* his eyes this morning are a bright, polished bronze against the walls of books, laughing at me, shining in lieu of the sun.

I've knocked over a precarious pile of books to the floor, where squares of black and white marble form a set of Borromean rings, beautiful interconnected circles. It reminds me of when I met Nolan, when books littered the ground because of my surprise. That was *yesterday*? It feels so long ago, time standing still and more—rewinding, reworking, regenerating—in this castle. A place long lonely, but now, in these moments when I hold my breath, feeling less so.

"Find anything yet?" Nolan questions, stepping back. Behind him the jewel-toned door to the library's still open. Dressed in practical shoes, dark jeans, and that thick navy coat with the collar turned up, Nolan's gaze ratchets between my eyes and the locket I'd forgotten I was clutching. I cover the emblem and slip the necklace beneath my shirt. "Something you want to tell me?" he asks.

I sputter, searching for a way to not be undone under his intense scrutiny and his windswept short blond hair too long on the top, and this attraction pinging through the air.

"Your father explained his predicament last night..." He hesitates.

"Papa told you about Declan? About his shop?" I ask, needing confirmation.

"My uncle threatened you, and I'm sorry for that."

I tamp down annoyance that Nolan spoke with him for less than an hour and Papa told Nolan what he never intended to tell me.

"Your father wants to protect you, but he sounds like—"

"Like he doesn't know what to do with his life outside of his work?"

A nod, then Nolan asks, "So that's why you're here. To save your father? That's it?"

"Sterling asked me to—"

"I know. After our lack of success finding the *Oirdera* in the Gated Library yesterday, I asked Mrs. Lucas to arrange for an expert to search here. Can't believe it's you..."

I tamp down my smile. "Coincidence?"

"So you followed your father, but how did you know what he was looking for?"

I decide to just tell him. "Lenora—Mrs. Hayes—told me about Mr. Hayes's plans." Nolan's eyes widen, but with so much to lose,

I need someone to know. "Papa's heart... I don't want him up in thinner air."

"Like your..." He palms a hand above the center of his chest. His lungs.

I pretend he's only talking about my fainting last night, and not the locket resting against my breastbone. "Yes. Asthma is tough enough with a young heart." But when you're broken-hearted, old, and your health is dipping, and your vasculature isn't what it used to be? I sigh. "Like I said last night, I'll find the book. But why didn't *you* look here first?" I circle my hands. "I suppose you don't seem the rare book type."

He raises an eyebrow. "You pegged me the moment we met. My lawyer said he'd heard a rumor about my uncle searching for it. I wanted to check the university first, and we failed there..."

It takes effort not to over-blink. "Who's your lawyer?"

"Professor Figgleston."

I laugh and try to be mad, but fail, because *Sterling*. "*That's* how you got into the Gated Library." *Sneaky professor.*

"How *did* you find the first book?" Nolan asks.

The first *Oirdera* was a miraculous accident in Penelope's bookshop, so I say, "Magic." At my bold assertion, Nolan barks a laugh, and it strikes me how uncomfortable he looks. "Like you, the steward's son, appearing out of thin air when all this business gets stirred up."

It's amazing how easily I've accepted who he is. But it isn't just his word—though words have power and only someone wild enough to use them deserves them—it's the way he carries himself.

He knows the castle like only one who explored it while bored as a child could.

Tracing the edges of silver threading a set of matching navy spines, I peruse the southern wall's shelves carved with grapevines, containing what appears to be varied textbooks in at least four languages. "The second *Oirdera* must be here somewhere," I mumble.

Mr. Hayes is after Nolan's home; Lenora is after mine.

"Wait—you want the book to *find* the hidden heir, and Mr. Hayes wants it to ensure there's *no* hidden heir to take this place from him..." He wouldn't have brought this up without being prepared. I doubt the Lord Chamberlain missed a detail, lawyer that he is. "So you want to thwart him? Just in case there's some hidden bloodline? What if there *is* no such person? There wasn't anything about it in the first book, Nolan," I say honestly. "I checked. No hidden heir. It really doesn't appear to contain a genealogy. All we have is just you...the steward's son."

If Nolan reveals himself, he'll be a target, and he'll have enemies. What does that make me? An interloper, an outsider, an uninvited guest? Nolan has a right to this place, whatever his reason for hiding. And there are more secrets here. Untold stories that came before, long before.

"This all happened because the professor—as my legal counsel—told me he heard there was another interested party. Your father has confirmed that." For a second I'm startled by the obvious fact that Nolan himself must be wealthy and for some reason, it makes me shrink. He doesn't seem to notice my reticence as he continues. "My uncle wants that book, same as me." His stance is faking-relaxed. If anything, it's defensive, arms crossed, in the center of the room.

"Your aunt wants it too," I admit. The witch with the scary white roses and sharp nails wants the same book as her lecherous, conniving husband. What a pair. Though it's the lady I fear most, I need to find a way to outsmart them both. I need time, another letter, word, page. "She wanted me to come here too, if you can believe it."

Nolan's eyebrows rise. "I never did like my aunt. What is in it for her?"

"Treasure."

"That's absurd."

"Is it?" I say. "If it's real, and there's no steward in the direct line, Declan Hayes will take over the rights to the mine below us. Makes sense she wants to beat him to it. She hates him."

"This is why I want that book!" he blurts. "If there were an heir, it would take my whole family out of the picture. If there's someone out there, I'll find them," he says seriously.

"Why can't you step forward? Isn't that why you came back?" I ask him.

"I can't—"

"You're so complicated!" I'm rewarded with a poof of dust as I sit on the settee. "You want to avoid revealing yourself this badly?" Nolan's eyes blaze and I lean slightly away, unsure if the heat in his eyes is anger at his Hayes relatives or me. Either way, it's unsafe to get to near, combustible elements and all. "The Council is ready to give in to Mr. Hayes, but they can be stopped—by *you*." The son of the Hayes's who'd lived here and died that night. "So what? Your being lost was fine *without* a villain like your uncle causing trouble, but now that someone's about to interrupt your solitary life and steal your hoard of treasure—"

"That's not why—" Something dark lances through his eyes. "There's no treasure. It's just you and your stories."

"It's not just a story." I balk. "And don't blame me for yours!"

His Adam's apple moves as he swallows, rubbing a hint of stubble on his chin. "My aunt is a piece of work," Nolan mutters. He raises his eyes to mine. "Greed makes people blind, and she'd never imagine I would come back. Would she do something like this without being certain?" The thought hovers between our trapped gazes, trapped in history, trapped in this very room.

"No." The treasure is a myth, a fable, a fairy telling a tale that *doesn't exist*. A dark one, at that. But...either I trust Nolan or nothing happens, and I like my stories to move forward. "To hear Lenora, you'd think there was a real map and real treasure, and I've promised her I'd find them. I don't know how she knew to ask. Maybe she's just chasing rumors too. But Nolan"—I wait for his eyes to meet mine—"fairytales aren't real."

He barks a laugh, incredulous. "You're telling me. She sent you here for...what?"

"The same stupid book! But not for any genealogy. She thinks it's the map." I think of the motifs of my locket all over the castle. "I can..."

"You can what?"

"Draw one! Make one up! Anything, so I can go back to my home and be able to turn the lights back on," I huff, standing, shaking my head. "I don't believe it exists, so we pretend...unless by chance I unearth the fabled—" Nolan groans. "Long lost," I amend, holding in a smile for all I'm worth, unsure how I went from frustrated to smiling so quickly.

"Never-truly-dead..." he inserts.

I meant the treasure. A smile splits my face and it's a bit heady, the magnetism I feel toward him and how utterly distracting it is. "...hidden heir of the citadel. It does have a nice ring to it."

"But alas, I'm not the heir," he corrects. "Our family took this place when the lord disappeared. The Dark Year; remember lecturing me on it? If the only way to stop Declan is to reveal myself, then..." He dips his chin, examining the ground. I follow his gaze and notice his shoes. Like yesterday, dirt covers them, edging the gray leather of shoes meant for collared shirts but also worn to chop wood.

I try to draw him out. "Nolan Hayes—what was the name you gave me in the university library?" He shrugs strong shoulders, and I'm reminded of how it felt to be carried in his arms last night. "Nolan *Neville Carter* Hayes? The son of the stewards." He nods affirmation, which clearly pains him. But it makes me smile. I love uncovering unintentional stories. "What if you reveal yourself? What's stopping you? Surely people are over the past."

"Are you over yours?" he asks in a rough voice.

I can't hide my flinch. He watches me circle the first level of the library. I mentally catalogue more books on the side farthest from where he stands—north shelves now, with palm leaves and engraved thoughts of different lands. I'd always loved the thought of being this high. Feeling so close to the sky makes me feel more alive, and I am carried by the feeling—boldness.

"What's up there?" I point beyond the spiral stairs to the second level. The books there are both smaller and bigger than modern books, not the usual standard sizes from the last two centuries or so.

"Memories."

Peering down at the awe-inspiring vista framed by windows for a moment, I turn back and raise my eyebrow at him. "Whose?" I hold his gaze, determined to win, but the moment becomes thick, like a dark mist crept through the floor when we weren't looking.

I want to go up those narrow iron stairs, to follow the double curve and see what the view is like from higher up, but in an annoying slit of time, compassion slices between the halves of my heart and I remember Nolan's fear of heights. I exhale, loudly, so he hears, and I swear his profile is stone. *That's* why he needs someone to catalogue the books. *That's* why he's standing in the center of the room. He isn't defending Fairhavens, he's protecting himself. The display case behind him, solid. His location specifically chosen with the stairs curving above him, as much away from the windows as possible and only a few strides away from the door, which he left open. Not accidentally, like me, but on purpose.

The dark mist leaves the room, and his fair lashes flicker as he blinks and turns his face away. He inhales deep, and his chest expands in a thorough way I'm a little bit jealous of, though he still avoids looking toward the window.

"The lord who built Fairhavens, the bloodline may not have been entirely cut off. If there was a descendant...*they* would be the true heir. They would have an older claim to this land. You can see their crest everywhere. That's why I wanted to find the *Oirdera*. That's why Uncle Declan wants it, to destroy any evidence that an heir might exist. I still think it's our best chance to beat both him and Lenora. If there's treasure, let the heir have that too."

"Would he want to destroy that heir, should they own up to their bloodline?" I ask.

He nods, once. "Don't you think your question shows why I wouldn't want to expose myself?"

"What if Declan finds out you're here?" My mind whirls. "If you're back in Gabreville, surely someone will recognize you?" Nolan shrugs at my question, mumbling *not yet*. And then it clicks. Everyone assumed he was dead. "Are you officially..." My voice betrays me. I can't ask it.

"No, I'm not dead. Not officially or otherwise. Besides"—he makes a show of slamming his palms into his firm chest—"they never found a body." His laugh is hollow, speaking of that terrible night, which makes it more painful—I was in the forest the night of the fire too. But I can't say that, not yet.

"You're saying there's no proof you died, but no one discouraged the rumor?

"To be precise, I think the newspapers said I ran away." He almost smiles.

"Oh my word, *Sterling*? Don't tell me your legal counsel—"

He nods. "Him and the Lucas's helped me go abroad, to boarding school, to graduate under a different name: Neville Carter." His mouth tightens around the words. He *is* a few years older than me, so I suppose I wouldn't have known him as a child before the fire to be able to recognize him now. "Gabreville authorities didn't search for me because my godparents, the Lucas's, were my guardians. And they couldn't share my location with my aunt or uncle, as I was a minor and I had a good lawyer." He looks away.

"No one knew where I went, and Mr. and Mrs. Lucas helped me keep it that way. They always had nephews visiting in the summers, and they let people assume I'm one of those boys. The fire destroyed so much—I only had the clothes on my back. But, though the mine was shut down and I later found out he was in debt, in my father's safe there was enough gold at the time to support me and the Lucas's. Now? I don't want to be a steward. I left who I was. I hid for long enough that I hope they won't know me."

"I'm sorry." I cannot cry. Nolan's family died in the worst way, yet he said he *survived*—he was *there*. I can't tell him how my mother and my grandmother died, not yet.

"If Aunt Lenora or Uncle Declan saw me on the street now, they probably wouldn't even recognize me."

Hmm. I recall the way he ducked away yesterday on the sidewalk, in front of the bookshop when Lenora cornered me. "What of their sons? Were you close with your cousins? Wouldn't they know you?"

He shrugs broad shoulders. "I've avoided them when I see

them." He shoves his hands in his pockets and I tilt my head, examining his disheveled fair hair and think of Mr. Hayes's olive coloring, with hair like both his sons—Darragh and his similarly straight and slicked style, Percy with his sad, dark brown eyes and wild, inky curls. If those Hayes men are dark, then Nolan is light—not white, but golden, tinged with fire in the sunlight.

He presses the bridge of his nose between his pointer finger and thumb. It looks crooked enough to have been broken more than once. "It might be too late. I legally changed my name, so it will take time to prove my identity. The professor has quietly started the process...he still has my original birth certificate. But Declan already set the Council in motion."

"And you don't want this."

"Right. Which is why we need to find that heir instead."

I want to fiddle with the scarf around my neck, but I took it off earlier. And I can't tug on the locket—Nolan's too fixated on it, and it can't appear in our story again for another few lines. "So," I ask, "we're going to do this? Find a book, find a map, find a treasure? We search every corner. If there's any sort of secret door, or compartment somewhere, it's an accident waiting to happen in this dangerous, crumbling, unkept castle—"

"It needs work." His tone is defensive.

I dig in a little more. "It needs another century." He grunts, uncrossing his arms, but something clenches beneath my ribs. He *does* love it here.

Heavily, he drops his gorgeous golden gaze toward one wall then the other, still avoiding looking at the windows. Warmth fills my chest, because he's suffering the gorgeous view that scares him to be near me, and compassion fills my heart, clouding the emotions that I'd intended to keep well in check. "Maybe we'll both find what we're looking for."

"I'll help you." As he looks at the ground again, his voice carries a promise. "I'll keep you safe."

I may be proposing the partnership, but every line is still my story, and there's nothing false about that. "We have less than a week to find the book, the map, and the treasure. Maybe find an long-lost heir."

His eyes glimmer again with a hidden, inner light, as if I'm the one to have given him hope. "You think it will be enough to stop them?"

Oh, never. "We have to try." My mother's words echo in my mind from her diary. *Moved hearts move the ground.* Fabled treasure isn't the problem, nor is it contested ownership. It's what owns the hearts of our enemies that makes this scary. "If we have no book, then we have no heir and no map, and there might as well be no treasure."

"They can't have it." Something a little like fury burns his tone. Where there's smoke, there's fire. "Not the mine and not the castle—I don't care if there's treasure or not. It isn't theirs."

"Agreed. You know..." I swivel and take in the books surrounding us, the dust motes in the air from our shuffling feet, the red scarf not the only vivid color in the room. "The library at the university is great, but this dusty, neglected graveyard of books is begging for resurrection."

He scoffs. "Hopefully the other *Oirdera* is here."

"If it is, I'll find it."

"You're strange. And that's coming from a man who's been hiding for ten years."

"Something tells me there's more to that story."

He shrugs. "I'm not the only danger lurking in these woods."

"I'm not afraid of you," I huff, hiding a shudder at the memory of the wolf howling. I look to the huge, ornate mirror, hating it for the reflection resembling my mother, wondering if others cursed it for the truth reflected in its depths. No one needed me before, not like Nolan does. All of me wants to save my father, but there's another growth in my heart, a vine with thorns that seems altogether dangerous, a bud ready for spring, determined to help this young man in front of me who's afraid of heights yet stalks the lonely hallways of the tallest castle in the region nonetheless.

I hope Nolan cannot see the truth in my gaze. Danger or not, I think in another story I might choose him every time, even if Papa's shop and our home weren't at stake. Without him, though... It feels like this is the best thing for me and I'll have the strength to do what I must, whether or not Nolan was supposed to be in my story.

"Do this with me?" Nolan says, formally. It's a proposal, only as real as a story in a book, ink blotted into words—no more. Right?

Something squeezes my chest. Nothing is more real than words on paper. Nothing more true than a story. What will happen if I write myself onto the pages of his?

THE WEST WING

Wednesday, three days later, in the West Wing

THERE ARE ALWAYS FORBIDDEN SPACES for children. The forbidden section in the university library. I found my way there through academic excellence and attention to detail. A forbidden jewelry box, which Papa never imagined his sweet daughter would steal from his own home. A forbidden castle, with its imposing towers and foundations, cracked. And the forbidden West Wing of said castle.

Nolan left me in the library after our conversation on Sunday, but for all my searching, there was no aged white book with ornate gold lettering hidden in plain sight. At the end of that first day, he returned to drive me down the mountain because I stayed too late. We've not said much, for which I'm glad, to avoid sharing any more of my search *or* heart with him. The pull for both in his aloof presence makes me want to share more of myself to try to find more of him. I've been steadily avoiding that by searching and not finding anything for three straight days.

Not that I've suffered—without being able to return to my own home, there's been a steady rhythm of quiet mornings walking up the mountain, Nolan arriving with lunch, and Mrs. Lucas finding me for afternoon tea. She and Martin have welcomed me into their home, and seeing them with Nolan at dinnertimes—he acts like a godson in their warm company—has been a balm to my battered heart. The only thing missing has been my own papa.

I've settled into another day of pulling out every single book and checking for empty shells beneath book covers like happens in mysteries, but I've found *nothing*. I was so certain the *Oirdera* would be here, because the greed of Mr. and Mrs. Hayes seems too strong for lies, but am now convinced it's somewhere *else*. I've combed through the library itself. Against the backdrop of the valley-view out the picturesque window, my fingers trail the triple shelves of the north side of the library. The library is arranged like the castle, as if perched atop a compass, for order or simple directions. *Why then is it so hard to find what I'm looking for?*

I feel like I'm walking in circles. Over and over I've climbed the spiral stairs, and after taking my daily moment of silence to appreciate the unparalleled view of the mountains and river valley, I pause at each section, stewing. I've already inspected the backs of the over-tall shelving on the top level, hoping for an accidental button to push and for shelves to just...move. But no luck. There are fewer books on the second floor, and even fewer in English. Books forgotten among old, painted pottery and tarnished bronze figurines of war-horses. Tomes not for touching, not for enjoyment. Stored for what they used to be worth, having lost their meaning and hardly holding on to memory.

I belong here, but still no *Oirdera*.

But nothing isn't an option. And though I remember Nolan's warning that first day, I know where I need to go.

After leaving the untouched stone of the library corridor of roses, I brave the westward hallway toward the living quarters. Up a half-flight of parquet-floored stairs, which are less charred and black than I remembered seeing my first day here. There's quite a bit of broken glass, and the tapestry on the far wall is as burnt as the rug.

The first door is a master bedroom with a carved, four-poster bed and framed oil portraits of proud ancestors with blackened edges. Peeling plaster is all that's left on the walls. I creak open another door to a scorched but working washroom. I brighten. Of necessity and fear I'd gone down the crumbling, curving stairs alone, and hated each time I need the restroom. This is much closer to the library, and had porcelain of what must've been the purest white. Burnt, monogrammed hand towels moth-eaten with holes, hanging sadly on wrought iron decorative ware. How rich was this family? What luxury, to live in what this castle must have been like before the fire's hot hands left claw-marks along the ceilings. Ashen speckles are like blackish blood, everywhere.

Here in the newer part of the citadel, hallways seem to have been eaten by the fire. Walls once paneled with wood and alternating with charred frescoed panels now seem dead. Memories of burning, memories of flames licking a path through bedding, the mattresses mostly gone. Fabric strewn in stitches on rugs no longer rugs, but eaten into plague-like sores from the fire. Above a tall table with empty vases full of dust, I move aside a frame. The faded brocade papering might have once been gold, or yellow, but is now sepia and unsavable.

Welcome to the West Wing. *Forbidden*. Wrong word, wrong letters.

It only sounds ominous. Surely it isn't worse than the rest of the wreckage in every hall and corner in view. But as I finally walk down the corridor, there are fewer windows, less light.

It's a hallway of doors. And it seems impossible, but they're all engraved. Not runes or letters, but with faces. The master bedroom has a wide tree-face. Other doors hold long flower-faces, slitted mountain-faces. One, two, three...I peer down the dim hallway. Seven. And if all these doors are so unique, so gorgeously not grotesque, then the rose emblem of my family might also be somewhere. There are servant tunnels within these walls, and it's occurred to me that there might be *other* tunnels. A sign-post, a marker, another way into the mines from within the castle. If I was a treasure, that's how I'd want to be found.

Best to start looking where I'm not supposed to.

I open each door as I pass. Every window was broken here, too. The blackened walls and floors, worse than anywhere else, indicate the fire started here in this wing. There aren't water stains like in the rest of the castle. No one could have come this way, the flames eating their fill before ending on their—

I gasp aloud and step back. *They aren't real.* But they're lifelike, nonetheless.

Bracketing each wall are suits of armor. Blackened, bent by smoke and a story so bad that it looks like...someone knocked them over on purpose. Empty shells, with no one to guard.

I wish Juniper could see this. I wonder how she is today? Will she go to classes and have afternoon tea with Penelope? Will she be lonely when she walks over Concorde Bridge? Will she accidentally come across Darragh—the awful boy who broke her heart, the worst sort of character to be so privileged with worldly riches and deemed eminently young and virile and handsome—at the tea cart where she works? Is my father at his shop, tinkering on the same old piece of broken clock that will never work again? How did he sleep? Was he warm enough last night, like I was?

I take slow steps, avoiding the soldiers. They're comrades of the bodiless guards downstairs, knights all fallen. Were they proud and tall and fearless? Were they silver-sheened, before? With the destruction of this part of castle, it looks like a mob knocked over anything in sight. Which makes me wonder what, or who, started the fire? Did they cause this mayhem?

I shake myself and just end up sneezing. Find the other *Oirdera*. Find the map. Find the treasure.

Is life trying to make me believe in fairytales? Force faith where I have none? I run my fingers over the engravings on the third door. Trees, flowers, mountains, but no swords with thorny rose-stems. No Ludovici death-emblems. My feet crunch over glass. Four more doors to go.

"Paige?" Nolan's voice startles me again.

I scream, then spin, clutching my scarf to my throat in a grip for dear life. *He scares me every time.* "Nolan! Appearing out of nowhere again?" I gasp, refusing to lose my head but *oh my word* his silhouette is both reassuring and imposing against the dim hallway.

A dark hallway I'm most decidedly *not* to be in.

"You shouldn't be here." Revulsion and abhorrence flood his deep voice, making it hot and scratchy, making *me* testy.

"Would you rather I pretend I wasn't?" I sigh. "*Of course* I was going to look here, Nolan. It's me—you tell me not to go somewhere, I'm going to go see what's there."

He rubs a hand along the back of his neck. He's dressed well, as usual, in dark tones but never black, with dark jeans and an unbuttoned light gray coat and Aran blue sweater. "You don't do anything without a reason." There's a bite to his words. "Why are you here, specifically?"

I hate feeling like I've done something wrong, when I've done the right thing. "Searching the castle for a lost book is my only job. I'm following clues." Clues? What am I even saying? "The edging on the mirror in the library," I hurry to explain, "had the—" *Long lost emblem.* I struggle for words. "There's a motif that matches the crest inside the *Oirdera*." That *also* matches the locket heavy against my chest, and my mother's sketches, and the drawing Lenora gave me. The crest of those Ludovician lords, who built the foundations of this castle until the ancestors of the young man in front of me took it.

Life might be much more difficult if I say it like that, so I don't. We have a search to pull off, and we can't even be friends, but I'm trying. It would be easier if his presence didn't make my stomach flutter in absolute botheration.

"Less than a week," he mutters. He hasn't entered the hallway, but even at this distance, his eyes are intense, polished bronze.

"And?" I can't keep the challenge out of my voice, feeling proud at how unaffected I sound.

"I've known you since Saturday, and somehow I've agreed to stake my future on the most deliberately obstinate, stubborn person I've ever—"

"I'm acquainted with my faults," I interrupt, laughing at the scowl on his handsome face. "Your bad decision, not mine. We're a pair." I walk to him, leaving the West Wing behind. For now. Four more doors. Three more days until spring. "It takes a headstrong, bull-headed—" He grunts, like earlier, and I laugh again. "See that? Add 'beastly' to the list of your fine qualities."

He hides it well, but I decide to believe he's trying not to smile. "I can't call off the search?"

"Absolutely not. I won't let you. Not when we're so close." I peer at the canvas bag he's carrying. "Though...I might be making bad decisions from hunger."

"Mrs. Lucas is thoughtful."

One should never underestimate kindness. "Did you tell her your aunt and uncle are searching too?" I had warned him that if he didn't break the news to her, I would.

He coughs and turns on his heel for the stairs. But it isn't fear in his gaze, it's annoyance. I laugh at his discomfort, following his long-legged pace and avoiding the broken glass in the central hallway. I trust my leather boots in rain, but with snow or glass, perhaps not. "Where are you taking—" My words cut off as he grabs my wrist and steers me away from the curving staircase to the servant stairs. Nolan doesn't let go when he pulls me through the wall and down the narrow stairs behind him, steps solid and unyielding, thank heavens—

Blinking rapidly, I inhale light and free air when we emerge on the main floor. Small, dark spaces are the worst. At least there's no storm outside. Today, sunlight permeates the air, brightening the white stone balustrades and stairs on expansive terraces outside. There's no rain, it's all buttery light. This is a formal room long unused, with a bank of windows and the expanse of mountains and valley.

There is no mountaintop without a valley.

Nolan leads me through the most hauntingly abandoned dining setting I could've imagined—all cobwebs caught on the longest claw-footed long table I've ever seen. Tumbled, blackened chairs, black, peeling plaster, and worst of all, traces of feathers and foul-smelling empty bird nests. There are two sets of double doors hanging open, pointing into what used to be—

"A ballroom!" I exclaim, not even embarrassed at the peak in my voice.

"Some things in the old books you read are real," he grumps, gallantly extending a hand to assist me over the threshold of the patio doors, glass dirty and half the panes broken.

"Someday I want to explore," I bite back, surprised that I'd never thought to search the main level in the last few days. But the books. Books are precious. I was distracted, because *books*.

"You would say that."

Did I say that aloud about the books? "Not ashamed."

I walk through the double doors into the meaning of the word *open*, the world ahead of me, trees glistening and the mountain close enough to touch, sky soaring a soft blue that meets the lake in the valley beyond, turquoise water shimmering like it was made from melted gems.

I breathe in the mountain air, all crisp, clean, clarion. "It's all priceless. Value beyond measure."

"This awful place?" With that grudging tone, he leads us along the outside terrace.

It has a *ballroom*. "Well certainly *someone* has made memories here that deserve to be in books." I have a soft spot for abandoned places. What price can you put upon history barely preserved? What price can you place for what is begging to be saved? "It's better when it isn't raining. Glorious sunshine!" Especially considering my search inside was unaided by electricity. I have a flashlight—which I'd taken when I began this timeless journey away from home—since candles seemed both dangerous and improper, considering the setting, and history. "Less moody, too," I say pointedly at the broody guy beside me. He's staring out at the mountains, for a moment looking...peaceful.

If I were to believe the fairytale, treasure lies below us. Though I'm undecided, because in this moment, I can't imagine any riches that could create all this. I let my sigh over the last fruitless three days blow into the mountain breeze—the air is never still up here, why won't it blow some inspiration or hints my way?

"Do you begrudge the rainy season ?" Nolan asks, sitting on the top steps of the terrace that lead to the once-beautiful garden. White marble statues have fallen left, right, and center...save one. I admire the life-size archangel until there's a clink and crinkle from Nolan opening the bag and pulling out heavy mugs and assorted food wrapped in wax paper.

Removing my navy coat, which I have worn day in and day out inside the castle, I huff down beside him. "I really might, because this is the first sunny day since I've been here."

He pauses, face most serene I've seen, staring at the broken remains of a hedge maze and the fantastical fountain figure that's missing a head. "The sun sleeps, in winter, resting. Long shadows and angles of cool light."

"Poetic," I say. "But spring is coming."

"Winter has a foothold up here for longer." He pours me steaming tea without offering milk or cream. Apparently, we're needing to be warmed more instantly.

I wrap cold fingers around the proffered cup, and the heat almost hurts. "Since your home isn't the forest with the wolves"—he elbows my arm and a tiny bit of tea spills, darkening the stone stair—"or the gatehouse, where in Gabreville do you live?"

He hesitates with his sandwich midair. "A brick-faced townhouse. With a friend. Just moved there last week."

"Is he broody and morose like you?" I ask and Nolan coughs, pounding his chest. I do not try to save him. "Truth hurts, doesn't it?" I ask innocently, taking a sip. Tea scalds my lips. "I read you like a book."

A straight brow, but a crooked smile. "Like the story so far?"

"The tea is too hot."

"It's cold out." He doesn't look cold, though, rolling up the sleeves of his blue sweater.

My eyes avoid the sun's brightness, but yes, the air's chilly. It's sort of perfect, really. "And this is supposed to help?" I wrap my arms around my knees, resting my cheek against the thick knit of my sweater dress, enjoying the warmth of the sun on my face.

"You're not having any success finding the other *Oirdera*." He raises both eyebrows, one struck straight with a white scar. "You need a shock to the system."

I glance behind us, at the megalith abandoned castle that I've somehow almost grown used to. No longer, now that my neck aches from three seconds staring high, so high. Not sure if I'm more afraid of real people in there, or wolves from the forest, or ghosts from the past.

Nolan hands me a halved sandwich, and inside I bless Mrs. Lucas and her thoughtfulness. Sourdough bread, Dijon on thinly sliced beef with thinner slices of apple and sweet onion, and so much butter. And cookies—I eat three until the only taste on my tongue is the spiced warmth of ginger washed with the strongest black tea.

I'm fortified, though I'm still at a loss.

"Tell me about the fire." I'm abrupt, and I know I'm basically saying "Tell me about the night your parents died," but I need to know. I'm missing something. I fiddle with the chain around my neck. The locket feels cool and heavy.

"No." He doesn't even try to be cordial or soften his voice as he rebukes the idea of re-living that night.

"Why not?" What is he ashamed of? Grief?

Why don't I tell him about my grandmother and my mother dying then, I accuse myself.

"Because it's my fault," he says. I gasp, but he fumbles, "I didn't kill anyone directly, but maybe I did. I was there. I'm the reason they died. My parents. Those two women... I didn't stay for the funerals. I left after the fire and never looked back."

I'm taking Nolan's mug but pause, our fingers lightly touching as his words fail to settle. Lowering my head, hair falling around my shoulders like a curtain, I toss the dregs and stack his cup with mine, not sure if his admission is true guilt. No one was charged; not legally *or* criminally. I remember that much.

Stories are never that simple. I would know. He doesn't know that my mother and my grandmother died that night, because I haven't told him. And if he wasn't here in the aftermath, not here for the funeral my father never let us have, he couldn't know it was me who was left alone after that night. Just like him.

With effort, I disregard the initial blame that clogged my throat so easily. I don't remember Nolan from my childhood, and I'm quite sure I'd never seen his face until I met him at the Gated Library. But memories are strange that way. He might still be there, in my memory, if he was in this forest that night. Like a mangled reflection in another form. Is he the thing I fear? He was there. *Here.* And it makes sense—the steward's son with the weight of guilt, leaving, hiding, lost. It's strange to venture down that painful memory lane on this beautiful, bright afternoon, where the cool air practically smiles and rises with the warmth of the sun as seasons press from winter to spring.

Only three days until spring—when Lenora's threat will come to pass.

Nolan's attention remains on my eyes, trying to find answers on my face in the light of the midday sun. It should be warming my skin, but my cheeks are kissed by that lingering winter chill that won't let go.

I keep my expression sympathetic and neutral, though I am neither of those things. I can't say more, not yet. I wish I could say I was sorry for bringing it up, that it was rude of me. That it must be hard for him. That I won't bring it up again. But it wouldn't be true. Every time we talk about the fire, about the treasure... Death has hung over me like a bloodstained shroud.

His gaze roves my lips, perhaps worried what I might reply. He wouldn't be wrong...truth is the thing missing. *What a sad fate.* I say nothing.

Then he shakes his head, speaking what sounds like a eulogy. "Though they have been gone so long, it feels like yesterday that I heard their voices, felt their touch. But years have brought their mists, so many that memories fade. I'm sorry you're here, Paige. I'm sorry you're with *me*, here." His voice is raw. "I wish I could explain what really—" He swallows, keeping his gaze fixed on the broken garden. "Time passing is good, isn't it? That's why every day after is better, and today, more. Because *that* was an awful day, and because today is not." His gaze swings to me, intensifies.

His words make me want to weep, because he doesn't know it's a memorial not just of who he lost, but who the fire also took from *me*. "How is it good?"

He leans forward. "Because...today isn't special, because this normal day is like every other normal day that follows awful days." With the skies above and valley below, I suddenly feel hemmed in. Surrounded, by that rasping, broken-sounding voice as he says, "Because I'm still waiting in the dark. And like the sun so desperate in winter, it hurts to look at you, because you are blindingly bright."

I blink at the beautiful words. They're rusted around the edges like the gilded vines on the frame of the mirror in the library. Twisted, like an apology said too late.

Like the mirror in the library.

Wrong, wrong, wrong.

I gasp.

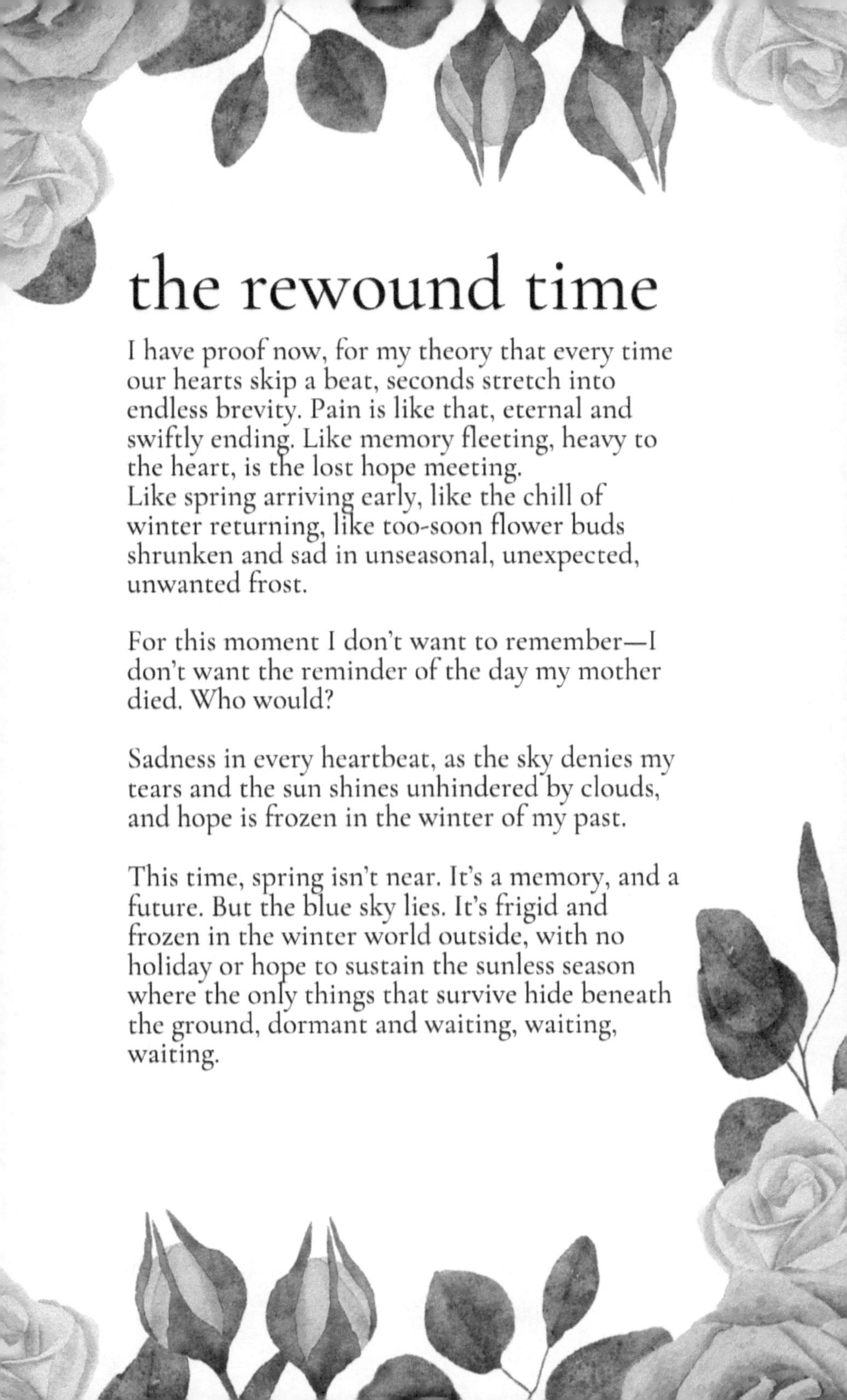

the rewound time

I have proof now, for my theory that every time
our hearts skip a beat, seconds stretch into
endless brevity. Pain is like that, eternal and
swiftly ending. Like memory fleeting, heavy to
the heart, is the lost hope meeting.
Like spring arriving early, like the chill of
winter returning, like too-soon flower buds
shrunken and sad in unseasonal, unexpected,
unwanted frost.

For this moment I don't want to remember—I
don't want the reminder of the day my mother
died. Who would?

Sadness in every heartbeat, as the sky denies my
tears and the sun shines unhindered by clouds,
and hope is frozen in the winter of my past.

This time, spring isn't near. It's a memory, and a
future. But the blue sky lies. It's frigid and
frozen in the winter world outside, with no
holiday or hope to sustain the sunless season
where the only things that survive hide beneath
the ground, dormant and waiting, waiting,
waiting.

THE POISON MAP

Minutes later, in the castle library, Wednesday

THIS TIME, THE MOMENT isn't spinning around us, we're spinning around each other. Round and round, up, up, up, but the curving steps, the ascent—it took us down into history. The circles, the upward spiral no longer dizzying or round. It's a straight line to heartache.

But I am not the only person here. A solid figure materializes out of the shadows, following me. Trailing me through the broken remains of a rich, happy home. Asking "where are we going in such a hurry" and "why?" It was so easy for him to say—the fire was his fault? Who does he think he is, saying awful things like that? What if it's true? I'm breathlessly ascending the final stairs, picking my footsteps with care. I lost loved ones that night. I lost my heart that night too.

I should tell him, or ask him all the awful questions, but apparently I'm too *obstinate*.

He's quiet. Dead silence in the halls, but he follows me into the library, where sun-streaks pebble the stone floor beneath our feet, where rings of circles in black and white marble overlap at the compass center of the room. It's pretty. It's painfully, breathtakingly beautiful. And in this moment, I hate it.

I hate the sunlight, for this day that brought up the memory I tried to bury. I hate the rose and the sword and the hammer and the filagree around the motif of that lost family from hundreds of years ago. Why must *I* be the one to find the *Oirdera?* Why must I suffer now for all what happened to them? What was done to them, or what they did? Will I also need to avenge them? Will I want to? What if the hidden books tell me stories I don't want to hear? Are we meant to tell them at all?

Nolan pauses beneath the library's spiral stairs, his eyes averted from the windows. My sympathy for his fear of heights has diminished. It's hard to find pity in my heart for this young man, no matter what he's lost or endured, because...the fire...what if he... He didn't say what happened, but he knows. It's like he's magically transformed into a monster before my eyes in the reflecting light from the mirror. Beautiful features. But the fire? If it was truly his fault, then it's his fault my mother and grandmother had no one to rescue or hear them, trapped, dying in the fire, in the smoke.

I plant myself directly before the reflection of myself in the gilded mirror, which is the length of my outstretched arm and stands taller than me, attached against the wall on a slight angle. I can't believe it took me so long to realize, but this mirror has a twin in *Azalea's Treasures.* The intricate vine and rose design are the same, the full-length size the same. Beautiful, unusual.

I'm not sure who I'm talking to when I say, "Step out of the dark. Stop hiding." The quest for answers—suddenly close—thins my patience. "Nolan, look in the mirror." I wait for his denial, but he obeys, stepping out of the shadow of the stairs and into the rays of sunlight, across the burgundy Persian rug beneath the settee, the shiny floor-squares making circles.

"What do *you* see?" he asks, low voice rough in his way.

For all the rational reasons that I should smother accusations it would be far too easy to place on him, he's still someone I can blame—a beast from memories not mine, nightmares of darkness I'd never seen.

"The day we met, when I found the first *Oirdera* in Penelope's bookshop, it was hidden in the storage room of all places," I explain. "There's a mirror just like this there, too. She'd said—much too vaguely—she had received a collection from an estate with too many boxes and antiques. The *Oirdera* was in an indestructible-looking chest. Near this mirror. Not this one, but the sister, the *pair*."

"I haven't been in this room since the fire, not until being here with you." He sighs, focusing on a black marble square beneath his feet. "I guess the mirror was there, before..."

I scoff. Not remember details of a library? Sniffing, I focus on his reflection, meeting his eyes in the mirror. "Let's take it down."

Without another word, he does as I say. His long fingers wrap around the bottom, his grip hardly able to surround the thick bronze edges on the lower half. Hefting a few times to check the weight, with fluid motions of his strong musculature, he lifts it up and away from the wall, setting it against the nearest bookshelf.

About six feet from the ground, a horizontal opening is cut into the stone. A square, with a book leaning on one side.

Breath leaves me. "It's here."

Nolan reverently removes the white book. It's an exact replica of the first, with threaded Latin phrasing on the cover and the single rose on the spine. He hands me the book and I flip the first page, finding exactly what I expected. There's a torn-out page—the title page from Lenora that shows the motif of a long-lost family, from whom I am the recipient of this burdensome, precious locket. It pains me, so I tuck the thought away like I'm keeping the locket hidden beneath my clothes, even as I pull out the missing title page and return it to its place.

"How will this lead us to treasure?" he asks quietly, examining the crest. Even as I see the book in front of me, I doubt. I doubt finding a hidden heir can save Nolan from his uncle. And I doubt the validity of his aunt's task, the absurdity of finding a map no one knows about to a treasure no one believes is real. "Or is *this* a map? Could there be a way into the mine through the castle? These swirling...things...are almost like the servant tunnels." His fingers trace the vines surrounding the crest like lines, as if they represent tunnels beneath the ground—which is exactly what I think they do. I take out my journal, where I'd traced the title page from the other *Oirdera*, and place one page beside the other. The vines on the pages overlap perfectly, making it clearer, looking more and more like—

The poison map before me, the sight making my blood boil. A freezing fire that burns.

It's hard to imagine humans living in the castle when it wasn't always cold, dim, and incomparably silent. Halls rush with hesitant wind instead of healthy flurries of regular footsteps. Daylight creeps in broken windows, but never quite reaches the charred black of the fire's fingerprints. My hands cover my heart. The locket is warm beneath my clothes, hidden in the dark, heavy against my chest, as I hesitate to show Nolan the symbol that's littered all over his castle.

"Nolan? I think the map is real."

He raises his eyebrows as I hold the books sideways so the vines align with the design around the mirror. It lines up, but nothing tells us how to overlay it on this castle in a way that makes sense.

"Hmm..." While my voice sounds breathy, my ears are buzzing with that desperation for answers that's been fueling me. I snap the book closed.

Nolan wipes dust from his palms onto his jeans. "Uncle Declan has one book with an incomplete map he doesn't know about and no trace of an heir"—he coughs a low laugh—"but what he doesn't know he's missing won't matter. The book alone should make him happy. But this map doesn't actually make sense..."

No, not without the key. A *ruby-red key*. My fingers itch to brush the clasp of the locket beneath my sweater dress. "Lenora asked for a map, so I'll give her a map. She can find her own treasure."

"You think it's enough to save your home and your father?"

"I hope so." I have to. Taking a seat on the settee, I trace the lines from this book into my journal beside the other page from the first *Oirdera*, careful to mark the variations of the two crests. Unfortunately, while the vines on the crest match the mirror, I need to see it beside my locket and Nolan's right here. I want to take the locket out and hold it to the sunshine, but…I'm not quite ready to step into the light. Yet how else can I discern how to overlay the map over this castle?

"Paige?" Nolan's quiet voice reminds me of the wolves outside. Even when they're far away and the sound is low, it still sends a tingle down my spine.

"Yes?" I resist moving to touch the locket that's hidden down the front of my sweater, suddenly feeling too warm. "I'll read the book and finish making a copy of this tonight."

When he doesn't respond, I risk a glance. His golden tone and golden eyes are darkening like the heavy sun eclipsed by the horizon at sunset as he asks, "What is it?" Suspicion filters an edge into his husky voice, making it deeper.

I tuck the book and my journal into my book bag and stand. "You'd better replace that mirror."

"What aren't you telling me?" he presses. "You think I'll follow you without question? You think I can't read the distrust in your eyes?" He takes a menacing step into my space. "And now you think I'm going to let you risk your life seeking a lost passageway in these awful ruins?"

Heat from an angry part of my heart flares in my cheeks. He admitted it was his fault—but he doesn't know the women in my family are dead *because of the fire*, and now this locket that belonged to them and is now mine is *a key to a map to real treasure,* and it's too much, and as those words become lines and paragraphs and pages in my story, I can't breathe. "I don't know where to go." *Yet.*

With less effort than it took to take it down, Nolan puts the mirror back on the monstrous set of curved nails that held it up. Clearly, anger or guilt or whatever is fueling his strength. Well, strength isn't merely physical. With effort I fill my lungs, again and again, focused on the rock hammer and sword forming a cross atop a single rose, my mother's locket, the key. Surety fills me, lengthening the bottom of my breath as I go to leave the library, filling my veins with purchase. There's somewhere I haven't finished searching...seven doors. I'm not done in the West Wing, and if I have to find my way without Nolan's help, so be it.

Nolan stalks past to stand in front me, blocking the stained-glass door with those seven snowy roses, his breath hot on my face. "We're supposed to be partners, but how can we be when we're"—he draws a bold line from his chest to me—"like this with each other?"

"This?" I fail to think of a better word. Annoyance leaches from my teeth to the back of my jaw. "We're here now," I state, refusing to be resigned to anything.

"You want to save your father, but that isn't what's chasing you. What aren't you telling me?"

I wanted to save my father, but from the beginning, it felt like lying. Letters making words I spoke, and promises I wasn't planning to keep. Letters, curving into language. Hiding things, twisting. Nolan hasn't bought any of my lies, and it's a relief and pain, pain, pain.

But I'm not the only one running. "How did you survive the fire when they didn't?" I know my question is cruel as I ask aloud,

"Were the rumors true, that blamed you?"

Nolan steps closer. "You should hate me," he rasps. "Everyone else does. You *are* looking at me differently, but I can't take it back. It's my fault." Wondering at the very important issue of *how exactly* it's his fault, I look up. But his eyes are shut for a piercing moment. "Better you see me as I am and blame me how I deserve."

I remember my mother saying how mirrors work, and how not to be deceived by appearances. Beauty isn't on the outside. It is found within. And within, regret is a vicious creature, leaching pain, spreading anything that stifles peace and love. Am I any different?

"That's not an answer," I say.

He pulls back at the look that must make that feeling plain on my face, yet he doesn't seem to care. "Doesn't it occur to you that you should be afraid of me?" I bite my lip, refusing to breathe *fire* because it's unfair. I have no answer, for I can't truly imagine he directly killed anyone at all. Though...the thought of his being responsible for the fire does seem like enough to warrant fear. "Look at what you think of me now! I am a beast to you and what—you still won't leave? You're so stubborn! Digging all this up might not be worth it."

He has no idea.

I can't decide if it's a good feeling or not, breathless fear and anticipation alike when it comes to my body's response to him. He's an antihero, but he's no villain. That role has already been filled. "I'm not afraid of you," I lie. I want to run, fast and fearless, away from this place with the memories that should be dead but that keep mirroring my own sad past. Repetition is an inescapable infinity.

He rubs his chin with his thumb, drawing my eyes to his sharp jawline, to his lips set in an angry line. "What if you aren't satisfied when you reach the end of your search?" His gaze follows a trail from the tips of my hair to my lips, to the chain he can see—holding the locket he *hasn't* seen—dangling against my collarbones. As his burnished eyes linger on my lips, his mouth forms tense words. "How much are you willing to give?"

Hesitation thins my breath, so I use bold words. "I would give myself." I cannot move, or part of me would touch part of him, his torso aligned with mine, head bent and unforgiving, not allowing me escape. I'm reminded once again that fire isn't the only thing in this wild, beautiful, dangerous world that burns. There are cold things, steaming things, that boil skin and scald the air. "I will go wherever this path leads."

"Reckless." His words steal my false bravado.

"Brave," I respond. "Undaunted. Courageous."

"It will take more than that for you to survive the mine...if that's where the map ends up taking you," he threatens, but steps away, giving me space to breathe. He rakes a hand across his short hair, voice raw as he says, "If there's no heir, then..."

The only tales older than time are those of loss and sorrow. But Nolan doesn't know that the women of my family died here, and I'm not sure our tenuous partnership can withstand the knowledge—our mercenary need for each other isn't built on solid *anything*. So, I promise, "Our deal remains, no matter what you did.

We'll find the hidden heir, for both our sakes." *I know we can.*

Leaving the library, Nolan explains that Anne informed him that Penelope has something for me. Like a ray of sweet lemon light, the mention of Penelope brightens my mood for a blessed moment. Whenever Penelope has something for someone, things take a turn. Nolan says he'll drive me to town tomorrow, and I laugh under my breath as I wonder which of the two lovely women guilted him into offering.

But as we leave the rose corridor, my resolve crumbles like the neglect throughout the rest of the castle. My body is meek, weak at the knees when we take narrow stairs carefully down, down, down, but something sharp rattles inside, raging at the unfairness that brought me to this moment that felt less like a choice and more like a sentence. Irritated at my inability to voice further questions, for fear the beastly young man might ask questions *I'm* not ready to answer, I keep my peace while he escorts me down the servant stairs, holding my hand as always. Safe, narrow, secret.

We emerge on the ground floor beside the closed-off ballroom. I don't look at him while we leave the castle, sitting without its family. Nolan and I represent both the start and the end. Strangers, enemies from an old story, who in another tale might be lovers if my flighty heart could have its way. If there's another cycle, which one of us will begin again?

He isn't a cursed prince. I'm the princess, and I'm the one who's cursed. The map isn't lost—it's poison to all who want it. Even those descended from those Ludovicis who drew it.

Including me.

The Time Spell

The next day, Thursday at 11 o'clock in the morning, in Upper Towne, Loirehall

AT THE BOTTOM OF THE STEPS to Penelope Garcon's townhouse in Upper Towne, an upscale neighborhood of Loirehall, Nolan balks. "Am I going to regret this?"

There was brooding, *complete* silence during the short drive from the gatehouse, through Gabreville, and over the bridge to northeast Loirehall. Nolan's car is black and fast and too low to the ground for comfort—if it hadn't been already, it became apparent to me this morning that wealth is not his problem.

"*This* is why I don't sit beside you at dinner," I mutter under my breath. Mrs. Lucas makes delicious meals and Martin talks nonstop throughout them—sitting beside him means I never have to pause my eating to speak.

"What?" Nolan calls to my back.

"Your words." Or lack thereof. Yesterday, we parted with a tension I wasn't ready to decipher. This question was his first words since he opened the sleek car door for me twenty minutes ago and the scent of pine and warm leather and luxury car enveloped me. I was annoyed, but comfortable.

"I don't talk much at dinner," he says. "I'm just hungry and eat and leave."

I roll my eyes and lift the flowery, starlike knocker. "Will you behave? We're just picking up something and then I'm going to the bookshop. Penelope means a lot to me, and you're someone who wants to remain...unnoticed." I don't say *steward* aloud, for we're not in an abandoned castle any longer. Couples walk on the street, a young mother pushes a baby in a black pram, and an old woman walks slow and serene across the five-cornered roundabout, stalling traffic on all sides.

It would be comical if I didn't think the old lady with the heart-shaped glasses wasn't spying when we parked.

Nolan takes the stairs grudgingly. The air expands when he's beside me, *perfect* him and those wide shoulders fitted in a crisp gray suit jacket atop a designer, striped crew neck sweater. Rich, but uncaring. That's his vibe and it goes well with the messy, straight, sand-hued hair at odd angles on top, the clean shave below short sideburns revealing a clenched jaw with that thin scar, narrowing to a chin with a prominent dimple, the only soft thing about him.

Nolan's golden eyes arc down to drill into mine, and my gaze is caught on the freckles on the imperfect bridge of his nose. Before I can talk back, the door swings open in our faces.

"Just look at you two!" Penelope flourishes, dressed in a classy A-line skirt and silk blouse, both a deep silver hue . "Mr. Hayes, I've heard so much about you from Anne. And Lincoln." Heavens, two mornings ago, while I had come to Loirehall to check on Papa and get necessities and clothes from our freezing Gabreville home,

I saw Penelope as she opened her bookshop. From that rushed update, what did she discern from my tone or description to make her this...

"Charmed." Penelope grabs a silent Nolan's hand to shake it. Not quite how I might describe Nolan. Mysterious and intriguing, yes. Aloof and standoff-ishly handsome? Absolutely. Rude? Sometimes. But *charming*?

"Penelope!" I go between them, hugging her and saving a silent, ungrateful Nolan. *Botheration.* "I'm so curious about what you've got for me—"

"What a striking couple," Penelope croons. "You with your lush dark waves, and his"—Penelope's hand circles a halo in Nolan's direction—"trendy, uncaring style and a backdrop of storm clouds." She nods, completely satisfied.

Storm clouds gather on Nolan's brow as Penelope calls to a passerby, "Percy! Percy!" She breezes past us down the stairs to greet the tall, lanky boy, laden with bags and boxes. "Oh, I double-booked myself. See? I'm lost without you Paige! Oh, well. We're all here!"

Tension spikes a rod down Nolan's body. "What's with you?" I whisper, though I'm surprised to see Percy too. Nolan's slack-jawed expression hardens in a second, so I say, "If you're rude to Penelope, lightning may strike you. Don't you know who she is? I'm unconvinced she isn't an angel."

"Percy is my *cousin*," he hisses. "He can't—"

"I know! I'm sorry! But it's not like I knew he'd be here," I return. "And it's not like people aren't going to see you now that you live in Gabreville!" Nolan's family relations are a detail I'd avoided dwelling upon, as Percy and Darragh share the Hayes name, with their father Declan being Nolan's uncle. Because sometimes details on paper mean pain in real life. And *Darragh* being Nolan's cousin, him having hurt Juniper so deeply, is like the fountain pen tip stabbing out my story, instead of telling it in smooth brushstrokes.

Nolan huffs and steps back as Penelope and Percy join us in front of the door. Both young men tower over me, but Penelope is unfazed by the rippling in the air, all the angst reserved for characters in stories trying to find their way. She's already survived her story, so seems to look upon us poor young leads with amusement and pity. The Hayes boys nod—Percy first, as recognition splits his face in surprise, then suspicion, then a mask of gentility. Nolan shakes his head once in an obvious signal that he's ready for a challenge if it comes. Percy doesn't echo Nolan's jerky motions, but keeps silent all the same.

Hayes boys are going to kill me.

"Hi, Percy." I attempt to sound like this is a completely normal situation. *Why is Percy here?*

"Percy's here to take pictures of the cherry blossoms!" Penelope ushers Percy and his mussed hair through the foyer. "Just one moment, Paige. Come inside, Percy. I have this marvelous idea for your photo spread, but before that, set that box here—no, not that one..." Percy obeys her as we all would, humble and obliging at the force of the aged woman who can be commanding when she wishes.

I consider the tall, dark-haired boy who'd entered Penelope's home. Having been the same year in school, I knew Darragh's younger brother, Percy. He wasn't the worst—wiry and lean, perceptive and quiet, and he's got those gorgeous black waves that girls loved, not that he paid them mind. Not black like bleak, just unknown, but *definitely* not my type. After a lifetime with him in the same class, we haven't spared more than a sentence or two a year for each other, and then only when necessary. I kept to my books—not sure what occupied his mind. He isn't the worst, if only because he always keeps his thoughts to himself.

Today, he's hardly said a word after seeing Nolan—a cousin he'd possibly presumed dead. I wonder if Percy knows his parents are getting a divorce. How much strife must there be in their family? Regardless...Percy's lack of malice always made me hate his older brother more. Darragh was a bully in school to any child who wore hand-me-down clothes. He irrevocably hurt my best friend, too, stringing her along, breaking her heart. I don't like letting those feelings go.

What if that hurt could happen again?

"I'm not going in there," Nolan gruffs in my ear.

I want to slam my forehead on a wall, or laugh till I cry, because the pen is stabby still, but I'm surrounded by people and can't. "Afraid of a wall of clocks?"

"She's busy anyhow. Take what she has for you and let's go."

From inside her house, Penelope raises a brow and looks over her shoulder to wink at me, then disappears.

"We'll come around back," I call, breathing in the warmth that whispers quiet before the storm beneath low, promising clouds. Beside me is Nolan in all his gorgeousness, with those sad eyes and a crease between his brows that draws my gaze to the cleft in his chin and his lips...

Then he speaks, and the heat of my attraction dims. "This crazy, stupid idea just got worse. I don't care if she's giving you a hundred-pound chest of gold. I should have dropped you at the door and left while I had the chance." He closes the door to Penelope's pretty white townhouse and starts walking down the stairs to the sidewalk.

"Oh my *word*," I hiss, following him around the side of the townhouse, which sits on the corner of the street. "He's your cousin—and the nicer of them. The only person resembling nice in their family, may I say." *Including you*, I add silently in a glare. Nolan glares right back. "He works for the *Gabreville Gazette* and *The Loirehall Times*. Papa mentioned printed papers are cutting costs, so it makes sense Percy takes photos for both papers..." My voice fades at Nolan's severe expression, but it doesn't stop my rambling. "I've seen Percy's name on the captions, and he always hid behind a camera lens in school, but—"

"Fine."

"Fine? Just like that?"

"If I have to say any more, it won't be."

"Fine."

He leads me toward the white-washed stone walls edging Penelope's tall townhome and hiding a garden full of trees. Because it's a mild day, it feels like spring. Though the sky has many a dark cloud, there's a thin break above the western horizon, and warm sunshine spills through it.

"Pretty," I murmur, peering into the garden over a simple gate, taken aback at the sight of a pretty inlaid path of stonework, the arbors and trellises begging for summer, perfect trims of hedges and spring bulbs not yet safe from frost. "It's changed so much since I was here last fall—"

Nolan crosses his arms, leaning against the stone wall, watching cars go by. "Her nephew is my friend, Lincoln. My housemate." At this information, a question that'd been niggling sizzles out—this explains Penelope's warm welcome to Nolan. The woman doesn't hold grudges based on names. Nolan continues. "Lincoln designed the stonework, everything. It means a lot to him. He worked hard, it had been overgrown and unused for years."

"I want to go in."

"No," he says, crossing his arms, and I cross mine too. "What have you told her?" Nolan hisses.

Goosebumps hide beneath my navy brocade coat and the thick black turtleneck beneath. Wool warm and itchy. "Everything. Don't blow your top off." I cross my arms in the universal gesture of a huff. "Besides, I'm unsure whether or not Penelope doesn't just magically *know* everything, anyway."

Penelope encouraged me to go to Fairhavens to find its secrets, likely knowing I would discover Nolan's identity and hoping we'd fall in love. Classic Penelope—chasing a love story. I think she knows who my mother is, about the white roses that make me who I am by blood. But not *just* that. I believe Penelope wants to thwart Mr. Hayes and Lenora. For what deeper purposes or history of their own, I do not know. What I do know is that every fairytale-land has a villain. Lenora and Declan, mirrors of each other. Nolan and I, mirrors of loss, and without a place in the world to call our own. And the mirror in the castle, pointing us to something deeper.

Penelope sees us and waves. Beside her, Percy stops taking pictures and dips his head to listen as Penelope tries to draw him out of silence . She pins him with a look, then shifts her warm gaze to us before brushing forward and calling him to follow. As if to obey her command, the cherry blossoms shift and drop into the air, floating to avoid the ground in the swift breeze.

When did Percy get so tall? He's as tall as Nolan, maybe an inch more, but lankier. Give him six months and the lanky might—

"Pardon me." Percy snares Penelope before she slips over an icy spot. In a shockingly smooth motion, he lifts her by the waist and deposits her on the other side of the arbor. "There you are."

"Oh, what a dear. And strapping! What a lad, thank you for saving my shoes!" Penelope disdains the muddy puddle for daring to only *partially* freeze over. "The weather missed the memo that winter is over. Spring is coming," she says. "Percy, I need to discuss a few things with these two, so have a look around and start as soon as you like. The article will mention that my nephew's company designed this heavenly place, so do it justice."

The tall boy lowers his head in deference but wisely remains silent. Or is he fixing the camera lens? His eyes are clear of guile and filled with only mild curiosity. I get the distinct impression that whether or not he knows every detail of Nolan's return or my visiting Fairhavens, he's trustworthy, like a vault.

"For the bookshop," Percy says, tossing a paper bag at Nolan, who catches it with a huff. Then he walks away, preparing his gear and looking around for the best angles.

My mouth is gaping. I snap it shut.

"Considering his family"—Nolan clears his throat—"he's least bad."

I stifle a smile. With a pang, I suddenly miss my friend—how I wish Juniper could see this. I snatch the paper bag from Nolan. Happily, I peek in—Percy's brought a box of Peckles from *Peckle's & Praline* candy shop, and I nearly swoon. "Can I bring a few of these to Juniper? They're her favorite."

"Do yes. The whole thing." Penelope reaches over the wall and places a very tall but narrow envelope into my hands.

"Why am *I* here?" Nolan asks, leaning back again, crossing his ankles.

"You're perfectly moody aren't you! Can't even come inside for tea!" She sighs at Nolan's silence. "I told Anne to send you so I can ask you how you're doing, young man. And I see you're the same. Less broody, more protective. Nolan, my boy, truly you and Lincoln are a pair."

Penelope is unfazed at his brooding, which is why I love her. I rub my tongue over my teeth, tasting the mint tea I had earlier, feeling an unfair amount of pleasure at seeing him so put on the spot. I tuck the unusual envelope into my book bag.

"How was your meeting with the professor this morning?"

Penelope asks Nolan. "Did you get your papers in order?"

"Yes, ma'am. But what's with that guy and umbrellas?" Nolan grumbles, and *that* is why I love Sterling. Can't pin the old man down.

"It could rain at any time, and it's a distraction. That's why he's a good lawyer." It *is* a good thing that Sterling Figgleston is Nolan's legal counsel. The legendary Sterling Irwinaeus Figgleston won't make any mistakes in re-establishing Nolan's identity before Gabreville Council meets Sunday. Then Nolan, the closest Hayes steward, can take what he's owed, if he wants it. Which he still says he doesn't.

Mr. Hayes with the other *Oirdera* has taken the heat off Papa—Declan thinks there's no heir to worry about. If only he knew there was an heir *and* a steward standing here, both loathe to step up and take their due. Not that Nolan changing his name back to Hayes officially changes anything. You can take back your family surname, but Nolan's unwilling to own it. Just like me.

The strap of my book bag is heavy across my chest. Carrying that second *Oirdera*, because I'm unwilling to let it out of my sight. I wonder what's in that unusual envelope into my book bag. Penelope never gives gifts without a reason. Will it help when spring comes in a few days? When my time will be up, and Lenora will want her treasure. I need to distract her with a map, false if need be. If there's *real* treasure, and we find a way to it beneath the mountain, in the mine...if there's a tunnel that isn't blocked. So many ifs.

Crazy, stupid idea, indeed. And me? Beyond the locket, there's no way to prove who I am, not that I've even *accepted* that I'm the heir, or told anyone—

"It'll rain later," Penelope interrupts my reverie. "You two best be on your way."

The same moment, on the sidewalk outside Penelope's townhome

PENELOPE WAVES GOODBYE as she returns to Percy in the garden, reminding me over her shoulder to visit Juniper at the bookshop, as my friend misses me and has something for me as well. Nolan and I are left alone outside the garden, with melancholy birdsong beneath bruised, tempest-tossed clouds.

He stares at me—a silent conversation boils between us as the clouds overtake the peeking sunlight. Our shared need to reveal something. A hint, the start of an answer. A secret. Something private and precious that won't get us killed. I let my gaze trace the narrow angle of stitching on his collar, to his Adam's apple and a muscle ticking in his sharp jaw as he refrains from speaking.

I need you. I carry the force of my need to help my father who's never saved me, who left me at the castle, lost in his broken inner world and unable to share his hurt or healing. *You need me.* All the years in a house with a father who let his broken heart forget his broken little girl. But now, now I thought I was strong enough, but the thought of relying on another man who might abandon me when it gets tough—

As if he hears my thoughts screaming, Nolan straightens and comes up to me. "Ready to tell me what you're hiding?"

There are clouds yes, but it's a feeling too. I smell it: the petrichor, the promise of rain, the scent of a coming storm that promises to be so much worse. A crackling in the seams between the fabric of the sky, seeking a place to land.

"Why do *you* hide? What happened during the fire that made you leave and never come back?" I ask right back.

"I'm back *now*." Nolan reaches for me before hesitating and dropping his hands. "And it isn't my fault you've been drawn into this mess, is it? Why do you run into danger, every time?" Gold eyes blazing, it sounds like he's angry.

I stare at the neck of his sweater. "Stop avoiding my questions."

"Start answering mine." His whisper is more of a huff, and we're close enough that his breath blows warm against my forehead.

"I *do*." Not my fault he doesn't know the question to ask that would blow apart my secrets. Obstinate heroine indeed. I really am a hypocrite.

"In a way that makes sense. All this for treasure?" Nolan's cheek nears mine as he whispers in my ear. He swallows, and my eyes follow the motion down his neck to the collar of the asymmetrical sweater. It reminds me of the day we met, how he leaned around me to reach a book, how his skin is pale and ruddy and scattered with so many freckles. But today—with him this close—his sunshine scent, still warm, is incongruent with the clouds above. I inhale the scent of his skin, something like woods and lemon and purely masculine.

I suck in cold air, and my head clears. Pulling away, I whisper, "All this for freedom."

Nolan clears his throat. "I'll answer your questions if you tell me about that necklace you keep hiding."

How many stories didn't turn out right for me to stand at the tip of the next wrong step? I close my eyes and count to three. Then, lifting the cuffs of my forest-green cardigan, I remove the locket from beneath my shirt.

He leans in, but not too close. "Where did it come from? It looks old."

"It was my mother's." She wasn't wearing it, that night when she left. *Leaving* being a euphemism well used in memories and histories and stories. Leaving, dying. You don't have to see someone leave *or* die for them to be gone from the pages of your life forever.

"Your mother, she's..." His question falls away, leaving space between us. A magnetic feeling of gravity trying to pull us down, toward each other, to our end.

"She's dead." Smoke kills. His parents died, there in the castle, too. His family, his home, his life, all taken in the flames. Which he is supposedly responsible for? And for what did they all perish? Kingdoms have fallen for less. Riches, treasure, gems. We all have a prize, and we all have a price. Still, I want to say I'm sorry. For loss.

There's his sharp intake of breath as I lift the locket to the light. Caught by the rubies on my locket, a ray of sunlight makes delicate, quivering designs on the ground. Nolan's golden gaze follows the ruby reflecting, dancing as I twist it about in the sunray—

Suddenly, the sun sinks behind the looming clouds.

"You have a locket that matches the crest of the lost lords." Astonishment lifts his brow, but it isn't threatening. "You're not, are you?" Then, "Who *are* you?"

The best, most important questions are hardest to ask.

Did my mother know about her lineage, if that's what this locket and all these symbols represent? All I know is that her parents are gone. Papa said that other than Grandmother, she had no family, which is why he and I lived such a quiet life after she left. No more mother's soft shoulder to cry on, no grandmother to visit with sweet buns to pester me about schoolwork. I feel just like the Ludovici crest on the gold locket, hidden but adorned with red rubies, weighty and silent, waiting for someone to tell my story.

I step away from him, an arm's length away. "Not me, who my mother was. Or rather, who my great-great-great-great grand-mother was." I'm not valuable but for what I hold. But for my blood, in my hand—my *lineage*. "Seven generations back, if the names etched here"—I hold out the locket and show him the tiny lettering on the back—"are any indication."

He examines it with a furrowed brow. The gold in his light brown eyes is like a fire in a forest, so far from calm in the coiled stillness of his strong hand holding mine, not taking the locket, just looking at it as it sits in my palm.

Holding history between our hands like a time spell.

"You're perfect," he whispers, lifting his head, eyes wide. Awe is not the response I'd expected. "The family who built it re-mains—and it's *you*." The chord in his voice remains serious as his tone rises, asking, "What do you want to do?"

Will I dare?

"You are the son of the last stewards of the mine with the closest ties to the citadel, but you're *not* the heir with the longest history, if this is true." The ruby looks as old as the stained-glass windows, which my family on my mother's side built. Those towers, the hidden ties she tried to bury— "It's too much, isn't it?" I scoff. "How *could* it be true? Even if it was—I don't want it!"

He frowns. "Why not?"

"Because it's a castle of death."

He flinches, and I immediately regret my words. "As if I could forget," he says. His hand wraps more tightly around mine, covering the locket, then he lets go. "My parents died there! Did it ever occur to you I don't want it either?"

"I can tell!" I sigh after my outburst, looking away, frustrated that we want the same thing. Or *don't*. If only he knew what I lost that night, he would understand—but no, I can't go there yet. If either of us were more selfish, this might be easier, but we're just too scarred. Too *scared*. Afraid, afraid, afraid. And I'm the worst. "You want to stop your aunt and uncle, though, and I am willing to do anything to save my father."

"Saving Fairhavens won't save your father." He pauses until I glance up, a sense of knowing in his raised brow. "You don't just want to save your home, you want to save everyone. Because you *believe* there's treasure, don't you?" He smothers a laugh, crossing his arms. "All your talk of books and you're willing to risk everything for a *story*. One that others who told it before you ended badly."

I'm annoyed he's figured me out so easily. "What else can I do? Papa's business means the world to him. And he means the world to me. It's that simple."

"Simple? Fine—*don't* tell me."

"It isn't like you're telling me everything! *Would* you even tell me? What really happened the night of the fire? What is so bad that you can't talk about it?" I'm berating myself, asking the very questions I would never answer. Then I think of books he knocked out of my arms in the university library when we first met. How he saved me from falling down the stairs of the castle and showed me the way. I release a sigh. It annoys me that I feel like *I'm* being unfair.

"It doesn't even matter. There's nothing I can say to make it better. Every word makes it worse." He fists the keys to his car, parked across the road. "I'm sorry."

I don't think "sorry" will be enough if he had something to do with starting the fire—or spreading it. It's the only reason I can think of that he won't tell me what happened. The shattered windows are a hint that someone deliberately *made* the fire violent. What if it had started malevolently, too?

"No," I disagree, "no words are worse."

"Tell me when you're ready to take your own advice, and we'll talk."

I clutch my book bag and scarf. "Can I have that, please?"

He hands me the bag of Peckle's treats. "Where are you going?" he asks behind me.

"Bookshop. Juniper," I say over my shoulder. He steps back, clearly getting the message that I don't want *him*.

"I'm sorry." I don't know why I try. He raises his fair brows and I look away. "This has been a long week." My breath leaves a puff of steam in the cool air.

Nolan must see the frenzy of pain in my eyes, a rabid sort of thumping deep in my soul that I'm trying oh so hard to hide. And I need to hide. *I need my best friend.* Spinning on my heel, I run off as it starts to drizzle. Rainfall blends with the sound of his voice calling me, and that strain inside tightens because he doesn't follow.

THE RED LETTERS

Twenty minutes later, a rainy Thursday afternoon at Azalea's Treasures

AFTER PASSING OVER THE HEART of our cities, the Valais River, then avoiding the historic district near Château Fleur, I skirt through alleys from the Yorkson Memorial in a hurry. It's chilly, right before the spring equinox. I hardly feel it. I'm running, running away from Nolan, running to find the one person I can truly vent to.

Juniper is exactly where Penelope said I'd find her on a rainy afternoon. She must not have classes today. Working at *Azalea's*, one would expect staff to be bookish, but Juniper is the opposite. Rainy days don't mean reading with a comfortable classic and wool throw—no—to her, quiet days at the shop are for organizing. Alphabetical, or color-coded, or whatever new insanity she wishes to mischievously employ to madden shoppers accustomed to the last layout. It's amusing, until you're looking for a particular book and can't find Juniper.

I pause outside the door and try to act normal. Not like I'm living out the slow-burn, enemies-to-lovers trope I despise, not like I'm here burdened with secrets I'm dying to share. No, no drama whatsoever. Then someone slams open the door with a rush of hot air. A young man with a black baseball cap and too much wind in his sails walks off without even noticing. Chimes announce my sopping entrance.

"Look. At. You." Juniper sees the story without me telling it.

"Who was that?" I've never been so thankful for a friend. "Also, help."

"First, that's Penelope's nephew who nearly bowled you over. So cute, so grumpy. Seriously—he writes review cards of new release biographies for our displays. Can you even believe it? Doesn't look like a reader, that one. He speaks in grunts, and I'm amazed he does this. He seems so put out every time he comes by." She shrugs. "Penelope pays me to be discreet and ignore her nephew's madness, I suppose."

Oh, *that's* the boy who designed Penelope's beautiful garden? The landscaper? Nolan's housemate and friend? Wonders never cease. I take off my coat, hanging it and my scarf nearest the blessedly warm radiators.

"Go dry off. One pot of tea coming up." Curls bouncing, Juniper dashes to the back.

"No Azalea today?" I shout after her.

"Just me!" she calls from the other room. "Much less work when she's not around, batty old lady..."

I imagine my best friend rustling about in the kitchen, choosing blackcurrant tea and muttering on my behalf against whichever antagonists made me sad. Tears slide down my cheeks.

She swiftly returns, placing tea on the low table in the front corner of the shop that she insisted on making into a reading corner, though she *does not read*. Flicking her ringlet bangs from her face while the rest of her curls protest in a soaring ponytail, she pours our tea and leans back on the deep juniper-hued—the color, not styled like the friend—Queen Anne chair, and I mimic her languid motion onto the lavender chaise.

I feel as though I can finally process. In a rush between three cups of tea, I explain the story thus far. How the perfect pair to the book in the castle was hiding in Penelope's bookshop the first day I met Nolan. What a stroke of luck it was that Penelope asked me to find something in the storage room! Juniper requires details—how it was uncovered while moving an old box of dresses and an even older chest of who-knows-what from the Gregson estate. She makes a humming noise and stands to immediately try on the dresses, but with even more theatrics, forces herself to sit and hear the rest of my tale. She even refrains from chastising me for not telling her when I found the book. Good friends are gold.

In spite of where the *Oirdera* lead me, Penelope was certainly right—those old chests *seem* indestructible. Jumper is riveted, deciding it survived the fire or someone stole it—a far more interesting story to *her*—neither of which I ever stopped to consider. We may never know how it ended up *here*.

"So," she summarizes, after seeing the locket and hearing of the motifs reflected everywhere in the castle, "finding the books helped your father's situation for the moment. You're *not* being threatened by Declan Hayes. And, those books showed you a map, like Lenora needs, and you'll give her a basic version of said map while discovering the treasure on your own, because"—she pauses for effect—"you're likely descended from the lords who built the citadel?"

"That's about it." I don't mention Nolan.

"But none of that helps you, unless there's a key."

I inhale my tea without drinking it. "What?"

"It's a meaningless map without a key. A legend. A box with something like an explanation? 'X' marks the spot? Anything?"

"I don't know." It feels like the answer is staring at me from a blank page with invisible ink. *What is the key?* Another false book, empty of pages, empty of story, empty of treasure.

Juniper drains the rest of her tea in a long gulp. "You plan to return?" At my nod, her eyes narrow, the first sign of worry creasing the edges of her prettily-lined eyes. "What if there *is* treasure? Have you considered you might succeed? Will you let someone else take that wealth, control the mines again? Will you not step forward with your legitimate claim? It's yours, if you want it."

"I think I need to finish this first," I reply around a mouthful of vanilla macaron.

Juniper brightens. "Aren't they divine? And so nice to have sweets that aren't chocolate. Isn't there enough cocoa in the world already? Uninspiring lack of creativity in candy bars is all I'm saying. *Peckle's* never stock enough of those macarons either. They even run out of the Peckles, sometimes!" she complains. Poor, bittersweet Juniper. "It's such a long line, but worth it. Sometimes I wish I worked at a candy shop rather than a bookshop. Clearly I love one more than the other."

I throw a Peckle at her—it's a nutty, caramel candy that's chewy and altogether perfect. Her squeals are worth it, and she gobbles up the sweet. "I cannot imagine the terror your organizational play would inflict upon the ten-cent candy displays," I inform her.

"I wish." Her inner light dims as I slump across from her. "Castle that depressing?" she asks, sympathetic.

"I'm not *trying* to be morose. It's just...dark. And for all those books, can you believe there's nothing good to read?" A slap of wind flings a line of rain against the window.

She snorts. "Oh, I believe it."

"Did Penelope mention anything about what she left here for me? She gave me an envelope that's in my bag and I wanted to open it with you." I peer at my tea, not sure what I'm asking. I'm shushing myself, cutting off my words, because suddenly all I wanted to say was "I want to go home" and it scares me, because I'm not sure if I mean the castle or Nolan or both.

"Oh! A box! My gracious madness, she *did*." Juniper rushes over her words while hurrying to the stairs that take her to her apartment above the bookshop. "You're on the clock if a customer comes in!" she calls over her shoulder. "Just because Penelope keeps all the clocks in the world at her place doesn't mean time doesn't count!"

"No one's coming today; this place is always empty when it rains like this," I call right back.

Tiny bits of plaster drift into our teacups from the banging above, and I get up and holler from the bottom of the stairs, "Are you all right?"

"Nothing to see here." Her voice is muffled.

I try to shape my eyebrow like the top hook of a question mark. It's been doing that a lot lately, and I think I've mastered the curve. Who cares that she doesn't see? "The ceiling landed in my tea!"

"Could've been worse," she says, smug at the top of the stairs.

I want to hug her. The tea and sugary macaron with the cozy ambience of the bookshop is vastly improving my outlook. "What have you got for me?"

"It's a shoebox." It fills her arms as if larger than life, but she's really just holding a very petite box with two careful hands.

I try not to appear suddenly deflated at the small item. "I can see that." From Penelope, one could imagine a pretty paper box holding something beautiful and unavoidable and likely uncomfortable. Unimaginable memories, hidden for now. This is an innocuous tan-colored box of boringly normal shape and on the smallish size.

Something brightens Juniper's dark brown eyes as we settle into our seats again. "But it's what's inside. Oh, the rose symbol!" She eyes the envelope I'd placed on the table between us and emptied—it held a brooch of a silvery-white rose with the crest imprinted on the back. "I've always wanted to read a forgotten box of old letters."

"June..." I hesitate to touch the faded red envelopes with tattered edges, which seem oddly delicate. *Red letters.* But she dives right in, dumping them to scatter across the table. "Juniper Crescent!" I admonish.

"What?" She ignores my tone, shuffling the letters like a puzzle, or a deck of cards.

If I had pearls, I'd clutch them. Or a fan would do nicely. "Don't *hurt* them." I start making two piles for us to read.

She pauses, looking up at me from beneath thick, dark lashes, suddenly serious. "Whatever hurt lies here is long past. Don't be afraid. It has no power over you." Unbidden tears blur my view of her. "All right?" she asks gently.

I nod, brushing my eyes. "All right. Okay." I drag out the short word. Many words seem to be dragged out in recent days, and filled with meanings not their own. Or maybe I'm simply speaking an innocuous word into a situation as it becomes uncomfortable because of my soaring imagination. I can be okay, no matter what these letters say.

I take a deep breath and wipe the pads of my fingers on my denim skirt, feeling overwarm with my tights beneath and my hair and extra-long-sleeved cardigan dried after the rain earlier. I fan my face with the cuffs. "I have no mascara left."

Juniper laughs and opens a letter from the top of her pile, valley-like crinkles emerging at fold crevices. "Well, let's see what Penelope wants us to find."

One, two, almost three hours later

THE LETTERS PAINT a very *different* story of my family. In the shoebox, letters are memories preserved, stories told in the words of one of the descendants of the founders of Gabreville's council, where there has always sat an empty Ludovici seat. Keeping a memory then has made it come to life, now.

This must be what Nolan was looking for all along. The moment when I met him in the library, he was looking for *this* proof that one hundred and fifty years ago, someone survived the downfall of the Ludovicis. My long-lost family tree, rotten at the roots.

History is its own theme. It's a bittersweet thing, to have memories black-painful and bright-joyful. Tearing, plaguing things that stir up sweet or sad sickness with the season. Blocking one might block them all, and then we'd lose the white light that keeps us upright in the present. History is unfair, that way.

Is that why Penelope gave me another way to save Fairhavens? It doesn't matter how, but she gave me this gift. In this shoebox, amidst a pile of red letters, is proof of my family tree, bitter roots and broken tips and all. But a literal family tree in ink, stamped and dated and *official*. Maybe history *is* a gift to those who'd use it for good. And the only thing left for me to do is return to Fairhavens and bring history to light, no matter how it hurts.

I don't need to wonder which Ludovici drew this family tree. They all did. Each name is inked by a different woman. Generations of women hiding who they were, until the name of my grandmother, then my mother, and a space at the bottom. Blank, left for me.

Now that I'm forced to face that I'm a direct descendant of them, the questions flood my mind. Did the Ludovici line abandon their ancestral home in the Dark Year, or were they beaten out?

What happened to bring the Hayes family to power and left my ancestors hiding their name? How many mothers and grandmothers hid the secret that my mother kept from me?

Juniper and I read the letters. Some read like a collection of written stories, with mentions of spoken history. Most, though, are recollections of a girl in love, written to her beau. Tragic letters sent during the Great War, with little detail beyond what her *own* grandmother insisted she pass on and remember.

The red letters are written by my great-great grandmother. Her name was Rose. She was occupied with painting a picture in pretty words for her absent love. Whatever battles in the stories she'd heard came through in scattered lines of poetry, most of them hopeful. She'd turned the history into a song. Letters, their own language. Most of what I read was the hope seeded in her husband's heart by a young mother alone in her world, which I hope gave him peace when he died—we haven't gotten to that part yet, but they're long gone.

How comforting and startling to read what my great-great-grandmother and great-great-grandfather never intended anyone to see. Did my grandmother give these to Penelope before she died? Has Penelope known this all along? How did she find out? Was it her position in the royal family? She seems capable—she'd kept her own father's journal hidden in the shoebox I brought from her house. I think she'd forgotten about that; the small, midnight blue leatherbound book with exceedingly slanted handwriting, which had the famous poem from the epitaph, scrawled additions to the poem, and notes before the indecipherable lists of numbers in the back pages…

Notes about the notorious Augustus Finley, the claimant to the throne of Loirehall, who'd killed the captain of the guard, then himself, on the night of the abdication over forty years ago. Notes of how Penelope's father Monsieur Beaumont famously saved the Crown Prince when the floodwaters rose—but no. Juniper succumbed to tears at finding a part of the story we'd never heard before, that Penelope never shared in her famous newspaper articles following the historic events she was a part of so long ago. It wasn't just Nicholas who'd been saved that day, but his younger brother young Pierre too, who hadn't yet been noticed missing amidst the chaos at the Chateau when Monsieur Beaumont returned the boys to the palace.

Penelope's father saved both princes, the day of the Yorkson Tragedy. He saved them, and for some reason, Penelope kept it secret that he'd saved *both*. Juniper sniffled—for someone who didn't like romance, she was a puddle of sopping nostalgia when it came to things—and speculated it was because of Pierre being young and out of the spotlight more than Nicholas, the prodigy Crown Prince. Penelope must not have wanted to bring Pierre into the scandal at the time.

We might never know, and we hide the journal away in the bottom of the shoebox, both of us agreeing not to be brave and ask about it, ever. Coincidences indeed.

Ten minutes later, there's nothing.

"Is my family tree so rotten there's nothing left of the roots? Nothing at all?"

Juniper lowers what she's reading. "I'm reading plenty of 'something'," she says. "These are from your—I can't keep it straight. How many greats?"

"Two. My grandmother's grandmother's mother."

"Well, she's a spark if I may say. Better handwriting than me..." At my silence, she prods, "Why do you sound disappointed? I spend weeks reading law textbooks, and these are about to convince me that romance is better than any non-fiction or academic reading."

"I want to know *why*."

"Why what?"

"Why it started! Whose fault it is that my ancestors faded from history. Why they hid." I take off my locket and place it on the low table between us. "This crest is on the brooch. It's all over the castle! And it's on the seal for these letters. But there's nothing *about* it."

"The woman was in love, Paige. For once, accept the genres you read and stick to them. She doesn't talk about the past because she lived in the present." Juniper takes a sip of tea and grimaces. "Cold tea! If this is about to be a sad ending after an hour of reading love letters to the boy she loves who goes off to war, I'm going to cry into this tea until it's warm."

My smile feels like the crack it is. There's no mention of the Hayes family. There's no mention of treasure or Ludovici or—

"Why are you sad? We're not done reading yet! And don't you dare say it's because they're already dead! I don't care!"

"I wanted to know about the Dark Year. Why it started."

"If you're looking for a reason to stop falling for Nolan Hayes, you're not going to find it in any history book, Paige. You and your double-great-grandmother are stuck in the romance genre and there's no escape."

I mime stabbing my heart, and we both dissolve into a fit of giggles. Finally, I collect myself. "Maybe I was hoping for a reason to justify lying to Nolan," I say. "If our families really hated each other in some epic feud of royalists and council members during the founding of Gabreville in the Dark Year, and his ancestors killed mine, then..."

"Then what? You'd be a perfect Romeo and Juliet?" Juniper scoffs. "Don't you think that there's never going to be a good enough reason for your mother and grandmother and every woman before you to keep this secret?" She sits up. "It's probably a tale as old as time. There was gold, and gems in the mine, and people fought over it. War, Paige, just like in all the books. Maybe toss in some royal feuding and political instability too, for the professor's sake? When Gabreville and Loirehall split and Prince Nicholas's ancestors kept their throne while Gabreville ceded from their crown lands... It's always the same. People suffered, and it was unfair. Even on a small scale, in this small region, it would still hurt. Look at you," she says quietly. "It's still happening. People still die, like your mom, and Nolan's parents, and it's still unfair."

"Stop making me cry," I mumble, wiping my face.

"Clearly you needed it."

"I'm not sure if known history is more frustrating than the unknown. There were these books—"

"Paige, no! You? Books?"

"—the chronicle books that I read when I met Nolan that first day in the Gated Library." She makes a choking noise, then fans her cheeks, but I ignore her. "The lists I had no context for—and might *never* have context for—of whatever happened in the Dark Year. If I'm not supposed to find out what happened to my family all those generations ago, then why did Penelope give me these, then?"

"Maybe she wasn't giving these to you to show history." Juniper picks up my locket and tosses it gently on my lap. "She wanted you to see your *future*."

"You think I should reveal who I am?"

"Doesn't Nolan?"

"He should be the steward!"

"You both want to stop Lenora and Declan by using each other. Talk about rewriting a history with family feuds."

My blood-red dynasty. Nolan's greedy family. Juniper be-ing...Juniper. "Friends are most annoying when they're right."

She harrumphs and reads her next letter aloud. It's from the war office, dated in the year 1919. "If this wasn't already tearstained and sepia-toned, we'd make it that." She gets up to retrieve tissues, then cleans up the tea-things as I keep reading.

Strange how those memories cause a moment of silence to those who hear them...the noise too much, for the silence the dead leave in their wake.

I keep reading. Then— "Juniper! I found something!"

She returns around the corner of the stairwell. "What?"

"Okay, it's only a single sentence, but she says her mother gave her the locket when she died and said, 'the locket is the key, so we leave it be.'"

"Whatever that means." She flops down into her chair.

I pause, then say heavily, "It's also what my mother said to me, the night she died."

"What?"

"They fought that night," I admit hesitantly, feeling strange to say the memory aloud when it had been silent for ten years. "Her and Grandmother. It was about treasure. Grandmother kept saying she'd had enough of hiding. That they didn't need to be poor any longer. Mother disagreed."

Most of what I remember of the argument between my mother and my grandmother that night in Grandmother's cabin in the woods is that my mother cried and my grandmother, in her haste to leave, dropped the locket. When my father found me alone in the cabin the next day, he'd taken it from me and locked it up. But my mother... "She said this. I'd forgotten until now, but this is exactly what she said to me, I'm certain."

"If there was a way to the mine through the castle," Juniper says, "then maybe the locket is key to everything because there truly *was* a map. Because there was treasure. *Is* treasure?" She frowns. "I don't know which tense is true now."

the past time

I have yet another, much scarier theory, that
every time our hearts skip a beat, seconds
stretch into a brief eternity. This endless eternal
circle of snowfall and dandelion wishes and lost
time, spinning, swirling, sifting. Every
everlasting moment a hint of heaven, reminding
us we're not there yet.

Once again, we're going round and round, and
I'm unsure if I'm going backward or forward.
For time doesn't stop, does it? Time never
leaves, never waits, never fails to spin, ready to
pour me out for the sake of the story.

I'd seen dew diamonds on evergreen needles,
impossible and beautiful, but today, there is no
sun to warm frost fractals on frozen leaves.

This time, the rain isn't pouring. This storm is
whipping sheets of sleet away from the ground,
freezing rain falling up, disappearing into the
waiting atmosphere, clinging to any solid strand
of earth, because the saturated air can't hold in
the water any longer.

THE HIDDEN ROAD

Some time later, late in the afternoon, on Thursday

WALKING THROUGH TOWN, I'm near *Peckle's &*
Praline, the source of the Juniper's favorite treat, but not
even the Garamond ampersand of the candy shop can lift my spirit.
Shops are officially closed on Saturday, the eve of the equinox, so
the streets are busy now with people rushing beneath umbrellas
and hoods. They're too distracted to note the girl sitting beneath
the two gray poplar trees cornering the grounds of Gabreville's
cathedral, as I sat and sat and thought and thought.

I'm soaked from my wandering, where rain turned to washing
sleet, my red scarf beneath my hood covering my head. I consider running into the woods, the land of my ancestors. But now?
Now...I'm afraid to go back.

Cars drive by, the trolley dings past. The busyness is gone,
and people smarter than I have gone home. Puddles of rain have
time to settle between the car tires that muddy them, reflecting
the vivid-hued canopies above, the colors a poor substitute for a
sunset. I hold my hand out to catch the raindrops that fall ever
slower. Mild and thick, the promise of coming danger. I have no
watch, and I've probably only been wandering for an hour since
my time with Juniper at the bookshop, but it feels like forever until

someone calls my name.

I'm huddling away from the downpour beneath a small awning in the quaint lane behind the candy shop with its striped canopy of burnt orange and clotted cream, where a lone lamp-post straddles the varied cobblestones between the north and south sides of the alley.

"Paige!" his voice calls, harsh in relief, as Nolan joins me beneath a canopy. "What were you thinking? Where were you? Why are you this soaked?" He touches the edge of my wet hair, brushing my coat at my shoulders, then re-wrapping my neck in the scarf. He's soaked too, but he doesn't seem to care.

"Too tight," I breathe, tugging the scarf looser. I have always hated the hour between four and five o'clock in the afternoon. It's a dreary time. "How did you find me?"

"Driving down every street, that's how," he retorts. "You weren't at the bookshop and you weren't at your father's shop. I thought you were going to go back up the mountain to keep searching..." If there is a question, he leaves it unsaid, hands shoved in his pockets. "I looked everywhere. Ready to come home?"

I shake my head. I'm not ready to speak the fear that's dangling inside.

He extends a hand from his pocket, offering a small flower, a silk rose on a keyring with two keys. "Anne made it for you. It's the key to the gatehouse, so in case you're ever lost..." Behind the frown with a hint of genuine amusement, is vulnerability. Is it because I've practically invaded every corner of the estate, his home? His home, which I've basically said I'm entitled to, lost Ludovici heiress that I am. And while he's hidden behind the disguise of his arrogance, I've hidden behind my secrets, so I can't judge. Genuine concern creases his brow as he asks, "Are you okay?"

I think I love that hard-won concern that he seems unable to douse, like a fire that won't go out. *Wait, love?* I sniff. "Why white roses?" I ask, my voice sounding a pitch higher than it should, but I'm done with the pale roses, a continuous and gorgeous motif to my loss. Lenora and her stupid white bouquet, all the colorless floral motifs of stone inside the castle.

Sincere confusion darts across his face. "They don't have them anymore—do you not know? They stopped growing after the fire—" His voice catches, but he goes on. "Fairhavens had the best roses in the region, but the garden was destroyed when the older side of the castle crumbled after the fire. The soil was diminished, the flowers stopped blooming. No one rebuilt the wall, nothing's reclaimed, just like the rest of it," he says pointedly. "But the flower shops in town honor the loss of the prize-winning flowers. That's why Martin tends the new garden so tenaciously. He's so close this year. He claimed a few reached enough maturity to make a single bouquet that the flower shop sold—but I won't believe it till I see it."

I swallow thickly. Oh, I saw it. "I try to avoid shops with plants, or being outside when things bloom." I sniff again from the cold, but the effect works.

"Well, it's reputation or history. Not sure which people care about most." He frowns. "But how do you not know this?" With a dip of his head, he attempts to give me the wretched reminder of the white bouquet, and I bat his hand away half-heartedly. "Paige," he grumbles. "You *need* this key in case something happens. You're not safe, you'll be in danger the moment they find out who you really are. That it's your *right*—"

"No." I don't let him say it aloud. The past *hurts*. I accept the simple, adorable, flower keyring with the word "enchanted" embroidered on the back of it. The present hurts too. Those artificial thorns are reminder enough of that. "I hate flowers. Everyone I love knows I'm allergic." Oh, why did I phrase it that way?

He blinks, but doesn't step back. "Really?" Golden eyes smolder. Surely he heard my slip—*love*. He cannot know how strongly I feel for him, or how entangled and thorny my feelings are. How I want to avoid them, and yet somehow stick my face in a real-life bouquet of them, to keep in a vase until it dies and even then, flatten the soft petals in a thick book so they can be passed down to my granddaughter in a small, golden frame.

It's my turn to blink, but he doesn't push. "You're the heir to the empty council seat. To Fairhavens itself." He's suppressing what appears to be a smile as he crosses his arms. "Ironic then, that your family's title and inheritance is symbolized by the Ludovici crest, dominated by a *white rose*."

"I really don't appreciate your literary criticism of my life."

His knuckle brushes my skin, lifting my chin. "It's too early to call it a tragedy," he says kindly but all I can think is *it's also too early to call it a love story*. Tragedy has an ending we expect. But this? Between us? Uncertain, but his next words come with a smile. "You and your locket with the emblem of my castle on it."

"*Your* castle?"

"Now you're saying it's yours? You *want* to claim it now? Why *do* you hate it so much?"

What if Nolan knows something about my mother? But I dismiss the thought—he didn't know the lineage of the locket before I showed him, and he wouldn't connect it to my mother even if he *had* seen her the night of the fire. Did he? Do I want to know, if the truth is terrible?

"What now?" I adjust the scarf and reassure myself the locket remains beneath my soaked coat.

He doesn't miss a thing. "Keep that hidden. Where's the box?"

"Juniper kept it." I really must tell him what we found in those letters—Ludovici stories of treasures and tunnels and a family tree, which might be proof enough of my lineage.

Raindrops trickle from his hair onto his forehead, and he swipes at his eyes. "You probably think I can't understand, hiding who I am when you want to find out who you are. Before, I wouldn't let myself hope there was a better reason for what happened. But what if your returning is the best thing to happen that none of us could have imagined?" Along eloquent words, the blame weighing his broad shoulders is tangible, perhaps because its apparent fate made me share the heaviness of it. Lenora after me, and Declan after Nolan. Broken mirrors reflecting shards of glass, distorting reality. If they united against us, we'd lose quickly.

It's like the strange chemistry to precipitation. It's just dirt surrounded by a force—an encounter that makes the speck of something into a drop of rain, swirling into flash floods and spring sprinkles and living water. Our world wouldn't survive without it, but it's all just dirt or ash or debris, encircled by water, floating in the atmosphere. It's just all gravity.

But the puddles, the glass of the shop fronts. They reflect Nolan and I—the road is empty and suddenly I realize it's quiet enough for the waters to still. Too quiet, for the color of the clouds bruising the sky. I'm afraid, in the strange mild warmth from those low clouds that promise a storm after this calm. "What's all this really for?"

"Truth, not treasure," he responds instantly, and his assurance twists something old in my stomach, straining my soul.

"Are you enjoying this?" I almost say, wanting to throw his words back at him, the way he accused me of mocking his life when all I was concerned with was my father. But now—now is painful. Now I care about Nolan too, and I want an outcome better than we all can hope for. Maybe better than we deserve, considering the truth I've been keeping from him.

If I tell him now that my mother and my grandmother died in the fire, he'll never tell me what really happened that night. Even now, I'm not sure I want to blame him. I just wish I knew if I *should*.

Nolan leads, and I follow. He carries my book bag. I hadn't noticed, but his car waits a little up the street. The rain returns from darkened clouds with a pounding thunderclap, wet sidewalks become slick beneath my leather boots, and we run.

It hasn't taken long for the storm to fall, but I might fall first—the itch to curl into a ball and cover my ears and block the noise that's coming nearly overtakes me. It reminds me of the night of the fire, when I hid in Grandmother's cabin. How I stayed there and never left. Not when there was a fire and I didn't know, and not when a storm came and all I wanted was for someone to save me. Someone to come, so I wasn't alone.

Instead, I'd cowered while thunder and lightning broke the sky overhead, walls of the cabin shaking, a wolf howling outside in the dark of the night after it was all quiet, and I'd missed my chance to save them. I can't miss a chance to be bold now if it means I might save my family.

I think Nolan calls to me, but I can't hear his voice as the air claps with far-off thunder, making me flinch and raise my hands to my neck, covering my fear. Trying to escape the memory. I pause to catch my breath beneath a light post, red and gold striped flag flopping in the rain, and use my puffer, leaning over so it doesn't get wet. Then I realize he's here—he makes a hood of his hands above my forehead, trying to keep me dry, sheltering me.

It isn't just me. The choice I have is mine alone, to continue the painful path or leave the woods behind. The clouds are crying, rain falling. I close my eyes and count to three—three seconds of fear until I make myself be brave. How many times have I done that this week? Run away, or stay? Before I can open my eyes, Nolan's hands move to cover my own over my ears, covering the shaking fear with solid warmth.

"Paige, let's go," he begs. Asking me to come inside, get in the car and out of the cold. With his forehead hot against my own, he asks me to stay with him. Not to leave.

I wish I wasn't afraid of storms. So angry at them. My vision blurs as rain begins to pour, thick drops that pound empty, slippery, cobblestoned streets that reek of petrichor. No one else is wild or stupid enough to venture into the sudden storm. And Nolan doesn't know what I haven't told him, and that bit of me, that little girl still stuck in her grandmother's cabin—she needs someone to carry her guilt, and that blame for him is festering. I feel reckless, like he says I am.

Digging up the past does that.

His fingers press into my scalp, his palms covering my ears as if he senses my fear, and I grip his wrists. He's someone like me, who's crazy and stupid enough to stand in the rain and get soaked. I look up at him, the young man with the expensive clothes and luxury vehicle who acts like he's not comfortable in his own skin. For if he was, why *wouldn't* he want to leave his life in the forest and return to the world? Part of me doesn't *want* to know what he can tell me about the fire.

Because he might know how it started, and how it ended, and knowing the first and last pages of a story means you can shut the book and move on.

A breath later

AS GENTLE AS HIS TOUCH, sleet lands on my lashes. Warmth grasps my hand as, leaning down and opening the car door for me, his fingers hold mine. And I hesitate.

The custom leather interior is getting soaked, the door left open to the downpour, though he's thrown my bag into the back seat. He steps away, releasing my hand and pointing up the mountain. "Is all this worth it?"

The thick, freezing rain finally becomes the hail it promised.

I remember Lenora in my face, taunting me with my father's livelihood, tempting me with answers as if I was the only one who could get them. Nothing else could have so forcefully drawn me to this quest, and to say I hate myself for following her so easily is an understatement. Yet I feel tied to Nolan and the castle and the locket, which feels heavier with each smack of white hail-drops against my coat. I've spent every day this week escaping into another library because my home is dark and cold.

"I wasn't doing this for my father. It was for *me*." I don't say I was determined to prove I wasn't so broken that my father wouldn't want me back. "If he kept his shop, then I could stop worrying..." If he kept his work, maybe he would keep me—stop forgetting about me. *Look* at me.

"You're afraid to go back?" Nolan guesses correctly. "Why?" He steps closer and puts a hand on my shoulder. I look away and up to the mountain, to those spires of Fairhavens in the distance, holding back tears that say I need to *try* more.

Nolan's voice softens without whispering, for the hail is too loud. "Your value isn't determined by—"

How can he know? "You can't possibly..." I brush wetness from my cheek. Melting hail, tears. "What do you know of my worth?"

With great tenderness, he tries to tuck a strand of my damp hair behind my ear. It doesn't work, but he brushes off my cheek all the same. "I know you keep trying to prove it, ever since your father left you without a backward glance in a dangerous castle on a hopeless search." Nolan grabs my wrist and I let him tug me to the car, which, when I allow myself to finally sit in it, is so warm.

I will myself to be brave, as we drive across the Valais, past Gabreville's Main Street, wanting to get back to the gatehouse, where beyond the Endilwood Gate a tangled forest path ascends the mountain. Waiting for the next turn up the mountain road, waiting for where it leads there between the mist and low clouds, waiting for the end of the hidden road.

The deep roar of the engine fills the space between us for swift miles toward the bottom of the mountain. The heavy rain lessens the higher we go, then Nolan says, "Your father, he didn't say a word to me, or threaten me to keep you safe." His freckled knuckles turn white around the custom leather steering wheel. "Are you okay with that? You shouldn't be."

He's so right it hurts.

"Having a parent alive, but forgetting to care for me, is better than having none," I stab back. I regret it instantly. No one deserves that haunting reminder. I want to ask harshly if he really *did* start the fire, to voice the one fear hanging on, hoping for anything to get away from the pain laid bare in his eyes.

Nolan parks the car near the gatehouse, hands still on the wheel, sitting in shattered silence for a dark moment that he can withstand more than I. Slamming open the door, I get out of the low seat and walk in a huff up the road near the gatehouse, rushing around the back of the house toward the hedge walls and the Endilwood Gate, blindly continuing being crazy and stupid and bold and maybe even brave. I may be torn apart by the wolf if I find one, but I want to face it nonetheless.

Nolan's perspective, his pain that started with that fire, it's leeching into my own cares and it's annoying, humbling, and infuriating. Breathing in, his stricken expression as I run away is inescapable. Breathing out, I imagine making him smile.

"Paige!" Nolan's voice carries between the forest and the gatehouse.

My father never called for me. He *never* has tried to stop me. He never said a *word*.

The rain has eased, but dark clouds remain. I run around a crisp corner on the path and abruptly trip, noting too late that my emphatic escape is thwarted by a vase. I land hard on my knees and right arm—my face barely misses hitting the sharp edges of half a yellow plant pot. Only a few breaths away and I'm falling all over myself, right into a puddle. Above my pained cry, I hear Nolan call my name again, followed by quick footsteps. Then he stops near me.

Any indignant comment I may have made is cut off by his hushed command.

"Paige, don't move." His tone holds enough tension that I mostly obey, lifting my cheek from the ground and wincing at the pricks of pain stabbing my right hand. My soaked, smarting backside is now equal to my aching wrist. I shift, then stop, my whole lower body throbbing. As I survey the sodden path, I am momentarily shocked enough not to move another fraction.

The stone-laid path into the square courtyard is covered end-to-end with glass and crystal vases, huge terracotta pots, dainty plants and flowers, all smashed into a sea of broken pottery. I recognize one from beside the front door of the gatehouse; a white ceramic pot with ivy designs that once held a little fern. The air is lifting rain and waiting. All I hear is my breathing, too fast, and Nolan's, too controlled. The scent of freshly churned soil lingers.

But that isn't what makes Nolan freeze—he stands stock-still in a defensive position in front of me. Inhaling through the pain from the ceramic embedded in the heel of my right hand, I look beyond the brokenness as a sarcastic voice breaks the haze of misted rain.

THE LONE WOLF

In the square courtyard of the gatehouse, Thursday evening

"WHAT A SHAME." Across the sea of jagged edges sits a young, lanky figure, lounging on a bench farther down the path. Cloaked in a long dark raincoat with a black fedora hat tipped down, he seems to be picking his fingernails clean of dirt, legs crossed and his foot lazily kicking the air.

Nolan inhales lightly. He is trying very hard to appear unaffected, and I would have been able to believe it but for the stiffness of his shoulders and a twitch in his fingers. My grandmother's kind but gnarled fingers stilled that night, before she left me alone, and I remember in an uncomfortable flash of memory that she used to twitch like that, too.

When she was afraid.

"Paige's outfit, I mean." The shaded figure gestures in my direction, and I immediately recognize his tone and long limbs—Percy's cruel older brother, Darragh Hayes. Darragh's is the kind of face you remember seeing for the first time and not liking. Smooth skin, beautiful in long lines, deep-set eyes against skin too pale to hold a gaze so dark, and an ungraceful litheness to his frame that makes you immediately know that he's a predator. Which makes one of us the prey.

"Nolan. I couldn't believe it. You've come back from the grave, the literal dead. It's been years—"

"Long years," Nolan replies, a harsh edge creeping into his voice, words sounding more like torture, or torment. He has an admirable skill for giving words meanings they most certainly don't have—I just hope he never turns that skill on me. And suddenly I hope very much that he'll hide me, hide who I am—the hidden heir who shouldn't be here.

"We all thought you died! Imagine what Mother will think of me, to have come here for *her* and find a better prize instead? Didn't expect to see you here again." Meaning infuses Darragh's words, enough for me to think that whatever lay between these young men won't be enough for Darragh to keep silent about Nolan's identity. Still seated, Darragh says, "Such a sorry passing of years without seeing my dear cousin. A decade..." It sounds almost like he's enjoying the morbid topic.

The cut on my hand hurts and I want to whimper, but stay silent. The rain is more a mist now. *How did it get so dark so quickly?*

"What brings you to our home, *cousin*?" Nolan asks, distaste tainting the word claiming Darragh as family. My eyes rocket between Nolan's fiery glare and Darragh's implacable audacity. Nolan wanted to keep his identity as returning steward a secret, before next week's council proceedings. Darragh Hayes is incapable of keeping this secret. *What terrible timing.*

Most of all, I didn't miss how Nolan said "our" home. A sorry, wild hope in me wants the *our* to include *me*.

Impervious to Nolan's contempt, Darragh continues. "Your

caretaker will be upset by this ceramic carnage, but I never really understood the appeal of this estate. Neither did you, if I recall, cousin." The word seethes through his lips, making his young voice uncannily resemble his father's. "But those clothes really are ruined, Paige." He sneers. "Running around like your crazy grandmother? Your sad mother? Here I am, sent by my own dear mother to see how your search fares at the abandoned castle, and now you two are..." He looks me up and down. "What *have* you two been up to?"

Clearly annoyed by the suggestive nature of his tone, Nolan steps forward, his brown leather shoe crunching a chunk of blue and white mosaic pottery. His right leg partially blocks my view.

Enough. I'm done being a silent, fainting damsel in distress. Nolan may be trying to protect me, but chivalry is not something I'm going to count on while crouching between broken glass and dark family secrets. My hand is bleeding, and I avoid looking at it as I lift myself up, despite the swaying of light at the bottom of my vision—I *hate* red blood—and Nolan reaches to help me rise.

Darragh stands too, striding forward with long legs until he stands a pace away. With a subtle step, Nolan is ever so slightly in front of me, and I let out the breath I'd been holding. Give me fair eyelashes and a ruddy complexion over this dark, brooding, possessive-looking boy any day.

I tilt my head and consider the son of the greatest scoundrel I know. Some years older than me, Mr. Hayes's eldest son Darragh is a chip of obsidian off the old block, the resemblance to his father uncanny. Percival—who would've been endlessly teased for his unfortunate name and quiet personality but for his cruel and uncannily shrewd older brother—has that black hair and the dark eyes, but something about Percy's quiet smile makes him stand apart from his older brother and awful father.

Can I forget Lenora's sharp white nails from when this all started, pointing at me like she owned my family because we had no value of our own? *She practically does own us now.* The Hayes's wealth and desire for fortune, their greed, all seeped into their oldest son like it lives through the father and mother—foreclosing our home, threatening to take Papa's livelihood.

But I can't stop myself, and prying into this might shed light on the Lenora issue. "Your mother sent you—do you *ever* make a decision of your own?" I nearly spit my question, vehemence stirring from somewhere within me that's terrified of Lenora finding out who my family really is, through my mother's side. Ludovicis, lost.

"You think my mother only made an offer to you? Who knows what deals she's since made with your father?" His eyebrows rise in the worst imitation of innocence since Macbeth. "What she made him promise if you fail."

I don't know if he's telling the truth to scare me or planting lies to trap me. *Would* Lenora connive yet another threat against my father? Wasn't it enough she wouldn't leave me alone? My papa can't handle both Mr. Hayes and Lenora. But I need something, some fleck of gold, some wisp of air to follow. "Haven't I done enough? Why can't your parents leave him alone? Aren't they busy in their own fight?"

Nolan flicks a glance to me before refocusing on his cousin as

Darragh says, "My home is hell enough even with them keeping their divorce quiet." I almost say I'm sorry. Like he senses it, any vulnerability on his face hardens. "But this isn't about my family. It has *everything* to do with your family, Paige, but I don't know or care why." He sneers, but it's affected. Darragh is dark and brooding and impossible and *sad*. In the books, he'd be the perfect anti-hero, the tortured soul who chooses right at the end. I don't want to hope for that for him, but maybe a book could save him.

Then, to Nolan, Darragh's voice sharpens. "What were you *doing* all these years? Partying after sleeping the day away? What trouble you've gotten into, when you started so well at it, so young. Good thing your parents didn't live to see you wasting your days, or know what really—"

"Enough." Nolan is forceful and familiar with this version of Darragh. I thought I'd seen Darragh's cruelty at school, even without first-hand experience like Juniper. "You don't know what I've done or who I've become. You'd never understand."

"I could say the same. But your fortune was never enough for you. No, you ran away. You're *still* running away." Darragh's voice is so cold. For the first time, I see his mother in him.

"If you want to compare wastrel lives, you've come to the right person." Nolan's words break my heart, he means them so forcefully. Does he think his life is a waste?

Fingers tap against his leg, as if a habit. "Your dear old father didn't deserve this estate, the mine, *or* the family fortune."

"This again?" Nolan cuts Darragh with a look. "And yours did?" I wonder if this isn't the first time their families have fought over stewardship of the mine.

"Precious metals mined from this mountain were what made the Kingdom of Loirehall rich, and look at us now! Nothing from it! After it collapsed—thanks to mismanagement from *your* family, my father said—it hasn't been mined or scanned in this age. How lucrative might it be if it could be reopened?"

"No one knew, Dare," Nolan runs a hand through his rain-soaked hair. "Back then, no one knew the mine had already partially collapsed. Yes, my father hid it. I remember it as well as you. It was *dangerous*, and it still is!"

"You're afraid of something good coming from here, more than something bad." He points in my direction. "Which is *she*?"

Nolan growls, aligning his shoulder in front of mine, the width of him a slight barrier that blocks Darragh from seeing all of me. I don't mind. There is only one side of this story I want to be on. "You don't know anything about me. Not anymore."

"I see enough. You think you can change? You are a Hayes, and Hayes men are dark hearts and greedy hands." Darragh's gaze flicks to mine, but the predator eyes gleam without glory. "We want, and we take."

Pain tightening his face, Nolan shifts farther to shield me, twisting his hand from my shaky fingers to wrap around my wrist, holding my arm with his body in front of mine. "There is nothing left here for you."

Darragh takes a step toward us, stopping where piles of fractured glass and mangled flowers lay scattered on the path. He nudges some pieces with the tip of a fashionable shoe—which is covered in dirt and scuffed—his all-black attire turned rakish. Apparently, Hayes men have a thing for being stylish, come what may. Staring at Nolan, Darragh's eyes are calculating and dastardly. I'm immediately glad for the few feet separating us. "I tend to disagree."

These young men fill the air with so much silent contempt, it makes me wonder about their history. Nolan was a young teen then—how much trouble is Darragh insinuating? Nolan has avoided mentioning his family, full stop. Would he speak with reverence at their memory, or with distaste like Darragh feels toward his father and mother? My splotchy childhood memory doesn't recall much but my own tragedy, but now it seems Nolan's history as a Hayes, like Darragh's, is hovering above the mountain and mine like this fine mist, quiet and sopping. Was there more to the fire than an accident? Was there more to Nolan's teen years, something darker? Something more on that awful night?

A few breaths later

A SUDDEN SHIFT in conversation pulls me back to the present. "Would anyone accept you, having come back from the dead? This town lives on memory and suspicion." His hands fist. "Such a fraud."

Even without the familiar weight of my book bag strap, my chest feels too tight, and I tug on my ear, trying for truth. "Nolan is no fraud, and you know it."

"But you and him, there's the lie."

How does he know it's a lie when even *I* don't? "You have no idea what you're talking about."

Darragh scoffs, looking down on me as I shiver. "Maybe *you're* using him."

"I love him," I want to say. For real, to Nolan, when we're alone. I don't know if Darragh or his mother know I'm the inheritor of a lost line with the most real claim to Fairhavens. But it doesn't matter, because I'm finding the present and possible futures more important than the past. I shake my head, rain dropping from the ends of my hair.

"You won't survive this," Darragh tells Nolan. "Haven't you realized the people who were once nice to you, those people who thrive on gossip, will become a mindless mob to kick you senseless if they find out the truth of what you did?"

At Darragh's harsh accusation, Nolan's hand tightens on my wrist. "What we *both* did."

I balk. What did they do—what did *Nolan* do, really? But something deeper doesn't want to ask those hard questions. It says another thing. *I think I love him.* All this drama between us three standing in the rain, and none of us seem to have changed since that awful night. Darragh is immovable—still walking his parents' footsteps. I'm still afraid. Nolan's still hiding. But I *want* a transformation. *I don't want to be the same person I was before.* Before I met Nolan and tried writing a new ending to the same terrible story.

So instead, I push back, like wind along the mountainside. "What does that make you? Your family are made of blackmail and threats."

Darragh steps back, running a hand through his long, soaked black hair. Wolfishly handsome. Pity is a sad feeling. It means I think I was wrong, and I see the sad more than the bad. Here in real, rainy life, he's very nearly a monster, and I'm wishing myself back into the chamber of civil records, safe between rare manuscripts and aged city records that no one cares about. Where no one can see me behind the walls around my heart keeping out good and evil as if there were no people stuck between them. Now that I care to see, that daring hope to understand is making me weak.

Neither of the broody Hayes boys can know. Wishing Nolan would save me, yet feeling a terrible sense of guilt for not telling him my mother died in the fire, I push Darragh a little more. "You can stay out of this, you know. Our parents are bad enough, and honestly, I'm not trying to stop yours, just save my father's business."

He considers me, a step down from the aggressive attitude he'd cornered me with. "Have you found anything?"

"Maybe," I almost lie, but he raises a rain-soaked eyebrow as Nolan shifts closer. Again. I blow a breath into the rain, ignoring Darragh's impatience. "But we need more time. It's a mess up there—"

Darragh simmers, white rage reaching the surface. "My life is a mess right now!" Whites around his eyes, then he deliberately unfists a hand. "She'll find out if you're lying. And your father will fall first, because *my* father doesn't have the qualms Mother does about the sanctity of life. She likes to keep people under her prissy thumb, and they have to be *alive* for her to control them."

Lenora has qualms? "Are you threatening me? Or is this you helping?"

"I'm warning you! I'm saying you're already under siege." He takes a breath and fixes me with a dark stare. "Just do what they want."

"Do what they want?" I ask indignantly, and Nolan's grip on my hand tightens. Darragh's raised brow digs at the questions plaguing me. If Nolan will reveal himself to stop his uncle in a few days, if it comes to it. If I'll give Lenora the treasure, if I find it. I struggle to believe Darragh's twisted sincerity, but mostly it's his awful parents I will never trust. "They truly didn't know their nephew was still alive?"

"Believe me. They had no idea—they really didn't know him when he was a kid, and they've ignored me all my teenage years. My good friends, my bad friends—and Nolan is *bad*."

Nolan interrupts, "Darragh, stop—"

"You judge me, Paige, but you should turn and judge him too." Darragh looks at me like I'm the one missing something. I'm so afraid he's right. "You don't know how desperate my father is. The Gabreville Council is set to approve mining again, and when it resumes, how wealthy would the owner be? Beyond comprehension. And if there's treasure, like Mother believes, even more so. You really want to fight them for it?"

It strikes me that Darragh finds this arrangement unfair. How twisted is their family? Lenora wants something not just for her-self, but for her children: treasure, on an estate with land above untapped riches. Yet, part of me understands. There isn't much a mother won't do for her child. How can I blame Lenora, when she's doing exactly what I wanted to have a mother do for me? What *did* my mother do for me? Did she die to save me in a way more priceless than treasure?

Nolan is decidedly silent on that fact that his being here changes literally everything. But...he's still holding my hand. "It doesn't matter what happened back then. Right now, this place isn't theirs. Not yet." By some rights it's Nolan's, but more than that, it's mine.

"This is your chance to leave this place unscathed." Creepy, but definitely dependable. What an awful combination. "Take what you get."

I don't want any of it. Nothing like that would matter to a girl who spent her teenage years in a single parent family. Papa tried to pay the bills, but his skills brought only the occasional lucrative contract. I worked at a coffee shop since I was thirteen to pay for books, for the heating bill when there was a deep freeze, for extra tins of loose leaf tea, for trolley fare. All this talk of land and riches—it's too much.

Darragh waits until I look up at him, and once again the pitiful strain around his eyes pulls at my heart. The despondency, the acceptance of whatever darkness exists. Sympathy rises unbidden and I don't want it. I don't want to feel any hint of understanding or, heaven forbid, *mercy*, for this young man who tormented me as a child, hiding insects in my desk at school, and later leaving a

dead mouse inside my locker. Anger beats my heart faster. Never mind how he tortured my best friend when she was only fifteen by leading her along as if he loved her, then using her and forgetting her, and if that wasn't enough, *mocking* her—

"And why do you think I'm here tonight?" Darragh sighs. "This is me doing what I must to protect my stupid brother."

I startle and clutch my scarf—*Percy?*

Darragh nods once at my reaction. "Our father saw Percy leave Madame Garcon's house earlier today. He saw you, *both* of you. I had to retaliate right away, and if it wasn't me against you, he would've taken his anger out against Percy instead."

"I'm sorry." I truly am. Sorry for Juniper's pain, sorry for Nolan's loss, sorry for Percy's oppression, sorry for Darragh's pain, and his attempt at stopping one wrong. Sorry for everything.

"Don't be sorry. Stop being stupid. Toss this. Stop it all."

I hold my cut hand to my stomach, stinging. "I have to see this through."

"Good luck keeping the treasure from my mother. Don't blame me if the story doesn't end the way you want it to." My skin crawls as Darragh speaks. "Mother wanted to remind you that she's got more flowers—"

"Stop," Nolan says, husky voice low, and harsher for how quiet it is. "You don't deserve to speak to her. Coming here with threats—"

"And you do? It is *just* like you to be caught up in all this." Darragh shifts his weight, casual and superior, to face Nolan. "This was her warning—it's all taking too long. Mother wants to know if you found a map."

"It's okay," I whisper to Nolan. He's with me, so I'm not afraid to speak up. "I think I know where it is," I say. I'm just buying time. I'm a diligent girl, they think. Obedient. But I am also bold and unafraid when I need to be. "I need another day. The citadel is so big..." I let a sigh escape, not totally faking because I felt a trickle of blood slide down the side of my palm and it's *not dripping off*.

"Do better." Darragh says threateningly, taking a step toward us, but Nolan doesn't cower, protecting me. Both young men are locked with defiant gazes. "Don't lose it, when you find it. Your father will lose everything if you're empty handed." Darragh flicks his fingers lewdly at me, his tone derogatory and sleazy. "I'll tell my mother you're working well together, because you're clearly...something."

Momentary panic floods me, but Nolan's grip tightens on my wrist, his steady strength comforting as he challenges Darragh. "You don't know *anything*."

I raise my injured hand to grip Nolan's arm—I don't want him to leave me, I don't want him to do anything to aggravate Darragh more. Pain ripples from the ceramic shards pricking my hand, through our connection, between our hearts. Like all these broken pieces are a shattered mirror reflecting the only thing they can. Pain.

Darragh curses, dark eyes flashing between us. "I don't even care what is real and what isn't, so long as my father doesn't think *anything* is happening here that can stop him. Because you know who he'll blame if you succeed? *Me*." If I didn't know better, I would say I heard an undercurrent of fear beneath his brash tone. "Your lies better be good enough, or something in the forest will eat you alive—"

"Dare," Nolan's voice is steel.

Darragh's sharply handsome face twists into a smile. "What should I tell my father, then? You've been alive this whole time and returned to challenge him for the steward seat? You have no idea—he'll do anything to leave Hayes Manor now."

Nolan's arm I'm gripping has turned to stone, and if this statue came alive, it would explode in a thousand fiery pieces. I squeeze my hand on his bicep, not afraid for my sake, not even for Darragh's—maybe he *does* deserve to be taken down. But I stay at Nolan's side, tears pooling in my eyes, as if their liquid is enough to prevent the flames of Nolan's wrath, for his sake.

Because he saved me once, I will do anything to save him. The realization floors me.

"We're done, Dare," Nolan grinds out. "You said what you wanted and have no reason to be here anymore." His eyes are hard as he turns us to walk away. I would be more annoyed at being man-handled if our adversary wasn't a walking reminder of the awful days he bullied my best friend in school, and if my head weren't quite so light. It isn't blood loss, it's the sight of blood. All the red.

Nolan glances back at Darragh, deliberately avoiding my anxious glance. "If you approach her, the Lucas's, or my home again, so help me Dare, God himself could not judge me for what I would do to you. You know your way out." His fingers tighten around my arm, pinching my cold skin beneath my damp jacket as he starts pulling us down the path. *Crunch*. Pottery crumbles beneath my boots.

Darragh's cruel laugh follows us. "Ah yes, you sound just like your father, the steward. He swore to God, and look where that got him." His voice sounds farther away, as he steps back toward the road. Rats sure find their way to dry ground fast.

Nolan stops, turning and saying, "Tell Uncle Declan I'm here. That I'm back."

All the bad things people said of the steward son? I don't believe it, not anymore. The way he scoffs, the uncaring timbre of his voice, the lie that he doesn't care. He cares *so deeply* that no one can know. He won't let them have that power. Had he spent his youth fuelling their assumptions like this?

This version of Nolan is terrifying. "Tell him that I'm not dead. And tell him I'm being *myself*." Nolan uses his free hand to loosen my death grip on his arm, laces my fingers with his, our palms slick with rainwater—wait, no. *My blood*. Nolan turns us to walk away, and calls over his shoulder. "Tell him I'm being reckless."

A minute later

NOLAN KEEPS HIS GRIP FIRM as we round the corner and continue down the shadowy path. His long legs push us forward, dragging me along until I try to pry his fingers off and stumble.

"Stop! Let me go!" I cry.

He stops and looks down at me, and once more my retort is silenced. His face is grave, eyes wide and full of emotion. Surprise and fear, but mostly anger. Almost like he'd forgotten for a moment that I was even here with him.

"I'm sorry, I didn't hurt you, did I?" His hands are touching me again, but gently. His long fingers hold mine, and with his other hand he rotates my injured hand slowly. His frown deepens as his eyes trace the bloodied patch of scrapes below my wrist, barely visible in the deepening evening darkness. "Is there still glass in there?"

"It's fine, I'm fine. I won't faint again. You just walk too fast." I take a deep breath of the crisp air, swallowing in the fresh scents of rain and lingering mist and hopefully some courage. I resist the urge to look behind me as the squeal of car tires fades into the distance. "Do you think he'll come back?"

Nolan shakes his head, blond locks flicking angrily. "My cousin"—he avoids saying Darragh's name—"is deceitful and jealous. Like his father, all he desires is money and the power it gives him over people. There's this cruelty...my whole life, my uncle wanted it all—this estate and everything in it." Both hands gently hold my wrist. "I am sorry you had to see that, to *hear* that. I'm sorry you went to the same school and were ever near him." He pauses and looks at the darkening sky. There must be so many stars waiting for their moment behind those clouds. "If you had gotten hurt, *more* hurt—" The regret in his voice is tangible, making me wonder if there had been more of a threat in those moments than

I'd realized.

The shiver I've been suppressing finally breaks through. Nolan looks back at me, and without saying a word takes off his jacket and wraps it around my shoulders. It's warm and heavy and dry on the inside—he didn't get soaked through like crazy me, walking through the rain after the bookshop. My shaky fingers clasp the coat with effort—I hadn't realized just how cold I was. I hold it together with my uninjured hand in front of my heart, gripping the fabric tightly, its weight comforting like a warm shield protecting me against the dark, confusing night and the tall, confusing men. I realize, with a sad tilt of my heart, that I must include Nolan himself in that category. Tall Hayes men, troublesome in their own ways, varying levels of dangerous. Yes, I definitely want a barrier between Nolan and I, as we stand face to face in the swift twilight.

"Paige," he whispers, waiting until I look at him to continue. Miniscule specks of water line his lashes. "Are you okay?"

I close my eyes and shake my head, sadly, because there is no point anymore in denying how ripped apart my heart feels. I want to make sense of what I know of his voice and match that to this desperate attraction that I feel toward him. It isn't just his appearance, his strong jaw and hard-done-hero depth that makes him intriguing and vulnerable. But the fire. He was there...

I don't know how much more my heart can take. It should have recovered from this scare, but it's thumping faster than ever, traitorously pushing forward as if the person before me is the moon. Does that make me the tide? *No.* I shouldn't acknowledge my attraction to him. This guy with the warm hands and kind voice and dark history that we share.

We're standing so close. "But Paige, are you okay with me?" He holds his hand over his heart. "You know I would never hurt you? That I never meant to hurt anyone then?" I blink at his words, reminded that he's never told me what happened the night of the fire. "That I will keep you safe now, no matter what? That I..." Whatever thought he has, he leaves unfinished.

Staring at him, I take in his strong profile and the way his unusual sweater fits so perfectly over his wiry shoulders where his collarbone pulls the tightly woven fabric taut. His tall frame, and the way his fair eyebrows rise on his smooth forehead creased in concern. I think of his deep emotion held under such tight control. Hiding, hiding, hiding.

Looking down at my soaked scarf, I nod, not sure if I really believe in myself or him, but unable to deny the sense of knowing he clearly speaks of. "I believe you."

"That's enough," he says, quiet and relieved.

"Is it?" I whisper, turning away with more force than I intended.

Strong hands whip me around. "It isn't safe. This whole scheme just got scary." Nolan's hands shake my shoulders as he leans near my face. "We can't trust Darragh or believe a word he says. You know that, right?" His eyes arrest me. When did Nolan and I become *we*? And yet, it's undeniable. He's so close that I can see molten detail in each golden iris. His beautiful eyes fill my vision and, beneath the anger is burning fear. I recognize it, the fear of loss. But you can only lose what you care about—does he care for me? Or is it just fear that his secrets from the night of the fire will spill into the present?

I shake my head and strands of my damp hair brush against his chest. Light blazes behind my own eyes as I close them, hiding from his stare and the magnetism that pulls me to him. But without sight, my other senses heighten—my shallow breaths loud enough that I cannot hear the sounds of the twilight forest. Amid the scent of pine trees and evergreens on the overgrown path, there's a hint of his lost sunshine scent that didn't belong in the library and doesn't belong in the dark in this leftover rain.

For a split second, I feel the brush of his breath against my lips, the warmth of his skin so close I can almost taste it. But my eyes flicker open and, still so close, he holds my gaze for a searing moment before breaking away. Heat from the fires of fear sizzles between us, crackling like sparks before a thunderstorm, catching like embers about to burst into flame. Which of us will it consume?

The Shattered Glass

Moments later, in front of the manor house

A SNAP OF A TWIG shatters the moment. The dark woods, the White Forest, coming alive for the night, killing the embers that were about to catch between us.

But Nolan's hands cradle my upper arms, his breath still hot on my cheek as he touches his forehead to mine, then pulls back.

I frown. "What is it?"

His grip on me tightens. "Darragh was here. He *knows*." I take a shallow breath as his glower remains in my personal space. I step back as he raises a hand to point behind him. "You can't tell me you don't regret coming here."

I hear his words, but all I can think is Nolan regrets...me? The niggling thought finds purchase in my soul-soil. Why *shouldn't* he regret meeting me, when my presence at the castle brought his estranged relations into his life again, exposing his secrets, forcing his hand?

I thought I loved that hard-won concern he seemed unable to douse, like a fire that wouldn't go out. What I thought I loved, for a moment, now mocks me.

"Nolan." I sigh, the feel of the almost-kiss draining from my veins. Heat and freezing all at once. "It won't matter if anyone or *everyone* knows you're back. By Sunday your uncle will take everything from you, unless you step up and—"

"Unless *you* come forward and say who you really are!" Huffing, Nolan roughs a hand over his hair. "He saw me, but he was looking for you!" He shakes his head. "And now you're hurt."

I clench my teeth. "I'm just glad Martin and Mrs. Lucas aren't home right now."

"It's like he knew they were out of town. They'll be back late tonight. We can't tell your father...wouldn't want him to worry or worse, get involved." I can't help but agree as he leads me inside, saying, "Let's get you cleaned up."

Five minutes later

THE TEACUP CHIPPED when he returned.

We're inside the manor house with its homey halls, so unlike the castle in its barren, wastrel, forgotten state. It's an old home, and quiet. The floorboards moan a little by the front door—my word, it feels like an age, yet it's only been a few days since I first came to stay here. The entryway is a square room with a rug rich in scarlet hues, that separates two archways on either side. One leads into this inviting kitchen. Opposite is the living room. Both spaces take advantage of the large windows that cover the front of the house, but where the living room is darkened by walls of forest green, the kitchen is bright yellow—as any good kitchen should be.

My mother painted our kitchen yellow the month before she died.

The far wall is covered with white cabinets, filled with upscale appliances. Rich onyx covers the counters and the large rectangular island. I sit at a wood table, built into the wall like a breakfast nook with benches on either side. The cuts on my hand are stinging. I can't help but worry—getting the slivers out is going to hurt. But will it hurt as much as leaving them in?

I'm staring intently at that mist-damp hair, busy *not* being distracted by the different fair shades of blonde and bronze and gold that seems to encompass all Nolan is, when he raises his head. He's kneeling in front of me, our faces very close. Too close. I can see his pupils shrink as he gazes at me, squinting in the light from the sconce on the wall behind me. His burnished bronze eyes blazing, light and gold, like the sun in the sky on a freezing morning.

Nolan grimaces as he glances down, picking up a piece of the chipped cup and placing it on the table, pinning me with a serious stare. "Give me the teacup," he commands, eyes full of both annoyance and mirth. He reaches to gently pry the cup from my suddenly clammy hands and dabs it dry. He'd surprised me—having left me in the kitchen to scour for tea while he sought bandages, and when he returned, I'd knocked over a porcelain teacup. Now, he looks at me with this hint of kindness in his expression that makes me want to cry again, as he takes the saucer and dries it as well, setting it carefully before me. "See? All better. You can even name the poor thing."

"Thanks," I mumble. Because I feel frightfully awkward with him still kneeling before me. "You've shouldn't do that, you know."

"What? Save sentimental china from drowning?" He still looks serious, but it falls for a moment as a cheeky grin escapes while he casually leans back on his heels.

"Making me smile. Making me think things will be okay." Because Nolan's cousin came and shattered everything in the greenhouse to prove a point, and now he knows Nolan is back before Nolan's receives the paperwork to prove he's real and alive and who he says he is. And Darragh's comments about Nolan and I...

I couldn't process, so I dropped the teacup. Sad little thing.

Nolan's smile falters for a second, but then his straight lips quirk, replacing indecision with confidence and making him look roguish as he cocks one straight eyebrow. "Well, we've come this far."

I stay silent and push myself farther along the bench.

"You're sure Darragh isn't coming back?" I blurt. My need to fill the silence is unbearable, especially with the added curiosity about the family intrigue I've unintentionally been caught up in. Most of all, I cannot yet talk about the fire; it isn't a conversation we're ready for.

Why oh why didn't I tell him about my mother before this?

He shakes his head, the top front of his otherwise short hair flapping with the force of his denial. "No, he won't. He got what he wanted. He left his mark."

Well, this topic is a dead end. Nolan's shoulders are tense and his movements overly methodical and slow. Like the anger he's holding in will overpower him if he says one more word.

Surely, I have a right to know. How can I ask more without being rude or revealing my own last secret? Bold but kind, one syllable at a time. "I'm sorry for the mess out there. I don't understand why someone would do that." There. Maybe now he'll tell me why his cousin trashed the garden like a hoodlum.

"It isn't your fault. Maybe his dad put him up to it—he did say it was a warning." His eyes flicker to mine. "You should heed it. I'll help Martin clean up tomorrow."

Oh my goodness, the plants. Mrs. Lucas' husband Martin will be devastated at the mess. It was if the entire greenhouse tucked behind the house's sunrooms had been emptied and shattered on the pathway. Did Darragh have qualms about ransacking the property of another? Doing the dirty work himself? No...teenagers feared him in school. If his attention zeroed in on you, you lost something you valued. Something got broken. No surprise here then, filthy hands, steady threats.

I make a mental note to visit Martin outside tomorrow. I'll bring him tea in the greenhouse or something.

"But you don't need to worry," Nolan continues. "I won't let anything happen to you. You're safe here. You'll be safe here." The phrases sound similar, but they're not. I see that now.

"This isn't your fault."

He doesn't raise his head. "Isn't it? I'm the reason you're here. I asked for an archivist. I didn't know that day it'd be you..."

At a crumpling sound, I tilt my head slightly as Nolan removes a selection of small bandages, white strips of gauze, wrapped items, and a small medicinal-looking tube from his pocket. "So, will you let me check your scrapes? This is a lancet; I need it to get out any shards from beneath your skin."

The handwashing I did in warm water didn't seem to help—there are still shards beneath the pain. Skin is torn from the heel of my right hand to my wrist. I press it to my chest. My heart, my hand. It stings. But...

"Okay," I reply, pretending to be relaxed.

He clears his throat, keeping his head down as he reaches for my wrist, pulling his hand back to ask my permission to touch me. "Your right hand?"

"Uh, yeah, here." I push up the sleeve and extend my arm.

He turns my wrist gently and curses lightly under his breath. "These are pretty bad, Paige. You weren't just being a wimp." I glimpse a small grin as he glances up at me through fair eyelashes. My mortification is utterly complete when he grasps my arm and pulls my hand toward him. It feels so intimate, his gentleness and care for my scrapes. For interminable minutes he painstakingly probes for bits of ceramic. I press my lips together to keep in the grimace, while the sound of our breathing is cavernous between our bodies, so close.

My eyes never leave him, taking advantage of the opportunity to watch him unhindered. The light causes shadows to fall under his cheekbones and under his eyes. Freckles dust his cheeks, the white of the scars on his chin and eyebrow starker in the dim light. The hair on the top of his head lies flat, slightly damp against his forehead. He's removed his stylish sweater, and his black long-sleeved shirt is tight on hard arms. Every sinew is stretched between long limbs. Even his hands and fingers are covered in lean muscle, and I wonder what pastime keeps him so fit.

It seems he mumbles under his breath. "Scars..."

"You have experience with those?" I ask.

"Boxing," he says to my hand. That probably explains the eyebrow scar, and how he looks so fit, and possibly the irregular ridge on his nose which mars the otherwise stark angles of his handsome face.

Diligently, he removes the third shard of the plant pot—incredible how miniscule they were compared to the discomfort they caused. With practiced efficiency, he dabs on cream and flattens another bandage to my skin, which blessedly provides immediate relief to the stinging. As he smooths the edges, he keeps going, thoughtfully tracing the small veins on my wrist. I have to focus on breathing quietly. The room becomes so still, so loud, so quiet.

I try not to enjoy how his hand feels holding mine, and ignore our past and the constant cold in this damp mountaintop. I will *definitely* be replaying the sensation of his warm hands wrapping around my wrist, steady and deliberate, forever associating warmth with Nolan. Is it the cold season and the cold stone of the castle that make him seem so opposite? Is the burning inside of him going to hurt me like it killed my mother?

I forget to breathe and blink away black spots.

"Better?" he asks, voice husky, like he too is making an effort to make this no big deal.

"Yes." I forget to thank him as he takes my hand between both of his and brings it to his lips, warm breath brushing my knuckles. His warm hands rest around my cold ones. Then his eyes meet mine and we stay locked in each other's gazes. It's like he's seeing into my heart, the fear and hope all tangled together. And I'm scared by the fact that I want whatever is drawing lines and writing words between him and I together to be real.

He steps away from me like a fire has been lit between us, likely to leave burn marks on our cheeks and fingers were we to touch, and all my hesitation peaks as he turns and walks away.

"Nolan," I say, knowing full well I'm asking what I'm unwilling to give. "You need to let me in. That day, you didn't…" *Die with them*. But Nolan's past is far from dead. It's resurrecting and coming to eat him alive. Even as I say the words, I remember how Darragh recognized him so easily, even after all these years, because they were close, before.

"What's so bad about coming back?" I whisper, but suddenly it takes effort to stifle the urge to simply tell the truth that my mother and grandmother died that night too. I can't ask because I can't know how I'll feel if I need to blame him for it, and what I should do if he deserves that blame. Before I lose courage, I ask, "What happened between you and Darragh?"

Nolan finally looks up from making a hole in the ground with his intense stare. His beautiful eyes are cautious and sad. Haunted, and hunted. In that moment I would have sworn to swim an ocean to make him happy, but he drops his hands and steps back from me. "Darragh and I were there when the fire started, but it was *my fault.* Don't you see? This is why I can't take the stewardship! He knows it, and *now* he knows I'm not dead."

The next morning, Friday

NOLAN'S HOLDING ME beneath the shimmering light of the chandelier in the entryway of the castle. I think we're dancing, for my fingertips brighten against his as we turn in smooth circles over the polished floor. There's a song, and it sounds a little sad. Our entwined hands swing between us as we walk down the shining halls, with the vivid banners of history heralding the future...which is what we are.

Together, at home, and in perfect silence—where did the music go?

There should be others. My father, Juniper, Mrs. Lucas and Martin. There's no Penelope and Sterling, no houseguests or housekeepers, no social events.

Where are they? Has something else happened?

Our footsteps become silent. Why are we alone? I seek Nolan's face, those beautiful eyes cast in liquid gold, and reach for his hand, but he's gone, and the hallway ends.

I'm standing before a wall, the locket heavy against my chest—I haven't taken it off since starting my search for the *Oirdera* and the treasure. Has it almost been a week? It feels like I've lived here forever, like I know every monogramed banner by heart, know each engraving on the unique doors and stone floors like I've lived here my whole life.

Did I see those designs before, when it was so messy and covered in debris?

Every hall has a different motif, as I walk the floors. I'm looking behind as I glide forward—*it isn't real*. I know it isn't. The derelict castle doesn't have polished floors, and there's no one to play music. But I somehow see it, and it's powerful and true. They look so similar, each hall I float ethereally down, but each flower inscribing the floor is different. Swords and hammers, chiseling through my memories.

Only one hall has the white rose. The West Wing.

I startle awake. *It was just a dream.*

Deep tones from downstairs echo through the floorboards. Nolan's voice, and quieter breaks must be the responses from Mrs. Lucas. A guffaw breaks through, and I realize Martin is there too, keeping things sane.

I push my cheek against the pillow and pull the covers over my head. I'm in the manor house, and it's nearly ten in the morning. Last night, Mrs. Lucas and Martin arrived with a great fuss of surprise, shock, and worry over the vandalism and for Nolan and I. After many assurances, Nolan stayed in another old spare bedroom, and I remember falling asleep to the sound of a gramophone blasting old-fashioned music. This morning, the world feels quiet, as it often does after worries are loud and danger visits.

Once the voices below quiet, I venture to peek out the little square window, my breath fogging the glass. Wretched, predictable cloudiness. I can see a spire of the castle above—the tallest, the one in the west—but the rest is in the clouds. Low, looming clouds.

Nolan walks down the hill toward his fancy car, spinning keys in his hand with his collar turned up against the elements. A figure follows at a hurried pace, and beneath a navy and white striped umbrella strides the classy figure of Mrs. Lucas. *Did they fight? Is he leaving without her? Would he dare?*

She catches up to him and thwacks his arm with her purse and a snort bursts out, mirth freeing something tight from deep within my chest. I didn't know that happy place inside my heart was still awake after Nolan's explosive admission regarding the fire last night.

I decide to forgo the citadel for now, and instead see what I've been curious about but too distracted to devote time to. After last night's disaster, I care very much about the greenhouse and plants and flowers that Darragh so carelessly destroyed. What's *left* of them. How much was there in the first place? What possesses someone to enact that kind of specific destruction? I've never seen the greenhouse—and now I want to. So, back I go into my long denim skirt with an overlarge red sweater, a pair of borrowed woolen tights, boots, coat, mascara, and my mother's scarf.

From where I'm standing, Nolan has paid more dearly for whatever happened the night of the fire than Darragh ever did. And the enmity burning between them had little to do with me. I'm not sure if I'm relieved or concerned by that fact.

Or by the fact that Nolan said, clear as cloudless skies, that he started the fire.

I stifle the confusing emotions that arise at the thought, because it feels as hard to describe as my dream does now. Does Darragh mean to hurt Nolan's only remaining family for the secrets he's been keeping? But no, Darragh had planned to come before knowing about Nolan's return...

This is *my* fault.

After a quick jog through the rain and an unfortunate step into a puddle deeper than it appeared, I head to the greenhouse. I hope desperately that the damage isn't as bad as I remember it being last night.

Last night. When Nolan almost kissed me. When he took care of me, then admitted the fire was his fault and his worry that Darragh knows he's back. When I didn't reply with the fact that my mother and my grandmother died that night. I should have—every moment I delay makes the truth inside scrape deeper, louder. But Nolan's preoccupation with Darragh having known no one was home, that Darragh was checking on *me*...it frightened me. Then Mrs. Lucas and Martin arrived last night before I had a chance to say anything.

But the longer I'm silent, the harder it is to speak.

Round the corner is the courtyard, and it's clear. Too clean.

Whatever glass was broken, whatever pottery shards, they're completely gone. Who cleaned it? And so early in the day? I step gingerly over the stone path. It's a little too clear, a little too sparkly. I can well imagine Nolan helping Martin this morning, and after clearing the worst of it, crushing any dangerous leftover shards with the sole of his shoe, over and over and over.

It's what I would do.

A modern glass and steel door—entirely incongruous with the texture of the thatched-roof structure of the original building, and sporting a taped-up hole above the handle—leads into a large greenhouse of opaque glass with black steel supports and a curved roof. It's an indoor garden on the side of the house, and I smile at the thought that Juniper would hate it. For someone named after a tree, she's always been jealous of girls named after pretty flowers—like Peony, that perennial that can be given to celebrate any occasion, or Autumn, named for the season of decay and coveting all things richly colored. Flowers are for giving, and fall is about dying, as I love to remind her, but she'd only complain of the boring quality of trees. How I wish she were here, on the cusp of the equinox, as the fresh scent of soil and rain tickles my nose, with a retort about the nearness of life in spring.

But alas, our names are ours. Mine particularly apropos and hers...well. I tell her it's evergreen, and she complains about pine needles in her shoes. Juniper, the tree who's meant to be here among the flowers that she hates—I snicker and open the door.

No one *lives* in this greenhouse, though technically it's attached to the home. I haven't been in the connecting sunroom yet. It's a private sanctuary for Mrs. Lucas, which her husband Martin built for her, and I can see it through a glass window that's slightly fogged.

Looking back and forth one last time across the property and finding the view empty but for me and the rain, I push forward and step into the greenhouse, jumping as the door swings closed with a thud. *That's what you get for sneaking around.* A tinkle of glass on the ground from the broken door—that's how Darragh got in here last night and cleared out all he could. *Hard work, being a villain's son.*

The floor is warm-hued stonework atop dirt. It's natural and classy all at once. Comfortable, as the temperature is warmer and the cool breeze gone within the protective glass encasement. Hanging baskets dangle from the ceiling, and what look like pots of herbs line the far wall on layers of wood shelving. Two white wicker chairs sit beside side tables that are just begging for teacups and books, and bending over their shoulders are a pair of potted palms. I stand taller and take a deep, life-scented breath.

I lift the locket from around my neck and hold it next to the row of roses. These haven't bloomed, but they're almost ready. Most of the plants in here are green, green, green. But like outside, the floors here are swept unnaturally clean, and the shelves emptier than I suspect they were before. At the reminder of Darragh's destruction last night, my eyes are drawn to a stack of empty, chipped vases, porcelain adorned with intricate designs so like the white roses that Darragh's mother gave me. The white would be lovely, but for the thorny stems and the reminder of Lenora giving me one when she cornered me into this story in its first chapters.

Abundance. That's the word. I sniffle and cover my mouth and try not to sneeze—

A loud bang startles me, and the locket drops heavily against my chest as I spin around.

"Harumph!" Martin exclaims, juggling two buckets in his arms with a huff as the door swings back from the wall to bump him.

"Sorry!" I hurry to help but don't need to, for he steadies easily with a wink.

"Oh, it's all right, you just gave this old man a start." He smiles good-naturedly, putting the buckets on the ground. As he straightens to his full height, well over six and a half feet, with shoulders as wide as a river, he catches my wide gaze at a rose lying on the ground. "Oh look, I forgot one. This is my specialty; a hybrid tea rose. Long-stemmed Pope John Paul II. It took years, but it finally bloomed again! I'm going to surprise Anne with it. Doesn't it smell divine?" He bends to grab it, then tries to hand me the white rose.

I hold the flower away from my face, then sneeze. It is indeed the breed that Lenora managed to get a bouquet of. "Flowers always make me"—I wave my hand in front of my nose but it's no use—"allergic," I finish self-consciously. For all my time here, I've only said greeting in passing with Martin, never having a chance for a conversation with the jolly older fellow.

"Sorry about that." He places it in the empty bucket. "Ironic for a girl with that locket." His tone is knowing, but non-judgmental.

I tuck the locket back beneath my sweater. "Why don't they smell like—"

"Roses?" He chuckles. "It's more of a tangy scent, isn't it? Orange in a shade of pale. Why should roses all smell the same? Why is one better?" He looks at me kindly.

I don't deserve kindness. Whatever I'm doing with Nolan, everything I'm doing to help myself and my father, is a failure in this moment, so I apologize. "I'm sorry this mess happened because of me. And I'm sorry for coming in here without asking."

"Not your fault, and not Nolan's either. Not that he didn't clean up with a frenzy of guilt." Martin peers at me. "Did you find what you were looking for?"

"Um, yes. No. Not really." My heart thumps heavily, and my hands almost shake as the burst of adrenaline fades. "It's just…"

"Young lady, you must be shaken after what you've seen. You have a lot of questions?"

I sigh and look into his kind eyes, lined with a lifetime of wrinkles. "So many."

"Well, it's a good thing I'm such a wise old man. Take a chair in my humble office and let's have a chat." He sits down contentedly, the wicker chair creaking. I sit more slowly, gazing at the door as I move a stack of travel books from the chair to the floor. I'm not sure if I'm ready for this conversation, whatever it's going to be.

A few heartbeats pass as I sniffle and stare at my hands. Martin is silent, so I look up. He's leaning forward, elbows on his knees and hands clasped, thick arms unsuited to the dainty wicker chair. His eyes are a little sad, looking at the empty shelving. I deliberately hold myself still to keep from squirming.

"Do you know why I love plants?" he begins.

"Because they're *green* and—" Whoa. When had bitterness seeped into my good humor? Even though I'm struggling to deal with the events of yesterday, it's no excuse. "I'm sorry. I don't feel like myself." *I had a bad experience with a witchy lady and your white roses.*

But he laughs, unfazed by my youthful petulance. He reminds me of a tree trunk, solid and sturdy and just there, regardless of the season. "You may not see it, but you're good for us, and for Nolan. He's like our son...the closest thing we've had to having children, and you with him is something else." He smiles affectionately.

I sniffle again and wipe my sleeve on my nose. It's sad that they never had any children, because Martin and Anne are so generous and kind. And this minute, I'm not so sure I deserve it.

He goes on. "I love plants, flowers, and trees because they're all living. And they all *die*. Even the grass, like the Good Book says. Just like us poor souls on two legs." He takes a deep breath and starts his homily with a story. "I grew up in a rougher part of north Gabreville. My mom was a nurse, and my old man, he wanted me to be tough, just like him. He worked at the mine, but not beneath the ground; he drove the trucks. He hated it. He gambled on racing and was often at the pub, which was better than him being home. I followed him into the mine at sixteen. I was strong, and I worked hard. My whole life seemed to be buried in the ground. My father's lungs filled with cancer, not working and angry until my mother passed. He was gone not long after.

"I worked odd jobs, mostly things outside that other people hated, like landscaping, finally landing here with the Hayes family at age twenty. The old groundskeeper took me under his wing—he remembered my sorry excuse for a father—and let me explore the land, which at that time was undeveloped and wild from the elder Hayes's neglect. Years later, when the citadel was in its full glory, Nolan's father kept me on after that groundskeeper passed. His wife loved her gardens and they had their social life to maintain, rich folk they were. They came by their wealth with the generations of mining, but also with hard work, good timing, business sense, and a bit of luck—until the collapse, and then the fire."

I remember what Darragh said to Nolan; blame lay at the previous steward's feet for the mine collapse the year of the fire. His grandfather, I suppose.

Martin peers keenly at me with pitiful eyes—a sorrowful combination—and I mentally prepare myself for the preaching part. "I knew green, you see. And this estate is full of it. Keeping the green beauty living is my purpose. Replacing it over and over with new seedlings, renewing the soil, and getting rid of the pests. There's something about being alive that the plants understand better than most people. They lean to the sun when it shines, they absorb the rain as a gift, they bow to their death gracefully, and embrace their demise, all so their seeds can thrive in the dirt of their death every spring."

The application part of a sermon is always the trickiest. I take a deep breath to shore up some courage. I try to believe it's somewhere dormant, under the surface, waiting for the rains...just like the seeds he's talking about.

Martin frowns and loosens his hands. "A plant's life cycle is easy to understand, to nurture. But our lives are messy things. I learned that a family tree is just as painful, or marriage just as cold, whether in a fancy country manor or a leaky row house. And Nolan Hayes is growing out his family tree as we speak, starting with his nasty uncle Declan, and I'm right proud of him."

I can't stay quiet anymore. "Martin, how do I fit into all this? I feel like I've stepped into the story without reading the prologue. Or like I'm in a river, getting pulled under every time I reach for a way to pull myself out." My hands have been gesturing erratically, so I clasp them in my lap.

He just smiles. "Love is a lot like drowning."

"Wait, who said this was about love? This is about me saving my father and my home and helping Nolan—the only real thing is waiting until Nolan gets some legal footing to retain stewardship of the estate. Not that he'll do it..."

"I don't think the look on your face right now is anything but real. And I *am* sorry about your father's troubles. I don't know him, but I see how you love him."

I frown at the stone-laid ground beneath my feet. "Then why is it so hard to find the true story?"

Martin looks at me with wise eyes, their blue pale like a lost winter sky, but still round and merry and twinkling with hidden humor. He's a sage and Father Christmas mixed into an aged rugby player. He's even wearing a rugby jersey, with the Gabreville red and gold colors, under his green rain jacket. It clashes, but for him it works.

"What do you think of Nolan?" he asks, ignoring my question and crossing his rubber boots in front of him. I spy a shard of glass in mud stuck in the treads. Relaxed, but obviously he has an agenda.

"Well, I don't know him that well," I say pointedly. "He's tall, and he talks back as bad as I do." I think of his angst. "He mentioned boxing, and he's probably one of those late-night running types—"

"Early morning," Martin inserts proudly. "He loved running cross-country in boarding school...was actually not bad, but stopped because he kept winning and didn't want the attention. He's fast." Martin avoids talk of the boxing—I get the impression *that* garnered less approval. I think of Nolan's physique and decide the length of his musculature, while pleasing, is too distracting. Is he still running from his bad past with Darragh?

"He *is* short tempered and often rude beneath his breath." I'm at once drawn to him and want to smack him. "Bitter and reclusive, but also protective of you and Mrs. Lucas and his home."

And his past. And me? Isn't he protective of me?

I refuse to say "but." *But* something about his sadness drew me. *But* his eyes haunted the ends of my dream, so it felt like I'd wanted to know him my whole life though I've only known him a week. But...I've felt more seen, more real, in our short, snappy, secret-kept relationship than with my father. "When I first came, it was like I either was supposed to be here, or supposed to stay far, far away." I pick at the bandage under my sleeve and sigh, the locket heavy on my chest. "I'm just not sure which."

"Well, that makes sense to me," he replies easily.

"Really?" I sputter.

Martin shrugs his massive shoulders and moves his clasped hands to his lap. "Love doesn't always make sense, and matters of urgency are most often matters of the heart." He winks. "Just as surely as you've tied Nolan's heart in knots, he's touched yours,

Paige-girl." I can't be mad at the sweet man when he calls me that.

"I don't know what you mean," I say, my eyes returning to the door, the broken glass. "I'm confused. And I wish I knew why…"

"Why those people died in an accidental fire? Why evil people want to take over an abandoned mine? What it's all really worth?" he asks gently, and my head snaps up at the implication that it was an accident.

Though I want to ask about how the fire started, so very badly, I think now only Nolan can tell me his side of the story. I shift so my knees face the door. "All that. And Darragh tore this place apart, and there was broken glass everywhere, and I feel so bad." My voice wants to come out sharp, because there's anger in me at Darragh, but it ends up sounding like a question instead. An overwhelming question, that leads to other overwhelming questions like the ones that my dreams exposed. Impossible thoughts, about how I would love to live and work and create a life here. "Can the treasure be real?"

"Mmhmm." Martin nods once. "There's always treasure to be found."

My head whips around. "You believe it might exist?"

His eyes remain merry and unchanging, which is no answer, but then he shrugs. "Maybe. But the one you're thinking about? You and Nolan need to find that yourselves."

"I would! But why does he refuse to tell me what really happened?" I ask, youthful petulance rearing its ugly head in my tone once more. I push myself off the chair and walk the four short steps to the door. Martin doesn't move as I pull it open, but his cheerful voice stops me before my hand releases the doorknob.

"Nolan is gone today, helping me deliver my order at the florist." I scowl back at the broken stem of the rose in the empty bucket as Martin's voice plays at something innocent but unavoidable. "He's there suffering with my sweet Annabelle. They order so many flowers every equinox, for some sort of charity tea every spring and fall. He's such a good lad, willing giving back to the community and all that."

Aiming for an expression of detached interest, my foot remains on the threshold. "Oh really?"

"He drove Anne into town earlier after helping me clean up. Not that he's avoiding you. Not at all," he chortles. "And he has a soft spot for Anne and I, to his credit." I don't know whether Martin's trying to make me jealous or make my heart bend. It mostly makes me curious, and belatedly I realize that was his plan all along. Then he mumbles, "You kids have a different life—never knew a monarchy, never survived without cell service..."

I waffle at the door, determined to go to the castle again, but afraid to go alone.

"Yet he's it, isn't he, the steward's son returned, back from the dead. All we need next is an inheritor of the old kind. It'd be just like a story." He's still smiling. "*Quite* the story."

It isn't *like* a story. It's our story. And it is altogether much too real.

Nolan, who's here in a place rich in broken-down everything, and unable to prove it all unless the council sees the documents proving he's who he says he is. Me, who's poor in everything except legacy, and still unwilling to say who I am.

"Then, what should I do next?"

"Up to you how you spend a lonely day on the top of this misty mountain." *Looking for the wrong thing*, he doesn't say. But it hangs in the air. "Spring is coming." He pats his palms on his tree-trunk thighs and stands. "I'm off. My carriage awaits."

We walk out into drizzle that will probably turn into more. As we walk, Martin chats enthusiastically about the local rugby team at the secondary school, then tells me all about the little pastry shop that is also a florist, hence, the flowers for selling. It's Anne's favorite place for socializing, it seems—I can't think of her as anything but "Mrs. Lucas," because of her dignified influence.

As he checks the load and closes the back of the truck, he tells me a hilarious story about a prank he heard about at the pub. The boys from the school apparently put some shockingly sticky clear tape on the arms of the chairs at the tearoom, and their principal had needed to leave his suit jacket attached to a chair.

I button my coat, and a smile takes over my face because he's still cackling about those boys and at my accusation that he's proud of them. The truck bed is full of white buckets and varied stemmed flowers—he'd loaded yesterday afternoon and parked in the garage, which is why they didn't get wrecked by Darragh. I want to ask why no red? Why only pale roses? So much white, so beautiful, maybe more because it's sad how they've been cut and will be sold—

I step back, but before Martin drives off, his soft voice stops me. "Paige?" I pause. He is serious, all traces of the jovial local guide gone as he beckons me back to the open window. "Don't be afraid to let your heart, not your eyes, guide you."

I nod mutely. Martin's truck smells earthy, with a hint of the caramel sweets piled in the cupholder—that candy shop in Gabreville has quite the reach. I lean in and take one. How can I describe the way that the black ash at the bottom of my heart has never stopped burning, and how desperately I want to sweep it out? "What if I don't want to go looking again?"

"Don't you want to feel better? To feel better, first, you have to feel. It's *easy* feeling nothing. But that's all you get—nothing," Martin says, sending me the saddest, softest smile, reminding me that though tonight is the end of winter, this isn't about the amount of light or length of days changing overnight. The start of spring is simply hope for one more day.

I pull my red scarf into a hood over my head and count to three in the cold, misty rain. I know what I need to do. I need to talk to the other person who was never the same after the night of the fire. I need to talk to my father.

"Martin? Can you please give me a ride into town?"

part three

the huntsman and the treasure

THE FIRST HUNTER

Friday, a half hour later, in the home I shared with my father

"PAPA?" After notching my key in the door and finding it unlocked, I call through ripples of uncertainty. "I'm home." *I'm okay, in case you were worried.* A tear slips down my cheek. The hope for love in any way has freed me into letting me feel more of the hurting.

A voice responds from far off—or rather, far *below*. Lighting a candle in the dark, I descend ten rickety wood steps into the basement. A crinkled and water-damaged copy of last week's *Gabreville Gazette* lies discarded on the bottom stair. What story will it tell once this weekend ends?

Fingering the delicate silken-floral keyring Mrs. Lucas gave me, I consider all the roses in my life—sketches in my mother's diary, Lenora's white thorny threat, the *Oirdera* motif. The symbols of my long-lost lineage on that door that I saw inside the castle.

"You're so much like your mother," my father says while staring at his work, illuminated by a single lantern and sounding a sad mix of wistful and regretful.

I follow his voice to the workbench behind a large contraption of rusted iron and steel, a black thing with gears and exhaust pipes—*I don't want to know*. Keeping my eyes off a set of grounding tools, small chisels and other tools. Devices for inventors, or diggers of gems. Treasure.

"Isn't it a good thing I sound like her?" I come up to him and speak my heart instead of my mind. "Will you finally tell me what happened?"

He sighs, then tucks a hand into his pocket and removes a very slim book embossed pink, red, and hints of green, limned with gold filagree and scribed on the front in Latin. This is the book he'd taken with him that fateful day at Fairhavens, when he got locked in the tower and I'd exchanged his treasure hunt for mine.

I take the small book and flip through softened pages. It's an illustrated book of Psalms, the kind artisans would spend lifetimes creating. It lands in the middle, naturally opening and easily flattened. I flip to the front pages and then to the endpapers, then gasp. There's a map sketched in sepia-toned ink, very faded, but exactly like the one I traced from the combined *Oirdera* books. Yet *this* map is overlaid with black, dead roses at the tips of the vines. Their texture is drawn to be fractured and frail like withered parchment. Like delicate pages falling to pieces. It's the same...but not. Because *this* map has a compass rose drawn on it.

"No one was supposed to find it," Papa says, his voice thin, like our weak breath often is.

"Find *what*?" I struggle to breathe normally; it's like the ceiling is lower than it used to be. I've never liked it down here. "What is this?"

"Your mother took it from *her* mother. She told me the day before the fire to hide it. She likely meant for you to have it someday, but I just...couldn't. Not with knowing how the treasure split their family apart." He took as deep a breath as he could. "Your grandmother suffered so much that I can hardly blame her. Her husband raged against her—"enraged" is not a strong enough word for the terrors your grandmother and mother lived through in that house in the White Forest. As if any treasure could make up for his black, rotten heart. He found out about the treasure not long after I married your mother. But it was *he* who died—a cliff claimed him. The town thought it was an accident, but I knew better and so did your mother."

"Grandmother?" I try not to show how sad or afraid or ashamed I feel. Mostly confused. I don't want to show anything that will stop my father from sharing this story with me.

He nods, wispy gray hair lingering where the rest is balding at the top. "After that, your mother was worried. She'd told me before that greed drove their family to ruin in the Dark Year. Legend has it that the war was over the gold and gems the Ludovici's hid, refusing to help when there was a famine and a plague. Not helping those in need. It's not a legacy worth resurrecting, your mother used to say." His eyes don't leave the locket. I hadn't realized I had taken it into my hands, clasped tight against my chest.

Not a legacy worth resurrecting, my mother thought. Just like my ancestor, the lady who wrote all the beautiful love letters. Rose, my great-great-grandmother. I love that she never dwelled on anything but her true love. And Papa saying that she *and* my mother tried to hide their Ludovici legacy both fills my heart and drains it. Is what I'm doing now betraying them?

Something in Papa's expression now reminds me of the look on his face that day ten years ago, when he found me alone in Grandmother's cabin and took me away from the forest. Stark and empty.

"Your grandmother was raving mad." Papa pounds his workbench. "Especially after her husband's unfortunate downfall. People thought she was crazy, living alone in the woods. And that night was simply an opportunity. What better chance to search for a way into that mine than during a party at the castle? Your mother followed, probably trying to stop her, and they both paid the price! She wanted to let the Ludovici line *and* that cursed treasure be forgotten, so it couldn't ruin anyone else's lives. What else could I do but honor her wishes? I didn't want this for you—"

I gasp at his words, the admission. It's real. *It's all real.* "You didn't tell me!" I'm angry because he's riveted on the locket and the corner of the map and he will not meet my eyes. "If I had known it was real, maybe I—"

He finally looks at me, all sad now, though perhaps a bit angry too. "Would it have stopped you? Wouldn't you have gone there anyway?" He shakes his head wearily. "I'm sorry that my reticence led to your being caught up with this...with *them*. But you should not reveal any of this! Not that the treasure is real, and not who you are. It's *dangerous*."

I swallow thickly. "I've already been in danger—Mother and Grandmother *died*! They were hiding, and it put them in danger.

Don't you see?" I want to be free, I want to live, I want to stop hiding and cowering and shrinking. "I want to be an open book, not a hidden one." He flinches like my words slap him. "*Seven generations* in hiding. And you hid my mother's identity, her position, her history from you own daughter. I want my own future, and if I need to reveal her history to get it, then I will."

He wrings his hands, eyes downcast. "I already lost her. I couldn't lose you."

"I still felt alone!" Suffering without response to my cries, or comfort to my cares. In the same room, doing wrong by doing nothing. As if by doing nothing things wouldn't get worse.

"Do you know how they got into such a grand party without anyone seeing?" he asks, and I shake my head, frustrated that now, *even now*, he won't acknowledge his own wrong. "While there are many servant passageways, there are secret ones, known by the emblems of Gabreville." I nod, reluctantly. Those, I saw. "They likely never got into the mines themselves. Your grandmother didn't have this map. Whether the treasure is in a hidden room or in the mine itself, I do not know." His chin tremors. "I think your mother did, though." He touches the book in my hand. "Your mother gave me that book for safekeeping."

My mother's locket fits into the mirror because she was the heir of the citadel, the daughter of the builders. The white rose, amid the black ones. Like the words in those old books of chronicles hinted at. *Indestructible chest. Ruby-red key.* It's a key. The key to the maps in the *Oirdera*. A hundred and fifty years later, and finally this locket will show me, the true heir of the Lords, the founders of the Fairhavens, where their lost treasure is.

Treasure my mother lost her life trying to stop anyone from finding.

"Paige, listen to me. I was wrong. I lost her, but I won't lose you." His voice cracks as he says, "What kind of father would I be if I didn't try to stop you from following in those deadly footsteps? Leave it where it stays, near hell. Let it lie."

"What if I can find it? It could change our lives!"

Now his head shakes, vigorously. "Even if you find a way into the mine, it will be dangerous. Rock walls can loosen unexpectedly, rotten wood might fall on you—" He cuts himself off, covering his mouth with a trembling hand. Seeing him this broken isn't making me angry like I thought it would. I feel sad, yes. Pity. But mostly I want to turn back time, to stop him from hurting himself all alone like this, for so long. Alone.

Then he murmurs, "I always thought if your mother hadn't followed your grandmother, she might have survived. That fire ruined everything." Truth makes my emotions hurt even more. Part of me thinks there was ruin before the fire started. That there couldn't have been a happy ending to that story that night. Papa's gaze shutters in memory. "I knew you followed me, Paige. Last winter. At the entrance to the mine. I just went to the forest alone, to talk to her."

I cannot stop the pain lancing my words. "You could have talked to *me.*"

His head whips up with a ferocity I've never seen from him. "I *don't* want you going down there." He mutters under his breath,

"You're too much like them."

"Was it worth dying for? Tell me, please." My breaths are shaky and when he doesn't respond, I push more. I will not give up, not this time. My mother must have hidden herself from the past for a reason that she deemed worthy. "For all these years you've been hiding things to protect me, but now I've been trying to protect *you*. If you have a way for us to make all this end, then let me go. Whatever it is, the treasure is real—you have to let me find it."

He laughs, bitter. "*She* wanted to save me, just like you. Money and gold can't save me from bad accounting and a job that doesn't pay enough, because the world changed too fast for my skills to keep up with."

Tears prick my eyes like thorns. "Your skills are all that's left of a world most people have forgotten. It would be sad to lose them—what would happen if there was no one to change the headline font on the press, or replace the overused "E" with the proper Garamond shape for the *Gazette*?"

"No one would notice—"

"*I would!*"

He looks up at me, shoulders sagging. "I should have noticed you more, Paige."

Tears trickle down my cheeks. "Then hear me now. *Help* me now. Nolan is the real steward, and—" At my father's surprised expression, I wave my hand. *Wait.* This next part is like a twisted reflection, the one you don't want to see. "And Lenora, I hate to say this—she's *right*. She thinks there's something down there. *I* think there's something down there, something Mother and

Grandmother died for. Maybe it wasn't just a box of treasure? What if there's *more*?"

Father's shoulders lose their slump. "If your mother thought it was worth protecting, then you *should* be the one to find it. Not Lenora."

"I can do this. There are marks on the map. Seven passages, just like the council, right?" I peer at the black-ink roses on the little psalter's endpaper. One, two, three, four, five, six... Are they meant to be black, or red? "I can try to find them all. Though I don't know which one—"

"She wouldn't have had me hide it from your grandmother it she didn't believe it was real. The map, and the treasure." He sighs. "I hid it from you to keep you safe, but you ended up there anyway, tangled with the Hayes family, and I've done *nothing*..."

"It was my choice, Papa." I reach for him, but hesitate. So many things unsaid over the years, so strangely unable to fill a second of silence. "You're helping me now." I lower my hand.

"The locket is yours by right," he says. "But if you go down there Paige, I don't know what you'll find. I don't know if *any* of the passages are safe to venture through, no matter what that Nolan Hayes boy says he knows of the castle. The mine collapsed *before* the fire. Who knows what effects the fire had on an already unstable mine?"

My spine straightens. "Nolan will help me." Like the storm that knocked me off course pushed me in the right direction, toward Nolan. I still need to hear his side of the story, and I need to tell him mine, but a tick deep inside gives me certainty. "He will keep me safe."

"You trust him?"

"More than myself, at least in that old castle." At the skepticism but kindness—the worry that I've always craved from my father's attention—I try to smile, but it wobbles. All I want is to rush away from my broken, detached father who's tried so hard...now all I can do is pity him and hope the future is less tarred by the past, now that we've aired it. Safe in the basement with my father's inventions, I want a better version of the story.

With Nolan's admission about causing the fire—accident or no—it's more painful, but also, more true. The past becoming clear. Words shifting into real things, or perhaps just the real things making my words alive. "I think I love him. Though it hurts, too." It hits me, the admission aloud a resounding depth like the unknown, endless chasms beneath the earth.

Papa clears his throat with effort. "Well then."

"Thank you for this," I clasp the psalter with the map tightly "And Papa?"

"Yes, sweetheart?"

"You cannot spend your life hiding and alone."

He tries to smile, rubbing his eyes. "Neither can you." And for all the years I've resented him for not noticing, I realize I'm more like him than I've ever wanted to admit. "Now, give me that locket before you go. It needs a good cleaning."

I hug him, and he's still warm, like I remember, like he's always been. He's still my father, and I'm thankful for him. "Thank you, Papa. Pray for us."

THE FORBIDDEN WOODS

Almost three hours later, Friday afternoon

I'M NEARLY NUMB, walking through the cold afternoon, skirting the main path and staying under the trees. But nearby, the gates feel so familiar, like the sway of the trees, because now walking into the White Forest feels like home.

When did I start thinking that? When did I start believing shadows over figures? When did I want truth over lies, even when it hurt? I can't say I regret it.

The path narrows up the side of the mountain, branches coated with freezing rain just like yesterday. I'm praying there won't be a thunderstorm. When I leave Gabreville proper, the rain still holds off. Then, up familiar footpaths, through the public park that ends in the shadow of the endless forest. Jagged gates forever eclipsed from sunlight amidst the dense trees—and just here, past the gatehouse, lies the path to the citadel lands beyond, less travelled in the last decade than in the hundreds of years before.

The Endilwood Gate remains ajar from when I first ascended this path on Saturday, following Papa. On that sunny day, the air still seemed dim and thick with threat. The creaking of the gate is a hinge in my memory as I walk through the aged tree line.

I may be afraid of those dark clouds, but there's no thunder yet, and I have enough fire inside to get me up the mountain if the promise of rain is the only thing chasing me. My father finally shared what I needed; I have my mission. I have an overlay to those maps in the *Oirdera*, to a treasure that is *real*. I'm certain that when I get into the castle, I can figure it out, that this illustrated psalter will decode what we've found so far. I have to.

The hum of an expensive car sounds beyond the footpaths as I emerge from the tree-covered road to see the towering castle spires. My heart thumps at the sound, but my asthma isn't acting up in the mountain air. I must be getting fitter, I'm hardly winded.

Where the curving road to the castle crosses the footpath, I avoid it, choosing instead to walk farther east. Toward the abandoned cabin my grandmother used to call home.

On a grade down the mountain, a car door slams. He's coming. Nolan's found me.

I can't help but think of the generations-old shoebox filled with letters in red, all those written memories from my great-great grandmother Rose. Like the books of my mother's. All the dairies, all those hopes, her love for my father. Those two women placed love before treasure. Ironic, then, that my grandmother killed her husband and became so mad with grief or pain that she ventured into the castle to find riches that would never soothe the hurt.

Nothing is valuable enough to replace loved ones, or fill that space inside. No matter how many generations of Hayes lived in the castle instead of Ludovicis or how unfair that was, if I find any treasure, it won't be to use against anyone else.

I only want to stop hiding in a dark forest.

Nolan's footsteps sound behind me on the forested footpath. I don't slow, because now that the doors are open in my mind, I don't know where to look. There's no break in the trees. I'm a bit lost; it's been so long since I was last at Grandmother's old, abandoned cabin.

My father went back once, to clear out her things. Grief-stricken and reminded of being trapped inside, I'd refused to go with him. He sold most of the furniture, and she had little else of value—clothes went to charity, and the cabin wasn't worth selling. It was too complicated, as the landowners were all dead and the cabin grandfathered in from generations before.

Trees cover the pink-and-gold-brimmed sky painted by the setting sun, but other bruised-looking clouds have rolled in from the east, making the air darker than the hour would dictate. I have about an hour of light left, and a flashlight for when it gets dark. Something magnetic has drawn me back here, a long-buried connection with the women with whom I share blood.

I'm beside an unremarkable bit of undergrowth when Nolan finally calls my name. "Paige!"

His face, when he appears, is set as stone. Unyielding, steps confident and sure, prepared for whatever level of conflict I desire. The nearer he gets, any high ground I had lessens, his towering presence before me almost in line with the old castle that's visible behind the soaring trees. Bruised, broken, and still unflinching.

I can be just as stubborn.

"Paige, wait!" My name echoes through the cold air and the forest. "Paige!"

"Stop following me!"

"Stop being reckless!" He slows now that we're in sight of one another, roughing a hand through his hair and making the coarse, short locks stand on end. Through a filter of rain, I wait for Nolan and his unyielding gaze, my arms crossed fruitlessly against the cold. If he wants to dredge up the past, I'm ready. There's no choice now but to lay out all the dark branches I've been clinging to.

I resist going to him, but I resist saying "I can't do this."

His hands raise like I'm a skittish animal as he halts before me. "Paige, let's go home."

"No. I need to go—" I stop myself. If I say this, he'll know what I've been keeping from him. The death of my mother and my grandmother—the fire's fault, thus his fault, though he hasn't told me *how*—and the fact that I avoided bringing it up all week.

The fact that I lied.

"Paige," he pleads, a crack in his voice, "don't you remember your grandmother warning you about wolves in the woods?"

"What? How do you know—" And it comes rushing back—the *beginning* of that awful night. "How do you know who my grandmother is?"

My mother took me to Grandmother's cabin, like she had so many times when I was little. But that night, we ran. I didn't know the fire was coming. No one did. My mother and my grandmother, dying of smoke inhalation. People at the party didn't know they were there, were surprised when they were discovered much later at the top of the stairs.

My memory of being trapped in the cabin during the storm, while all the tragedy in my life happened elsewhere, has overshadowed the first pages of that night. I've always hated returning to the memory of my eight-year-old self. That night's thunderstorm and the childish feeling of a black fear of thunder; it's no wonder I hadn't dwelt on the hours before.

There was too much weight in the hours *after*.

But now, I remember. I *let* myself remember. The running. The sharp ache prodding my side and the muffled pounding of my feet beside my mother's on fallen foliage on the forest floor—up, up, up the same path I just trod. The vibrant red of newly loosened dead leaves. The storm coming up the mountain. And fear.

My mother, afraid.

Because our footfalls weren't the only calls in the woods that night.

"Wolves still live out here," Nolan interrupts the terrorizing forest of memories, standing a pace away from me, stock still.

I glance up—thick trees—and the looming storm clouds. "I almost want to take my questions back. I don't want to ask about the fire or that night at all," I whisper. "I don't want to know. And I want to know everything. It's all I can think about."

"I didn't believe it was possible," Nolan says in a voice so quiet that I take a step toward him to hear. "I didn't know your dad was married to the woman I saw that night. But when I took him to his shop last Saturday, the day we met, I saw her picture on the wall of his workshop." His chest expands with a deep breath. "I didn't just see her in the castle, Paige. I saw her before, out here. In the forest."

I shiver. Rain trickles from the sky, kissing my face gently. The air is cold. But not as cold as the blood in my veins at his admission. How much tighter will the thread of our stories bind us?

"Earlier that evening, I saw you and your mother—I didn't realize it was you, just this little girl... You ran through the forest." His voice carries, though it's low and raw. Half his face is cast in shadow. I feel my lips quiver, my eyes water as he repeats, "I was *here*."

He doesn't need to say it for the memory to come to life between us, because suddenly, I fully realize he's not talking about the fire or the citadel. It's here, this thing between us.

Because he was there, then.

"Before the fire, I was in the woods. I was fourteen. I was coming back in the dark. I'd been avoiding the party, but I knew my friends would be there—Darragh had called me, and I was going to join him and our friends and cause trouble. We were young and dumb and had no idea of the consequences. But before, I saw a light in the house off the path, as I always did, but there were wolves out that night. I stopped by to make sure the old lady who lived there would stay in."

I'm not sure what to say to that. He's talking about my grandmother—no other elderly women lived in those woods.

"I wasn't sure of her name, though I'd seen her before," he hedges, sensing the storm from what we're finally saying out loud. As if the rain falling between us could heal us as we finally release it. "She was your grandmother." Not a question.

Why is he doing this now? It's like I'm alone and trapped in the dark all over again.

He hesitates. "I—I barred the door just in case, so the wolves wouldn't get in."

My spinning thoughts are revolving around the fact that teenaged-Nolan was tromping around the White Forest on the night of the fire. Grandmother had made split-pea soup for dinner, and played cards with me in her simple, single-room cabin. She and my mother fought, then left me alone. No one knocked on the door when they were with me. That happened after...which means Nolan must have come when it turned dark—when I was on my own.

My words fly like accusations. "*I can't believe it was you!* You barred the door, you *trapped* me! My mother *left* that night to follow my grandmother." And then, the thunderstorm, the smell of smoke from the fire hours later, when I was alone and afraid with no way to escape. And all through the night, until my father found me the next day, crazed with worry and grief. "Do you have any idea how terrified I was? Twenty-four hours of fear and I *still* want to hide during a thunderstorm." I can't even muster embarrassment for my fear, because it's visceral and angry and old and *finally*, I have someone to blame for every scattered thorn of pain.

His eyes close and his face is anguish. Then his golden eyes flame open to find me once more. "I don't regret it."

I'd expected apologetic entreaties, excuses. He is immovable, statuesque and unnerving. In any other situation, his steadfastness would be reassuring.

But his voice is tight. "I'm not sorry you're here and alive. Your heart, beating. Your tears, falling." I brush thickly gathered tears away from my mouth as he continues. "Everyone else died, but *you didn't*. You can hate me all you want for saving you." Any wavering in his tone vanishes as he swipes at his eyes with his wrist. "But no, I'm not sorry."

My question is weaker than I want, "So, what, you watched over my grandmother's cabin in the woods, and watched me grow up?"

"Yes, I had seen you before—I *lived* here. I knew every mile, every path. I still do. This was my land. My *home*! But it wasn't like that. I just had a sense that night. I was afraid."

"And then you burned it all up!" I cry, all those questions finding release in the harshest of accusations.

"You don't need to remind me! I loved it here before I ruined it! What I lost—what *you* lost, because of me—" He rubs a hand on the back of his neck. "It wasn't safe for you that night to leave the cabin."

"You saw my mother?" I ask, my voice not quite sounding like my own.

"I saw her in the castle. And then she disappeared. You said your mother was searching for your grandmother?" He laughs, but it's hollow. "Of course." He pins me with a stare. "They were looking for treasure? Is that how they ended up there? And you—you're doing dangerous things like them. Crazy, bold, stupid you—that I might *stupidly* be falling for—would have gone running through the dark, a frightened little girl, and been torn apart by wolves."

Stupid? Love? I know he can't mean it, but the words rip open something inside. "The tearing apart happened anyway."

He was there. My blackest moment. But what my father said earlier? My mother was trying to save my grandmother from their history. *My* history. And what of Nolan? Was it that same stupidity that got out of control? That Darragh was part of? Even if it was mostly accidental, because I doubt even Darragh meant to burn the castle, I despise the thought of it. Thoughts are hard to control, and now that I've thought it, I can't un-think it. Nolan was *there.* He's *here.*

How much do I blame him? My frenzied thoughts collide in my head, pounding and painful, because I don't want them to be true. Though the trees above us shield us from the rain, some still lands on my face. It's freezing, and it's getting late, dimmer by the minute.

Nolan's eyes harden. "I regret every moment of that night, except this one thing." Two steps and he's closer than he was before. "You need to decide if being alive now is worth the hurt then. If your mother and Grandmother would've wanted you to lose everything, or save it."

"I did lose everything!"

"You can claim Fairhavens," he says. "We'll find a way to prove who you are, somehow." I haven't told him yet I have proof of my own bloodline and that I could take it away from even him. But he's not done. "You didn't lose yourself. You've finally found who you are; you should be grateful!"

But I almost did. This climb up the mountain has only lowered me to the packed ground of memory. "You think I'm selfish?"

"Yes! I made my choice to save you that night, and I'd make it again. I made such a huge mistake, it was the one good thing—"

"Trapping a child alone in a cabin in the middle of the woods? I had no idea you were out there, and back then I had no idea why they left me."

He steps closer and peers at my face. "And you know now? Why they left?"

"Do you have any idea how afraid—" I swallow and lick my wet lips, tasting lip balm and rainwater and maybe my tears.

"Look at the danger you insist on putting yourself in! Over and over!" He pauses, finally close enough that we can hear each other breathing, the rain the only thing between us, trees dripping around us. "I *know* we are using each other. Before you came, I didn't care if I lost the estate. But look at the people trying to tear down my life! And yours! We can stop them."

"One of us has to lose," I insist. "Don't you see that? They'll hurt my father if I don't give them what they want."

"I don't care anymore. Let me protect you—"

"How? What if I've already betrayed you?"

"You won't."

"I thought about it!" I cry, hugging my stomach. I'm already shuddering with cold though I'm bundled in my scarf and coat. My father's debt could've been paid, but at what cost? Doing the right thing *hurts*. "I thought about it, the whole way up this inglorious mountain! What if I gave Darragh what's weighing this bag down to appease his mother? What's weighing *me* down? I could let them throw you to the wolves and they'd pay me by finally leaving me alone!"

"But you didn't." Nolan reaches for me. "We just need to find the treasure first. Let them *have* the castle for all I care. Unless you want it—"

I step back, pulling at my coat collar, which rubs against my neck uncomfortably, but at least I'm warm. "Do you really not care that I seriously considered it?" I find the will to fight. Nolan isn't hearing the threat. He isn't *hearing* me. "Not only could I give Lenora the maps. I have a family tree, Nolan. It's authentic, as are the letters Penelope had for me. It's all enough. Old books and papers are what I *do*. Gabreville Council would accept my claim, and then I sell it to Mr. Hayes, and you would have nothing. Don't you see?" I clasp the strap of the book bag across my chest, which is pressed against the locket beneath my sweater. That crest shows *I have the right to claim it all.* "I could undo all of it!"

Impervious to my fight, Nolan reaches for me again. "You didn't, Paige."

"There's too much at stake, and they're going to take it away from you—" I can't swallow and cough instead. "What will your uncle do now that he knows you're alive and could take the wealth and position he thinks he's entitled to? Last night was terrifying, so what will he do to you, or accuse you of—"

"Do you think I'm afraid of him?"

I raise my voice. "You aren't hearing me!"

He doesn't reply. He stands across from me, silent. But now that he's waiting, giving me space to speak, I don't how to say what I really want to. What if I die alone, like my grandmother did and my mother did? Would it feel like that night I was left alone in these woods? When my father wasn't with me, when he didn't come to rescue me, and I was scared...

"Is it better to be alone and alive?" I ask. "Is it *wrong* that part of me wants to have gone with them below the ground?" I don't want to return to a time when no one hears my cries. No one was there to hear me when it mattered most. No one cared.

But, then I'm reminded...Nolan *was* there.

"I heard you," he admits. "I heard you that night, whimpering, after I watched your mother and grandmother leave. I was on my way to the castle, and there are always wolves, and you were too young to be out there alone. When I locked you in, I told myself I'd make you cry again if it meant you were there and hurting but still alive. Still safe, even if you were scared. One good thing. Because I had already given up on myself, I wasn't going to give up on you."

Part of me is glad, and it hurts to be glad. I shiver. "You survived that night."

"So did you."

My lips wobble. How must my face look, now that I'm letting myself *feel*. This ugly anger, the thing beneath it hurting, like when you're screaming in a dream without making a sound. All those who've ignored my voice—I want to make them feel the emptiness, the despair and helplessness when they most needed rescue.

Nolan's a story I want to keep reading, but I can't reconcile my new thoughts and days with him with the memories I now associate with him, now that he's admitted to being part of my darkest hours. He was the cause of them, partly. His claim that it was to protect me only makes it worse, because above the pain swirling is the possibility that he may be right. That him keeping me from the castle and the wolves that night kept me safe—and I feel sad that I lived, and they did not.

His expression has lost the sadness, filling with mostly worry and a tinge of hope. There's that hint of him that's impossible to resist, that makes it impossible for me to believe he intended to hurt me.

Trapping me...saved me. If that's true, then my perception of that night is backward.

Backward, like the hand we think we're raising in a mirror. It's wrong.

And for a breathless moment, snowflakes swirl upward and around us in a frozen embrace. Winter's bare fingers reaching for the lost sun lowered past the horizon, clinging to a losing fate. But then, I look up, and a snowflake floats before me. *What...?*

Nolan steps forward and keeps coming, enveloping me in his embrace as if I'm the one keeping him tied to the ground. I need to accept that regardless of those who *aren't* listening to me, there is someone who *is*. And it's him I should focus on. It hurts. Like starting on the wrong chapter, or the wrong page. Will I ever escape this feeling of being chased by this fear that I'm losing them, all over again?

Would that my doubts had drowned in sleet. But it's snowing, and it's pretty, and that feels wrong.

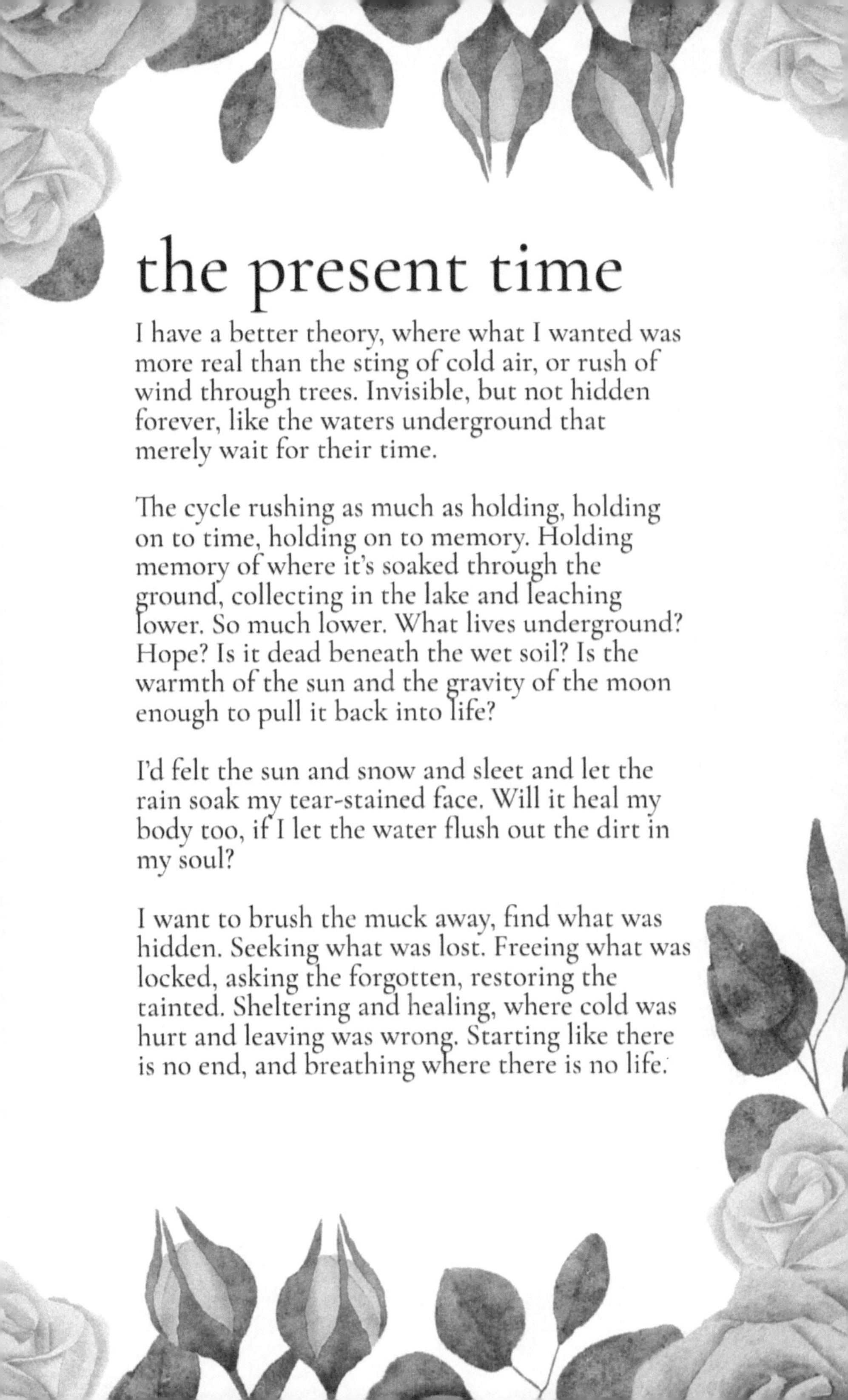

the present time

I have a better theory, where what I wanted was more real than the sting of cold air, or rush of wind through trees. Invisible, but not hidden forever, like the waters underground that merely wait for their time.

The cycle rushing as much as holding, holding on to time, holding on to memory. Holding memory of where it's soaked through the ground, collecting in the lake and leaching lower. So much lower. What lives underground? Hope? Is it dead beneath the wet soil? Is the warmth of the sun and the gravity of the moon enough to pull it back into life?

I'd felt the sun and snow and sleet and let the rain soak my tear-stained face. Will it heal my body too, if I let the water flush out the dirt in my soul?

I want to brush the muck away, find what was hidden. Seeking what was lost. Freeing what was locked, asking the forgotten, restoring the tainted. Sheltering and healing, where cold was hurt and leaving was wrong. Starting like there is no end, and breathing where there is no life.

The Deadly Chase

Moments later, Friday, in the white forest

ADJUSTING OUR EMBRACE, one arm holds me solidly against him, the other hand cupping the back of my head. A calloused finger brushes my hair from my wet cheek.

I choose to ignore reality for a moment. Ignore that he's this enigma to me, ignore that he's caught in the center of the storm trying to hurt my family. Instead, I memorize his strong arm bracing my back. Memorize the scent of never-fallen snow and citrus, as I press my face against the strong chest I'm leaning against. If I listen carefully, I feel his heartbeat. I memorize his grasping my waist, brushing my tears. How it feels, to be encircled and enclosed and safe.

How long can we ignore the future coming for us?

Fingers stiffen around mine as his hand runs down my arm, clasping my wrist and caressing my fingers. The air stills, snowflakes falling upon our shoulders in a hush. It's an unseasonal storm after the flowers begin to bloom—like that one there. A gorgeous apple tree that marks the path to the cabin—blossoms now dying as the buds fall with the snow. As the light of the forest dims, twilight descends and Nolan steps back, leaving me cold.

"I can't do this."

And in that second, my heart strings finally snap. Does he mean *us*? "What? I remind you of your past, yes? Well same! It's torturous—"

"Yes, torture. It's torture." He lifts up his hands and throws them down. I remember the sweet, uncomfortable way he tried to brush away my hair in the rain yesterday. His eyes blaze and his cheeks flush. "I don't care who you are or why we're doing this. This can't work because you'll end up hating me."

Hurt flows ice through my veins. "Then I guess I have nothing to say." I turn away.

A strong hand grabs my wrist, whipping me to face him again. "I have something to say to you. I don't *like* you. Your questions, your stubbornness—you make me rise to meet your challenges, and it means I can't be lazy or selfish, not the in the face of what you're willing to sacrifice for your father—though you should put yourself first, for once." His eyes are cold, like fury is cold, like passion chills away the fear that's left.

The ice is so cold it burns through my blood, pounding through me.

"I didn't want to, Paige. I don't want..." he repeats, eyes searching, but softer than the rejection I'd imagined. "It's always been you—I *love* you." His chest heaves with unspent energy. "I love you." I scoff, and he drops my hand. "How many times will I have to say it for you to hear it?"

Unspoken emotions light the fire between us, catching me unaware. Just like the flecks of snow that don't belong on the day before spring. "All this time, I'm not sure if you're pushing me away or protecting me—" My voice breaks.

"I love you so much I've felt ill, like something inside dies every time I can't kiss you. Every time I can't catch you—can't save you. Do you believe me now?" he begs, holding my arms as if I might run away. "What if I can't save you from this mess you're walking into? What if I hurt you again, like I hurt so many people that night?"

I shake my head, then nod, my eyes burning and my throat so tight that I couldn't say anything if I wanted to. Do I really want to know what Nolan did? No matter what, something deeper inside says another thing.

But I love him. I can't help thinking it. Repeat it, now that it feels real on my cold lips. Instead, I push back, like wind along the mountainside, undaunted.

"I will always protect you," he vows, a promise I wish I could believe. A tear slips down my cheek and the warm pad of his thumb brushes it away. "Even from myself."

No. I find my voice. "You tell me you love me and this—it sounds like goodbye. Or should I run away?" I could be a rose, thorns and all, as he stays back. A chill settles in my bones. Snow, on the day before the last day of winter. Falling, so thick, and suddenly very fast. "Will you just leave again—"

"I won't leave you now."

"What about later?"

"You are the most valuable treasure in my world. Ever since that night. It's always been you, and I will keep you safe." It's his past that's between us, and it kills me to have him not say it. "Please believe me," he rasps.

I step back at the force of his confession. I wanted love, but this? This is a storm, a blizzard, where up is down and the sky is falling and the whole world is bright and white with light. Night a mirror of day, a dizzying reflection. This mountain is the only thing that can contain him—Nolan's love is a *force*.

"You feel it too? *This*. There's more. All I care for is now, and all I care *about* is you." He is fervent and passionate. "This one second in time. Forget the rest, forget the past, forget the future. You and me."

No, never, and yes, always. His words echo around my throbbing heart. *Why should I love someone like you? Why torture my heart with this hope?* This aching hint of happiness is burning a hole in my chest. "How can I trust you after every time you hid the truth of the fire from me? How you still won't tell me *how* it happened?" I cough, but even I can hear it's forced and shallow, like the air in my lungs. The higher elevation, the dry air. I take out my puffer—*relief*.

"Every day this week, I wondered if you could know me enough now to forgive what I did then," he says, reaching for me, but I step away. "Then when you told me who you were—that this estate is yours by right more than any of my family? I should have been mad at you for lying to me, but it's a relief."

"Don't you think I am strong enough, or important enough, to tell me the truth? Doesn't it matter how I feel about you, too? How can I believe there's more for us if you can't leave the past? At least bring me there with you!"

His jaw hasn't dropped at my tirade. It's clenched in the opposite way. Not shocked. Or maybe shocked but covered with anger. Or maybe anger covering sooty ashes of guilt and sadness and sorrow. That's the thing between us, the past and pain deep enough to fill the mountains with bitter black drops.

Sorrow. Out of place in young lives, like snow in spring.

"You said it was your fault. Tell me *how* it was your fault. Tell me," I beg. "I'm strong enough to hear it." I may not be strong or brave in this moment, or big enough to carry the weight of the pages in this book. But now that I'm in it, the hurt in his story won't let me go. This chapter of my life is already so changed, I need to read on to reach the end. "Because it's too much—what more do you want from me if you can't tell me? What is this? What are we? What do you want? What!"

"Because I heard her die!"

"You—what?" History weighs on me, heavy like cold air, light as snowfall tickling my nose, memory sucking me toward the ground. My feet crunch pine needles and ferns as I back away.

"I was there, and I couldn't save her—your mother, or your grandmother. When the fire started—Darragh and I and our terrible friends were messing around with the cigars his dad brought us, burning old books in a barrel. Out on my balcony. But a curtain caught, and it was that simple. They rushed out, breaking windows as they went. They were drunk, and I couldn't stop them when it got out of hand." His voice is raw.

"We left, we all left, afraid to get caught. But I didn't get far, I already felt so guilty—I thought everyone would get out fine." He rubs a hand down his face, both of us soaked from the rain earlier and the snow just melting on our skin. "By the time I got back, most of the partygoers had gotten out... Then I heard the shouts. Your grandmother had somehow gotten your mother to the top of the stairs, but the banister was on fire and...and I think she was already unconscious." Sorrow lances his vocal cords, cauterizing his voice as if the fire were still burning inside him. "I couldn't get up to her quick enough," he repeats, "I didn't know how. I couldn't get to my parents either...the fire went through the newer section of the castle first and there was no way down. They were too high in the castle—a jump from those windows would've meant—" He closes his eyes. "They were up there to save me. To find me. Don't you see? It's not just all our fault—it's all *my* fault."

He turns on his heel and walks away, away from me, into the thick trees until he disappears.

I don't stay still for long. I run after him, the path he took disappearing through the woods. Snow falls heavily. White sky, white air, white ground. Needles on trees dark as black fingers, raking clawed accusations. Above and below, dazzlingly bright, and me, tripping and rushing like the only thing left living in the snowstorm's grasp.

I don't seethe, I don't accuse, I don't feel angry. I just speak to the sky and wander in the woods alone. "Nolan was there," I repeat to myself. "Nolan was at the cabin. Nolan saw my mother—" I don't feel anything but the cold and the woods. But my mother, she was in these woods, making her own decisions. Is this shock? Blistering words, alone and getting numb. He's one of those responsible for the pain in my heart that eclipsed all other hurts that day. Don't I deserve to blame him?

In my mind's eye, light is reframed from a mirror, making a grotesque mask of jagged edges over Nolan's face. Just now was the most *real* I've seen Nolan look. Instead of the fair, handsome young man who swept into my life with secrets and promises, he's been revealed as the central character in my nightmarish memories. Looking at the past through the mirror, with the castle and the fire and the threat of treasure beneath this mountain...

My soul used to feel dry without answers, but now it's caught fire, embers turning to flames along with Nolan. How would the mirror of the past—of truth—change me? How would I look under that unearthly spotlight?

Broken.

The branches sway above me, my breath comes short. I walk, for I can no longer run. His footsteps in the snow are already covered by fresh flakes. They shatter my hopes, and I should fear the elemental, frigid air, but all I can do is put one step before another. One word repeats itself, over and over.

Nolan.

I cry his name. I scream. I call and call and cry some more, until my feet fail and, staring at them, I fall like snow without wind to keep it afloat.

I don't see the ravine below—tumbling, voiceless and hoarse, I land hard against a birch tree, the wind knocked out of me as my back crashes against the trunk of the tree, cracking my head against the sandpaper bark of a broken branch. Agony at the back of my ribcage and slicing on the top of my head.

I touch my temple and forehead. My fingers are sticky. I wipe the red in the fresh snow coating the ground. The weeping hurts more, and I lay back, staring at the swiftly darkening sky. What once was white is darkening gray, every moment a touch darker.

Colder. Heat sears my back, and blood is warm where it's sticky, seeping through my hair. All else freezes—I'll freeze.

I'll die alone. Like my mother, here on the Hayes estate that generations ago was the right of our bloodline, Fairhavens swallowing us up in the shadow of the castle. Did the smoke clog her lungs as she spent her last breaths calling for help?

I shut my eyes. The forest was always meant to take me.

Then, a growl to my left. A reverberation, of unmistakable lupine sound.

Minutes later, in the White Forest

I HAVE NEVER stepped a foot off the path in these woods—that was my first mistake, looking at my feet and not the path ahead. I have never run through this forest. And yet...I have. With my mother, that night. I hated going to Grandmother's just like I hated the woods, because it meant my mother was leaving. I'd forgotten how in the weeks leading to that fateful night, my mother had left me with Grandmother before. Deep in the White Forest. Walking from the foot of the mountain. I hated being away from my mother, hated how my grandmother was so silent, so worried.

They fought so much.

HOWL.

This isn't the first time a wolf has followed me through the forest.

I get up and don't stop running. I press my hand to the back of my head to check where it throbs. Tacky, red, blood.

Once, I trip, my hand screaming when scrapes from last night catch me, but I push back up. A break at the treeline is all I need. In her diaries, my mother taught me the art of reading what's hidden between lines and words and spaces. Because she wasn't here for all these years, I became very good at it. She wasn't in my life to tell me her past, for I wasn't old enough to hear it before she died. All I had were the words she wrote me.

My mother looked back often. She described this place of her childhood as if it were magical, not a nightmare. Does hindsight make things so wrong, so different? But isn't that what a diary is? Looking back?

A crack, a husky breath? I risk a glance over my shoulder, but there's nothing to see. There's no glowing eyes through my dizziness, for there's no light to reflect off them. Musky dim hovers in grays and browns, and I move through it since I cannot get away from it. Grandmother's cabin can't be far.

And still, painfully still, the snow falls. Falling when it shouldn't.

Spring is tomorrow. Falling and swirling like it knows it will dissolve into nothing when it lands, turning the ground to mush and somehow still freezing the air.

WOOSH—sounds shatter the air like icy fingers of fear, as the wolf gives chase.

A lone wolf is the most dangerous, Nolan had said. Fear wants to hang on as every snagged branch on my coat snaps, and my feet slog and make too much sound. Can it smell my fear? It can, can't it? But because I read my mother's diary—because I read a *book*—I've been here before. There's something familiar. Frantic, I look up for the tall, strange, curved monkey tree, then the three half-stumps in a line marking the way home.

Just like she wrote.

I know the way. I know this story and how it ends. I run hard, and I keep low. My feet slip in the muddy snow—it isn't sticking and it isn't white. It's brown and dark and the world gets blacker and blacker, but I can't let the fear take all the light.

Just as I remember my flashlight in my bag, I find myself following a real light—flickering in the opposite direction of the sounds stalking me. I run like I've never run before, scrambling from the tree line to the clear space with an untarnished view of the snow-swept sky. Running on the forest floor my feet now recognize, Grandmother's cabin beckons—it's near the source of the light.

But the light...it's going the wrong direction. My steps falter. I sincerely hope Nolan heard the wolf, but if he comes looking for me—*I can't lose him.* I scream again, hoping against hope for him to return, but tingles break out on my skin when there's another howl at the same time as a voice, calling.

Hope pushes back, because it's *Nolan's* voice above the wind, calling my name. I follow his voice, which leads me to the light, and I stumble into a clearing—Grandmother's cabin.

Nolan rushes toward me, holding a blazing torch and shouting above the howling wind, "Get inside!"

I rush through the open space, feeling exposed and terrified as I push past. I stop inside the doorway and watch in horror as Nolan waits far too long for the wolf to approach, facing off against it, unyielding and strong and tall. In the second before it advances, he hurls the fiery torch in its face and sprints back to me, barricading us in the cabin as the wolf yelps in pain.

Moments later, in the abandoned cabin

WE CAN HEAR THE WOLF. First, it's a frenzy. Prowling around the cabin. Sniffing the rotted wood, hacking, banging at trash on the porch. My coughing seems to make it worse, as if it senses I'm weak.

SCRATCH—terror claws my heart at rabid snuffling and the crash of wood breaking.

"It's okay, it can't get in," Nolan reassures me in the dark. Not even his low voice can turn the raging in my heart down as I crumple in shock, clutching my bag and my scarf like they're the only thing between me and—

No. I'm safe.

There is no light but the reflections off the snow-full clouds outside. Huge, wet snowflakes make the sky slightly brighter through dust-caked windows. That meager hum, a bleak memory of light, is the lighter Nolan uses to look around. Ignoring the sounds of the wolf outside, he barricades the doors with old furniture and braces an end table above the kitchen window. He finds a single citronella candle, which sparks until he wipes it with a cloth and hands it to me with a tight smile. He takes yet more cloth and wraps it around another candlestick, dousing it with fluid from an old carton. At my curious expression, which must look terrified and comical behind the awful-smelling candle, he huffs a laugh.

"I've always been good with fire," he explains, "and vegetable oil dousing does the trick." For all his confident words, his voice is strained. He makes me settle beside him on the ground, our backs to the wall with us facing the door. "I'll leave this here, just in case." Belatedly, I realize he'd used the same trick earlier with a matching candelabra to create a makeshift torch. "It's going to be okay, he'll leave soon."

I am in awe of his fearlessness, that defiance. He kept me safe tonight, and he isn't done. The promise is in his hand reaching for mine, his steady breathing, his eyes watchful. Just like he kept me safe before.

I need him to hear this. "Thank you for telling me everything. You kept me safe then and I didn't know it, but I am thankful now." I mean it, though my voice breaks. "You came back, that night, and none of those other boys did." I don't ask why he didn't try harder to save my mother—how cruel would I be, when I know him now. When that night he was torn between finding his parents, saving my grandmother and mother collapsed on the floor above, fleeing with all the guests while his friends abandoned him...

A nightmare.

He would never *not* give his all. It's because he did—does—care, with all his soul and strength—that he covers the loyal nature with arrogance and detachment. No, my accusations now wouldn't be fair. He was young, he was so much more than a child at fourteen, but how much can one blame a wayward teen? And no person that young should be responsible for the terrible choices adults make, nor the consequences. My mother knew the danger, which is why she went after my grandmother.

Saving someone sounds worthy.

We can't protect each other from what happened in the past. But I will not hurt Nolan anymore. I will not put that guilt and shame on him. Not for another second. I take a breath and it's lighter, like the air is brighter. But he remains unmoving against my side, breaths deep as tension rolls through his body.

I whisper to him, "It isn't your fault."

He hangs his head, shadows and candlelight flitting across his face. "It is."

Letters are their own language. Lies twist them. But lies aren't everlasting. Brokenness and decay cannot overcome beauty and truth. Compassion is also its own language. Mercy fuels it, fuels my words for him and much as for me. "You've punished yourself long enough. I know you—you did not intend for anyone to get hurt. And my mother…she went there on her own. Her choice. You have to stop blaming yourself. I don't."

"If you say so." The rumble from his low, rough-hewn voice comforts me.

"Good." I tug the strap of my book bag and tuck it to my other side, grimacing at the pain at the back of my head now that the danger is less immediate. "I have a flashlight."

"Save it," he grumbles. "We've locked ourselves in a dodgy structure with a wolf dogging our scent, and you say things are good?" Worry snatches the end of the question mark, worry that he's trying to hide. "Why now?" He lets his head thud against the wall behind us. "Why did this happen? Why did this have to happen?"

"I don't know," I whisper, as if there were an answer I could give if I searched long enough or delved deep enough.

But he doesn't feel what I feel. I've been afraid before, but while running home should be the first hope for someone, I never had that. The need to run, yes. But *where* to run? The house I shared with my distant but loving father never felt safe, because I never felt heard. This week it wasn't even an option. It was cold and dark and empty. Silent. But with Nolan, I know he hears me. He *heard* me. He's with me, now.

Home is no longer where I thought it was. It isn't behind me, in the past. It's here, right in front of me. Nolan turns to face me.

"You're here," I whisper as freezing wind whips around our shelter from the cold, once forgotten and long abandoned, but now lifesaving.

A wild force tethers us, from a dark, craggy space beside my lungs to his broad, heaving chest. Does the line my love draws find an end somewhere deep near his heart? Is fate this simple? This painful? Can a single thread tie us together?

"You have my heart," he says at last, and I know he feels it too—this bond forged in snow and ice melting into spring, finally giving in to warmth so flowers grow with winter forgotten.

"My mother said something in her diaries that always struck me. I think it's why I wanted to study stories by working in the library. She said, 'A whole person's life of victory or tragedy can be summed up in a book. Sad, how such a long journey called life can be passed over in a single line.'" I sniffle, then go on. "Every time someone told me how sorry they were, or when friends teased that she left because we didn't have a grave for her...it reminded me of that single line. She's still worth more than that single line, *everyone* is. With her gone, I think I made it my mission to go into all the books I could and find those lines and give them the honor of reading them and remembering them, no matter how short they were."

He takes the candle and sets it aside, then kneels before me. "With everything you know about me, with the hold you have on my heart, only you have the power to hurt me. Only you can keep me safe."

What can I do? In the face of love, sheer, untamed, and fierce, I'm afraid. But there's something beneath the fear. Something above and behind and below it, circling like snow, falling like it's flying. Soaring, this *something* bursting in my chest, making my heart race in a crashing cadence unlike the restless, rushed, running rhythm that led me here. Heat bursts from my collarbone beneath my red scarf and it reminds me of the hot, red emotions I'd felt while tearing through these white woods, this fair forest so pure, so pristine, so filled with memory frozen in time.

Memory I haven't been able to let go of.

It's awe, awakening my mind to the beauty of branches bent with white weight. It's pretty really, the memories between us no longer crushing, like snowfall covering the branches with a layer of soft white.

I'm awestruck, blinking and delightfully alive, cold, yet burning from the inside.

We are aligned, face to face, with that thin line between our hearts pulled taut. But I am brave, and I am bold. I let my fingers trace his jaw. Both of my hands in his hair, drawing him closer, until his intake of breath against my lips gives me life and I kiss him. Pulling him to me, baring every secret I've disguised behind all the words I've read instead of spoken, I tell him.

You are loved.

One of his hands braces the wall behind me as the other moves beneath my scarf, cupping my neck ever-so-gently and tilting me to him. Passion engulfs me as my hands can't still, cradling his face, bracing myself against his shoulders as we taste one another. Like we crave each other's air, like there is no disguise or ugliness or beauty, but only truth in our touch.

As you are, you are loved.

He pauses and pulls back from another hurried kiss and hides his face against the front of my neck, breathing heavily until a small huff escapes. Our laughter becomes one gentle release of tension until he kisses me again, hard and short on a smile, and we hold each other like the world is spinning the wrong direction and our embrace on our knees is the only thing keeping us tethered to the earth.

His arms spread around me, a fortress. Not the abandoned citadel, crumbling from neglect but still imposing, impenetrable...the castle keep is now a shelter. He encloses me in safety. Nothing outside these castle-like walls could touch me. Solid and sure, his heart beats beneath my forehead and I close my eyes as the weight of his strength encloses me.

It isn't a trap, it isn't prison, it isn't fear keeping me here. It's love.

I won't leave you.

Neither will I.

Instead of night, behind my eyes, I see starlight. A dream like day dawning on a once-ruined castle of stone, long beaten, now burning gold and ruby against a rushing indigo sky, fading, fading, into the bursting rays of morning bright.

Love is a fortress, and nothing can overcome it.

THE WHITE SNOW

In the abandoned cabin, the next morning, Saturday

H AS THE NIGHT ALREADY PASSED? I breathe deep and feel pressure on my chest, unwilling to open my eyes.

Heaven's child, it's simply a storm. It's like Grandmother's voice, scolding with a hint of a smile, all at once. It's a memory that isn't real, but one I wanted to have.

"Just because there are clouds doesn't mean there was a storm," Mother wrote on the bottom of every page of her diary, an echo of the contented soul of Rose in her love letters, in those red envelopes generations ago. I never understood it. I used to think that if I wrote on the bottom of every page in a diary, I'd write. "Somewhere, there's always a storm." Now, I want something better to say: "storms never last," or "there's sunshine, somewhere."

Time can feel like a spell, but it isn't. Days can drag or fly and sunlight can lie where forests hide in shadow. As if the day ends before it should. The sun tarrying in its rising. But the day doesn't cut off the living, and the sunrise finds the horizon nearest. It rises. The sun always rises.

I inhale, sense the presence with me. Exhale, feel his warmth. Someday and somewhere are out there. If we are willing to search long and far enough, perhaps our faith in that always-rising will become unshakable.

Nolan and I held each other through the night, our coats and hearts and the single candle the only fire to keep us warm. He held my hand while the snow fell outside, until moonlight broke through the swift clouds. Nolan was calm, unafraid, humming a song I'd never heard before that I wish never to forget. His affection, like the dawning light of morning, and the spice of his manly scent with a hint of lemon and warm cotton, enveloped.

And my heart, burning, not smothered, breaking free. Because we survived, and when the sun finds its way through the treetops to dawn on this lost cabin in the woods, the world is peace. Snow white, like flowers bright. He *stayed*, and it feels like all that matters. Like nothing remains to stoke fear, not this morning.

It's so bright when I open my eyes, Nolan's arm warm across my middle and his head heavy against my shoulder. My backside is sore from the wood floor—at some point he stopped being my pillow and I became his.

The wound on my head hurts more, but my heart hurts less. I used my mother's scarf as a blanket on our laps, a vivid ruby hue in the dim cabin of medium brown wood and ratted tan rugs. I'm blinking at memories of years spent here, and somehow the rooms feel smaller, the ceiling closer. There's a blinding shaft of dawn-light, which glances from the window to a full-length mirror set against the corner, partially shrouded in a dirty white sheet. In its reflection, Nolan's face is smooth. No act, no mask. The arrogance becomes innocence, and the cynicism is smoothed away.

I brush his hair from his forehead—it's now familiar, wild,

blond hair coarse and stock straight—my pulse quickening at the memory of our kiss last night. I don't think any words best describe it except that the passion we shared was a promise. Something as simple as a kiss, and it said more than words ever could. Devotion. Adoration. Apology. *Mercy.*

Mercy is the closest to goodness I've felt in my life. The most like love. Now that I've felt the freedom of pouring it into my passion for Nolan, I want it to color my life, as if the red scarf is more alive than the drab, forgotten hues of the cabin's interior. I want the merciful red to cover everything in my life.

I look beyond the boarded-up windows, thankful for Nolan's quick thinking and protection last night. The wolf must be gone, and the wind has died, and the bright sun came up as if the storm clouds from last night were a bad dream. Winter, becoming spring. The sun, always rising. Even on a cloudy day it's there, breaking through the haze and sliding past the horizon steady as clockwork.

Annoying, intrusive, obligatory clocks with unreadable symbols and roman numerals. That's why we use them to tell time. Because the only time that matters is the present. So even if bronze clocks in far-off, tall castles might be broken, time is still going. Sometimes it needs an eccentric like my father to keep it ticking, and sometimes it goes on with ferocious tenacity.

I shake a drowsy Nolan awake, the dear, tired lump of a wonderful person who the world might soon discover is the steward's son returned. But the world might not care if I tell Gabreville Council who *I* am, instead.

Now I know what I need to do.

THE TRUER LOVE

Three hours later, in the white forest, the first day of Spring

NOLAN AND I ASCEND THE MOUNTAIN—after we went to the manor house to freshen up, he'd agreed that we had to hurry before Lenora came looking here on the first day of spring.

Our time was up.

It feels like we're always going up, but I desperately yearn to, and dread, going below. We spend an hour in the castle library, comparing the psalter my father gave me to the *Oirdera* maps I'd painstakingly copied. I tell Nolan everything I'd heard when my grandmother and my mother fought on the night of the fire, and everything my father told me of my family's sad history. I show him one of my great-great-grandmother's letters and the proof that I truly am the heir, to which he smiled and kissed me thoroughly.

Nolan draws a basic layout of the citadel with all the rooms and servant passages he knows—stealing a kiss or two in between. Our kisses sizzle between us, drawing fingers to brush and eyes to linger until I push his laughing self away and tell him to advise me from more than arms' reach away. Then we check all seven passages marked on my mother's map in the embroidered psalter. Except, there are only six dead roses on her map. I recognize the names of deadly sins inscribed below each: pride, lust, envy, gluttony, sloth, wrath. The detailed depictions from her map are perfectly aligned when compared with the map from the *Oirdera*, except for the seventh one that's missing: greed.

The women of the Ludovici line. Seven generations hiding, indeed.

We explore one passage near the library door, another in the kitchen, one more on the ground level near the ballroom. There's one beneath the grand staircase and one directly at the top. And the sixth at the end of the hallway where the bedrooms once were. That part is quiet, and I hold Nolan's hand against the memories and silence. But nothing. We go up and down, and the servants' stairs lead nowhere. It's exhausting, all the stairs and knowing we're missing one.

Back in the library after lunch, Nolan falls asleep on the leather couch, more satisfied after the meal Mrs. Lucas forced us to come home to the gatehouse and eat.

Be our guest, she'd said. *Breakfast this morning wasn't enough for you two to recover from last night*. She had not been okay with my running off yesterday evening, and she wouldn't let me leave this morning without eating a ginger cookie. She fixed up the cut on my head. Replaced the bandage on my hand and pressed a mug of herbal tea upon me. Her worry was sweet, and she'd cleaned my boots and coat while I showered, dear woman.

But after a morning wasted staring at sketches of maps and finding passages through doors that tell me *nothing*, I hardly touched my lunch. Sustenance is a recurring pain, and with my father's confirmation that tunnels and treasure are real...I was barely able to eat or drink, not wanting to enjoy Mrs. Lucas' comforting presence or Martin's jokes—the poor man can't stand a hint of awkward or uncomfortable. There was a fear of the unknown keeping me awkward, and I pulled back before the sweet older couple as they nourished our bodies and tried to encourage our souls before we returned to the castle, promising to cover for us if any nefarious extended family arrived.

All I know is right now, I want answers, and they're *here*. But time is running out. Declan might act immediately and dangerously now that he knows Nolan's back. The threat of either of us proving our identity will infuriate him, when he finds out the truth. *Why does it feel like our lonely haven on the mountain is about to shatter?*

And since when did I start thinking of this place as safe?

Since the tension broke between us last night, I'm constantly trying to be nearer to Nolan—staying close to his side by choice, because how I feel for him has to be stronger than fear. After lunch, when we crossed over the stone mosaic on the road up to the crumbling front doors, he'd held my hand and laughed into my hair and his teeth flashed in a rare, wide smile.

But not even tea and lunch have calmed my nerves, for we can only guess that one passage must have been unknown to my mother. The seventh rose—the rose that should be—isn't on the map. It's missing.

What if history isn't where my mother thought it was?

I linger by the library mirror, where we found the other *Oirdera*.

But no rose magically appears on the maps when I hold them up to the window-light, which dims as the afternoon progresses.

Nolan is still sleeping, peaceful, as if it isn't his life his uncle is after. Long legs crossed and propped over the armrest, brown leather boots dangling, arms crossed over his chest, forehead smooth in slumber. I'm jealous. But I take a moment to stare at him in the soft afternoon light here on the first day of spring—when did those dark clouds outside return? Had they ever really left?

He isn't a beastly reflection of the people in the past who were driven by greed—I know that now. I believe it with all my heart. He's willing to give it all up, surrender the rights to a mine that could produce wealth beyond imagining. If he didn't think someone like Declan or Lenora Hayes would take it, maybe he would step forward. But he wants me to, instead. Our impasse hasn't been solved by the silences that his lips covering mine kept causing. We fought again about it earlier, but the promise that we would search together soothed nonetheless. Because we agree on one thing.

Good people need to hold on when evil fights for the same prize.

My shoulders rise and the tension in them reminds me that I've spent fruitless hours poring over maps that do not make sense together or apart—

Boom. A rumble of thunder. Close enough to feel in my chest. I drop the papers, covering my ears. A storm is coming. And I just realized that it's my perspective that needs to change. The maps. I'm looking at them too closely. Suddenly, I know how to unlock the secrets of the incomplete map. It isn't how, it's *where.*

I press a kiss to the air and leave Nolan asleep in the library. I miss him when he's asleep, because I want to tell him so much more. I miss him, now that I know all he'd done to save me, when I was young and didn't know what dangers lurked in the forest. I miss him, now that I've come to know him enough to see that his heart isn't twisted or greedy like I'd thought. It's private, like everything about him, but it isn't dark.

Placing away my papers and putting my book bag over my shoulder, I accidentally brush the leaves of the dead fern in the kintsugi pot. At my touch, the fragile ends become dust, and I'm sorry I was the one to have made their death so final.

Through the stained-glass door, I enter the cool, dim hallway. The sun is gone in the deep halls of the old castle, the rose-and-gold-tinted windows empty of colored rays.

Something different than royal blood flows through my veins. We never had royalty here in Gabreville. We had a council. Long ago, they must have hated the Lords of the Citadel who controlled the wealth from the mine on their land. For a century and a half, there's been a guardian to keep the power of wealth in check—the Hayes family. I can't believe I'm admitting it, but here I am. Not everything they did or stood for was wrong.

Regardless of whatever happened in the Dark Year, the Hayes family *did* steward the mine as Gabreville grew. Gabreville prospered, without a monarchy. The Hayes might have had some right to take away the citadel from my ancestors, and I don't know if I blame them for that anymore. It's unclear to me if they were more just, more able to control the greed that blackens hearts. Here, in the West Wing, I'm seeing that the only thing my blood is colored by, is the greed of my family, who dug too greedily and brought disaster upon their own heads. If I want to figure out how deep they went to hide their greed, I must ascend to the highest point.

I trespass through the forbidding West Wing. It's darker, without many windows. What ones remain unbroken are darkened with clouds. I don't know if I've ever seen clouds this black. Storms like that should stay in the night..

BOOM!

Thunder rattles the windowpanes and the doors. It's like the storm is coming just for me for being where I shouldn't, for looking for what I shouldn't, for reading what I shouldn't, for *asking* what I shouldn't.

I step over the fallen soldiers that used to line this hall of power. All the broken glass, the toppled side tables, the debris that makes avoiding tripping nearly impossible. In the hallway of doors, there is no Nolan calling out to stop me. I peer into the rooms. The tree-faced door has a destroyed desk and many lamps—a study. The next is a conference room, slitted mountain-faces carved into the door symbolizing the leaders of the mountain, wielding power from behind closed doors. Now, the chairs are broken and burned, and the table cracked in two from a fallen ceiling beam. There's a guard here like the one downstairs—the only one with a spiked plume on the helmet. The whole place is this...husk. Dead chaff broken off. This shell of memory, keeping in the stench.

This room is blackest, for it's where the fire that consumed a castle began. Out on that balcony, Nolan said. Before, I wanted to be brave. To say I wasn't afraid of the dark. But I am afraid, so I need to face it. I need to face the storm, the greed, the memory—I pause and see the barrel still out on the balcony, charred. This fire didn't purify, it simply consumed. I know now why he didn't want me here.

I step out of the room, footsteps crunching on I-don't-want-to-know-what, no longer needing to dwell on the past. It smells bad and will choke me if I remain too long. I always thought that these special doors must be sign-posts, if the tunnels were real. But the marker for the right path might not be on a door. The rose emblem of my family is somewhere. I think I've seen it every day, treaded on it, ignored it.

I pass a final room. It's the door with long, sad flower faces. Not sunflowers, or peonies. No, nothing whimsical or summer-like. These are ice-roses, wooden figures of thorny stems and narrow-faced petals that droop under the weight of privilege and entitlement.

Another crack of thunder. I run, but keep my ears covered as I enter the servants' stair to the West Wing's tower.

Up, up, up.

I dislike windowless spaces, hate not seeing the world around me. Surrounding stone on the stairs—an unforgiving, lifeless gray pallor—and my breath comes too narrow on air too thin. Empty, fruitless nausea turns my stomach, the sick feeling making my head light as I ascend.

Maybe I should have woken Nolan. He wouldn't have wanted me to be alone.

My wrists weaken and my fingertips begin tingling, aches shuddering through my upper arms, gut clenching, dark fear slicing through my veins. The same dark fear that brings my heart to its knees. Like the first time I came here, I hate feeling like I've done something wrong, when I'm trying to do the right thing. The emblem of my ancestors, the crests inside the set of books making the *Oirdera*—and that book in the university library that pointed the way. Each person in our past is worth more than the single line they were given.

What will the letters form for the words of this part of the story?

Just minutes later, outside on the castle's highest balcony

NOWHERE IN THE CITADEL has a balcony as high as the one here. How high will I have to climb to find how deep the sin of my ancestors went? The west turret is open, the stone drains never clogged with detritus. The castle reigns over the forest here, high above the trees. I'd seen this balcony many times while walking up the long drive, and with Nolan's basic layout of the castle, I finally knew the way to get here.

I didn't ask him to come, because his voice tightened when he sketched this area of the map earlier. It's the height.

And...I didn't want him following me until I knew for certain that the dark side of the fairytale was *here*. I stuff the hand-drawn maps into my pocket and close the buttons of my coat—it's prob-ably going to rain, and I don't want to ruin them. I slam my shoulder twice against the old door at the top of the stairs, and the hinges creak before releasing me outside. I look out on an expanse of endless treetops, disappearing into dark clouds. The air crackles with energy as I turn my gaze down, to the ground beyond the imposing citadel the gates. There, below, far below, is the Ludovici symbol: the rose and hammer motif immovable and untouchable, written in stone.

Stonework, creating a motif on the very ground we trod upon, a mirror of the design on the locket, that aligns with the crest and vines of the combined *Oirdera*, that aligns with the map from my mother with the black-drawn roses of despair. This is it. The seventh rose.

In my mind's eye, I hold up the map from the psalter. Now, everything lines up. The direction of the halls, the location of the mine below the castle, angling down the mountain. I can't quite see the edge of the motif on the ground below, so I step—very scared and very carefully—between the turrets and hold on tight. Below, the storm batters the trees, turning them to war against one another and tearing off early blooms and leaves.

The Ludovicis hid the key to the map in plain sight, before the White Castle itself. Lies so loud they're beneath the first steps you take into Fairhavens, the first thing you see as you enter the castle.

This, my inheritance. A white rose, when the rest are black.

I gasp freezing air. There's no rain yet, only the thunderstorm surrounding the imposing, silent castle. Silent, against the wind of time and seasons thrust upon it. Silent, confronting neither good nor evil in unmoved stonemasonry, wordless, yet witness to history.

The white rose of the Ludovici line, the seventh rose, when all my mother's map showed were six black roses. Will this seventh, white rose lead us to our deaths, or is salvation the pure petals of promise?

Leaning so far to see the ground below, full of fear at the low rumble in the clouds, promising nature's anger—*BOOM!*—I forget where I am, lifting my hands from the immovable stone to cover my ears and losing my balance, screaming and crying for the unfinished end.

But before I fall, strength wraps around me in corded arms.

"I've got you," Nolan assures. His grip is desperate but firm around my waist and across my chest. Warmth surrounds me and relief makes me sag as he drags me back and we fall to the solid floor of the balcony. He grunts at the impact but doesn't let me go. The force of his strength is steadfast, though his hands are shaking as he pulls me up to prop us both against the wall. "You're okay. It's okay."

"You're here." My breath is a fog in front of my face. "You're here." I gasp my words, fear seeping out with the air through my freezing lips. I could have fallen. Far, so very far. Hope and amazement soar through my veins, pulling me down, lifting me up.

I start crying. He's afraid of heights, yet he came here to find me.

Once I've caught my breath and my heartbeat returns to normal, my mind registers the strength in his arms and the intimacy of his hold across my body. He's keeping me from falling, even as the danger has passed, and I don't want to leave the safety of his embrace.

Never.

The thought nearly strangles me. It's consuming me too quickly. *He's* consuming me.

It's all happening so fast.

And I feel shame—smaller and stupider—like I've always been teased to be. Bold and brave, or stupid? We're six—*seven?*—stories up in this tower. How is he okay with these heights?

I leave his arms with a jerking motion. Facing him, and needing to face what's going on inside. Needing to face myself, reflected in his eyes, which lock on mine in an uncertain silence in the crackling moment after thunder roars again, too close.

His hands wrap around my wrists, his fingers shaking, my own hands locked against my ears, against the sound. Emotion burns in his red-rimmed eyes, molten gold in his gaze. His voice rasps loudly over the storm, "How far will you go for this treasure? Are you crazy?" He drops my hands and ducks his head, his hands visibly shaking, roughing the scruff on his neck, begging to be touched—but I don't know if I deserve this desire to love or to be his comfort anymore.

I shake my head, my hair sweeping out in a gust of wind. He feels the same as me, and I hate it. "You didn't force me into anything. I chose this. I'm still choosing this." My heart whispers something about choosing him, always choosing him, but I stifle it with a squeeze of my shut eyes. Then I open them. "I found it, Nolan. I know where to go."

Something flashes through his expression, and it might've been lightning.

I lift my chest with a shallow breath. It doesn't feel like enough, not after the fear of falling, the split second when I thought I was dying. Not after a life of running from the pain inside while I sat, stock still, reading, reading, reading and pretending like the pain wouldn't turn to rot.

Pretending a thing wasn't there never made it so.

The cool of possibility shoots through my upper arms, tingling with the electric prospect of hope and risk, unable to see the difference between them. Just as how sometimes, I can't see the difference between raindrops and snowflakes. But my heart knows. They are different, each one of them.

Just because I can't see it doesn't mean it isn't so.

Can I break free of it? This old pain, the diamond-tipped dagger passed from generation to generation, doing this to him, doing this to me. I raise a hand to Nolan's face, feeling the scruff against my fingertips as he leans in and closes his eyes. Our calm in the storm.

Belatedly, I swipe tears from my jaw as rain begins pounding down. So quick, every blink releasing a feeling so like joy, it reminds me of sorrow. In this moment, between him and I, I don't know if they're truly any different. I can almost hear my mother, and if she were here, I hope she'd agree. This story needs a chance to figure out the ending, and no storm will stop me.

"Come on. We both know they're coming. Lenora won't delay. But I'll follow you anywhere." Nolan pulls me inside the narrow staircase, out of the downpour. Thunder rumbles and I freeze at the top of the stairs, my lungs shuddering, adrenaline fading and restarting memories of Grandmother's cabin. Inside is a storm, a deluge, engulfing—

"Nolan, I'm so sorry. I was so stupid—"

"It's okay." He shuts the door behind us, shutting out the storm, reaching for me. "I'm here." His arms enfold me, and I hide my face again in his chest, my forehead against the skin of his neck as he whispers soft words of love and kindness and my fear slips down, down, down.

How can anyone deserve even a second of such happiness? How can a body contain the delight of love returned in the adoring gaze of another? His feelings and mine will swallow us whole and I don't know where that river goes—how deep or wide that ocean is.

It's a little frightening, but I want to dive in. I shake my head, sniffing.

"I love you." His hand is cupping my jaw, wiping more tears. "But you can leave now, if you want. No one knows you're the heiress. You can go back to your father. Be safe, far away from this place." A sad smile touches his lips, and the dormant part of my heart he's brought alive responds.

But I can't say it, not like I did in the cabin. I *love* him. So much it hurts. But will he love me if we find the treasure—treasure that's torn families apart before? Will he love me if I insist upon this course, no matter how dangerous it gets? Descending below, to find the threads of the story, no matter what?

"I love you," he says, lips moving against my hair, his husky voice rasping and ripped through with resignation and the cold. "I love you." It's a plea. "I love you." A promise. "I love you." I shut my eyes and let his voice fall over me like a rush of wind.

I'm too afraid to say it back, but with my eyes still closed, I whisper the inevitable words that will lead us to the next chapter.

"I know how to get into the mine."

The Enchanted Mirror

In the castle library, Saturday afternoon

THE STORY OF BOOKS IS LONG. But the longer story isn't books, it's lives. They leave pages when they end. Like every letter of their days had a memory, pages of history make forgotten books, letter by letter, line by line.

I've never been here in my life before this week, but no longer can I deny that it's like walking through a museum of my mother's worries come to life, my grandmother's fears in a glance, and the secrets of all the women before me, come to light.

It begins with the design on the doors in the portals at the gate. The rose, on the ground beneath it. Roses on doorways, in palm-sized, stone-carved secrets marking hidden passages. Roses blooming as they used to, in the gardens tended by loving groundskeepers. Roses, even in the stitching on the tapestry above the human-sized fireplace in the ballroom hall, half-scorched, but sturdy. Like how Nolan kept me in the air, saving me from falling.

I stand in front of the library mirror, Nolan at my back and surely curious as to why I hesitate, since before I was so eager, so sure of myself. Why do I want to wander in the woods and through the leaves of pages in the library? How is it their call feels so similar?

When he first removed this mirror from the wall, I asked him to do it quickly, without question. This time, I stare and count to three, then count to three one more time, for good measure and for courage. When I nod, he moves toward the mirror. With a grunt and a heft, the mirror slides out, more easily than before, and he deposits it to one side. We stare at the empty stone shelves. It looks like another dead end.

But it isn't.

For a small second, I swear I smell apple blossoms, and I lift the locket and cradle it in my palm. "This is it."

Mother's locket proves that my grandmother was the great-great-granddaughter of Lord Ludovici's hidden daughter. Him, the Marquis of Gabreville, holder of the seat on Gabreville Council that was left empty *only* for one who could prove her blood. Which makes me further, and newer on the family tree, but attached to the rotting branches all the same. Nolan is the steward, yes, but my mother—and myself—are the line with the oldest claim to this mountain. This forest. This castle. Whatever sparkles beneath the ground.

I'm unsure if I should claim it, the gems, or gold that my grandmother died to find and my mother died trying to smother. That night, they knew the halls would be filled with strangers at the party. An abandoned mine, bereft of workers, smelters, laborers. A society party, a traditional ball on the eve of spring. Then evening fell, and the storm crashed on a spring night that should have been forgotten on regular society pages worth skipping.

A single line tells a whole story. A line which is stronger. It's older. It's truer. It's *mine*. In the picture of my mother in the locket, she's *also* wearing the locket. Is that our curse, to be chained to these roses? It's a confusing parallel, infinity in a mirror. A story I don't know, a story I've *always* known. It's keeping greed beneath the ground where it should stay. It's truer love, to die to keep others safe.

The locket. It's the literal key. "It must be here," I whisper. I stand before the mirror, propped against the wall, tracing the designs that match the locket on the very top. I peer at the stone in the exposed cleft. Peering above the topmost shelf, and *there*. A faint notch, a perfect match.

"This library matches the white rose in the stonework outside, but we were certain there was no tunnel here..." I may have nearly died in order to see the maps we'd collected reflected on the stonemasonry of the ground beneath the castle's gates. But I'm glad now, because finally, I think we've found it.

Nolan is quiet when I raise my gaze. Hope, burning. An angel afire, hair lit in a halo, all gold, truly the only warmth in the overcast world around us. "It's here?" he asks.

I remove the locket from around my neck, the chain tangling in my hair and the strap of my book bag across my chest. "The lost passage."

I untangle the locket and hold it against the indented shape. Just like in the center of the iron gate, far below. It fits this recessed stone, and as I press the locket into the embrace of a fissure in the stone, something clicks and I collapse forward.

Nolan snatches me by the waist as the shelves move in a violent, slow swirl of dust and creaking stone. As he pulls me aside, we knock the mirror over and it shatters, breaking, breaking, breaking. Because eventually, old foundations fracture, and the moving aside of the shelves made the wall a *door*. A narrow passageway descends to blackness, like all the old servant passages. But here, there's a cast-iron lever on the inside, and instead of a narrow hallway, a dark chasm opens before us in an echo of breath and unimaginable depth.

THE LIVING COFFIN

The same breath, in the tunnels

A TUNNEL BENEATH THE CASTLE, behind the hidden door in the old library emblazoned with my family crest. The way of the enchanted mirror, the white rose.

Nolan's hand brushes the painted, unfaded petals along the walls as they mark our descent down the stairs at intervals. These seem bleak, these black roses guiding our steps. And that's not just because it's getting dark.

There's something closer than memory stirring inside me. It's the pain of not understanding my mother, for all the times I've pored over her diaries. The rotting of doubt coats the bottom of my heart like ash, the taste bitter on my tongue as we descend down the solid stones to the black beneath the castle. It's familiar in a way that a story coming to a close finds the page turning on the exact moment we expect it. But in this, I'm the heroine, and I have no one to follow. Now, no one knows the way below ground.

Doesn't mean I won't try.

At the edge of the light, at the bottom of the first descent, the scents change. It's damp here, and smells of dirt. The floor is different, too. Wood now, rickety wood that echoes and creaks and feels entirely unstable. Nolan mutters about engine oil, pitching his voice low. I hear the strain, but then his voice evens out when he announces he's found wire cutters. He takes off his button-up, leaving just a white T-shirt beneath, and wraps the it around the top of the cutters.

I reposition my book bag across my chest and pull out a flashlight. "What are you doing?" Artificial brightness replaces the muted light, casting bigger shadows.

Nolan douses the cloth of his shirt with caramel-colored grease. "This can was sealed. I figured we'd find engine oil for the mine carts"—he points in a direction which I follow with my flashlight, and there it is, a narrow track and wheeled car full of ore—"for those." With a flick of his hand, he lights the new makeshift torch. We smile at each other.

There's no sign of any wreckage yet, not like it appears at the mine's outer entrance where my father went when he was sad. We skirt the minecart, and Nolan leads us down the long passageway. Heroine or not, he seems to know this place better that I ever could. I happily let him lead, my flashlight pointed to the ground. Before I can ask my burning questions, he stops and turns to me, the flame-light used by humans for millennia flashing before his caramel eyes. The torch illuminates his cheekbones, sharp with worry. But his eyes flash with humor.

"To answer your inevitable question, yes. I sneaked down here as a kid, before the collapse that year before the fire. It's still unstable, especially on this side. The equipment was my favorite part." His voice catches. "My dad used to let me take rides when I was little."

I smile weakly, resting the top of my much more recently invented torch against my chin. "That's sweet. But if you say that question was inevitable, it's only because of your troublemaking nature."

He looks to the side. "It's one of my best memories with him. He'd push me, and show me all the tools…" A heavy pause. "I had no idea there was an entrance from within the castle itself. Did my father know? What else didn't he tell me?" With his free hand, he musses his hair. "I never knew why the mine was shut. I don't know what we'll find."

I take his hand. "We'll be all right. Trouble like you knows how to get out of trouble, I'm sure."

He smirks, and suddenly all I want to do is turn out the lights and kiss him. Nolan's eyes darken, but suddenly, he grabs my hand and steps away from the wall. I hurry to catch up to his long strides, thankful for batteries and the modern bulb lighting the ground before my feet. "What's wrong? What is it?"

He takes five more steps before responding. "I don't know. You believe in this myth, this treasure, but now that we're down here I'm not sure." He squeezes my hand even tighter. "I thought I saw…"

I sigh at his silence, waiting as he stops and listens, unsure if I want to hold onto faith or let the dream go. He lets my hand go and lifts his forefinger, pointing to the air.

I whisper, confused. "What?"

"The dust."

"We're in a mine." But then I see it. The dust seems…alive.

"Watch it, it's dancing," he says in a voice so low, I nearly miss it. I step closer, needing to feel the length of him beside me. Then he turns to face the direction we came, moving his body to a defensive position before mine. "Stay behind me."

I listen and lift my flashlight to shine on the ceiling—which is lower here than I thought, and supported by beams of wood just like the platform as we came down. Cracking, soft wood. Rotting, above us. I regret looking.

"Delving too deep, nephew?" a sharp voice calls.

Nolan replies without hesitation. "It isn't enough for you to be the footservant of the Mayor of Loirehall? You had to return here, to the beginnings you despised?" He squeezes my hand, and I flick my flashlight off.

Declan Hayes, Lord Chamberlain of Loirehall, speaks from outside the circle of Nolan's torchlight. "My older brother wasn't ambitious." He steps out of the dark, and the flickers of the small flame only emphasize the dark crescents beneath his eyes. "Your father didn't like my ideas; he didn't *hear* me. If he had understood, he would've done more with this mine. With our future. So much more. Instead, he did nothing." Desperation fills his gaze as he looks around, not really looking at us at all. "How long I've waited to finally *do* something."

Now I know. As clear as diamonds, greed has returned to Fairhavens.

"The castle and this mine aren't yours," I say boldly. I don't know if Mr. Hayes has found out about the buried treasure, but suddenly I know how to start the next paragraph, and quickly.

Putting the flashlight back in my bag, I take mother's embroidered map book from my pocket and—holding Nolan's shoulder—lean around him and hold the slim volume open above the flaming torch. The edges of the paper catch. Flame wrinkles the edges, curling them black as orange flames glow through the pages, consuming them in mere seconds. I hold it as long as I can without burning my fingers then toss it on the ground, all the ink on the page dissolved into gray, lifeless ash.

Declan simply cackles. "Little girls, getting in the way, going into forests they shouldn't."

I lift my chin, bold and brave like my mother would've been. Relieved that, for the moment, he doesn't know I'm the Ludovici heir. "I do not fear these woods."

His voice is steady, but flat. "You should. It's swallowed seven generations of your ancestors, little heir." So maybe he *does* know.

Stepping between me and the villain, Nolan interjects, "Leave it to you to follow us underground. Are you more worried about my return, or the fact that a girl whose grandmother lived in this forest carries a secret strong enough to end your claim? What do you *want*?"

I wondered before if his will was immovable, like the foundations of the stone. And he is like this mountain: deep, untold riches, set in stone.

The creak of rotting wood on the last level of stairs announces another arrival. "He wants the same thing I do." In a wide flash of heavy light, Lenora Hayes points a flashlight at me, but beside it she wields a pistol. "And you two should be ready to give up everything."

Nolan raises his free hand, and I copy his slow, deliberate motions, raising my hands in surrender. This woman is crazy.

"You so badly want to exhume the dead gems from the living earth?" I ask.

A flicker as her flashlight jerks. "Let's go deeper," she orders, like a snake burrowing beneath the ground, away from the light of the sun and into the cold depths of the earth.

THE BLEEDING CHEST

Ten minutes later, at the end of the tunnel

"WHERE DO WE GO NOW?" Lenora noisily taps her black-manicured nail on the safety on her gun, as if Nolan staring her down would make mythic buried treasure appear. Which, truly, he deserves to do, after the acerbic baiting and criticism they've berated him with over the past ten minutes of exploring until we met this dead end.

My chest shakes as nerves and dust make a deadly cocktail. After begging for my puffer earlier—which the villains allowed a pause for—we've walked until we can walk no more. There was most definitely a cave-in here. The supply rail-line ends here beneath a pile of dirt and rock and rubble, where somewhere far on the other side my father grieved.

Lenora tosses her flashlight to Declan, then takes a shovel from the collection of abandoned work tools scattered around. We seem to be as far as we can go, but this isn't the end of the tunnel. It's obviously collapsed, with haphazard piles of lanterns, axes, and broken beams.

"This is where it caved in," Nolan says, "we can't go any farther.

There's *nothing here*." There's steel in his deep, steady voice, and a sharp edge on the husky tone. "Except maybe a sinkhole if you decide to start digging. Anything could happen! Stop!"

"Don't tell me what to do, nephew." Lenora points the gun at him with one hand and smacks at the pile of rubble with the other.

"Always full of terrible ideas." Declan sneers at his wife as she ineffectively wields the shovel. "Don't point it at *him*, point it at the thing he cares about more than the treasure." He wrests the gun from her hand, pointing it at me.

In a flash, Nolan shoves me to the side. There's a blinking-out of light as his torch falls to the ground, just as a shot fires. As the gun goes off, Nolan lands on top of me in a rush of breath.

The wind is knocked out of me, my ears ringing—I can't breathe. I can't hear. Inhaling through my teeth, tasting dirt, I feel my ribs in the worst way. I think one might be cracked, and Nolan's a dead weight on top of me, making my lungs scream for air and my mind shout because *what if he's shot*, but then actual shouting breaks through the cacophony of noise—new noise, smooth and long and deep like how I always imagined an earthquake would sound.

Lenora cries out frantically. "This was our one chance—idiot!"

More thunderous booms make me curl into Nolan, who rolls over and groans beside me. Something slick and warm coats my fingers as I grab his arm, squinting in the dark and taking out my flashlight to see, panicking at the blood. "Nolan—"

"Stupid woman!" Mr. Hayes shouts at Lenora, and erratically waves the flashlight. She screeches back at him, about fortune and success and the wealth that she deserved, about his failures.

They don't deserve to be heard.

I pull Nolan to the wall. We're upwind of the fighting, closest to the way from which we came through the mine. He shakes his head and grabs me, pushing with his legs so we're against the wall, as far away from them as possible. He's, cringing, and holding his injured arm. And as the terrible couple argue, not even the young man I love can hold my gaze, because there's something rumbling beneath the ground, *moving*.

With a bang deeper than the sound of the gunshot, and more like how I imagine a bomb feels, a sudden fissure becomes a sink-hole.

Lenora loses her footing. Shrieking, she clasps at Mr. Hayes. Nolan pushes me harder against the wall with his good arm, and I grab the nearest handhold. It happens to be a post of rotted wood that breaks the moment my weight pulls, leaving an angry and piercing splinter within the half-healed scrapes on my hands. Loose pieces of wood tumble into the hole past Lenora, who screams at her husband to save her as he scrambles away, to the far side of the opening rift.

Nolan's breathing heavily, probably with fear, for this must be like heights but worse. He shouts at me to stay back, then, beyond comprehension, leans forward to reach for *Lenora*. I reach to hold his belt as my other hand grabs around for—*aha!* A forgotten axe is bolted to the wall. I fumble, then unclasp it, using all my strength to smash it into the dirt for leverage.

Deep below, the earth speaks to those of us it would swallow.

"You would leave me here for *this*?" Lenora calls as she grips Nolan's hand. Her husband eeks along the far edge and passes us, making for safety. Running away. Coward.

Most of the light disappears with him. My flashlight's faint beam is our now only hope.

Lenora looks down, and Nolan desperately keeps a grip on her and I furiously tighten my grip, not willing to lose him for her.

"I see something," she calls, high-pitched in manic excitement. "It's a box! Ornate with an old crest—there's more than one. There's two, four, more! Declan, come back!" she screams in desperation.

Indestructible chest. Ruby-red key.

Breath locks in my lungs. My locket must surely be the key.

"No! Leave it!" Nolan cries, groaning even as blood seeps into his shirt, keeping her hand as she leans away desperately. I hold onto Nolan for dear life. I don't see the chests, but the ore lining the walls is different in that pit, touched with a sort of green that doesn't belong in ordinary rock. Sparkling, in a luster that feels as natural as greed.

Never mind a chest of treasure. This is a mine *full* of it. Copper.

Lenora grabs for the nearest box, but when she grasps the handle with bloody fingers, it seems unearthly heavy. With a heave, she tries and fails to throw it above her head. There's another piercing scream, and now she's barely clinging to Nolan.

Gold. Gold will drag her down. It's so bright, this close to death.

Then I realize that I'm seeing more clearly—*where is more light coming from?* Out of nowhere, Declan slams his flashlight to the ground and pushes Nolan aside side to grab his wife's wrist. "I've done nothing wrong," he grunts at us. "Remember that, when we escape here richer than we all intended."

Nolan heaves himself away as Declan takes over holding Lenora. Now he's lying on his back unmoving, with blood seeping down his arm. *What if the ground gives way?*

"Let the gold go!" I shout. "Nolan's hurt, don't you care?"

But then Nolan rolls over, spits dirt from his mouth and leans his injured arm against Declan as both men try to save the dangling woman. She must have a good grip on the box. I grab Nolan's leg and anchor myself to the axe. "You mean you've done nothing *illegal*," Nolan grunts to his uncle. There's still blood soaking his shirt, but now I suspect the bullet only grazed him. *Still.* "Not here, anyway."

Declan pants and struggles as his estranged wife scratches his arm. "Maybe, but I *always* have a backup plan."

I don't doubt that Nolan's uncle's other plan is equally vile. By the razor-edged glint in his eye, perhaps more so. I'll be happy if our cursed acquaintance ends here, but I also don't want to die. I don't want *anyone* to die.

The ground breaks away beneath their clasped arms, and the men wrangle themselves back, holding onto Lenora who won't let the wretched chest go. Declan's grabbing Nolan, and Nolan's blood is dripping down his arm and her wrist, and the handle of the chest looks like it's bleeding. But, if saving Nolan means saving them, I'll try and save us all.

For a second, I want to smile. It isn't just the villains who can change the ending.

The mine was a good thing, but it was the greed of men who brought up hell by digging too deeply and never sharing. I hate greed, especially when it comes with such a high cost.

I grab my flashlight and toss it with all my strength, breath whooshing from my lungs as it hits Lenora's fingers where she clings to the gilded box. The hit knocks the chest—with all the world's treasure, for all I care—into hades below.

Lenora screams as the light from my flashlight fades into the depths, and that's left are voices and sounds. Declan and Nolan yank Lenora up, and then it's all darkness. So dark. I push back against the wall, silent as I can be.

Nolan finds me with a hushed word. "Run." He grabs my hand, and I scramble to my feet. He pulls me to run, run, run as the ground screams at us in the same desperate tone as Lenora—*it's gone, it's all gone*. And though the world is black, Nolan's hand is strong, blindly pulling me away as the sinkhole grows and expands and devours, trying to pull us into the tomb of worthless fortune as the ground becomes a living coffin.

Beneath the ground, desperate for air

THERE IS NO BREATH IN DEATH. Papa said that life is debt and mistakes and regrets. That those are real life.

There is more to life, Papa. I wish I had a diary to write in. There are stronger sacrifices, better choices, lovely memories. Those are real life, too.

But it's dark and I'm afraid to move from the wall behind me and the minecart beside me. I can't find anything else in the dark. For all those times Nolan was there for me, watching me, guiding me, and guarding me, now he isn't here. Panic sets in. He was just here saving me—he was holding my hand—but now, he isn't here. How long have I been here? An age, an hour? Just minutes?

I cough, but can't call his name. I want him to be safe because I want a future with him. That's the only treasure—*he's* the only treasure—worth saving in this dark place beneath the earth. But I can't see him or find him. I can't see *anything*, and the fallout from falling rocks and shifting earth chokes my lungs in the dust, the lack of light making the space feel cramped, when for all I know it could be a cavern beneath the earth big enough to be lost in forever.

I cry for far too long, but once the sound of my own tears subsides—*are Lenora and her husband cut off from air? How long do they have?* I close my eyes to the dark and listen.

Breaths. In, and out.

All I feel is my own heart pounding, and the sound of my own breathing seems loud. As if there's now less space...*did the cavern collapse between us?* Slowly, I crawl and pause, listen, shuffle on my knees again. Then I find Nolan, and trail my hands over his dusty hair, his chest, which steadily rises and falls. His bloody arm. There's a gash above his eyes that's full of something warm and sticky. Red blood, but all around us is black.

Nolan isn't conscious.

I despair on my knees. "It's okay," I whisper, holding his head in both my hands. "You're okay. It will all be fine. All will be well. I'm here." Gently, I lift his head to my lap. I struggle not to jostle him, because I'm not sure how injured he is, but I can't let go of his face. I *cannot* lose him again.

It's so dark.

Tears loosen and I cry above him, my chest heaving inward with the pain that I could've lost him. That I *still* could, and now I'd give anything to hear his rasping, rough-edged voice.

"I'm here this time. You don't have to save me anymore. I want to save you." My sobs are a hiccup in the dark as the weight of my confession demands release, like the mountain above us is pressing for freedom too. "I love you, Nolan. I'm sorry I didn't say it earlier. I'm sorry I never returned these precious words when you spoke them to me freely." My voice is lined with dirt, raw. I curve over his face, as if my small frame could block his from the danger of the mine. The danger he isn't able to protect me from.

I breathe from my puffer. "How can it be beautiful, if it remains buried?" I start crying again, but then another sound startles me.

It's my father, calling my name.

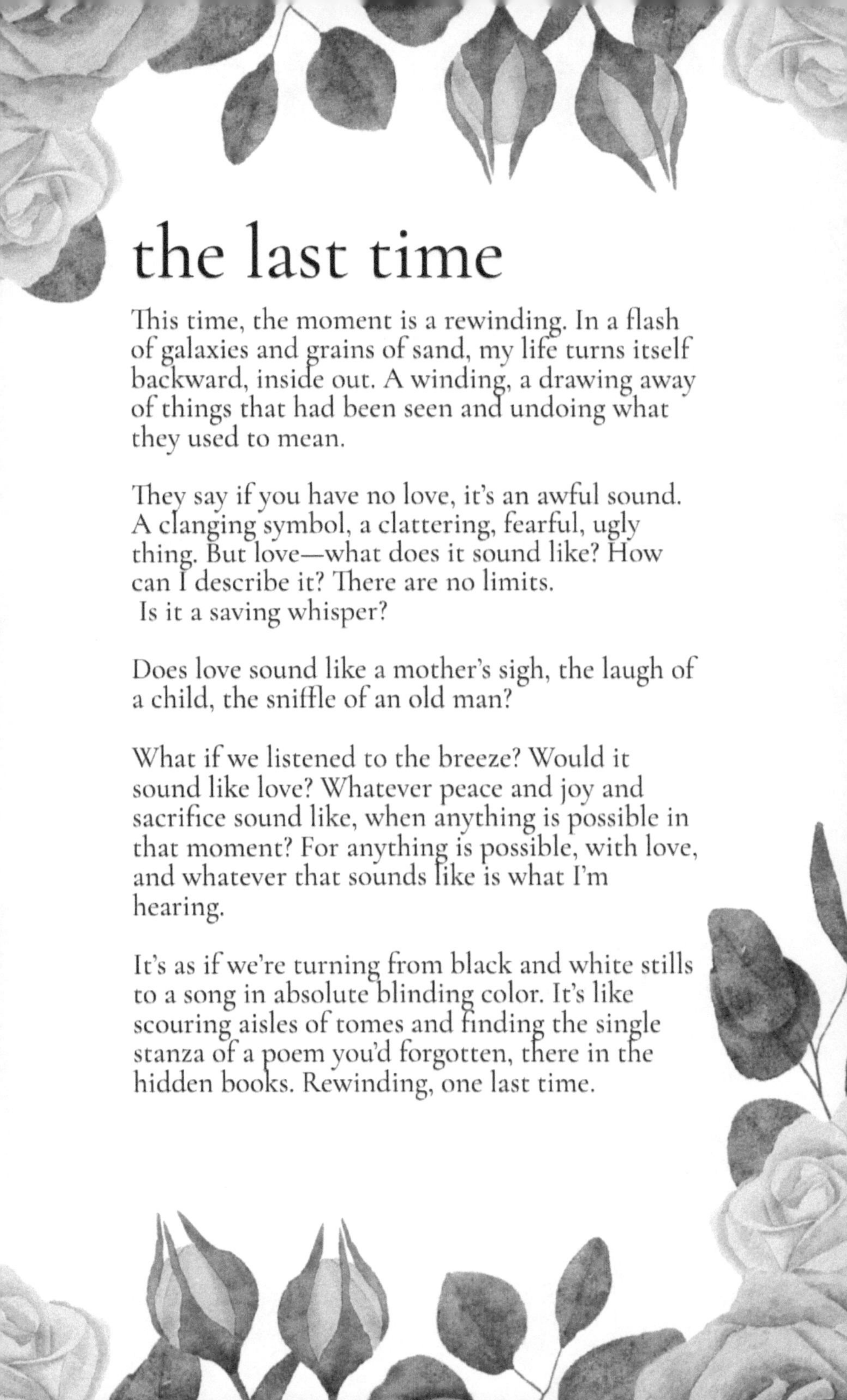

the last time

This time, the moment is a rewinding. In a flash of galaxies and grains of sand, my life turns itself backward, inside out. A winding, a drawing away of things that had been seen and undoing what they used to mean.

They say if you have no love, it's an awful sound. A clanging symbol, a clattering, fearful, ugly thing. But love—what does it sound like? How can I describe it? There are no limits.
 Is it a saving whisper?

Does love sound like a mother's sigh, the laugh of a child, the sniffle of an old man?

What if we listened to the breeze? Would it sound like love? Whatever peace and joy and sacrifice sound like, when anything is possible in that moment? For anything is possible, with love, and whatever that sounds like is what I'm hearing.

It's as if we're turning from black and white stills to a song in absolute blinding color. It's like scouring aisles of tomes and finding the single stanza of a poem you'd forgotten, there in the hidden books. Rewinding, one last time.

THE HIDDEN HEART

The rescue

COUGHING, HACKING, lack of air. There's no air, beneath the ground. There's no air, in a brush with death.

As I open my eyes, the wicked air is all I see. Skirting the fallen cavern walls, it's pale and ghostly and filled with debris. It's a visible evil except that even as it swirls, it settles. It cannot last, the foul dusty mess. Our mistakes, the ill designs of greedy people, it's all swallowed into the cavern below.

Hard ground hurts my backside, solid and uncomfortable beneath me. There's silence, as shifting rocks stop and swaths of fresh air sweep to replace the puffs of smoke-like, dirty air. And I can see it, which means there's *light*.

I blink at the bits itching the edges of my eyelashes. *How can I see?* It's astounding, how the invisible wind is so apparent—a beautiful shape, a moving presence above me in the dust cloud—and I wonder how I'd never appreciated the beauty of a breeze, never seen it so clearly until this moment. It's never been so apparent as when evil took a last gasp of air.

I never could see what was always with me—I never saw *who* was always with me. I was focused on the pain hurting *around* me, that it took me this long to accept the invisible good moving through my life.

There's a voice, and it sounds like my father. "Papa?" I whisper into the busy air, strangled with the hope of all hopes.

"I'm here," my father replies, somehow—miraculously—beside me. "Martin Lucas called, and I came as soon as I could. Others are here to rescue the Hayes." His voice breaks, like he's crying. "But what matters is that you're safe, and so is this boy. You're safe." Light streams behind him in an ever-growing halo, as others come to support Nolan and rescue us from the mine.

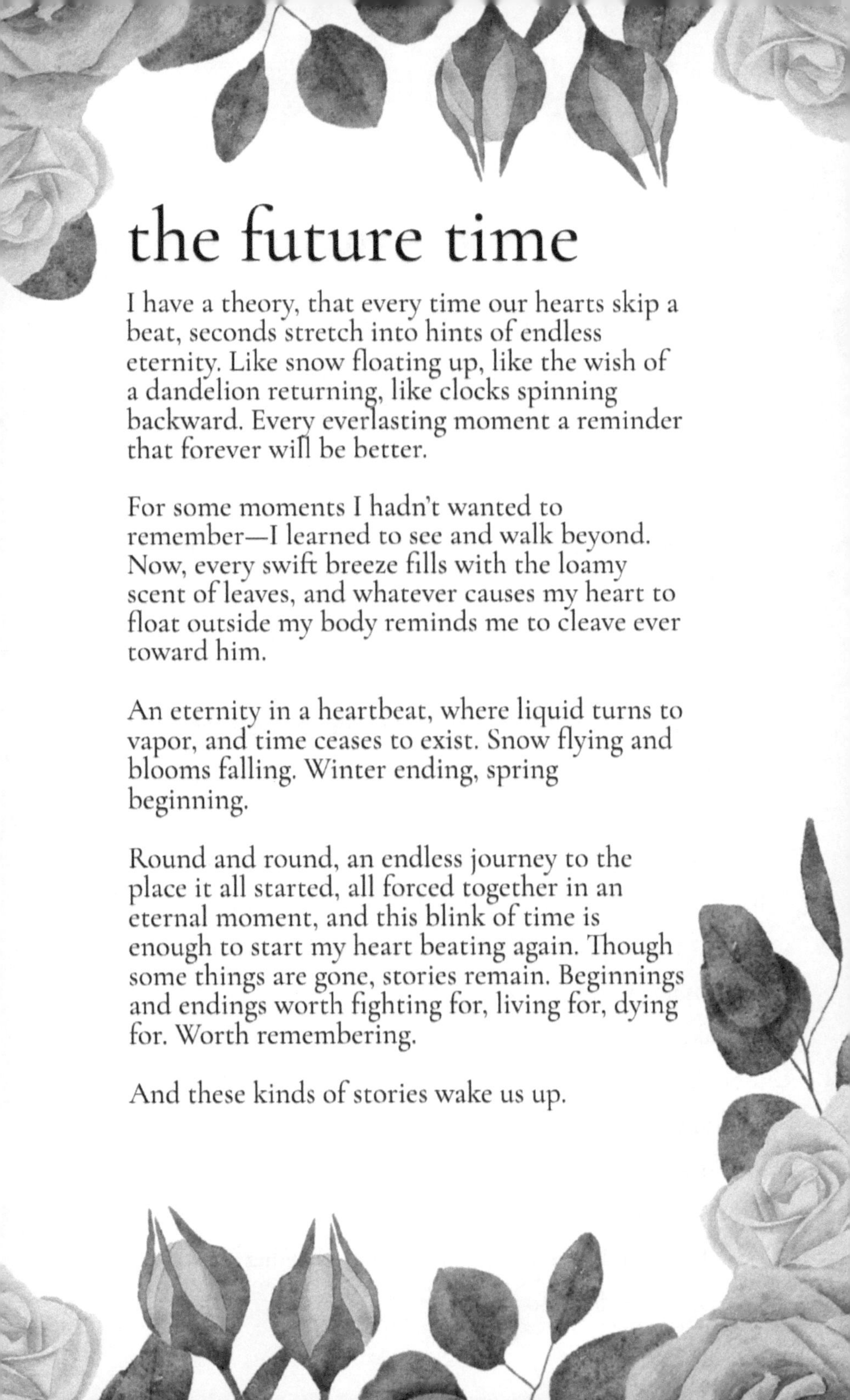

the future time

I have a theory, that every time our hearts skip a beat, seconds stretch into hints of endless eternity. Like snow floating up, like the wish of a dandelion returning, like clocks spinning backward. Every everlasting moment a reminder that forever will be better.

For some moments I hadn't wanted to remember—I learned to see and walk beyond. Now, every swift breeze fills with the loamy scent of leaves, and whatever causes my heart to float outside my body reminds me to cleave ever toward him.

An eternity in a heartbeat, where liquid turns to vapor, and time ceases to exist. Snow flying and blooms falling. Winter ending, spring beginning.

Round and round, an endless journey to the place it all started, all forced together in an eternal moment, and this blink of time is enough to start my heart beating again. Though some things are gone, stories remain. Beginnings and endings worth fighting for, living for, dying for. Worth remembering.

And these kinds of stories wake us up.

THE FAIREST BEAUTY

Three days later, mid-morning, at Azalea's Treasures

"HOW DID YOU KNOW?" I ask Penelope. Because *of course* she's been entirely unbothered and unsurprised at my tale. A vase of white roses adorns the countertop as we sit in the same chaise and chair Juniper and I claimed last week. Spring sunshine cheers dust motes by streaming through the window, warm and glorious.

But then my view of the bouquet is obscured as she adjusts her posture and says, "What makes you think I knew any of this could have happened or would happen? You and Nolan were meant to be, but I truly had no idea. Who could've known?" She tilts her head, as if ready for my next question.

I take a long time to ask. "Did you know about my lineage, though? *You* have the matching mirror. Did you know what my grandmother intended that night?"

"I'm sorry, Paige. I was at the party, but I never saw them"—she chokes up—"until the smoke cleared. Had I known her intent, I doubt I could have stopped her. You're like her: unstoppable, when it comes down to it."

Disappointment mingles with a strange acceptance of the truth of her statement. "And that's it?"

"Oh no, not at all." She smiles a sad smile. "Once upon a time, long, long ago, I first met my Nicholas." Her eyes flicker and she pauses for a heavy moment. I set down my teacup and lean forward as she continues. "The first time I saw him being all...prince-like in the palace, with people clamoring for his attention, an old woman caught my eye."

Penelope coughs delicately. "Now, I'm nearly as old as she was then, but at the time, it felt as though my whole life was ahead of me, and that was a frightful, uncertain thing. This woman dropped her pendant..." Her eyes light up. "It was a rose, gold-stemmed with silvery-white petals. Captivating, and unusual. But what truly caught my attention was her interaction with Nicholas. He treated her like a gem, that fragile old lady. Some time later, during our engagement, he brought me white roses and I was reminded of her.

"I asked after her, where she lived, who she was, and his smile—oh, his smile could light the sky. He was my sun, my starlight..." Her voice trails off into sweet memories that I dare not disturb. She takes a sip of tea, then brushes hair from her forehead, streaks of silvery-white between coppery locks. "He was so dashing and strong, so stoic, but at the mention of her, he softened. When I found out who she was, and that she wanted to keep her lineage a secret, I agreed. *She* was your great-great-grandmother...and I was blessed to call her my friend."

"Rose," I breathe, "That's why you had them? Those were her

letters. The red letters… Hers was a sad love story, wasn't it?"

Penelope nods, and something deep settles inside my spirit. "She would have been delighted that this story ended with the next steward and the true heir working together, trusting one another. Perhaps only you two could heal those old hurts. That old conflict."

"My mother was right to leave the treasure be, wasn't she?"

"So were you," Penelope says. "You let it go, just like she did. And that takes strength. Greed is powerful enough to pull the unsuspecting away from sacrifice and nobility. You resisted, and everyone was saved. Though, that part of the mine may yet be made safe again, from what I hear. If those chests are full of gold, it could be a boon, and you need not say no to a good thing in the future because of what happened in the past. But just like beauty and wealth are passing, illusions most often are too. Your mother knew treasure is where your heart is, and she banked all she had that you would someday end the hunt for that which swallowed souls and bodies until the end."

"Not Mr. or Mrs. Hayes," I mumble, thankful no one died, but annoyed beyond comprehension that they have no crimes for which to answer after all that's happened. But Nolan was determined that, just as him and his friends never had to own to what they did the night of the fire, no one else should suffer on account of Fairhavens.

He's hard to resist, sometimes.

"It is a relief that they still live. And why should they be locked up? What did they do but follow the coldness of their hearts?

No gold or gems are worth that! The risk! Don't fret, Paige, and sip your tea before it gets cold," Penelope admonishes. "Their comeuppance is coming. Be sad for your loss, but be proud that you stood strong for the same thing as your mother. She wanted to leave that treasure, and because of you, the strife it once represented is no more."

I paid so dearly, and yet, look what was uncovered. "I need time."

"Of course you do. You cannot simply *become* the heir your bloodline demands in mere days. But I will help, when that time comes. I'm just glad you're safe and that you found your own treasure."

I inhale a bit of tea and cough. "Nolan wouldn't like that analogy."

"Not him, sweet girl. *Love.* Like Fairhavens... That castle is from another time. It survived, like love survives."

I shiver at the thought. "It's scary having love like that, if I can't be sure it won't burn me in the end."

"Is every love note joyous? Is every picture perfect?" Her words echo Sterling's, from when all this started. "A love note means lovers are apart, and a picture, a painting, a sketch—" She places a hand on her chest, wedding ring glinting. "What less does art require, than the pouring out of a heart? Isn't that the best kind?"

I smile so much it hurts my cheeks, making a tear slip out of my eye. She pats my hand as I cry healing tears of thankfulness and sorrow for my mother, for my grandmother, for Nolan's parents. I cry for my father, for Nolan, and possibly even for Darragh as his parents continue in their broken ways, and then Penelope returns with a fresh pot of tea and lavender macarons. With *chocolate filling*. "Someday I need to meet whoever makes these," I say around a huge bite.

"Don't eat it all at once."

"But they're my favorite."

"Since you're indisposed, falling in love, and going back to school soon—"

"Why can't I go back this week?" It's an existential question, and I fail not to sound petulant. Term hasn't ended yet, and I'm a little grumpy, not having been in *any* library for *days*.

"Sterling told me you had papers to work through with Gabreville Council, and their meetings have always taken ages. *You* have caused quite the stir. Just pray they don't force you to attend every meeting now that you hold the seat. Patience," she advises, pointing half a macaron at me. "Now, I have a thought. It's been long enough..." The trail of her voice is full of obstacles, but she carries on. "Maybe I should restart it."

"Restart what?" I sip the last of my Darjeeling, then take half a bite of another macaron.

"*L'étoile dans les Ténèbres*," she says wistfully.

I drop my macaron in my tea. "Yes! You should!" I giggle at her perfect eyebrow raise, setting down my empty teacup as the liquid dregs swirl a timeless dance. With lavender speckles of sugar, no less.

I'm happy for the light in Penelope's eyes at the mention of her famed art auction, which she used to do before Nicholas passed. Her philanthropy and love of art may yet make a comeback. Then

I remember the storeroom with all its treasures here in the book-shop. "Return to the social calendar of Loirehall with a bang," I say seriously, "and put those absurd candelabras to good use!"

Her eyes twinkle. "They *do* look as though they crave a party."

"They really do. What with their being human-sized." And I laugh. It feels free and light and bright. Like the air can finally find a way through my lungs and chest, like the insides of me are blown fresh with forest wind.

"And not a cold-weather one like my December birth-day—summertime will be soon, and late summer it shall be." She swipes a finger at the crumbs on the table between us. "But who will headline the auction? Oh, I do love art, and there are some pieces in my attic that need the light of day."

"I would love to help! But..." Beyond my having a seat on the Gabreville Council and whatever that entails, there's also the need to address the heady relationship in my life with a certain hand-some blond Hayes boy—and there's also my studies, my goals. And yet, at the thought of Nolan...I grip the teacup handle a tad too tightly. "I haven't much time but maybe June—"

"Oh dear, I know. Juniper's drowning in Sterling's assigned reading, as she should be, and *you* are indisposed, distracted, smit-ten"—she smiles serenely as I sputter on my final sip of mac-aron-tasting tea—"and altogether too busy."

I swallow and press my lips together. But my grin spreads, be-cause I really, truly love him.

Penelope continues. "I need an artist to headline the event, but the only one I know of is—" Her voice breaks off abruptly.

It's the kind of pause that makes a body curious. "What? Who?"

"True art finds a way to be born new." Her eyes shut for a soft second.

"Maybe it should be someone young," I muse. I like eccentric art and trying to discern meaning. And while I prefer my thousand words over a single picture, I'm not beyond being convinced. "You need an assistant, like what I used to do for you." Planning a party like the kind Penelope is known for would be an undertaking.

"No, no," she demurs, "I'm a single old-ish lady with a modest home and an open schedule, especially now that you're back working here at the bookshop." I don't believe her for a second, but suspect a plan between those icy blue eyes that are somehow, magically, warm as she says, "I just oversee...*things*."

"You work too many hours here."

"Time doesn't count in the bookshop." She leans forward, and for a moment I fear she'll float into the air. "I tested it once. It simply stops."

I blink furiously then frown. "So, no assistant."

"I'll make do. There is nothing worth remembering. There is only everything," she declares. "These things tend to find ways of working themselves out, and I won't worry about that story today. It'll keep."

THE BOOK SHELVES

An hour and a half later, in the Gated Library

"STERLING GIVE YOU A KEY AGAIN?" I ask Nolan when he finds me some time later, four stories up in the Gated Library. Buds were blossoming on trees as I came here this morning, the promise of spring.

He grunts the affirmative, and I smile at this mirror image of our first meeting. "How do you feel?"

He stands before me, tall and strong and sure, late-morning sun highlighting the tips of his hair. His face is clean-shaven, golden eyes bright but rimmed with shadow. He's tired, and his injury is still causing pain based on the stiffness in his shoulders, but there's no doubt that the half-smile is just for me. I wouldn't have it any other way.

When he says nothing but a huff, I say, "It's a miracle." Lenora, surviving with only broken bones, a concussion, and mild breathing problems. And Declan, unscathed, when they both could have died underground.

Nolan puts one hand in his jacket pocket, shrugging his injured shoulder with a grimace. "How can miracles happen to someone like her?"

I smile and remember Penelope's response to that exact question when I posed it to her as I left the bookshop earlier today: *Who are we to judge the miraculous?*

I sigh, filling my chest with enough air to blow away the last of my cares. I know the unhappy couple will leave us alone or face charges. Sterling informed Nolan of his rights, which became exceedingly important with the discovery of copper—valuable, and now accessible thanks to the cave-in, if the mine is rebuilt safely. As the Ludovici heir, I own it, but...I don't really want to own it alone.

I tilt my head at the young man before me, and let my imagination wander into the future of possibilities. It makes me smile. My treasure isn't in the fortune below the ground. What I found is more precious than silver, more priceless than any amount of gold.

It's amazing really. Love is a heart that moves. Toward people, or for people. To protect, to carry, to uncover. Just like when the ground moves, or when the earth shakes, we find real, hidden treasure. Penelope and Sterling and Juniper showed me, and love keeps leaving me for Papa, for Nolan, and it hasn't returned empty.

But the sad story of others? It isn't mine to carry.

"I don't know all of Lenora's reasons," I say quietly, "but I'm grateful the Loirehall Grand Court ruled in favor of Papa taking ownership of the printer. I don't know how it *should* end. Only she can write her own story. Maybe she'll be different in another book? One can hope."

"That's ridiculous." His words would look harsh on paper, but they're tempered by his stepping nearer, by his fingers brushing hair from my forehead.

Are compassion and mercy ridiculous? Is grace ever wasted? I whisper, "It's sad, revenge and greed. All that wanting for things that aren't ours to begin with. I'm glad to just be here, with you." I lean into Nolan's hand. Thankful for unveiled faces and mirrors that help us see, but if they don't, I'm prepared to shatter the false images and the lies. Everlasting things don't find a home in mere reflection. What we behold, we become, and that is no lie. It's what remains, and it's the truth.

"I'm sorry for all that happened." He takes my hands as I inhale at the intensity of his stare. "Thank you. I love you. You're beautiful. You are my treasure." He laughs under his breath, holding my gaze. "I should have said all that first."

All I can do is shake my head as he places a hand behind my neck, then leans in. There's a scent of citrus and fresh air on his dark jacket, and my eyes trace the bandage showing beneath his open shirt collar. My heart pounds at the thought of our kiss in the cabin...but then he kisses my forehead. Silly me, thinking about something that isn't happening. My breath returns to normal, but then I meet his gorgeous golden eyes and warmth leaps into a hidden place deep inside my chest.

"I hold grudges, Paige. That's something I understand. And revenge? I want it, but I'll have to leave it. So instead...what can I do but spend every day chasing you?" His voice is a smiling rasp as mischief replaces the dark slant in his eyes. "I'll get my revenge somehow—there won't be a day I won't kiss you. I will never leave you alone, and I'll never leave you. I promise."

"I'll remember that." I'm embarrassed at the break in my voice.

"You still have to catalogue all those ancient tomes in the castle. You know that, right? I hired an archivist for a job. Not letting you leave until it's done."

"It may never be finished." Books fill physical spaces. Libraries, side tables, boxes, shelves. They fill liminal space, too, with stories that expand in the infinite plane of imagination and possibility. "I've always been partial to stained-glass. It's pretty."

He steps closer, until there is no air between us. "Pretty, like you."

Hmm. I murmur and lean my forehead into his chest, pleased he's here but distracted by the piles of books on the ground. There are two I've been eyeing for the last hour while finishing the last one, but I enjoyed that story so much that I hesitate to start another. At least I had plenty of time to read over the last few days of resting in bed so my father could stop worrying.

It's so nice that after all that happened, we got our house back. Turns out that being the heiress to Fairhavens carries weight. Our little townhouse—dead plants notwithstanding—holds so many memories, and I can't imagine Papa growing old anywhere but there. Concern aside, he's not a good nursemaid, so by this morning I had to leave the house for a little while. And the books *were* calling—

"Paige." Nolan's deep voice is wary as he embraces me tighter. The dark, husky sound is such a balm. It's nice to be reminded of the scent of summer-dried cotton and sharp lemon and something spiced and uniquely *him*. I shift and raise my gaze, knowing there must be a silly smile on my face as he says, "I love you."

It's like a trance. Eternity in a heartbeat. Spring arriving early, with the frost of winter clinging for a spell. We are not in heaven, not yet. But we see tinges of it, feel hints of it, when things become impossible and souls are freed, bringing breath where there was no life. When spring returns after a long winter.

It sounds like a song you've always wanted to hear.

He speaks words worth remembering. "You were my first love, and you will be my last."

"My first and last," I echo, happy to be falling in love in a library all over again, and not just with the books or the stories, but with a person. This person. "I love you."

All the broken pieces became perfect together, because he was there. He was there, then. And he is *here*, now.

"Why *are* you here?" I whisper. Sparks are heated disagreements and exhilarating adventure. "I'm not even supposed to be here. Honestly, I was sneaking. Trespassing!"

"I'm here for you," he says, laughing and pressing something cool into my palm.

I look down, then up, surprised and delighted at the ring, until it dawns on me what it means and surprise crests as I say, "Is this—" I cut off my own words as he snatches me deeper into the library, his strong arms and laughter surrounding me.

And there, between the "P's" and "Q's" and aisles full of books, he kisses me.

a preview of *Curses*

Juniper & Percy's story

THE GABREVILLE GAZETTE

SEPTEMBER 21ST

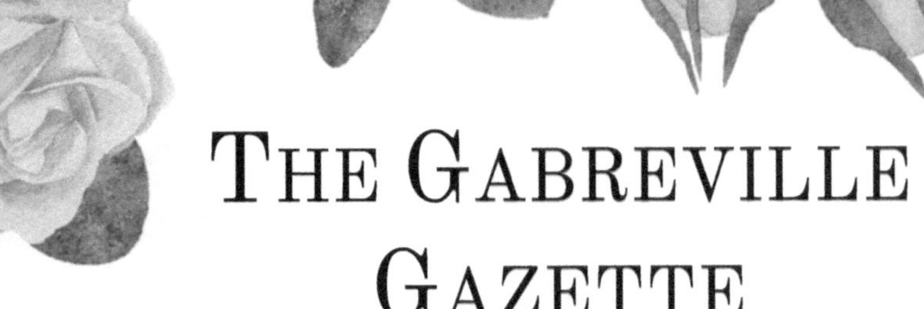

C ROWN JEWELS STOLEN

Article by Lucia Dooritt, photo by Percival Hayes

THIRTY YEARS AGO, THE HOUSE OF GARCON TOOK THE CROWN JEWELS OUT OF THE VAULT IN THE CENTRAL BANK OF LOIREHALL FOR DISPLAY AT THE LOIREHALL UNIVERSITY LIBRARY AND MUSEUM

Photo: The former Regent, Nicholas Garcon & his wife Madame Penelope Garcon, and his brother Pierre Garcon & his wife Odette Garcon, dedicating the Crown Jewels to the Loirehall University Library and Museum. (file photo)

In the four decades since our neighbor, the Duchy of Loirehall, transitioned from monarchy to elected governance, the history and scandal of the royal family never seemed to decline. Initially, the exhibit at the university was an equalizing factor, mixing young people in a heady blend of studies and chumminess that pervaded the public houses and fashion outlets with friends of all stripes. Placing the jewels there among antiquities from Gabreville and Loirehall's shared history seemed 'the closest thing to sharing the Garcons were capable of,' claimed a family member of someone who was employed by the family during the Monarchy days.

In light of the middle-of-the-night theft, battle lines thought forgotten are being redrawn. Our partner paper, *The Loirehall Times*, with whom we share a printing press, indicated before this article went to print that their editorial team would be casting a wide net of accusations, none the least of which are recent changes to the museum's regulations about access to the historical artifacts. One must note said artifacts are not limited to the Crown Jewels nor property of Loirehall alone. One thinks of the bronze statuaries from Gabreville's cathedral after the bombing in the Great War, or of the gold-plated incense burner engraved with the myths of Gabreville's founder, Sir Hale Grentham.) More is sure to come, and as the autumn season arrives, the shared history of Loirehall and Gabreville is certain of one thing: change.

Editor's note: As of printing, there was no indication from the Loirehall Historical Society or the university itself as to whether or not suspects were being considered. When they are, you'll hear the scoop dished here first, no holds barred.

THE LOOSE LEAF

September 21st, Friday, the morning before the Autumnal Equinox, in Loirehall's Wrenley Square

ORANGE AND YELLOW FIRE AND RED leaves hang on tight for their lives. Fall makes them brittle and unsteady, the pretty pops of color turning with the season. Above the trolley stop, where I sit at a surprisingly comfortable bench, golden morning sun spreads through my personal autumnal overhang, too pretty for so much death.

"Move over, Juniper!" A young voice breaks through the cheery gloom. "Hog the whole seat yourself?"

"Only on mornings you show up," I mumble, then say coherently, "Sorry, Chet."

"Only on mornings you're feeling sorry for yourself." The newsboy winks at me, all thirteen years of him the kind of cheeky that should be bottled and weaponized.

"Does anyone buy the paper anymore?"

"Both of them." He flashes his half-empty canvas tote at me.

Avoiding what I know the paper says, I look around Loirehall Old Towne, a block away from my second-floor apartment above

Azalea's Treasures. The bookshop is just below, and I left earlier through the back entrance so as to avoid conversing with the owner in case she came in—I'd not heard the chime of the doorbell but, coward I was, I decided not to risk facing Penelope. Too much going on in her world. I nod toward the other side of Wrenley square, the tips of my gabled rooftop attic visible through the trees in the park in the center of the civic square. "How do I know you didn't just sell those to Penelope?"

"I didn't. She's not there yet," he replies smugly, not seeming to notice my pause. I sat here in the cold for an hour before the trolley was due to avoid facing her—why wasn't she opening the store yet? "Have you seen the foot traffic in that bookshop?" he continues. "And from both sides of the river. And the news—not every year the Crown Jewels disappear! Sales are sales, lady."

"Oh, wow Chet. I'm no lady. I'm nineteen."

"Ancient and aged." He nods to himself like he's the one seventy years wiser. We both have a ways to go. "Why are you dressed all grown up and fancy?"

I look down at my pleated, plaid skirt. "I love all things dresses." And to be fair, all I wear is skirts or dresses, over pants if need be, to stay warm. I am nothing if not committed.

"Wait until you see today's paper! Midnight edition! Azalea—"

"I'm not listening," I interrupt. "I make it a vow not to read the newspaper or find out any news whatsoever until I've had at least one cup of coffee or three cups of tea."

He swallows. "That's weird."

"I know." I like keeping my mind free from sad new things

first thing in the morning if I can help it. But I can't resist the waif because his glasses are in such dire need of a clean, so with a well-timed swipe, I snatch the frames and sacrifice the corner of my honey-colored hexagonal scarf as wipers for the abominable situation.

"Oh look, the trolley," Chet crows, rolling a copy of the *Gabreville Gazette* and sliding it into my hands. "For the road. Exciting times, these days."

"You're telling me." I peer around the corner, handing him back his glasses and mumbling, "I can't see it."

Ding, ding!

"See? Just because you can't see something, doesn't mean it isn't coming." He flashes a dimpled smile. "You can have your seat back," he cracks merrily, and I narrowly avoid swatting him with the paper. Such sad aim.

He bounds up to the couple he's spotted, who are walking deep in conversation and in business attire, blissfully unaware of the incoming barrage of personality that is Chet. He's going to make double the profit—making deals runs in his blood, like his father who owns the hardware store. In this case, I give them about twenty seconds until they happily overpay to get Chet to stop talking.

The trolley dings once more as it draws up and I step lightly aboard, taking a mental picture of the old-fashioned transit vehicle in its vibrant-hued glory amidst a perfect fall morning. Kissable cherry paint, merry bells, and wheels that run on a track that marks a path through Gabreville and Loirehall and back, there and back, there and back.

I smile as I pay coins for the fare. They *clink*, and while I toss another coin at Chet as we pass by, the driver pulls the cord for the *ding, ding!*

Happy sounds. I cross my arms and harrumph into my seat. Who says I'm feeling sorry for myself *or* dressing like an adult? I'm just on my way to an *appointment*. Business, not personal. The large, folded papers in my purse? From my legal training at college so far, one year complete and counting, it's easily understood. The terms, that is. The *why*, and the *how it came to be*, are much harder to decipher. They're simply impossible to understand, as I have no reference. Then there's the timing of it all.

But one does not follow a lead on an attempted murder without dressing for the occasion. At least I look ready.

Because it's my birthday today, and no one but my best friend Paige knows it. Which is why she took me for dinner last night and I arrived home late. Which is why I also took special care this morning with the herringbone vest and plaid dress. It sounds wrong, but it's *so right*, because patterns that should hate each other don't when they're in the exact same shade of goldenrod and ochre. Earlier, I was confident, throwing my short, cadet-gray coat overtop of my ensemble. But now I wonder if I just look like a gloomy-covered clementine, undecided if she wants to stand out or blend into the shades of pumpkin-clad doorsteps hidden in the alleyways of Gabreville town.

Overtop of my thoughts screaming *I'm not ready for this*, the trolley has taken me to my destination: leaving Loirehall and over the Valais and into Gabreville, down Main Street, then stopping just beside the alley between the antique shop and the flower shop. Orange and red bunting flutters gaily in the near-autumn breeze. I send a prayer to the sky that neither owner will see me exit the trolley, busy with their own schedules and clients and customers.

Skipping the last step off the trolley, it's a struggle righting my balance on the cobblestones in my half-inch heeled black boots. I may love dresses, but heels are a step too far.

I'm not ready to answer questions about any of this as I step toward the building I now hold the deed to myself. I'd discarded the large manila envelope before leaving this morning, keeping the simple double-sided papers folded in three simple sections tucked in my purse, in case anyone questions my right to search the candy shop for a clue to a mystery that may be nothing but the fictional red-herring. And whether the news of the contents of these legal papers will be accepted by the people working in the shop when I reveal my name on the literal title to this brick-fronted building...that remains to be seen.

"Ready or not, deserve or not, this may be the start of something good," I tell myself, talking aloud, wishing I felt a little less sane. "This is something new. New is good." Surprising, unexpected, only good things. Like the candy shop I'm heading toward. With a spring in my feet, I beeline for the sidewalk as a car zips past, but—

SPLASH. As if in slow motion, puddle water creates a vast spray of imperfect droplets in a grotesque flower along the right side of my skirt. "Gah!" I cry, appalled at the damp damage, which, for the record, might well appear as angels or gargoyles for the improvement my swiping motions make on the mud splattering my beautiful plaid skirt.

I do nothing but the sane thing. I rant to no one in particular. "What did I ever do to you, sky? Why does my skirt have to pay for my transgressions, rain? Isn't my invisible ruination enough for one lifetime, ground?"

As if on cue, the back door to *Peckle's & Praline* opens, here in the brick-faced alley I escaped into to wipe the mess—

"Juniper? Is that you?"

I don't look up at the resonant voice, a voice too low even when it's happy. Who has a voice that deep at the age of twenty? It's unnerving. But even as it surprises me, it scares me, because it sounds so similar to his older brother.

I'm not afraid of Percy. He has his own voice. He isn't Darragh. I tell myself facts, to rein in the hiccup in my pulse. *This is the same Percy I spent every year in school with, in the same classroom.* I keep my head down as he calls my name again. Reminding myself this is the same Percy who never, ever did anything to make me uncomfortable even when his older brother broke my heart and spread the shavings through our high school hallways. I tell myself all these truths, and force air into my chest.

Swallowing thickly, I hesitate before speaking on this beautiful, chilly autumn morning before any leaf has dared release its clinging hold on the branches that gave them life. It isn't time yet. They won't fall, neither will I, not yet. And though it seems impossible, as I turn and face the boy calling my name—

I hang on.

read more

in *Curses*

candy, crown jewels & a crypt

ACKNOWLEDGEMENTS

We're at the end of another story! How is it that this part always feels like a new beginning? If you've been with me through this series, thank you! If you've left a review on this book or previous books, thank you ever more!

First, thank you to my early readers and editors, and in particular, thank you to Brigitte Cromey and Amber Kirkpatrick, who both at different stages brought the story up beyond I would have been able to do on my own. The best thing about friends who edit your work is that their official critique is so immersed in hilarious commentary, so many all-caps opinions, and insightful suggestions, that it makes the process all the more wonderful. It's just like Proverbs 18:24 says. Thank you both; this book would not be here without you but more than that, me as an author would not be here without you. You held me up when I fell down, and I am so grateful.

Thank you so very much to the talented authors who endorsed this book: Kaitlyn Carter Brown, Rachel Lawrence, and Ashley Schaller. Thanks also to all my editors! You know who you are and any remaining errors, you know who you are, and you made it through. I'll find you someday. Magic is in the editing, as the publisher of Quill and Flame April J. Skelly loves to say. And she's so right—writing a book is only the beginning and it takes hard work, a team, and a dose of humility to finish. She's also been the most amazing cheerleader of this series from the moment it began with me saying, "I have this Christmas novella," to "I need to take a year off publishing for my family." Now, we're keeping the series going and I'm so grateful. She was behind me in every turn on this publishing journey so far. Thank you, April! May there be ever more books!

Thank you to my husband, a source of constant support, and my kids, a source of inspiration and joy! And as always, thank you, Jesus.

Brittany Eden

ABOUT THE AUTHOR

BRITTANY EDEN GRADUATED from the National University of Ireland, Maynooth with a First Class Honours B.A. (Double Honours) in Greek and Roman Civilization and Political Science. She was awarded the Gerard Watson Prize from the Department of Ancient Classics for being the highest performing student in their graduation year examinations, and her work was shortlisted for the Global Undergraduate Awards in the International Relations and Politics category. Brittany has worked in Ireland and in Canada for government and on local, provincial, and federal election campaigns. A world-traveler, she's been to over twenty-five countries and has walked the Great Wall of China in Beijing, the Acropolis in Athens, Table Mountain in Cape Town, and Ipanema in Rio.

Now, she brings her highly-curated Pinterest boards to life through her trademark brand of atmospheric love stories. With a classic, feminine voice, Brittany is a poet who loves sad swoon as much as the timeless endings she crafts in her writing.

Brittany resides with her husband and three children in beautiful British Columbia, Canada.